PLUS ONE

ELIZABETH FAMA

SQUARE
FISH

FARRAR STRAUS GIROUX · NEW YORK

SQUARE
FISH

An Imprint of Macmillan
175 Fifth Avenue
New York, NY 10010
macteenbooks.com

PLUS ONE. Copyright © 2015 by Elizabeth Fama.
All rights reserved. Printed in the United States of America by
R. R. Donnelley & Sons Company, Harrisonburg, Virginia.

Square Fish and the Square Fish logo are trademarks of Macmillan and
are used by Farrar Straus Giroux under license from Macmillan.

Square Fish books may be purchased for business or promotional use. For information on
bulk purchases, please contact the Macmillan Corporate and Premium Sales Department at
(800) 221-7945 x5442 or by e-mail at specialmarkets@macmillan.com.

Library of Congress Cataloging-in-Publication Data
Fama, Elizabeth.
Plus one / Elizabeth Fama.
    pages cm
    Summary: In an alternate United States where Day and Night populations are forced
to lead separate—but not equal—lives, a desperate Night girl falls for a seemingly
privileged Day boy and places them both in danger as she gets caught up in the
beginnings of a resistance movement.
    ISBN 978-1-250-06294-9 (paperback) / 978-0-374-36008-5 (ebook)
    [1. Love—Fiction.   2. Social classes—Fiction.   3. Government, Resistance to—
Fiction.]   I. Title.

PZ7.F1984Pl 2014
[Fic]—dc23

2013028762

Originally published in the United States by Farrar Straus Giroux
First Square Fish Edition: 2015
Square Fish logo designed by Filomena Tuosto

10   9   8   7   6   5   4   3   2   1

To all those
unjustly torn from the people they love
then and now
and in the future

It takes guts to deliberately mutilate your hand while operating a blister-pack sealing machine, but all I had going for me was guts. It seemed like a fair trade: lose maybe a week's wages and possibly the tip of my right middle finger, and in exchange Poppu would get to hold his great-granddaughter before he died.

I wasn't into babies, but Poppu's unseeing eyes filled to spilling when he spoke of Ciel's daughter, and that was more than I could bear. It was absurd to me that the dying should grieve the living when the living in this case was only ten kilometers away. Poppu needed to hold that baby, and I was going to bring her to him, even if Ciel wouldn't.

The machine was programmed to drop daily doses of Circa-Diem and vitamin D into the thirty slots of a blister tray. My job was mind-numbingly boring, and I'd done it maybe a hundred thousand times before without messing up: align a perforated prescription card on the conveyor, slip the PVC blister tray into the card, slide the conveyor to the right under the pill dispenser, inspect the pills after the tray has been filled, fold the foil half of the card over, and slide the conveyor to the left under the heat-sealing plate. Over and over I'd gone through these motions for hours after school, with the rhythmic swooshing, whirring, and stamping of the factory's powder compresses, laser inscribers, and motors penetrating my wax earplugs no matter how well I molded them to my ear canal.

I should have had a concrete plan for stealing my brother's baby, with backups and contingencies, but that's not how my brain works. I only knew for sure how I was going to get into the hospital. There were possible complications that I pushed to the periphery of my mind because they were too overwhelming to think about: I didn't know how I'd return my niece when I was done with her; I'd be navigating the city during the day with only a Smudge ID; if I was detained by an Hour Guard, there was a chance I'd never see Poppu again.

I thought Poppu was asleep as I kissed him goodbye that night. His skin was cool crepe paper draped over sharp cheekbones. I whispered, "*Je t'aime,*" and he surprised me by croaking, "*Je t'adore, Soleil,*" as if he sensed the weight of this departure over all the others.

I slogged through school; I dragged myself to work. An hour before my shift ended, I allowed a prescription card to go askew in the tray, and I poked my right middle finger in to straighten it before the hot plate lowered to seal the foil backing to the card. I closed my eyes as the press came down.

Even though I had only mangled one centimeter of a single finger, my whole body felt like it had been turned inside out and I'd been punched in the heart for good measure. My fingernail had split in two, blood was pooling through the crack, and I smelled burned flesh. It turns out the nerves in your fingertip are ridiculously sensitive, and all at once I realized mine might be screaming for days. Had I thought through this step at all? Would I even be able to hold a baby?

I collapsed, and I might have fainted if the new girl at the machine next to mine hadn't run to the first-aid station for a blanket, a gauze tourniquet strip, and an ice pack. She used the gauze to wrap the bleeding fingertip tightly—I think I may have punched her with my left fist—eased me onto my back, and covered me with a blanket. I stopped hyperventilating. I let tears stream down the sides of my cheeks onto the cement floor. But I did not cry out loud.

"I'm not calling an ambulance," the jerk supervisor said, when my finger was numb from the cold and I was able to sit up again. "That would make it a Code Three on the accident report, and this is a Code One at best. We're seven and a half blocks from the hospital, and you've got an hour before curfew. You could crawl and you'd make it before sunrise."

So I walked to the emergency room. I held my right arm above my head the whole way, to keep the pounding heartbeat in my finger from making my entire hand feel like it would explode. And I thought about how before he turned his back on us, Ciel used to brag that I could think on my feet better than anyone he knew.

Screw you, Ciel.

Wednesday
5:30 a.m.

The triage nurse in the ER was a Smudge. The ID on her lanyard said so, but politely: Night nurse. She had clear blue eyes and copper hair. She could have been my mother, except my eyes are muddier, my hair is a little more flaming, and my mother is dead. I looked past her through an open window into the treatment area. A doctor and her high school apprentice were by the bedside of another patient, with their backs to us.

"Don't you need to leave?" I asked the nurse, wanting her to stay.

"Excuse me?" She looked up from my hand, where she was removing the blood-soaked gauze.

"I mean, hasn't your shift ended? You're running out of night."

She smiled. "Don't worry about me, hon. I have a permanent Day pass to get home. We overlap the shifts by an hour, to transition patients from the Night doctors and nurses to the Day staff."

"A Day pass, of course." My throat stung, as if I might cry with joy that she'd be nearby for another hour. As if I craved protection, someone who understood me. I made a fist with my left hand under the table, digging my nails into the palm of my hand. *Don't be a coward.*

I tipped my head lightly in the direction of the doctor and the apprentice. "Are they Smudges or Rays?"

"They're Rays," she said without looking up.

The pressure of the bandage eased as she unwrapped it, which was not a good thing. With no ice pack, and with my hand below the level of my heart for the examination, the pain made me sick to my stomach.

Her brow furrowed when she got the last of the gauze off. "How did you say this happened?"

Of course, from the doctor's point of view, the accident was more than plausible because I'm a documented failure. It says so right in my high school and work transcripts, which are a permanent part of my state record and programmed into my phone along with my health history. *Apprenticeship: Laborer. Compliance: Insubordinate. Allergies: Penicillin.* The typical Ray, which this stuck-up doctor was, would never think twice about an uncooperative moron of a Smudge crushing her finger between the plates of a blister-pack sealer, even if it was a machine the Smudge had operated uneventfully for three years, and even if the slimy supervisor had forced her to take a Modafinil as soon as she swiped her phone past the time clock for her shift, dropping the white tablet into her mouth himself and checking under her tongue after she swallowed.

I was lying on a cot with my hand resting on a pull-out extension. The doctor was wearing a lighted headset with a magnifying monocle to examine my throbbing finger. She and her apprentice both had the same dark brown hair; both were wearing white lab coats. I bit my lip and looked at the laminated name tag dangling around her neck to distract myself from the pain. *Dr. Hélène Benoît, MD, Day Emergency Medicine.* There was a thumbnail photo of her, and then below it in red letters were the words *Plus One.*

"*Elle est sans doute inattentive à son travail,*" the doctor murmured to the boy, which means, *She undoubtedly doesn't pay attention to her work.* "*C'est ainsi qu'elle peut perdre le bout du majeur.*" *She may lose the tip of her finger as a result.*

I thought, *Poppu is from a French-speaking region of Belgium, and he raised me from a toddler, you pompous witch.* I wanted to slam her for gossiping about me—her patient—to an apprentice, but I kept quiet. It was better for her to think the accident was because of laziness.

"Could I have a painkiller?" I finally asked, revealing more anger than I intended. They both looked up with their doe eyes, hers a piercing gray-blue and his hazel-brown.

Yes, there's a person at the end of this finger.

Seeing them like that next to each other, eyebrows raised at fake, worried angles, I realized that it wasn't just their coloring that was similar. He had the same nose as her. A distinctive, narrow beak. Too big for his face—so long that it lost track of where it was and turned to the side when it reached the tip, instead of facing forward. He had her angular cheekbones. I looked at the ID on his lanyard. *D'Arcy Benoît, Medical Apprentice.* His photo made him look older, and below it was that same phrase, *Plus One.* He was both her apprentice and her kid.

8

"Which anesthesia is appropriate in such cases?" She quizzed him in English with a thick accent.

"A digital nerve block?" He had no accent. He was raised here.

She nodded.

The boy left the room and wheeled a tray table back. It had gauze pads, antiseptic wipes, a syringe, and a tiny bottle of medicine on it. He prepped my hand by swabbing the wipe in the webbing on either side of my middle finger. He filled the syringe with the medicine and bent over my hand.

"Medial to the proximal phalanx," she instructed, her chin raised, looking down her nose at his work. He stuck the needle into the base of my finger. I gasped.

"Sorry," he whispered.

"Aspirate to rule out intravascular placement," his mother instructed. He pulled the plunger up, sucking nothing into the syringe. Tears came to my eyes. He pushed the plunger down, and the cold liquid stung as it went in.

"One more," he said, looking up at me. He was better than his mother at pretending to care.

"Kiss off," I said. He looked stunned, and then he glared. He plunged the needle into the other side of my finger, with no apologies this time.

"*Donne-lui aussi un sédatif,*" his mother said, cold as ice. *Give her a sedative.* Apparently I needed to be pharmacologically restrained.

To me she said, "What is your name?"

"It's on the triage sheet, if you bothered to read it," I said.

The boy took my phone from the edge of the cot.

"Hey—" I started.

He tapped the screen. "Sol," he told her. "S-O-L." He looked at me pointedly. "Is that even a name?"

I snatched my phone from him with my good hand. "Sol Le Coeur." My last name means "the heart" in French, but I deliberately pronounced it wrong, as if I didn't know any better: Lecore.

His mother said, "You will go for an X-ray and come back here, Miss Lecore."

The pill they had given me was beginning to kick in. I felt a light fog settle in my mind as the X-ray technician walked me back to the treatment area. The boy was there but his mother was gone. I sat on the edge of the cot, unsteady. My finger was blessedly numb and I was very, very relaxed. I wanted to lie down and go to sleep for the day, but I couldn't afford to rest: I had to get treatment and somehow find that baby.

After the technician left, the boy rolled the tray table over. There was a sheet and a pen on it.

"I . . . uh . . . the triage nurse forgot a release form," he said. "You need to sign it."

I looked at the paper. It was single-spaced, fine print, and I was in no condition to read.

"Give me the ten-words-or-less version. I'm not a Legal Apprentice."

He huffed, as if I were a complete pain in the ass, and then counted on his fingers: "You. Allow. Us. To. Look. At. Your. Medical. Records." He had nine fingers up.

11

He did it so quickly I felt a surge of anger at the realization that, yeah, the mama's boy was smart. I grabbed the pen and said, "Hold the paper still." I signed my name as if I were slashing the paper with a knife.

He put his hand out. "Now, may I see your phone again?"

I took it from my pocket and smacked it into his palm.

"Thank you."

He scrolled through. He was looking for something.

"You're underweight," he commented. "You should get help for that."

You're right, I thought. How about a home healthcare worker, a shopper, a chef, a housekeeper, and a bookkeeper? Oh, and a genie to make Poppu well enough to eat meals with me again. But silly me: the genie can take care of it all while Poppu and I eat foie gras.

"Are you taking any medications?" he asked, after my silence.

"Guess."

He looked up at me without lifting his head, as if he were looking over glasses. "Aside from melatonin and vitamin D."

"No."

His eyes drifted down to the phone again. "Do you want to think about it?"

"No!"

"It says here you took Modafinil four hours ago."

I opened my mouth, but nothing came out. He waited.

"I did," I finally said. I didn't bother to say it had been forced on me.

"Do you have trouble staying alert?"

The wild child surged in my gut. "It's repetitive-motion fac-tory work, after a full night of school. I wonder how alert you would be."

He studied my phone again, his brow furrowed. "Sixteen years old. Seventeen in a few days. You should be acclimated to your schedule, if you're sleeping enough during the day and tak-ing your CircaDiem."

I pinched my lips together.

He looked up at me. "So, you can't stand your job."

I rolled my eyes and lay down on the bed, staring at the ceil-ing. I had nothing to say to this guy. All I needed was for him to fix me up enough to be functional. The injury was supposed to be my ticket to the Day hospital, not an opportunity for psychoanalysis by some smug Day boy.

"What did you do wrong to get assigned to labor?"

There was something implied in the question, wasn't there? He thought I was a thug, with a criminal record, maybe. But I couldn't think straight. The adrenaline from the injury was gone, and I was feeling woozy from the tranquilizer.

His mother came in, and I didn't exist again.

"It's a tuft fracture," he said to her as they studied the X-ray with their backs to me. "Does she need surgery?"

"Conservative treatment is good enough."

Good enough for a Smudge, I thought.

"Remove the nail and suture the nail bed," she went on. "Re-pair of the soft tissue usually leads to adequate reduction of the fracture."

I closed my eyes and drifted off as she rattled through the

medical details. "Soft-tissue repair with 4-0 nylon, uninterrupted stitches; nail-bed repair with loose 5-0 chromic sutures . . ."

The boy's bangs blocked my view of his face when I came to. I had trouble focusing for a minute, and my thoughts were thick. Luckily there was no chance I'd have to talk to him. He was working with such concentration on my finger he hadn't even noticed that I was watching him. It was sort of touching that he was trying to do a good job with a Smudge, I thought stupidly. But then I realized, who better to practice on?

I closed my eyes. Normally I'd be cooking a late dinner for Poppu at this hour of the morning. Then I would read to him to distract him from the pain, and crawl into my bed with no time or energy left for homework. I sluggishly reassured myself that I had left him enough to eat and drink by the side of his bed. Everything made him sick lately, everything except rice and pureed, steamed vegetables. But what if he had trouble using the bedpan alone?

"Poppu," I heard myself murmur.

"What did you say?" The boy's voice was far away.

"Poppu."

When I awoke again, my finger was bandaged, and the apprentice and his mother were huddled together, whispering in French. I heard the words "la maternité"—the maternity ward—and I allowed my heavy eyelids to fall, pretending to sleep.

". . . I've had to do this before. It's a trivial inconvenience."

"Is the baby being reassigned to Day?" the boy asked.

"The mother is a Smudge." She said the word "Smudge" in English, and I wondered, groggy, whether there was a French equivalent. "Her son will be a Smudge. Being the Night Minister does not mean she can rise above the law."

"Of course," the boy said. "And she wouldn't be able to raise her own child if he were reassigned to Day."

There was an uncomfortable pause, as if his observation had taken her aback. "I suppose. Yes."

"So why are we moving the baby to the Day nursery?"

"She asked for him not to receive the Night treatment. That much influence the Night Minister does have."

In a moment, I stirred on the gurney and took a deep, sighing breath to announce my return to the conscious world. When I opened my eyes, the boy and his mother were staring at me, standing ramrod straight. The clock over the boy's shoulder said quarter past eight. I smiled, probably a little dreamily, in spite of everything. It was *daytime*, and I was *out of the apartment*. My half-baked plan was succeeding so far, in its own fashion.

An Hour Guard came to the doorway with his helmet under his arm. He had the Official Business swagger that's so ubiquitous among ordinary people who are granted extraordinary authority.

No, my heart whispered.

"Is this the girl who broke curfew?"

"Pardon me?" the mother said.

I stared at the boy until he glanced my way. *You didn't* was my first thought, followed by a swift *Why?*

He pinched his lips together and looked back at the Guard, who had pulled out his phone and was reading it.

"Curfew violation via self-inflicted wound?"

"Yes, she's the one," the boy said. His cheeks had ugly red blotches on them. "Her name is Sol Lecore."

Little Doe

I was a freshman the night they took Ciel away, and he was a senior. It was the beginning of the school year, and I had chosen a seat in the back of my class. If you're going to sleep through lectures and skip the readings, it's rude to do it from the front row. I'm at least a thoughtful reprobate.

My first period, American history, had started normally enough. I was busy drawing on my desk as the teacher droned on about the flu pandemic of 1918. That was the year the population divided into Day and Night, during the second wave of the disease. They teach you the same curriculum in first grade and sixth grade, so it seemed pointless to listen in ninth grade. The picture I had drawn was a landscape, and a pretty fine piece of art, if I did say so myself. It was a view from inside the Council Overhang at Starved Rock, looking out at a stand of trees. I could draw that scene from memory; I'd been there so many times as a kid.

There weren't many parks in Illinois that a Night family could visit for just a quick twelve-hour trip, leaving Chicago after dusk and arriving safely home before curfew at dawn. But Poppu was outdoorsy back when he could see, and he wanted us to learn to hike on the weekends, and to experience nature as he did when he was a child—or as much as we could with only flashlights and the moon to guide us. Starved Rock, despite its hiking trails worn by tourist traffic and graffiti on the layered sandstone, was still nature, and only one hundred fifty kilometers away by bus.

The new and amusing thing about the drawing on my desk was that another student had started adding to it in a class after mine. On the first night I had drawn the mouth of the cave, rocky and arched, and the silhouette of most of the trees by the time the bell rang. The next night the drawing had changed. Someone had added the moon for me—a gigantic, textured ball. No, on second thought it wasn't the moon . . . was it supposed to be the sun? But every Smudge in the world had seen the sun through windows before we went to bed, and in movies and photographs, and this was not how we would have drawn it, even abstractly. This was a roughly spherical orb, with an envelope of short, hairlike appendages poking out around it. I'd smiled then at having an anonymous partner in crime. It was expertly shaded to give it depth, and the appendages were so intricate it must have taken an entire period to finish it.

Before class ended, I'd added more trees outside of the overhang, intertwined and reaching for the sky. As an afterthought, I'd drawn an arrow pointing at the orb, and I'd written:

Moon.

Sun.

Alien ship descending to wreak havoc
on planet earth?

Now, sitting down at my place on the third night, my heart quickened to see that my query had been answered.

Yes, in a way. Spanish flu virion.

The handwriting looked masculine to me: it was print, not script, half upright and half slanted to the left, which I'd once read was a sign of independence mixed with reserve. The letters were small, which was supposed to mean the writer was academic, or a thinker. Even though I was left-handed, my handwriting leaned violently forward, and the letters weren't uniform in size, which supposedly meant insecurity and impulsiveness, with a tendency toward hysteria. I got back up from my seat, ignored the teacher when he paused his lecture to moan, "*Please* sit down, Sol," and went to the bookcase to pull out the dictionary. A "virion" was the infective form of a virus particle. I took my seat again. The student had also embellished the landscape with a beautiful doe in front of the trees, looking directly at the viewer, head erect with alertness, ears cocked. There was an arrow like mine pointing to it, saying,

Actual deer I have seen near the Council Bluff.
What shall we name her?

At the bottom of the desk, he had scrawled, "Class is obviously killing us both with boredom." Below that some jerk had written, "Get a room." I erased the comment and gave the deer a name:

Petite Daine.

Which means "little doe" in French.

There was shouting in the hall, and a jarring thud, like some-one had been tossed against our classroom wall, and every kid turned to look out the open door. A couple of men in neatly tailored black suits walked briskly past, and then two police-men followed behind, dragging a struggling student. It was all so quick that I couldn't see who it was they were manhandling.

"Where are you taking him?" I heard the contralto, raspy voice of the computer science teacher ringing above all the others from the direction of Ciel's first period class. I got out of my chair instinctively. I knew what was happening in my gut, even though I didn't want to believe it.

"Close the door, Sol," my history teacher said, as if that's why I'd stood up.

A voice blurted in the hall, "I didn't do anything!" It was Ciel, and he sounded panicked.

I ran out of the room and screamed, "Ciel!"

It's burned into my memory the way he looked back at me in that hallway, his shoulders scrunched up to his ears because of the force of the burly cops yanking him, his shaved head making him look like so much more of a thug than he really was. This was my brother, who washed and folded our laun-dry, and arranged Poppu's clothing by color in his drawers and closet so that he could dress himself without anyone's help. I exploded into a sprint in his direction. A teacher grabbed me, locking her arms around me at the level of my elbows. I shouted that it was a mistake, that he was the gentlest person in the world, and, "*You don't know him!*" Useless arguments when dealing with the police.

Ciel was almost out of the building, still struggling. I couldn't see his face.

"I love you, Sol!" he screamed, as if he would never be able to say it again.

Wednesday
10:30 a.m.

"Since when does an emergency room trip count as breaking curfew?" I shouted through the thick acrylic wall.

The Hour Guard lifted a black phone handset on his side, indicated for me to pick up the receiver next to me, and spoke calmly. "The doctors thought there was enough circumstantial evidence to investigate. They're just doing their job. If you're innocent you shouldn't mind the inconvenience."

"Their job is to heal people, not put them in jail."

And who was he kidding? It wasn't doctors who had done this, it was the freaking Medical Apprentice, whose gut I would sucker punch if our paths crossed again.

"This isn't a jail, Miss . . . Miss . . ." He looked at the name on my cell phone but gave up. "It's a detention center. Curfew violation via self-inflicted injury is a class B nonviolent offense—a misdemeanor if it's your first time."

"I want a lawyer," I said.

"Nope. It's a summary crime. The magistrate rules without a trial."

"Please, can't I have my phone? My grandfather doesn't know where I am. He'll be worried sick. He *is* sick . . ."

"The young man in the hospital told me." He looked at my cell again. Seeing it in his hand, through that bulletproof barrier, I realized that I felt naked without it—stripped of my identity and my connection to my grandfather, whose Braille phone was my lifeline to him while I was at school and work.

"It's 'Poppu' in your address book, right?" the Guard said. I wanted to slap his smirking mouth. "We've sent him a message. If you're innocent, he'll be texted to pick you up after your hearing."

"He can't pick me up. I told you, he's *sick*." I didn't bother to mention that he was blind, too. I slammed the handset down and slumped to a sitting position against the clear wall.

I had neglected to ask what would happen if the magistrate found me guilty.

I folded my arms on my knees and put my head down. The anesthetic block had worn off in my finger, and it was throbbing and hot again. I was bleeding right through the bandage—a bright, wet crimson that would have freaked me out if I hadn't had bigger worries. If I weren't so damned tired.

I closed my eyes, and I thought about that nosy apprentice in the ER. *What did you do to get assigned to labor?*

I'll tell you what I did, Day Boy: I was a screwup in school, that's what. I was a lazy, rebellious nothing of a student, and so I was assigned a drudge factory apprenticeship with all the poor slobs who *couldn't* do better. No one on this earth who pulled administrative strings—not the Night Ministry or the Day government—expected anything of me, or had any hope for my future. And once you're on the loser track in this country, it's impossible to get off. Only kids like D'Arcy Benoît, who had the genetic luck of being born a Ray, not to mention the personality trait of being an ass kisser, advanced to a professional career and a successful life.

Ciel was the one with the brains between the two of us, and I guess it paid off for him. When they hauled him off that night, he didn't end up going to jail, he got reassigned to Day. That's how brilliant he was.

Rotten Ciel. He knew Poppu was dying, but that didn't mean he'd skirt the law and try to visit us, or send us an uncensored text. He hadn't even visited us when he could have, legally, on Unity Night. The next Unity Night was two months away, by which time Poppu would be . . . I couldn't stand to think of it. Ciel used to be a troublemaker in school like me, too—you can't be Poppu's grandchild and not have a little fire in you—but when he became a Ray he also became a team player.

Ciel had always been a whiz with computers and wireless technology. He started tinkering practically when he started walking. His specialty became routing intact text messages around the censorship firewalls for all his buddies and their families—which was probably the reason he got chosen for reassignment after he was arrested. Only the most talented Smudges got to become Rays, and until Ciel I had never heard of anyone being selected from jail. But when you accepted the transfer—and everyone who had the chance grabbed it—you left the night, and your family, behind. Ciel was a Ray now, legally, and married to a Ray I'd never met, and all of his skills were being used to thwart and arrest the hacks getting around the censors. The very hacks he'd left behind who used to be his friends.

Until Ciel was arrested and Poppu got esophageal cancer, I didn't give a flying crap that I would never be anything in this world. It was enough to put my hours in at school without studying, and to clock in at the factory with as much attitude as possible while still not losing my job, to laugh around the dinner table with my family, to read with Poppu, and finally take my CircaDiem in the morning, to sleep my exhaustion away. Or try to sleep: no matter what the president and the Night Minister said in their speeches, even blackout shades and earplugs made REM in the middle of the day hit-or-miss.

The thing is, when you're with someone like Poppu—someone who sees straight through your battered façade and loves every bit of you, someone who makes you laugh until you pee your pants, someone who grabs you in a hug exactly when you need it—you don't crave any kind of approval from strangers. You don't need to "matter" in the world, because you already matter to the only person who counts.

There was a faint tap on the wall behind me. I turned around to see D'Arcy Benoît. He raised his hand and uncurled his fingers in a wimpy "hello."

Wednesday
11:00 a.m.

I stood up slowly. I was as tall as him, which I hadn't noticed in the hospital. He hadn't noticed it either, I could tell. Without his lab coat on, wearing a teal T-shirt and dark jeans, he looked like any other self-satisfied Ray I might want to push into a puddle.

He picked up the black phone next to him and put it to his ear. I didn't do the same. I glared at him, cocked my head, turned my back on him, and sat down, curled up again, hugging my knees.

There was another tap on the wall. I didn't move. *I have nothing to say to you.*

Rap-rap-rap. More insistent this time, authoritative. I turned around, fire igniting in my chest.

But it was the Guard. He was holding the phone to his ear. Day Boy was next to him. No, more like behind him. He was a sniveling coward, that one. I stood up and put the receiver to my ear, but barely.

"This isn't like an ex-boyfriend you can blow off," the Guard said. I scowled at the mental image of Day Boy as any kind of a boyfriend, even an ex. "We don't allow visitors in the detention center. He's here for a medical consult only."

I glanced at my mess of a bandaged finger. It was dramatic-looking, I granted that.

"Fine," I grumbled. "But I'll die of hunger before this kills me. Do you have anything out there I can eat?"

"You think you're in a hotel?" He held the receiver out for Day Boy, and I heard the muffled instruction, "If you need a physical exam I'll have to fill out a requisition to let you enter." The Guard disappeared through a side door.

Day Boy and I were quiet for a second, the captor looking at the animal in the zoo. I intended to give him the silent treatment, but I had always been more of a wear-your-feelings-on-your-sleeve type.

"You *moron*, I can't believe you threw me in jail! How can you live with yourself, knowing you're an arrogant ass who's really just a chickenshit inside? Is it not enough for you that you have *everything* while I have—"

"Can you please show me your finger?" he interrupted.

I jabbed my bloody right middle finger in his face through the glass. *Up yours.*

His irritation gave way seamlessly to a flash of worry. "I'll need you to remove the bandage for me."

I lifted my shoulder to hold the receiver against my cheek as I began removing the tape.

"I didn't actually come to see your finger," he said quietly. "But now that I'm here it looks like it might need attention."

"What are you talking about," I grumbled.

"I don't blame you for being angry. Well, I suppose I do if

you're actually guilty. But has it occurred to you there's a reason I turned you in?"

"Because you're sycophant Day scum?" Most of the medical tape was off, but the blood on the bandage had clotted, and I couldn't peel off the last bit without pulling at the gauze pad and hurting myself. I talked a big game, but I'd always been one of those kids who had to take Band-Aids off a millimeter at a time, with lots of rests and deep breathing to steel my courage.

"Like *that*, for instance," he said, proving some sort of mysterious point. I stared at him.

"Like *what*."

"'*Sycophant*'? What laborer uses that word? I couldn't figure out what you were up to, but all the red flags were flying at the hospital."

I was really starting to get concerned that I couldn't take the bandage off, so I put another effort into unwrapping it, pitifully peeling at the outer layer of the gauze pad, getting blood all over my good hand, but nowhere near exposing the wound.

"Listen," he said, as if he were running out of time. I didn't look up. He went on anyway. "I was in a lousy position. It's against the law for me not to report suspicious injuries—not to report curfew violations. And your phone records didn't help lower the flags. It was a factory station you've manned uneventfully for three years; you took a Modafinil, so you should have been alert; the accident happened at the end of your shift, with enough time to get to the ER before sunrise. Not to mention when I gave you the waiver to sign, you took the pen with your left hand."

"What the heck does that prove?" I couldn't ignore his babbling anymore. "Plenty of people are left-handed!"

"Only ten percent of the population. It just seemed too—too convenient that you injured your nondominant hand in such a mild way, but seriously enough to get you into the ER."

"Did you set me up with that form from the nurse?" He was nastier than I thought.

"Not entirely, no, I—"

I held up my half-undressed finger. "My 'mild' injury hurts too much for me to unwrap it. You'll have to come in here, where I can kick your ass."

He looked at the ceiling and huffed, like he'd had enough. He peered at the instructions next to the black phone and then punched two buttons that switched him to another line, killing the connection with me. He said something terse into the handset, hung it up, and waited for the Guard to come get him. He left without looking at me.

I was sure that I'd scared him off for good, but several minutes later the door to my cell was opening. The Guard and Day Boy stepped inside.

Homeless Guy

After Ciel was arrested he was in jail for two months, and we were not allowed to visit him. The judge refused to set bail—said he was a flight risk. I didn't know how a person could flee for long with the random curfew checks that happened all over the city. You could be shopping at the market or sitting in a movie and an Hour Guard would come up to you and politely ask to see your ID. That is, he was polite unless you refused, in which case he was empowered to arrest you, or disable you if you fled. Of course, when an Hour Guard fired blindly at someone's back with a gun, "disable" sometimes turned to "kill." Whenever an Hour Guard asked, you were required to hand over your phone, and he could look at your ID—and whatever else he damn well felt like looking at while he was in there—and most people I knew said "Thank you" after the experience.

A random check happened to me at least once every couple of weeks. I could only imagine how frequent it would be if I lived in the Day. I'd heard there were ten times the number of Hour Guards employed by the Day Ministry. Rays had more reason to be vigilant: no Day person in his right mind would want to switch to the Night, but plenty of Smudges had tried to forge their profiles and sneak into the Day. The only people I ever heard of who got caught out of place after dusk were Ray teenagers who were drunk at their buddies' parties and stumbled into the darkness instead of hunkering down until morning. They usually spent the night in jail and were released with a couple of hours of community service and not a blemish on their records. *Their* curfew violations were considered youthful hijinks, not felonies.

Before his trial, Ciel told me he knew a few people who had jumped bail and disappeared. They were neither Night nor Day now, as far as he could tell, or so good at traveling between the two that they never got caught. It was a mystery to him and to me.

In the weeks after they dragged Ciel off, the raging heartburn that Poppu had after every meal turned into nausea, and the nausea turned into vomiting blood, and he could no longer swallow without food becoming impacted in his chest, which was terrifying for him and for me. He lost fifteen kilos before my eyes and looked like skin hanging on bones. Even his hair began to thin. It took us a month to get an appointment with the state-insurance Night doctor, and he was admitted to the hospital on the spot because—as I'd been trying to say to anyone who might listen—something was horribly wrong.

Poppu's surgery happened while Ciel was in jail, awaiting trial. They took out most of his esophagus, rebuilt it with some of his colon, and stuck a temporary feeding tube into his jejunum until he recovered enough to eat soft foods by mouth. The surgery was seven hours long, and Poppu needed two blood transfusions. I skipped school for a month, nursing him first at the hospital and then at home, and going to Ciel's court dates alone. You could have pushed me over by blowing on me. I cried every morning when I crawled into bed. The apartment was so empty I could hear the mice scritching in the walls as they settled down with me to sleep.

It was supposed to be a trial by jury, and the lawyers prepared for it right up until the last minute as if it would be. The night after they finished choosing the jurors and the alternates, I was sitting in the gallery one row behind the spot where I knew Ciel would be. There were only a few other people in the audience, and two of them looked homeless—a filthy, young, wiry black guy with wild, roving eyes, and a lanky old man who was hugging a plastic bag in his arms—like they were just in it for the heat and free coffee. A petite Asian woman with a notepad stayed as far away from them as possible and may have been a news reporter.

Ciel walked in ahead of the bailiff—walked with baby steps because his ankles were restrained—wearing the clothes he had been arrested in. There were plastic ligatures acting as handcuffs on his wrists, linked to another ligature around his waist. He looked suddenly very different to me. He was too slim, and his skin color was ashen. His hair had grown in to a pretty red fuzz, and he seemed both younger than eighteen and wizened at the same time. He had a splotch of purple-blue on his cheek, and his eyes were swollen and pink, as if from crying. Confusion blended with panic and anger in a hot slurry in my chest, and I had to clench my fists to keep from standing up and screaming at everyone in the room, *Why aren't you taking care of him?* The two people I loved most in the world were disappearing in front of me. Without them I would become a walking corpse.

Ciel's eyes scanned the room quickly and locked on me as he made his way to his seat. They were so shadowed with feeling it was as if they were brimming with things he wanted to say. Things about him, and me, and Poppu, but he was mute. I wanted so desperately to read his thoughts, I found myself whispering, "Tell me." The bailiff shoved him into his chair. He turned around in his seat to look at me. It was the closest I had been to him since he'd been dragged away.

"Ciel," I whispered.

"Sol." His mouth formed my name silently.

"Mr. Le Coeur!" the judge said sharply. Ciel jerked forward. "If you look into the gallery again you'll spend the rest of this hearing in your cell, listening to your own trial on a pair of broken headphones."

What harm could it cause for us to just *look* at each other, when we hadn't spoken in so long? The judge was a control freak and a fathead. He had his collar buttoned tight, and his neck was ballooning over the top so that there was a crease below his ears where his skull began. Half a century of greasy foods and alcohol had probably filled up that neck, and I had the urge to find a needle and bury it there to see what would spill out.

I made as much noise as possible as I stood up—dropping my phone, gathering my coat, scraping the bench on the floor—and moved down the row to my left, so far that I'd be in Ciel's peripheral vision even while he was looking forward. He stared straight ahead at the judge, but his lip on my side curled into a tiny Mona Lisa smile. He still had a trace of defiance back then.

And then the prosecutor stood up and made an offer to the defense. The Day government would drop all charges if the accused agreed to reassign from Night to Day.

I had to shake my head to rattle myself awake; I thought I'd heard wrong. The black homeless guy laughed—a too-loud, hyena-like, mentally ill sort of laugh—showing several missing teeth and a bright pink tongue. The prosecutor stated the terms: Ciel would have to work for the state texting board, helping them thwart communications hackers.

The judge said, "I've had a chance to review the deal, Mr. Le Coeur, and it's better than you deserve. Thugs like you are a threat to civil society. You're looking at twenty years behind bars if you go to trial and are convicted. With this deal you not only avoid jail, you have a chance to redeem yourself by channeling your so-called talent into what's good and right. I suggest you apply yourself with passion to the cause."

The defense lawyer was a young woman, perfectly groomed. It was probably her first case. I guessed that she was a grind in high school who aspired to becoming a Legal Apprentice so that she could grow up to defend the downtrodden like my brother and "do good." She stood up and said, "Your Honor, my client has a minor sister with only a terminally ill grandfather at home to look after her." I sat up straight and held my breath. "Given the rarity of this sort of transfer, and the family's precarious circumstance, it seems reasonable to request that the girl be reassigned with him."

The girl and her grandfather, I corrected her in my head. Why would she leave Poppu out?

"Objection, Your Honor," the prosecutor said without hesitation. "Retention of familial integrity is not a consideration in cases of reassignment, per section 85-D of the Day-Night Code."

"The objection is neither sustained nor overruled," the judge said. "I have no jurisdiction over reassignment. This deal was worked out between the Day and Night Ministries and authorized by the Day government. It makes no provision for a sister."

"She'll become a ward of the state if the grandfather dies before she reaches the age of majority," the do-gooder said. It was sort of brave of her to press the point, but also hopelessly stupid. What I heard the judge say was the equivalent of "That's not my department," and in a bureaucracy that's the same as "Get lost."

Wednesday
11:30 a.m.

The Guard tossed a cellophane-wrapped sandwich at me, which I caught with my left hand. Day Boy followed after him carrying a medical bag—one of those black leather satchels with a buckle that you only see in old movies—and a paper cup of water. The Guard stood right in front of me. He pointed up to one corner of the ceiling, where there was a video camera.

"See that?" he asked me. I nodded.

"And that?" He pointed to the opposite corner, where there was an identical camera.

"Yeah," I said. "I'm being watched."

"That's right. By *me*. And if you touch a hair on this kid's head"—he pointed too close to Day Boy's face—"I'll come in here and treat you like a violent, resisting offender. Got it?" I nodded again, but I rolled my eyes.

After the Guard left I blurted, "You squid, you told him I threatened you!" Was that all this guy could do, snitch on people?

Day Boy smiled with closed, smug lips, handing me the water.

He *smiled*. "In fact, I may be an arrogant chickenshit, but I am *not* a moron." He said "in fact" the way Poppu always did—a literal translation of the French tic phrase *en effet*.

I gulped down the water, dropped the empty cup on the floor, and unwrapped the sandwich, while he held the satchel under his arm and pulled on a pair of latex gloves. The sandwich was room temperature and soggy. There was more mayonnaise than meat—a meat I couldn't place.

"What is this?" I said, peeling the supposed French bread apart. "Turkey?"

He leaned over to look. "I don't know. Food. You asked for food."

I tore off the rubbery end with my teeth and spoke while I was chewing. "Thish ish not fuhd."

He searched for a place to set his bag, but there was no furniture, so he put it on the floor. And then he held his left palm out, as if he were expecting a tip. I looked down at it, taking another bite of the sandwich.

"*What.*"

"Your injured finger?"

"Oh." I took one last bite and laid the sandwich on the floor. It was too gross to eat the whole thing. I plopped my right hand knuckle side down in his, guarding the middle finger. "Be careful."

"I will." He began picking at the bandage, looking for an opening. He quickly got that same look of calm concentration that he'd had when I groggily watched him stitch up my finger in the hospital. It's a look I've probably never once had on my face in my whole life.

He tugged at the bandage, and I sucked breath through my teeth, ripping my hand away.

"That hurts!"

"I have to get it off." He tried to take my hand again, but I held it behind me, and he said, "Don't be a baby."

"You're a quack! Look how much it's bleeding, and it's throbbing like it's going to burst. You're the one who screwed up my treatment the first time, why do I have to get you again?"

"I told you," he said in a low voice as he bent down to open his bag, "I didn't come to follow up on your injury." He pulled a small pair of scissors from his bag, blunt and rounded on one side, and stood straight again. We were exactly at eye level.

My finger was hot and painful, and I needed to know it was going to be fine, so I put my hand out for him. "It's too late for you to apologize."

"Didn't come for that either," he said. He slipped the scissors under the bandage on the palm side of my finger and gently snipped the blood-soaked gauze. I winced, but I resisted the impulse to pull away. "I came to find out why you deliberately injured yourself."

I clamped my lips tight. Why did he care? The deed was done, my plan was ruined. I was making Poppu's life more miserable, not less. Besides, the room was probably bugged, and that bully Guard was listening and eager to lock me up for life.

"It's safe to talk," he said quietly to my finger, as if he'd heard my thoughts. "The officer told me that I should call him on the phone when I was ready to leave, or if I needed help."

I was silent. There was no way I was going to confide in the very person who had busted me.

"If I hadn't turned you in and you decided to go AWOL, I might have lost my apprenticeship. They would have looked at your records and seen what I saw." He paused. It was creepy the way he anticipated me. It made me trust him less, not more.

He had finished snipping. He pulled a tissue out of his bag, spread it on the floor, and then set the scissors on it. He stood up and started to peel the gauze back. He looked at me briefly. "But if it helps, I feel like a shit."

"If it helps, you *are* a shit."

He let out a cynical puff of air through his nose. "I knew you were going to say that. You're so easy to read. Except in this one way: why did you deliberately hurt yourself?"

"Why do you keep insisting that I did?" I countered.

"I've already told you why. Do I have to say it all again?" He had peeled most of the bandage loose, except the part directly over my nail bed, where the blood had dried hard. He lifted my arm by the wrist. "Hold this up, it will ease the throbbing."

He rifled through his bag, looking for something. He stood up with a small foil packet of Polysporin and a cotton swab. I gave him my hand and watched him work. He was being gentle, at least. He pushed ointment carefully under the gauze to loosen it.

And that's when I realized that he was a sucker. Or at least that I might be able to manipulate him. He had come all this way to tell me that he felt forced to report me; it was plaguing him that he didn't know whether he had made the right decision; and he couldn't do the manly thing and just rip my bandage off. My hopelessness burst into irrational optimism that I had to cover up. Maybe I could salvage something from this whole ridiculous mess I'd gotten myself into. I closed my eyes and took a calming breath.

"What will happen if I tell you?" I said after a moment, trying to sound vulnerable.

He looked earnest. "Nothing bad will happen. And maybe I can help."

Bingo.

I gasped, as if stifling a sob. I wasn't sure how believable it would be without tears, but it was worth a shot.

"It has to do with my brother. He was reassigned to Day two years ago. I haven't seen him since." I kept my voice weak, to sound wounded, but also in case the Guard was listening. "He couldn't visit us on Unity Night." *He wouldn't visit us,* my brain argued with me.

I said the rest in a quick run-on, as if I were trying to get the whole thing off my chest. "He got married a year ago, and I've never even met his wife, and now they have a baby, and I only wanted to see her, to maybe sneak in and hold her at the most." In the end I had actually worked up some wetness in my eyes. A drop spilled onto my cheek, and just like in the movies I left it there. I hate the way actresses do that, because when you *really* cry you want your tears gone—it's all about wiping them away as fast as you can. "I wasn't going to break any other laws. I just wanted to hold her."

The gauze was all the way off now, but dangling by a couple of threads that were still stuck in the wound. "I'll do the rest," I said, sniffling.

He put the back of his hand on his forehead and pushed his hair up, thinking.

40

"I get it now," he said.

My nail bed was bleeding. Even I could see that a stitch had popped. I held it out for him.

"*Zut*," he swore in French, taking my hand in both of his and examining the finger. "I was so careful."

"The Hour Guard was rough at the hospital," I lied. I wanted him to think I trusted him and his amateur work. "Shouldn't we go back to fix it?"

"I think it will be fine if I bandage it well."

"Won't I need antibiotics or something?"

"My mother can send over a script, just in case, but so far there's no sign of infection."

I lowered my voice. "If you took me back to fix it . . ." I tilted my head, imploring.

He furrowed his eyebrows at me. "What are you suggesting?"

"It's just . . . I might still be able to see her," I said meekly. "I mean, the baby."

He shook his head before I finished speaking. "I can't do that."

"You can."

"I won't jeopardize my apprenticeship."

"You wouldn't be. You'd just be treating a patient. All they'd have to see is this!" I held up my hand and a drop of blood fell dramatically, perfectly, on the floor. He got another gauze pad and some surgical tape and began re-dressing the wound. I pressed my point: "You'd be doing your job conscientiously— they'd blame it on me. *I'd* be the screwup who slipped away when we got to the hospital. They'd find me in the maternity ward and take me right back here, and nothing would be different . . . except I would have seen her."

He finished his work as I drove the last nail in. "If you do this for me, it will make up for turning me in."

He stared at me, thinking, weighing. His hazel eyes were really quite striking. There was a bright splotch of green in his left eye, and a rim of black around both irises. His long, hooked nose was elegantly dramatic. His bone structure was good. His skin had just a hint of olive from the sun. It all worked well together, but in an unusual way—a way that made you want to study him. My insides churned with irritation; he was such a lucky bastard.

I smiled hopefully at him.

He went over to the phone on the wall and punched a button.

"She needs to go back to the hospital," he said into the receiver.

Who's easy to read now? I thought, sticking my tongue out at his back.

On Fire

Before Ciel and I were assigned apprentice jobs, we lived on Poppu's pension alone. We patched clothes instead of buying new; our vacations were camping trips; we didn't eat at restaurants, we cooked together at home. It was pretty idyllic, really.

When the weather was good, we'd walk to Wooded Island after dinner. It was a small lagoonlike park with willows along the shores, gnarled live oaks and scrub in the woods, and an improbable, beautifully manicured Japanese garden in the middle of it all.

Poppu called our after-dinner trip *"un digestif,"* since walking sometimes helped his fussy stomach to feel better. He always brought his ukulele, too, because the island was as close to being in the wilderness as you could be in the city, and his music wouldn't violate the nighttime Quiet Ordinance the way it might in our apartment.

Poppu had taught Ciel and me how to swing dance, which is how he danced as a teenager, and Ciel was great at it. He was one of those guys who wasn't afraid to use body parts like hips and shoulders and wrists in fluid, graceful ways, and he had a lazy coolness to his syncopated steps. Since we only danced with each other, we got to be pretty good partners, and I was just a slip of a thing, so Ciel could toss me around in dips, flips, and jumps that had daring names like Waterfall and Cannonball and Shin Buster.

Whenever Poppu started plinking on his ukulele he'd eventually come around to a tune that a Smudge quartet called the Ink Spots covered in 1941. The song became hugely popular even with Rays, making the Ink Spots some of the first cross-over musicians.

One time when I was twelve and the moon was full and Wooded Island was so magical the owls were calling, I led Poppu to a bench, and he started on his ukulele, and within minutes he launched into that song, his voice rich and gravelly:

> *"I don't want to set the world on fire*
> *I just want to start*
> *A flame in your heart*
> *In my heart I have but one desire*
> *And that one is you*
> *No other will do"*

I swooped in on Ciel and grabbed his left hand with my right, leading him into a slow Lindy Hop. When he didn't put his right hand around my waist, I took his arm and made him do it, and I started crooning the second verse:

> *"I've lost all AMBISHUN for worldly acCLAIM*
> *I just wanna be the one you looove*

And with your ADMISHUN that you feel the SAME
I'll have reached the goal I'm dreaming of"

And Poppu finished:

"Believe me
I don't want to set the world on fire
I just want to start
A flame in your heart."

This was the point in the song where Ciel usually jumped in with a spoken solo, like the Ink Spots did, while Poppu and I hummed the tune in the background. It was corny, but Ciel was good at it. He'd extemporize some heartfelt thought on why the only important thing in life was winning someone's love, not being famous or saving the world. Or he'd go totally off-topic and chant dirty things about how hot the girl was whose heart he wanted to set aflame. Sometimes he made it so outrageous that Poppu and I couldn't keep humming in the background because we were laughing so hard, and I'd lose my step and crash into Ciel or trip over his feet. This time, he was barely moving with me and refused to open his mouth. I'd never seen him look uncomfortable dancing, like his body weighed more than he wanted to bother lifting.

"I can't stand this song," he groaned.

"Oh, please!" twelve-year-old me begged. Poppu gamely kept humming, in case Ciel decided by some miracle not to be a killjoy.

"I can't do this anymore," Ciel said, dropping his arms, motionless now with conviction. "That song is simplistic bullshit."

Poppu stopped strumming. His face had gone limp. Ciel was moody lately, and it wobbled our family orbit in a way I didn't understand. He sometimes stayed out of the apartment all night with no warning or explanation. When he was home he worked in his room with the door closed well into the day, when he should have been sleeping.

On the path to the south I could see dark figures approaching us. The moonlight wasn't bright enough to identify them, so I took my flashlight from its holster and shone it on the ground near their feet, which was the polite way to assess strangers among Smudges.

I took a breath when I saw in the halo of my beam the black clothes and red shoes of a pack of Noma. And now I saw that their body language was Noma, too: even in silhouette they had a distinct swagger, a willingness—maybe an eagerness—to hurt you.

The Noma were an itinerant population of thugs. Physically, they looked part clown, part goth, part serial killer. The girls always chewed gum; their hair was black and spiky, with a mullet in the back; they wore pancake makeup so that you could only see skin-color differences in their extremities, and red rouge circles on their cheeks, plus red lipstick. The men had crew cuts so short their heads were nearly shaved, and they all bleached themselves blond. Piercings and tattoos abounded. Noma clothing was as varied as the outfits ordinary people wore, but it was all black, with occasional red accents, and always red shoes. No one understood their social structure, but they were at least loosely formed into tribes, and there was a rumor that Noma barely trusted Noma—that they'd just as easily kill each other as other Smudges and Rays. The Noma were supposedly all Smudges; at least that's the way it was when I was twelve.

Ciel said, "Put the flashlight away."

Poppu's eyesight was already too diminished to see anything without bright lighting, but he sensed something was wrong. "Come sit by me, Sol," he said. I obeyed. He found my hand with his and held it down against the bench.

A girl Noma said, with no preamble, "Gimme the little guitar, old man."

"I . . . Do you really—" Poppu stammered, obviously trying to think his way out of giving up the instrument.

"C'mon, guys," Ciel spoke up, making his voice friendly but confident. "He's had that since he was a kid."

I wasn't prepared for the suddenness of their attack. The girl slammed into Ciel and knocked him over, the boy fell on him and began punching him. The girl turned her attention to ripping the ukulele from Poppu's grasp while the others hung back and laughed. Stealing a ukulele from a senior citizen was apparently just a two-man job.

It turned out there was a reason Poppu was holding my hand down. It was to prevent me from doing what I did next. I wrenched away from him and leaped onto the back of the boy who was beating Ciel. I clawed at him like a cat, pummeled his stupid shaved head, and finally resorted to biting his shoulder so hard that I felt something sinewy crackle between my teeth.

Until that bite, I was an annoying fly, not even worthy of

shooing. After the bite, I was a violent menace, and I saw with a little flash of regret that the searing pain of the wound had flipped a switch in him. He lashed backward with his arm, grabbing my shirt, and in one motion threw me to the ground. He climbed off Ciel and onto me, punching my face, shouting, "You little Smudge bitch!" The weight of him was crushing me, and the blows to my face made my teeth cut into my cheek until I tasted blood. I closed my eyes and felt a massive slam against my nose, causing a burst of brilliant red behind my eyelids that turned into a bloom of stars.

And I was dazed enough not to care. Somehow, each blow came to represent exactly what I would do for Poppu and Ciel. Each blow turned the confusion of my world into a pain that I could suffer on my body instead of in my brain, trapped, where it had no way of getting out.

"Sol!" Poppu cried. "Ciel!" He heard the commotion but couldn't see what was happening.

Someone pulled the boy off me, and he grabbed at me so hard, wanting to finish the job, that I was lifted for a moment, suspended in space and time. When I returned to earth, I felt him being peeled away from me like a dead layer of my own skin.

I opened my already-swelling eyelids to see that it was his compatriots who had stopped him from killing me, and that both Poppu and Ciel had been restrained during my beating.

"What the hell are you doing, Dice?"

"She's a kid!"

"She's just a kid, you psycho!"

The guy holding Ciel said, "Gimme your phone." He was hoping for some liquid assets to steal—something to make the inconvenience of our fight worth their while. Another boy with a tattoo of a crucifix on his forehead frisked Ciel, took his phone from his pocket, tapped it on, and in a moment said, "Holy shit!"

We were so poor, almost none of our money was stored as cash. I personally had enough to buy two banana chew candies at school.

But that's not what he meant.

"Listen, my bitches!" Crucifix said. "This little prick is none other than Ciel Le Coeur."

The girl stopped plinking a non-tune on the ukulele and said, "Who the hell is that?"

"He's the hacking genius Dice's brother has been looking for."

Ciel shouted, "Give it back!"

Crucifix entered something on Ciel's screen, hit one final tap distinctly like a "send" command, and said, "Let them go."

Ciel lunged for his phone. Crucifix gave it up willingly. I was on the ground, unable to get up on my own. The euphoric emotional release of Dice's blows had morphed into a throbbing, nauseating agony that my body desperately wanted to escape with unconsciousness.

Crucifix pulled out his own phone and it pinged with a new text message, which spiked a disgusting grin on his face.

"Sweet. I have his contact info. I bet Dice's brother will pay a pretty penny for it." He barked at the girl, "Say thank you to the geezer for your new toy and let's roll."

"Fuck you, geezer," the girl said sweetly.

They loped off, pushing and shoving, as loud as Rays, arguing over who deserved the reward.

Through my good eye I saw that Ciel had squatted down over me, with his arms folded on his knees and his face buried in his elbow. His shoulders rose up and down in quiet sobs. But he wasn't crying from the beating. It looked more like . . . grief. As if he'd lost something he loved. I closed my eyes, suddenly afraid of how much I depended on Ciel's strength.

The Hour Guard took me from lockup to the hospital in a squad car. Day Boy sat up front with him and I was in the back, where it was ridiculously hot. There was a partition between the front and the back, with two clear bullet-resistant sheets and a metal screen in the middle. Aside from the heat, and a gas pain in my stomach that was stabbing me, I was just as glad not to have to talk to either of them. Their windows were open, and the rushing breeze was enough to dull the sound of their conversation but not enough to refresh the air in the back seat. I took off my hoodie and shook my T-shirt away from my chest.

The sun was blazing, and I had never traveled the city in daylight. It was like a different world—laid out like my world, pretending to be my world, but with an explosion of detail and colors and an overexposure of light that made me dizzy and a little queasy. There were millions of individual bricks in the buildings, limestone lintels above doors, and terra-cotta flourishes; there were flowers in garish colors planted in pots and in parks and in the median strips, and billions of leaves in dappled greens on the trees. The newer buildings were made of glass that twinkled blindingly in the sunlight. The skyscrapers thrust boldly into a crisp sky, surrounded by puffy white clouds, instead of being the hulking, lurking giants of my world. Lake Michigan was a giant sapphire, with an achingly beautiful green band closer to shore. These were all sights that were usually muted or cloaked in shadows for me, illuminated only by the moon, dim streetlights, or my government-issued flashlight. At a stoplight I noticed that the mood was different, too: vibrant and carelessly loud instead of hidden and furtive. Even though the Smudge population had grown larger than the Ray population, we were supposed to keep quiet at night when we were out and about. But apparently birds and cicadas were allowed to sing at full volume during the day, and Rays could shout to each other at will. The sun stung my skin through the window. It always surprised me that its rays could hurt.

"The fact that we used your Plus One patient-transport perk unfortunately means you have some responsibility for her while she's in the hospital," I heard the Guard say as the light turned green.

Plus One patient-transport perk.

The white noise of the wind kicked in as the car sped up. I leaned forward and cocked my ear to the metal screen. "But it would have taken hours to fill out the paperwork for a government Day pass, so I'm glad you had it."

"Great," Day Boy muttered. "I have responsibility for a loose cannon."

The Guard snorted.

No, really, I thought, *have a laugh at my expense.*

After a second the Guard said, "So. How long do you think she'll need?"

Day Boy looked sharply at him. "To do what?"

"To get that finger fixed."

"Oh! Uh. Not too long, provided the ER isn't crammed with patients." Day Boy sounded suddenly flustered, exactly like he was lying. The dummy.

"I'll talk to triage and get her check-in expedited," the Guard said. "I can't have a juvie out of lockup for more than three or four hours or my sergeant will flip a shit."

So I didn't have much time. And of course I had no plan. I had to quash a feeling of panic. Maybe the Guard wouldn't let me out of his sight? And if he did, how would I sneak off to the maternity ward, past security and receptionists? I was suddenly nauseated. I could feel sweat beading on my forehead and upper lip, and my hands started shaking.

"Guys," I said. Either they ignored me or they didn't hear me.

"*Guys*," I said louder. "I think I have to puke." Day Boy turned around at this.

"Are you sick?"

I nodded. I really was.

"We're almost there," the Guard said. I saw the circular emergency room driveway ahead. Too far away.

"No, pull over," I said. My mouth was already watering, which for me was the end.

"You'd better pull over," Day Boy said.

"Just hold it in a few more seconds," the Guard ordered, looking at me through the rearview mirror.

"Open the window!" I cried. *You can't "hold in" vomit.*

"Almost there . . ."

Bastard, I thought, as the sandwich and water and all my hope in the world came pouring out of me.

The Guard held my elbow and practically dragged me through the sliding doors into the crowded emergency room. Day Boy stumbled after us, carrying his satchel and a wad of fast food napkins containing some of the bigger chunks the Guard had made him clean up from my accident. He went straight to the garbage can to dump them, and then slid his ID through a reader next to the treatment room, where I assumed he was going to wash his hands and tell his mother what a freak I was.

The triage nurse was a Ray—it was afternoon now—and she was talking to the wife of a cancer patient who was having a racing, erratic heartbeat, fever and chills, and a bloated, tender belly. I should not have heard this information, except that the Guard refused to stand behind the patient-privacy line. Over the nurse's shoulder was the window into the treatment area, and as predicted, I saw Day Boy's mother pull him aside for a private conversation. I felt a pain in my stomach. Maybe it was the bad sandwich, but probably not.

"Excuse me," the Guard started to say to the nurse, with a tone that sounded like he was the one being inconvenienced.

"I'm with a patient," the nurse said, handing him a clipboard with a sign-in sheet. The wife turned to look at us, her eyelids swollen and her mascara running. The Guard scrawled "Sal Lecor" on the sheet and handed it back to the nurse.

"Just make sure this one's next," he said, pushing me forward. "And send a facilities custodian out front to my vehicle, with plenty of antiseptic and rags to clean up her barf." Then he called over her head into the treatment area: "Binoyt! Get your ass out here."

I looked through the window just in time to catch Day Boy heaving a sigh, like he wanted to do anything else but deal with me again. His mother glanced out at the triage desk and her gray eyes found me. They had such a look of disgust, I had to turn away.

Day Boy pushed the door open and came to stand next to me. He was wearing his lab coat again and wiping his hands on a paper towel. He smelled of soap.

The Guard held out my phone to him. "You'll need this to check her in, but she can't touch it."

My phone. My identity; my connection to Poppu. I couldn't take my eyes off it.

"Uh, okay." Day Boy held it like it was coated with Spanish flu virions. "But where are you going?"

"I gotta make sure the janitor cleans every drop of that mess up. And then I'm going back to the station until you call me and tell me she's ready, which had better not take more than a couple of hours—I don't care how full this waiting room is."

"Because, you know, I've missed a lot of work . . ."

"You're an apprentice," the Guard sneered. "We have dozens of them at the station, using up air. Believe me, the doctors can live without you for ten minutes."

Wednesday
3:00 p.m.

The glass doors hissed shut after the Guard left, and without looking at each other Day Boy and I both stepped back until we were behind the privacy line.

"How's your stomach?" he said, after a moment.

"Not good."

"You should sit down. I can get you a paper tray if you're going to be sick."

I turned to look at the waiting room. It was crowded with people who needed to be seen more than me. There was a shoulder-high partition between it and the door the Guard had just gone through.

"Let's sit," I agreed. I led him to the few unoccupied seats that were behind the partition and out of sight of the door.

"It's late for you," he said. I wasn't sure why he was making conversation with me. "You must be bushed."

I cut to the chase. "You want to be nice to me? Give me my cell."

He shook his head and put the phone in the front pocket of his jeans. "You know I can't do that." He leaned toward me and said in a low voice, "I'm sorry to have misled you. I didn't realize until we got here how hopeless your plan is. There's no way you'll be able to sneak off, and there's no way to get into the main hospital without proper ID."

"*You* have proper ID," I whispered angrily. "And I heard the Guard talk about the 'Plus One' that's on your badge. I think it means you could take me there."

"This is my *job*," he said almost viciously. "It's not a game. It's a *real career*—one I hope to keep. I won't let you involve me in a scheme that's doomed to failure. You may have nothing to lose, but I have *everything*." He sat straight in his seat and blinked a couple of times, as if he were surprised by what he'd said, and then took a breath to calm himself. "In fact, I'm very sorry about your niece." He wiped his palms on his thighs. "But while we're here at least we'll get your finger properly treated."

"Right," I said bitterly. "Make sure the Smudge is patched up physically and you can wash your hands of her real troubles. That's what being a doctor is to you, isn't it? You have some grand notion that you're caring for people, but in the end it's all about you."

"There's a big difference between helping someone and breaking the law," he said, keeping right up with me.

"Yeah"—I spat the word—"that's *always* true." I got up and moved over a seat.

While he stared at his hands with pinched lips, I sat fuming. There were plenty of times in history when breaking the law to help people made sense. And then, all at once I remembered the conversation he'd had with his mother about the Night Minister's baby. My eyes grew wide. He was such a hypocrite!

It didn't take long for me to figure out exactly how I was going to get him to do what I wanted. I slid back into the seat next to him. He looked sideways at me, wary. I draped my left arm around his shoulder, intimately, like we were best friends and not enemies. A woman with a bloody gauze pad taped on her forehead watched us.

"What are you doing?" His body stiffened. His eyes searched mine.

I rested my cheek next to his. His hair smelled like lavender. *Imported shampoo*, I guessed in my head. *Probably his mother's favorite.* I put my lips near his ear and said quietly, "I heard you and your mom talking about Night Minister Paulsen."

"You're like a wild animal, do you know that?"

I put my hand on his neck and pressed my cheek against his, to keep him from pulling away. There was a hint of stubble, but it was sparse, and softer than Poppu's. "You spoke about her baby." I could feel his body rise and fall with shallow, quick breaths.

"That conversation was in French."

I whispered, "You moved it from the Night nursery to the Day."

"You were asleep."

I dropped my arm and pulled away from him. His body slumped—barely perceptibly—with relief.

"So apparently it *is* sometimes okay to break the law to help someone," I said at normal volume. The woman with the forehead injury stared.

He looked at my face like I was an alien—his eyes darting from feature to feature. I enjoyed the moment, however brief, of having this power over him, of his wondering exactly what sort of monster I was. A French-speaking, blackmailing, curfew-breaking monster. And he didn't know the half of it: he didn't know I was an aspiring kidnapper.

"Take me to the Day nursery," I said calmly, "or the moment I step into my summary hearing I'll tell the magistrate what you and your mother have done."

When Ciel got married, Poppu and I received text message announcements. Like all of Ciel's texts, they had censorship stamps, and the photos were set at legal resolution—which is to say, pixilated as hell. But I could see well enough to tell Poppu that Ciel's new bride was black, she was wearing a flippy white dress, she had short dreadlocks that poked in all directions and a lovely high forehead. I could see a symmetry in her blurred face that seemed pleasing, and a wide-open smile. It was the sort of smile I'd only ever felt on my own face at dinners with Ciel and Poppu, or hiking with them in state parks, before jail and cancer.

For a second, staring at them holding hands in the photo, I remembered what it was like to have Ciel love us.

They took Ciel away directly from the courtroom that night—the last night of his trial, the first moment of his reassignment. He was not allowed to say goodbye to me. He was not allowed to visit Poppu in the hospital. It was exactly like he died, except for the infrequent, vapid text messages that were worse than nothing: "Happy birthday, Sol. You're growing up too fast." He was an expert at getting uncensored messages through, and yet he wouldn't do it for us, the people he used to pour his heart out to. Ciel the rebel had become Ciel the yes-man.

Wending my way through the hospital corridors now, trying to keep up with Day Boy's determined march, I realized with an odd nervousness that Ciel could be in this very building, at this very moment. His wife had delivered less than forty-eight hours ago; it was daytime, so Ciel was out and about; it was normal for a husband to visit with his wife and newborn as often and long as possible. And then something else occurred to me. The baby might be in the room with them, not in the nursery. How would I deal with that? How could I steal their daughter right out from under them? Just thinking about speaking to Ciel—or meeting the woman who had happily made her life with him *without* me and Poppu—made my stomach clench and my mouth dry.

"Hey," I said to Day Boy's back. For some reason I couldn't bring myself to say his real name.

Irritatingly, he read my mind again. "D'Arcy," he said over his shoulder.

"Whatever. I'm wondering what we do if the baby is—"

He turned and stopped so abruptly that I almost crashed into him. "Not *whatever*. D'Arcy."

"Listen, Day Boy," I said without thinking. "There's no point in first names between us. In twenty minutes you'll never have to deal with me again. And won't that be a relief?" I tried to walk around him, even though I didn't know where we were going.

He stepped in front of me. "What did you call me?"

I looked at the ceiling with a huff. "Forget it."

He closed his eyes, summoning patience, and then opened them again. "The way I calculate it, in twenty minutes we'll have seen your niece and be on our way back to the ER, where I'm going to remove that popped stitch, re-dress your wound, and get a script for some non-penicillin antibiotics, and you're going to obey all the rules and stop extorting criminal favors from me."

He had remembered my drug allergy. Was he a machine or a man?

"Right," I said, realizing that I had slipped up by revealing that I thought I'd never see him again. How *was* I going to shake him loose after I stole the baby? I scrambled to cover my tracks. "I didn't expect that you'd automatically get my case. There are other doctors in the ER."

"But it was my mistake, and I want to fix it." He looked at me then as if he were trying to see inside of me—to figure out what made this wild animal tick. He gave up, turned, and started walking again. "You know, I could also be called to your summary hearing. So *you* may not be rid of *me*."

We approached a set of doors and Day Boy held up his ID to a reader on the wall, which had the effect of releasing the locking mechanism with a quiet *sa-shink*. He pulled the handle and held the door for me. And just like that, we were in the main hospital.

A few meters in, we had to pass a receptionist sitting at a high desk, staring at a computer screen. She was a teenager—on the Administrative Apprentice track—which meant school was out for the day for Rays. I wondered for a second why Day Boy hadn't been in school this whole time.

"ID, please," she said, not looking up, as we tried to walk by her.

Day Boy grabbed my good fingers below the level of the desk, out of her view, to stop me. I nearly snatched my hand away until I realized what he was doing: my inclination was to barrel right through, looking as guilty and suspicious as I felt. My heart was beating so hard, I could feel it pushing against my ribs. He didn't let go of me as he held up the badge on his lanyard with his other hand. "Day Emergency Medicine. And I have a Plus One," he said.

"Is the patient Day or Night?" the girl droned mechanically, bored with her job.

Try factory work, you spoiled Day brat.

"Night," he told her. "She's being transferred."

"Where to?"

He hardly paused for a fraction of a second. "Psych ward."

I scowled at him, and he raised his eyebrows—a facial shrug. She looked at us then, finally taking an interest. I must have seemed believably nuts. I was internally frantic about my lack of a solid plan, my ponytail had more hair out of it than in, I was greasy and stale, my stomach was still upset and ragingly empty, and I hadn't slept in—how long had it been?—more than twenty-four hours. A corner of her glossy pink mouth turned up.

Her eyes moved from me to Day Boy, and I saw her face change—I saw her scrutinize him and reach across the desk for his tag, checking his face against the photo. He moved closer to her, leashed by the lanyard around his neck, and stood patiently, whereas everything in my body urged me to run. I couldn't bear the tension, but he seemed to be in his element. He squeezed my fingers, either to scold me or to reassure me. It had the desired effect of keeping me still.

"Are you coming back this way after you drop her off—um"—she glanced at his tag again—"D'Arcy?" Her voice was fluid and deep; her eyes were as wide as a Kewpie doll's. She fondled his badge in her fingers. *She was only flirting with him.* I slowly breathed out a lungful of air.

"Alas, no." He smiled at her. He had a narrow space between his two front teeth. Another perfect imperfection, the little bastard. "I'm off duty and I'll be leaving through the west exit."

She dropped the tag and leaned back in her chair. "Another time, then."

He let go of my hand and gave me a gentle shove. "Let's go, Plus One."

There may in fact be a god, because I prayed for him not to let my niece be rooming in with her mother, and lo and behold, the baby was in the Day nursery, swaddled and sleeping in one of dozens of clear plastic bassinets.

We had walked through the maternity ward past most of the patients' rooms, and I had studiously ignored the ones with open doors, not wanting to catch a glimpse of my brother.

Day Boy stopped at a cabinet before we reached the nurses' station and took out a hospital visitor's gown for me. It was two sizes too big for my emaciated frame, which was just what I needed. I slipped it on over my hoodie and tied the strings behind my waist. He looked clinically at my hair—which was disgusting by this point—and handed me a scrub cap made of a fibrous cloth. He pulled out two pairs of disposable shoe covers from a pop-up box, one pair for him and one for me, and two surgical masks from a box on another shelf. We put the booties on and left the masks dangling from one ear.

"Let's get this done quickly," he said. "Officer Dacruz will expect to pick you up in the ER in the next couple of hours, and I'm the one who will take the heat if you're not mended by then."

We walked up to the window of the nursery to study the babies in the bassinets. It was a room full of new life: innocent, mostly napping, new Day life; little people who didn't yet know they had the world wide open in front of them. There were two nurses tending to the babies, one male, wearing a surgical mask, and one female. My heart sank. There were too many people here for this to work. The male nurse looked at us through the window. He was black and skinny, and his eyes locked on mine for a second before he turned away, oddly flustered. I thought with despair that he'd gotten a good enough look to identify me.

"Why didn't you try to see your sister-in-law and brother as we passed through the ward?" Day Boy said to the window.

"Why don't you mind your own business?" I asked, mimicking his clandestine, curious voice. It was a handicap for me that this guy was so observant.

"Did you lie to me about having a brother?"

I looked at him, shocked. "No!"

"Take it easy," he murmured. "It wasn't an unreasonable question given everything that's happened."

And he was right. He had no reason to trust me, based on what he knew of me: that I had deliberately hurt myself, that I'd broken the curfew law, that I'd eavesdropped on his conversation about the minister's baby, that I was forcing him to protect himself and his mother by compromising his own apprenticeship.

I was something of a shit myself, it turned out.

I said grudgingly, "Ciel and I don't get along anymore. But that doesn't mean I don't want to see his baby." This last part was a lie, of course. It was Poppu who needed to know the baby; I didn't really care one way or the other about her. "What's going on between us sucks, and I don't want to talk about it." *That* was the truth.

He was quiet. No chafing, no lectures.

"Will your brother have used your last name?" he finally said, searching the name tags on the bassinets.

"I think so."

"Let's see." He pretended to ponder. "Was that Lecore, or Le Coeur?" He pronounced it the correct, French way the second time.

"There she is," I said, pointing to a bassinet. "Baby Girl Le Coeur." My voice cracked as I said it. My throat was hot, and I felt a sting of tears. It must have been because I wouldn't have to deal with Ciel after all. I hadn't realized how anxious I'd been until that moment.

Day Boy assumed it was the emotion of seeing the baby. "You're determined to hold her."

I nodded with that vulnerability I had mastered in the cell.

The female nurse began to wheel one of the bassinets to the door. Day Boy took advantage of the opportunity and moved to greet her.

"Hi," he said as she opened the door. He held up his ID and smiled, I had to admit it, disarmingly. "Could we step in for just a second? This young woman would like to catch a glimpse of her niece before curfew."

It was the first time I had ever been described as a young woman rather than a hooligan, and the first time anyone had passed me off as Day. In fact, I felt more Night than ever—strung out and hollow.

"I'm sorry, visiting hours are over."

"I know, but she only missed the cutoff by a few minutes, and she has a bit of a drive ahead of her before dusk; she's cutting it too close as it is."

It was the most humane lie I'd ever heard. I spoke up, fortified by his generosity. "Oh, please? Tomorrow I leave for college. The next time I see her she'll be walking."

The woman pursed her lips, debating with herself. Then she smiled at me. "Just a quick peek." And to Day Boy she said, "You'll both wash your hands and put on your masks, right?" She pushed the bassinet out the door and let us walk in.

One nurse down, one to go. I had to admit that having Day Boy with me—an official employee of the hospital—was a boon. I'd lose a lot of cred when I managed to ditch him.

We washed our hands side by side at the sink. Or rather, Day Boy washed his hands, and I did the best I could on my left hand and the four good fingers of my right.

"College?" Day Boy said softly, a gleam in his eye. "Almost no one goes to college anymore."

"I'm going to college," I said, low enough that the male nurse wouldn't hear me. "Dwight Correctional University."

He laughed; a real laugh, not a cynical huff, not a snort through the nose. It came from his belly, the way Ciel's did. God, I missed the old Ciel.

"Now hurry up," he said, as we dried our hands and lifted our masks on.

I scooped up the baby as gently as I could. I had no idea how to hold an infant, but it was surprisingly easy with her swaddled so tightly in the blanket. Even her neck seemed to be supported by the wrapping. Only her face showed, with a little pink-and-blue-striped knitted cap on her tiny head. Everything else—her torso, arms, and legs—was a diminutive, taut bundle.

It was a mystery how anything could be so small and so light and still be a complete human being. She was asleep, with the most peaceful expression I had ever seen on a living thing. Her jaw was slack, but her lips—perfect and full—were closed, with the lower lip sucked in slightly under the upper. Her smooth, round cheeks sagged near the corners of her mouth from their own weight. Her large froggy eyelids were completely wrinkled, but they were new, fresh wrinkles, not old. Her nose was tiny and broad. Her ears looked like little sculptures.

The second nurse had his back to us the whole time, standing at a procedures table, shifting nervously from one foot to the other. He was working on an infant whose fussing was becoming insistent.

"Everything okay over there?" Day Boy asked. The mask made his voice slightly muffled.

The baby's cry turned to a guttural, hysterical scream.

"I think I got it," the nurse said, not turning around. His tone didn't inspire confidence.

Day Boy moved to join him.

I looked at the chart on top of the metal box below the

baby's bassinet. She had been fed only fifteen minutes ago by breast. Another close call: if I had arrived sooner, she would have been in the room with her mother, and I might have had to face Ciel. The baby's full belly explained her sleepy contentment. For a brief second I had a pang of jealousy. What was it like to nod off whenever the urge came? My thoughts were getting thick from my own exhaustion. I wished I could curl up somewhere, anywhere, full to distension, and close my eyes.

I looked at the rest of her chart—she had been fed at roughly two-hour intervals. So she was about an hour and a half away from needing to eat again. The metal box below the bassinet had a sliding door that was open, showing stacks of tiny diapers. I slipped one into the left back pocket of my jeans, out of sight under the visitor's gown. I hoped I wouldn't need more than one diaper; I was pretty sure I could complete my kidnapping-and-restoration mission in ninety minutes. Or maybe: my kidnapping-and-go-to-jail-for-life mission.

There was a baby boy asleep to the right of the Le Coeur bassinet. On his metal supply box was another chart, but also, miraculously, a stray stethoscope. A nurse or a doctor must have left it there after filling in his data. It might prove useful to me.

"Whoa!" I heard Day Boy say. I stiffened. And then he said, speaking to the nurse, "You're doing that too close to the calcaneus. Use the lancet more on the side of the heel. What test did you say you're collecting blood for?"

"CBC?" the nurse said, uncertainly.

"Well then, where's your microtainer? Have you done this before?"

I guessed not all Day employees were brilliant, which figured. Rays are only human, too.

All at once—or as "at once" as my sleep-deprived state allowed—I realized *this was it*. This was my chance: Day Boy and the other guy had their backs turned. I scanned the ward through the windows. There was a nurse on the phone at the ward station, completely distracted. A doctor and a Medical Assistant were in the hall, but conferring with a maternity patient who was taking a slow, painful walk with an IV pole.

I lifted my visitor's gown to the side. I unzipped my hoodie. I put the baby against the cavity of my stomach. There was an advantage to being skin and bones and too tall: my "pregnancy" wouldn't show much. She felt warm through my T-shirt. Even though she was swaddled, her little mass was somewhat pliable, and for the first time I was frightened by the fact that she was a living person. I would have responsibility for keeping her safe if I pulled this off. I zipped up my hoodie just enough to hold her body securely in place, but not so much that there wasn't room for air to circulate around her face. I fumbled to straighten the visitor's gown over my belly. My movements were so numb and inefficient, I worried whether I could pull off any escape that required gross motor skills. I wondered what the hell I was doing—why I was ruining my life in the span of a single night and day. But then I thought about Poppu in his bed, his beautiful eyes becoming shadowed pits in his skull, his scarred body all knobby joints and loose, ashen skin. I thought about what it would mean to him to kiss Ciel's baby. And then I thought about how Ciel acted like he wasn't part of our family anymore, like this baby wasn't part of our family, wasn't Poppu's flesh and blood, and the anger gave me strength.

I looked at Day Boy and the male nurse. Both were leaning over their crying patient, hard at work. I had one last moment to cover my tracks, and to buy myself some time to leave the hospital undetected. I snatched the stethoscope from the bassinet on my right. As I shoved it into my back pocket, I noticed that the sliding door of the metal box was open a crack, and a fragment of something blue was peeking out from the stack of diapers. I didn't have time to dawdle, but there was something familiar about it. I pushed the door open, lifted the stack of diapers, and pulled out a blue-and-white lanyard strap.

It had a Day maternity nurse ID attached to it. The photo was of a Japanese woman, Yukie Shiga.

It was like finding a diamond ring on the sidewalk. It seemed impossible that a nurse could have lost it, yet there it was, a gift from the universe; it was the only lucky thing that had happened to me in years; and it was suddenly absolutely essential to my escape. What would I have done without it? Maternity ward security is notoriously high. I put it over my head with shaking hands and tucked it inside the neck of the visitor's gown.

I glanced out the window of the nursery: the nurse was still on the phone at her station. I finished my task quickly: I picked up the baby boy—Baby Number Two—and gently tucked him into Ciel's baby's bassinet, so that it wouldn't be empty. All newborns look pretty much alike, right? All were wrapped in the same pink-and-blue-striped blankets and wearing striped hats. The switch would only be discovered when they were unswaddled and their ankle bands checked. And then, since Baby Number Two's bassinet was the last one in the row, I ripped off the blue patient-information card that was taped to it and stuffed the card in my front jeans pocket, hoping that it looked more normal for the last bassinet to be empty. I braced myself and closed my eyes, dizzy.

"You okay, Plus One?" I heard Day Boy's voice.

"No, I . . ." I looked over my shoulder at him and the nurse, trying not to turn my body. "I think I'm going to be sick again."

"I'll get you someth—"

"Can I go to the restroom instead?" I said, before he could finish his sentence. "I saw one next to the nurses' station."

Day Boy made a quick decision. "Sure. I'll come knock on the door in a second."

"Thanks," I said, heading out—bent a little as if I were sick, but really to hide my new baby belly. If I could get past Day Boy, maybe I could get past anyone.

"Plus One!" he called to me.

I froze. I put my hand on my sweaty forehead and looked over my shoulder at him. Had he seen the bulge? My heart was exploding inside my chest.

"I'm sorry you're not feeling well," he said.

The *Morazan*

For the two years after Ciel was reassigned, drawing on my desk helped to keep me from going mad in school. My sketching partner in crime never failed to have at least one classroom in his schedule that overlapped with one of mine, and to sit at the very same desk. I always sat in the back, and apparently so did he, although I couldn't figure out why. I did it to hide from teachers, to avoid being called on, and to catch up on lost sleep without being noticed. But it was hard to imagine that he was a truant, like me, given that he tossed around words like "virion." So instead I decided that he was brilliant but cripplingly shy, this was his only social outlet, and I was helping him to cope with his handicap while he helped me to survive Poppu's chemotherapy rounds.

His family must have liked nature as much as we did, because he seemed to have visited every one of our favorite nature haunts. Once, the Monight after the principal had made me scrub our last creation clean from the desk during lunch, I started a new drawing with this single word: *Quiz*. Below that, I wrote a number 1 and drew giant cedars as viewed from below in a forest, with ropy ridges of bark, and impossibly thick trunks triangulating to meet in the sky.

On Tuesnight he had written, "Muir Woods National Monument?" He had drawn an anatomically detailed brain next to that, with comical sweat droplets flinging from it at every angle. But I had never been out of the Midwest, so I crossed out his guess and gave him the hint "Not redwoods, giant cedars." And then I wrote a number 2 and drew a lighthouse above a rocky beach—the way I remembered it, bathed in the moonlight— towering over the little fog-signaling shack below it, and a cistern of fresh water in the foreground that was a garish fire-engine red if you shone a flashlight on it, so I filled it in with a colored pencil.

On Wednesnight he had written, "Gah! So many lighthouses in the world!" and he had drawn a picture of himself hanging by the neck, with x's in place of his eyes. Totally gruesome, but it made me laugh out loud when I sat down, causing everyone to stare at me, so I set my books on top of it until they turned away. I smiled every time I looked at that cartoonish self-portrait, and I spent the rest of the week trying to figure out which boy he might have been. I could only rule out the blondest ones, but that probably left something close to five hundred guys, none of whom would have tossed a crust at me if I had been starving to death in front of him in the cafeteria. Toward the end of class I wrote the number 3 and drew a sketch of a tent and a campsite. "I know, I know," I wrote. "This is not helpful."

On Thursnight, I wrote the number 4 and drew—as best I

could from memory—the half-sunken hull of the *Francisco Morazan* as seen from the beach.

The *Morazan* was a Liberian steel freighter with cargo destined for Holland through the Saint Lawrence Seaway. It was the end of November 1960, and the sailors were a multinational Smudge crew plus the captain—a Greek who was only twenty-four and commanding for the first time. He wanted to complete his run before the lock system in the Seaway froze up for the winter. The forecast was for strong winds in the next few days, but being assigned to a Night dock meant the captain couldn't leave until after dusk. Once a ship was in open water, there was no Day/Night jurisdiction, but the curfew laws applied in every harbor in the country. So he waited, hoping the winds would hold off until he had passed through the Straits of Mackinac into Lake Huron.

The first night and day of sailing were smooth, but as the *Morazan* passed the Point Betsie light at Frankfort, Michigan, the winds picked up and waves washed over the deck. Snow, fog, and darkness blinded the crew, and the ship ran aground one hundred meters from shore, in less than five meters of water. Everyone had to be evacuated by helicopter and taken by ice-breaker to Traverse City.

The *Morazan* became the nesting site of hundreds of cormorants, which I drew as black, goosenecked forms, totally out of scale with the ship. I was no Audubon. Night visitors were allowed one fifteen-minute period of viewing, during which bright floodlights illuminated the ship and the cormorants grunted and croaked like walruses at the disturbance. Poppu had taken us out by dinghy, anticipating the light show. I was so small, I had to peek out over my life vest to see the dead metal hulk, eerie in the artificial light, with its empty portholes, winch hoists that were arched like gnawed ribs, and straw bird nests poking out around the smokestack. I remembered feeling exposed on the water, chilly in the breeze. I tipped back and forth in the inflated raft, wishing the birds would stop growling at us. Now I realized that the cormorants had profited from the shipwreck. Nature had stepped in to make good use of the Day/Night insanity of human beings.

When I sat at my desk the next night, my partner in crime had written in excited letters, "Weather Station Campground, South Manitou Island, Sleeping Bear Dunes National Lakeshore! I can't believe you've been there, too!" And he had added an adorable picture of one of the ubiquitous island chipmunks pulling an entire sandwich from a lunch sack, like the little thief it was. On South Manitou Island, campers were instructed by rangers to hang their food in trees, because the chipmunks were as aggressive as bears.

At the end of class while I was packing up my books, I realized that, like the drawings of the deer and the brain, his rendering of the chipmunk was skillful and accurate, and it led me to wonder for the first time whether he might be an Artist Apprentice, a coveted and rare assignment. I startled when my teacher said over my shoulder, "It's Frinight, Michelangelo. Come back at lunchtime to wash off this graffiti."

"Transient art," I corrected him.

"And if you'd only snitch on your little friend, I'd gladly force him or her to do half the cleaning. I don't know why the two of you insist on contributing to the reputation Night students at this school have of being disrespectful punks."

I threw my backpack over my shoulder and looked him square in the eye. "I don't know why the Day students have no souls."

I walked past the nurses' station straight and tall, striding purposefully but not hurriedly. It took every effort not to hunch and scurry like the Smudge rat I was sure everyone saw when they looked at me. I passed the women's restroom and found the stairs. There were red letters on the door warning "Alarm will sound," and the security reader on the wall to the right had a bar of red light. I reached inside the neck of my visitor's gown and pulled out the ID. I waved it near the reader as I had seen Day Boy do, holding my breath, and after a fraction of a second that felt much longer the light turned green. I left the ID dangling around my neck, but with the photo facing my chest, and walked down to the next level, the first floor. It was no longer maternity here, it was radiology.

I ducked into the public restroom. In a stall, I took the stethoscope out of my back pocket and draped it around my neck, casually, like a doctor. I slipped off the blue booties and stuffed them into the feminine waste container. But I left the cap on my head, because the color of my hair was too memorable. I went to the sink and splashed water on my face, which had the hue of the papier-mâché paste Poppu and I made when I was little, and blue bruises under pink-lidded eyes. Seeing myself in the mirror, I wished the nurse on my stolen ID had been a redhead. I wished I had my phone. I wished I didn't look so wounded and young. I wished for a lot of hopeless things, and then I took a deep breath and put everything out of my mind except Poppu, at home.

I headed toward the west exit. There was no way I could slip through the east exit with Day Boy's girlfriend manning the desk; she might recognize me. The baby stretched against her bindings, poking my rib with a little grunt. I ought to have been panicked she would wake up and start wailing right there in the middle of that cavernous lobby. But in my rubbed-raw brain her movements became oddly comforting: I was taking Poppu something real—making a final moment of joy possible for him, a little miracle. And if I was being honest, that baby's jab also reminded me that for the next hour and a half the tables would be turned on Ciel. I would be the one taking something precious away from him.

There was a mass of people—families, outpatients, and staff—milling toward the revolving door, funneling into a line. The sun was low in the sky, streaming through the glass entry, leaving beams on the floor, illuminating dust motes in the air.

I almost choked on my own spit when I saw two Hour Guards on either side of the revolving door, wearing their stupid helmets even inside, tapping people as they passed.

A random Day check.

It felt like a rubber band was strangling my intestines. My heart beat against the baby. I had to concentrate on slowing my breathing, on not running in the other direction. I had such an urge to step out of the line, to give myself a chance to think, to figure a way out of this, but I knew that I mustn't call attention to myself. My feet continued shuffling toward the door, while I was mentally paralyzed—too afraid to bolt, too confused to troubleshoot.

I focused on how they were choosing, and whom, and how long it took to check their phones. They were trying to be random, but it seemed like they were selecting men more than women. Each time they tapped someone, that person had to step out of line, a phone had to be produced, the Guard had to activate the phone—twenty seconds for each encounter, at least. There was a good chance I wouldn't get chosen. Like a wildebeest in a massive herd, the odds of my being taken down by either of those two lions were objectively slim.

That's the thought I held on to.

The baby squirmed. It was hot in the lobby.

A squeak.

The man in front of me turned around. I coughed. When he turned away, I rubbed my belly—the baby. I patted her. So solid. So warm. She settled down.

Three people in front of me now. A female doctor got chosen by the Guard on the right. *Score*, I thought. What were the chances they'd pick another female staff member to harass, which is what I hoped I looked like? I hid my bandaged finger in my front pocket. I told myself that the hospital lanyard and ID would help me pass as Day, as long as the Guards didn't flip it over to see the photo. The door kept revolving, and I was almost there. I felt a warm breeze waft in as it spun, smelling of the outdoors mixed with exhaust fumes from the line of cars waiting to drop off or pick up patients. Through the glass I could see valets running with keys toward the parking lot. There was a pigeon roosting on the steel support of the overhang, dirty and haggard, like me.

I was next at the door. I saw my hand go out to give it an extra push. I felt a tap on my left shoulder. I turned to see the black uniform, the helmet, the visor. It was so unexpected, so last-minute, even the woman behind me bumped into me.

"Really?" I said to the Guard, immediately regretting how belligerent I sounded.

"Destination?" he said, slightly annoyed, slightly mechanical. The people behind me were impatient. They wanted to go home; most of them probably had long commutes before curfew. But I wouldn't step out of line. I refused to give up. I was *so close*.

And then I realized that he hadn't asked for my phone yet. He hadn't reached for my fake ID. Thank god, I hadn't been caught yet.

"I'm going to stand *there*"—I pointed to a cement urn outside filled with sand and cigarette butts—"and take a five-minute smoke break, or go back upstairs right now and kill my Mentor by strangling her with this stethoscope. Which do you think I should do?"

"Get out and calm down," he said, like my crassness made me the scum of the earth, which it probably did. But it had also freed me.

When I was sure the Hour Guard wasn't checking on me, I pulled the cap off my head and slipped in step with the crowd of Rays making their way to the train, still putting my faith in the wildebeest strategy, despite the fact that it had already failed me once. The travelers around me had their heads down, with empty faces. They were missing the sights around them, taking their gifts for granted. I wanted to shout at them, *Try having cancer, or never seeing a bee forage for pollen*. Dopes.

I had roughly an hour and fifteen minutes to make the round-trip home and back to the hospital, but I hadn't anticipated losing my phone and therefore having no money for the train. I walked with a crush of people into the station, and when I was next in line for the turnstiles I made a show of checking my jeans pockets. The young man behind me looked like Business Apprentice material all the way: short hair, suit and tie—the kind of kid who already had a firm handshake and knew how to trade in the pits.

"Crap!" I said, catching his eye. "I lost my monthly pass!"

He scanned me quickly, taking in the enormity of the

disaster in front of him. He shook his head like he couldn't believe his rotten luck for being behind me while everyone else was on their way up to the tracks, couldn't believe that I was smart enough to be a Medical Apprentice.

"Oh, please," I begged him, "I won't catch my train if I have to stop to buy a ticket. Can I share yours?"

"Step out of line," someone called behind him.

People stopped queuing behind us, choosing the faster lanes instead.

"How can anyone be such a mess," the boy said rather than asked, shoving his card into the slot.

"It takes more effort than you'd believe." I felt the turnstile unlock against my weight. I pushed through, grabbed the card on the other end, leaned as far as I could to hand it back to him, and said, "Thank you. You don't know what this means to me." I hurried up the stairs to the train, and then stopped short when I reached the platform.

There was another pair of Hour Guards boarding the first car as arriving passengers disembarked. Running into a random check twice in the span of ten minutes—that had never happened to me at night. I stepped back, lingering, watching through the train's windows. The cars filled quickly; passengers found their seats and began reading, checking their phones, settling in for a nap, while others stood, holding poles and handgrips with blank faces. The Hour Guards inspected the phone IDs of their first victims, and then moved down the car slowly, examining the passengers, choosing their prey. There was no way I would survive that scrutiny. I looked down the length of the train. Should I board the last car? Would they make their way all the way to the end before my stop, which was only about eleven minutes away? The four-tone gong sounded and an automated voice said, "The doors are closing." I held the baby firmly through the hoodie and visitor's gown, and I hurried to the first door of the first car, boarding right behind the Guards. It was a gamble, but I hoped that they wouldn't turn around and start over, I prayed they'd just keep moving.

A man got up to give me his seat.

"That's okay," I said, shaking my head, panicked that he was calling attention to me. And then I remembered I was pregnant, so I forced a smile and sat down. He moved to reach a strap, which put his body squarely between me and the view of the Guards. *Such luck.* My shoulders relaxed; I hadn't even known I was clenching them by my neck.

As the train jolted to a start, I closed my eyes. I wanted to see my night world rushing by in sunlight, wanted to savor the one day I'd ever had, but I was being crushed by lack of sleep. Hot tears pooled under my lids.

I opened my eyes. The man who had given me his seat was staring at me. I couldn't blame him; I was hard to figure out.

"May I ask another favor?" I said, my words slurred as if I were drunk. He shrugged, which I took to mean *That depends.*

"If I fall asleep, would you be able to wake me at Sixty-third Street?"

He nodded.

I had no choice but to rely on him: I couldn't keep my eyes open.

* * *

I felt a tap on my shoulder, and I was aware of my body leaning as the train slowed. The wheels screeched. I had missed the announcement of the stop, but the stranger had remembered.

"Thanks," I said, my eyes taking a moment to focus. "And for the seat, too. I didn't know how much I needed it."

The doors swished open. I stood—too quickly. I was dizzy. My brain craved REM, and eleven minutes of sleep had only been enough rest to whet its appetite. I gripped a bar near the exit for a second and then stumbled onto the platform, one of only a couple of passengers to leave the train at that stop, the rest of them on their way to the suburbs. The baby was squirming now. I had sweated through my T-shirt in my sleep; she was such a little furnace next to my body. The late September weather was too warm for a hoodie. But I was almost home. I lowered the zipper more, to let in the evening breeze. Her grunts were growly and hoarse for such a tiny person. If I had been a more sensitive, maternal type, I might have found the sound miraculous.

I headed straight west, at a steady clip, and turned north on my street. I could see our apartment building in the distance.

The evening light revealed just how run-down our block was, in a way that dull amber streetlights didn't. There were torn screens and peeling window frames. Our building needed tuck pointing. Grass sprouted from cracks in the sidewalks but refused to grow in the parkways, where the only green was the broad leaves of dandelions. Still, it didn't matter to me. It was home; it was the place that sheltered Poppu. I braced Ciel's baby and broke into a jog, needing to be there. If only I were returning for good. If only it were night, and I had my phone, and I was failing school as usual and getting yelled at by my boss, and Poppu didn't have cancer, and Ciel hadn't left us. If only.

I had no keys—the Guard had taken them away with my phone and the rest of the contents of my pockets. But I knew how to get in. I slipped down the stairs to the gangway between the buildings, lifted the door with a quick jerk until the lock gave way, walked through the musty brick corridor with the smell of cat urine pinching the back of my throat, and came out in the concrete backyard of the apartment building next door. Normally I would climb the fence between the properties to get into our yard, but not with today's cargo. I went out to the alley and reached my hand through a hole in the mesh of the back gate to unlock it. I retrieved a spare key from under a dead potted plant and climbed the back porch steps. I now felt like every horrible thing that had happened since last night might possibly be worth the payoff. Crushing my fingertip, getting arrested, mercilessly using that Day Boy, kidnapping my own niece—it was all in service of the next half hour of Poppu's happiness. I felt the way I used to feel as a kid handing Ciel some silly home-made gift on his birthday: the anticipation of pleasing someone you love makes you practically shiver with joy.

A cry came out of my mouth when I reached our third-floor apartment. The window of the kitchen was smashed in, and the back door was ajar.

Sun and Sky

When I turned thirteen, Poppu prepared his special tarte au maton, which he only made for our birthnights. It was a kind of Belgian cheesecake enclosed in a puff pastry. Poppu was a good cook in general, and the tarte was his signature dessert. It took twelve hours to prepare because he had to curdle whole milk with buttermilk and then drain the mixture through a sieve lined with cheesecloth. Every couple of hours he would go to the pantry and stir the contents of the sieve, to encourage the whey to flow through. He called it "coaxing the curds," and in my mind the pleasure of eating that gently sweet tarte was inseparable from the pleasure of watching him create it. The other ingredients were eggs, ground almonds, and sugar, and the filling was so light and dry that it nearly melted in your mouth. But the secret ingredient was love.

Over the years I had realized that it was clever of him to restrict such an unassuming dessert to our birthnights, because if we had eaten it on other occasions it would never have acquired such a fantastic lore. On the other hand, I wouldn't have missed it so staggeringly when I turned sixteen and he could not stand often enough or long enough to coax the curds.

On that thirteenth birthnight, after our bellies were full of tarte and all that was left was a pile of burned cake candles, Ciel pulled a small purple velvet box from his vest pocket. The box was almost square, with rounded corners, and was tied with a white cloth ribbon. Poppu raised his bushy eyebrows when he saw it. He had only given me his usual gift: a stack of books that he and I would read together every night after dinner while Ciel washed dishes and shouted, "Louder!" from the kitchen. Poppu had discovered long ago that I didn't do homework, but I did do family book time. Really, why would any person do homework when they could read great novels—and trashy comics—with Poppu? There were also books about science and history and art, and Poppu tried to sneak some poetry in there when he thought I wasn't looking. We had an understanding: he ignored my lousy grades as long as I wasn't outright failing, and I was supposed to pay attention in the one subject we never covered at home, math.

The book on the top of the stack that year was the *Odyssey*.

I untied the bow of Ciel's jewelry box, and the ribbon slipped off the way it does in the movies, gracefully, as if in slow motion.

"Do you get it?" Ciel asked happily after I'd cracked open the hinge.

Inside was a necklace. It had two dangling charms on it—a sun and a moon. The charms were attached to different bails, so that as they slid along the chain the moon rested halfway over the sun, as if it were about to eclipse it, Night trying to dominate Day. The moon was full and made of white gold, with a relief of the major terrae and maria. The sun was yellow-gold, with pointy rays blazing in all directions. The rays that spread out underneath the moon had tiny diamond chips embedded at their tips. They were meant to be the stars.

"It's night and day," I said, because it was obvious.

Poppu took it from me and examined it. He brought it to the kitchen and pulled a magnifying glass out of the utility drawer.

"No, it's *you*, Sol," Ciel said to me.

Poppu sat down and studied the back of the charms and the gold lobster clasp.

"Eighteen karat," he murmured. "Later we will talk about where you got this." Then he handed it to Ciel, who had his palm out.

Ciel admired it and went right on talking to me. "I mean, sure, it represents night and day, too. But I got it because your name is Soleil and you live in the night." He looked at me intently then. "You know there's a reason Mom and Dad named you that."

"Ciel," Poppu started. There was concern in his voice, or a warning, and when I glanced over I caught the vanishing remains of furrowed eyebrows.

Soleil is French for "sun," and it's my real name. Poppu was the only one who used it. My phone ID, my official state document, listed the nickname Sol. Most people pronounced it "soul," which was not quite French but close enough.

Poppu said, "Your mother named you Soleil because you

were her sunshine." He looked pointedly at Ciel. "And you were her sky."

"She's thirteen, Poppu. It's time to stop dumbing down the story. She needs to understand her world." He stood up, opening the clasp of the necklace, and walked behind me, saying, "Our names are a symbolic rebellion, Sol." I looked up and back at him as he lifted the necklace over my head, maneuvering around my ponytail to join the ends together. "There was an act of rebellion in everything they did."

Wednesday
5:00 p.m.

My mind raced through possible options. I couldn't go to a neighbor for help: the Night neighbors were still under curfew, and I didn't know any of our few Day neighbors. Besides, they'd want to call the police, and I'd get arrested.

Within seconds I knew I was overthinking this: Poppu was in the apartment, possibly hurt. I had to go inside.

I peered through the broken window. I could see that no one was in the kitchen, at least, or the hallway beyond. I pushed the door open a third of the way with my foot, knowing it would creak if it went as far as halfway, because I'd never found the energy to oil it.

I unzipped the hoodie and was grateful that my charge was still asleep. I wriggled out of my sweatshirt, carefully ladling her from one arm to the other to peel off each sleeve. I stepped inside, avoiding the broken glass so that my sneakers wouldn't crunch on the wood floor. I left the door open for a quick escape. There was a deep drawer under the counter to the right of the fridge that was nearly empty and traveled on smooth glides. I quietly pulled it open, bunched my hoodie inside a fry pan to form a nest, and lowered the baby into it. Then I pushed the drawer almost closed. I was too exhausted to wonder whether it was a good plan. I didn't want to encounter a burglar with a baby in my arms.

I held my breath and listened, my heart thumping in my chest, but the apartment was silent. As I let out my air, a wave of nausea came over me, along with the strangely lucid thought that I wasn't strong enough to find my grandfather murdered. I stayed like that for too long, frozen, and then the fact of being a coward snapped me to my senses. I had to do this, and I had no choice but to do it alone. I made a fist of my good hand to stop it from shaking. I walked as light-footed as possible down the hall. I paused before getting to Ciel's room, and then slowly peeked around the door frame. His room was the smallest of the three bedrooms. He had traded his old room with me as a surprise on my eleventh birthnight, skipping school to paint it a color the can called Sunshine. The window and door casings were Dove.

His room, with its landlord-beige walls and trim, was as hollow as it had been the night they dragged him away. Poppu and I had cleaned the sheets, made the bed, and straightened up after the police ransacked it for evidence. We didn't know then that he'd never come back. The electrical equipment and tools that the investigators *didn't* take fit in a shoe box.

I swallowed but my throat was so dry it caught on itself. I continued down the hall to my room. The door was open, as I'd left it so long ago on my way to school. A lifetime ago. There was nothing but the usual: dingy white sheets, dingy white comforter, books stacked on books—two-deep in shelves, on my night table, in piles on the floor—like a mad witch lived there. I moved on to Poppu's room. The door was closed, but it shouldn't have been.

I turned the doorknob. I knew the door would stick, that it swelled in the summer. I pushed hard and it scraped open. The smell of dying wafted out, sweet and musky. But that smell was always there lately. His blackout shades were closed, and the room was as dark as night. I closed my eyes and flipped on the light switch.

I opened my eyes just as an animal mewl came from the kitchen. My whole body startled, causing my bandaged hand to flail against the doorjamb. The pain ricocheted through me at the very same moment that I realized Poppu's bed was empty.

I rushed into his room and ripped the duvet off his bed. I flung open the closet. I ran across the hall to the bathroom and threw the mildewed shower curtain aside. I continued down the hall to the living room and hurried through the patio door to the screened porch. He was in none of these places; nothing was disturbed. I ran back to check closets, and then I stopped all at once, a vision flashing in my mind. I turned back to the table in the middle of the front hall. There was a stack of unopened mail—I hadn't paid a bill in months, or even thrown away junk mail—and on top was a note scrawled with a green magic marker on a piece of lined paper taken from my room.

WE WILL EXCHANGE YOUR GRANDFATHER
FOR THE BABY. A SMOOTH, QUICK
TRANSFER WILL BE SAFEST FOR BOTH.
INSTRUCTIONS BY TEXT.

I got so dizzy I had to kneel to keep myself from fainting. I sat on my heels, curled forward, and put my face on my hands on the floor. I heard a moan and realized it was my own voice. And then a dam burst inside my head and liquid poured from my face—tears from my eyes, snot from my nose, spit from my mouth. I wailed at full volume, not caring who heard me. At that moment I was as alone as I had ever been in my life. Poppu, who was too sick to walk across the hall to the bathroom, had been taken from me. Ciel was gone. If Poppu died—*when* Poppu died—the apartment would echo like this. My heart would echo like this.

The front doorbell buzzed, rude and toneless and insanely loud. I couldn't move, as if my body had given up on everything but breath and a heartbeat and mucus. *No one ever rings our bell*, I thought sluggishly. I had forgotten even what it sounded like.

I heard the awful bleat from the kitchen again and remembered the baby. She was stirring. I sighed. I wasn't alone after all. I had someone with me who was not only of no help and no comfort, but a catastrophic liability. A liability I had brilliantly inflicted on myself. The doorbell buzzed, long and irritating, then pulsed, and then sounded a seemingly interminable note again. I willed my torso up until I was on my knees, realizing it might have something to do with Poppu. I went to the screened porch to spy down at the door, lifting the hem of my T-shirt to wipe my face with it. The baby's whimpers became a bona fide cry—not insistent, not continuous, but I could hear in her voice a primal recognition that she wasn't being heard, and I knew her cries would soon escalate in volume and urgency. I ignored her.

The room was designed as a sleeping porch in the early 1900s. With a flat tar roof above it, our third-floor apartment was a furnace in the summer. There were knee-to-ceiling screens on three sides of the porch to catch a pitiful cross-draft when Chicago's temperature soared into the high, humid nineties. I sometimes still slept out there, running one small air conditioner in Poppu's room only.

I edged over to a screen and looked down.

It took me only a second to recognize the teal T-shirt and disarranged dark hair.

"Day Boy," I whispered, stunned. I stumbled back. Like a bloodhound, he had followed me home. I peeked out again to see whether there were police cars with him. If it had been night I wouldn't have been able to see much, but in the rosy evening light I had a clear view all the way down our street in both directions. I searched, but I saw no cops.

He pressed the buzzer again, and then he peered at the names on the brass plate. He was checking for apartment numbers but wouldn't find them. He stepped back and raised his head. I saw his nose bob with a systematic inspection of each window. First floor, second, third. His eyes passed right over me. I was muted behind the dark screen.

The baby cried now, lustily. Day Boy cocked his head, hearing her. He pulled something out of his pocket. It was my phone. He touched the screen, scrolled, and I knew what he was looking for: my complete address with the apartment number, 3S.

He looked directly at my window, caught the shadow of my form, and called to me, "Goddammit, Plus One. Let me in."

Wednesday
5:30 p.m.

I let him in because he had my phone. That was all I was capable of processing. I tried to think through the ramifications of opening the door, to imagine how I might instead escape with the baby, but my brain was broken with exhaustion and grief. And he had *my phone*.

I leaned on the entry buzzer long enough for even a pampered Ray to figure out that he had to shove through both the front door and the vestibule door before I released it. He probably lived in a high-rise on the Gold Coast with a doorman who greeted him by name and kept biscuits in his pocket for his mother's miniature poodle.

Depending on how out of shape he was, it might take a minute for him to climb three flights of stairs in an old, high-ceilinged apartment building like ours. I decided to retrieve the baby from the kitchen drawer. She was what he came for, I was sure, and with all the wailing there was no way to hide her. Her cries had become hysterical, painful to listen to, so I jiggled her lightly and made whatever sympathetic shushing noises I could, but my heart wasn't in it. By the time I got back to the front door I saw, through the peephole, Day Boy stepping onto the third-floor landing. He didn't hesitate between the two doors, ours and the neighbors', either because of a good sense of direction or because Ciel's daughter was like a foghorn. He knocked hard. I took a breath to steel myself.

I opened the door, our eyes caught, and I saw and felt in that instant that he was just as wary of me as I was of him. I was dizzy, unsteady on my feet. My finger was exploding through the bandage with every squirm of the baby. And all at once my mind tricked me. It had something to do with the juxtaposition of my abject aloneness of the minutes before—sobbing on the floor—and the fact that there, standing in front of me now, was a human being I knew. I didn't know him well, and I wasn't even fond of him, but by now I was accustomed to him, to his superior attitude, his type-A personality, his French tics. I knew that he didn't like me or trust me. That he wanted nothing more than to be rid of me to get back to his privileged life. I knew that he was honest about it, that he'd been honest with *me*, even when he'd called the Hour Guards. And those facts were enough—my desperation and that mild familiarity, combined with holding a miserable, writhing infant that I couldn't console because there was no one there to console me—those were enough to make me reach out to my enemy, the only available life preserver in a world that was drowning me.

"Please help me," I said. I handed him the baby as the room spun and the world went black.

I awoke on the couch. Day Boy's back was to me. He was rocking the baby in one arm and texting with only the thumb of his other hand. He was good at both. My head felt stuffed with cotton. I wanted to sleep, but I needed to focus.

He turned around and saw I was awake.

"You have a fever," he said. And then, "What the hell were you thinking, kidnapping a baby?"

"Who are you texting?" I asked, trying to sit up. "Are you turning me in? Don't turn me in—"

"I'm trying to figure out *what* to do. Are you still light-headed? Lie down."

"You don't understand, they took Poppu," I started incoherently.

"I saw the note." He came and stood over me, and now he looked pissed. He was still rocking the baby, who seemed utterly soothed. "I came here on a million-to-one shot, hoping you'd have run to your apartment and I could cart you back to the hospital before Dacruz got back, and go home for my off shift and forget this whole horrible day. But then on my way here your phone started receiving texts threatening your grandfather and demanding 'the baby,' and *ha la vache!* I don't know how you did it while I was right there, but I understood that you must have kidnapped your brother's baby, and this is—*so*—*messed*—*up!* Are you trying to destroy my life, or am I just collateral damage in your death spiral?"

"Wait," I said, catching up. "You mean you didn't know that I stole the baby while you were in the hospital?"

"Thank god, when I left no one had noticed her missing yet—but that was almost an hour ago."

I wished my brain weren't so sluggish. Who was texting me?

Who took Poppu? "If Ciel's baby is not officially missing yet, how does anyone know I have her?" I wondered aloud.

Day Boy's brain switched gears instantly. "You're right. If the hospital doesn't know she's missing, we might be able to put her back before we go to the ER."

"That's not what I meant!" I said, sitting up too fast. I put my hand on my left temple to stop my brains from bursting out. "We have to *keep* her. They have Poppu. And that stupid baby is all we have to get him back."

"This 'stupid baby' is a human being, and someone else's child. And stop saying 'we' when referring to this disaster."

"Let me see the text messages."

He stared at me. I could see his mind chugging away behind those hazel eyes. He wanted to stay in control.

"I'm not going to run away with my phone," I assured him. "I can't run anywhere with my head exploding."

He reached into his pocket.

My phone. I had been so long without it.

The first text was from Poppu:

Réveille-moi quand tu rentreras, n'importe l'heure.

I felt a pressure in my chest. He wanted me to wake him when I got home, undoubtedly to read together before I went to bed.

"Your Poppu is French," Day Boy said sullenly.

"Belgian," I said, scrolling to the next message. Unknown number.

Your grandfather is visiting with us. He is well. Please text when you receive this message.

The words were so polite. So benign. Such a lie. Poppu was

never well anymore. There was a CPI censorship stamp on it: Approved.

The next message was time-stamped only ten minutes later. Unknown number. Censorship stamp: Approved.

We must see the baby before your grandfather returns home.

Reply by text and we'll give you directions.

And soon after that, a message without a CPI censorship stamp. The corner of the screen that usually contained a little check mark was empty. I had only ever seen messages like that on Ciel's phone. It was a felony if an Hour Guard or a cop discovered an uncensored communication in your phone records.

The Committee on Public Information had shut down voice calls a decade ago. It was too tedious and expensive for the state to redact verbal conversations, and on the customer's end, the ten-second time delay necessary for the redaction—along with frequent, irritating bleeping of content—spelled the death of person-to-person calls.

Perhaps we weren't clear, the uncensored message read. **Bring us the baby immediately, or you'll never see your grandfather again.**

"Why do they want her so badly?" I asked Day Boy.

"Who is 'they,' Plus One?"

"I don't know!"

"What are you mixed up in?" His voice had risen a couple of pitches. "Is it drugs? Day Assignment forgeries? Trafficking in infants—?"

"Shut up!" I interrupted, a fire burning in my chest as well as my head now. "You know exactly who I am. I'm nobody! I'm a moron who injured herself on purpose to get into the hospital. I wanted Poppu to hold his great-granddaughter. *That's* what I'm guilty of."

"Where are your parents?" he asked, reaching for something—maybe a way to extricate himself.

"They're dead. Didn't you see that on my phone?"

"I didn't read your personal records. Why couldn't your grandfather visit the hospital, like a normal grandparent?"

"Because Ciel is a Ray and we're Smudges!" I rolled my eyes, which caused the muscles of my eyeballs to ache in protest. "You know that!"

"I forgot." He took a breath to calm himself, and when he spoke it was with his supercilious, educated Day voice. "Well, then, photos are all you and your grandfather were legally entitled to until Unity Night."

"Photos are worthless because Poppu is blind," I spat. "And he won't live to see Unity Night. He's terminal."

"He's . . . ?"

"Esophageal cancer. Metastasized. To his lungs and liver. He's a week or two away, at the most." My eyes flooded. "I don't know how they moved him."

Day Boy was silent. A stunned sort of silence. His guard was down, and in that moment I saw the face of the boy who whispered "sorry" when he stuck the needle in my finger.

My spinning head threatened unconsciousness again. I held the phone against my heart and lay back flat, wishing the thumping in my ears away. Closing my eyelids caused the pooled tears to spill out, and I wiped them away before they could trickle into my ears. I said in a low voice, "When Poppu dies I have nothing."

Day Boy was silent. I could hear him swaying nervously with the baby, the floor creaking in time. I told him the full truth, although there was no way he could know the difference between that and my lies: "When I crushed my finger it was because I didn't mind going *straight* to nothing a few nights earlier, so that Poppu could hold his great-granddaughter before he died. Everything else could kiss my ass."

I started to drift. It was a blissful sort of anesthetic, removing me from the world. I heard Day Boy say something about the baby's diaper being soaked. I had not even considered that her crying meant she needed changing; I must have been the least maternal being on the planet. I tipped to the side and pulled the diaper out of my back pocket with my good hand, accidentally dropping it on the floor. "There," I heard my voice murmur.

I fell asleep then, or my mind slipped into a semiconscious state. Because even though I heard Day Boy's voice, far away, I didn't process what he said.

"Oh my god, Plus One. This baby is . . . he's a boy."

My next moment of lucidity involved Day Boy's knuckles, clinically resting on my forehead, then my cheek.

"What?" I gasped, lurching my head and shoulders up, seeing first a cone of blackness, and then pricks of stars in the periphery as the room came into focus. I still had the phone in my hand. He hadn't taken it away.

"You're burning up. You need antibiotics." He looked at the baby in his arms, who was perfectly swaddled. "I need to get you both back to the hospital right now and pray it's not too late to fix this."

"How did you do that?" I mumbled, disjointed thoughts pushing ahead of coherent ones.

"Do what?"

"Wrap her up the way the nurses do after you changed her diaper."

"I've done a few rotations in the maternity ward and the NICU," he said impatiently. "Get up, you're in big trouble."

"We're in big trouble," I corrected, closing my eyes, easing back down.

"Stay with me." He shook my shoulder again.

"You can't turn me in," I murmured. "Now I can say you not only switched the Night Minister's baby to the Day nursery, you also helped me kidnap Ciel's baby."

"Listen to me, you *impulsive, blackmailing*—" His voice was so sharp I forced my gritty eyes open in a squint. He fought for composure. "This"—he held the bundle out—"is Minister Paulsen's son."

He waited for me to answer. I had to repeat the words in my head twice. *This is Minister Paulsen's son. This is Minister Paulsen's son.*

My brain clicked into a vaguely functional gear. I propped myself to sitting, head swimming, finger in agony. My phone fell to the floor.

"She's a *girl*," I finally said.

"His penis argues otherwise."

"That's impossible—" I started. I put the back of my bad hand to my forehead. Even I could feel it was dangerously hot.

"The ankle bracelet says Baby Boy Fitzroy. It's the temporary ID my mother made for Minister Paulsen's baby. Fitzroy is my mom's mother's maiden name."

"I took Ciel's baby," I reassured myself. And then I looked up at Day Boy, needing to convince him, I didn't know why. "I wanted *Ciel's* baby. Yes, I moved another baby in the bassinet next to her—I mean *him*—but I took this baby from the Le Coeur bassinet, I swear."

I remembered something. I reached into the pocket of my jeans and pulled out the wadded blue patient-information card I had taken from the last bassinet.

Baby Boy Fitzroy. *But how?*

Day Boy took it from my hand, glanced at it, and muttered, "I'm screwed."

"You don't understand!" I insisted. "This baby didn't come from the bassinet with that card!"

"I don't care how it happened," he interrupted. "This is Paulsen's baby and we're getting him back to the hospital *right now*. Can you walk?"

I scooped my phone off the floor—bending made my head throb. I touched the screen.

"What are you doing?"

I pulled up the last text and hit the reply button. By virtue of whatever illegal technology the sender had used, the composition screen popped up with no censorship warning. It would be a first for me, sending an uncensored text. But I needed to get instructions from the people who had Poppu.

"Oh, no, you don't," Day Boy said, snatching the phone from my hand, even though I saw the movement with plenty of time to dodge him. My reflexes were shot. Hopelessness surged inside my belly, hot and angry.

"Take the baby," I said bitterly. "Bring it back to the hospital, but leave me alone with my phone to find Poppu. Can't you pretend you lost me? That you got to the apartment and found the baby here, abandoned? They'll believe you! Look." I pointed down the hall to the kitchen. "The back window is smashed. It will confuse the police. Let the break-in buy me some time." I heard my voice turn to cowardly pleading. "Please let me go. You don't understand how much Poppu means to me."

"I'm beginning to, and it's . . . impressive," he said, in a voice I didn't understand. "But you're sick, you're currently under arrest, and you're my responsibility. *Levez-vous.*" He ordered me to stand in French. It didn't escape me that he used the formal, respectful "you." He grabbed my elbow, easing me to my feet. I wrenched my arm away.

"*Lâche-moi.*" *Let me go.* I deliberately used the familiar form.

My brain had severed its connection to the lower half of my body. My legs were heavy and dead. I lost my balance, falling into him and the baby. A bloom of lavender, laundry soap, and sweat filled my nose as my vision darkened. He twisted to unpin the arm that held the baby and held his free arm around me to steady us both.

The curfew alarm rang on my phone in his hand, and on his phone somewhere in his pocket. It was Night. All of my muscles relaxed just a bit, in the reflexive way Pavlov's dogs had supposedly salivated. After almost seventeen years, my body associated that sound with the freedom to move about the city. But for Day Boy it should have signaled confinement.

"You can't leave anyway . . ." I whined.

"I have a Night pass to get myself home and you to the hospital."

My eyes pooled with hot tears at the word "home"; my throat swelled nearly shut. Even if I didn't go with him, the cops would be at my apartment as soon as Dacruz figured out I wasn't in the emergency room. Day Boy was trying to cut our losses by returning us. For the moment, the hospital didn't know a baby was missing, and Dacruz might not have come looking for me. I should have been grateful for what he was trying to do.

"My car is outside," he said, having recovered his bedside manner. "You only have to walk down the stairs. Can you do that?"

I leaned on him hard, focusing on what he wouldn't: there was no good outcome for me from this point on. Poppu was going to die in the custody of strangers, away from his home, without me by his side. A gasp of a sob left my mouth as Day Boy practically carried me to the door.

Stardust

One night when I was still a freshman I came to class and there was a new drawing on the desk: an exquisitely rendered human heart. It was not the kind of heart that little kids draw and cut out to make valentines, with two plump cheeks at the top and a pointy V at the bottom. It was an anatomically perfect sketch, tipped slightly as real hearts are, showing the aorta, the pulmonary artery and veins, and the vena cava—although I wouldn't have remembered the location of any of those if they hadn't been carefully labeled. My desk partner had drawn the heart as if it had been sliced almost all the way in two by a sharp knife, which was no small feat since the drawing was three-dimensional and looked like real muscle tissue. Below it was a poem. But it wasn't one I would have ridiculed, or forced Poppu to dissect to expose its pretentiousness. It was raw, an open wound, and it brought tears to my eyes.

> I am empty
> I am released from a ship
> In space
> I am unmoored

Vast nothingness
Aching for what was lost
Wanting what will never be
And suddenly
The after-moment of now versus then
The paradigm shift
The world in too sharp relief
The past and future overlap
In front of my eyes
Death and life
Love and its mysterious absence
A knowledge
I am not a player
I am a spectator

I read it again and again until I had it by heart. I heard nothing my teacher said the entire period, not a word. I had no comfort to offer my friend, even though it's what I most wanted to do, and in that way I felt an impotence that matched the tone of the poem itself.

A worry forced its way into my mind. Was it a girl he was talking about? Wasn't that a broken heart he had drawn? Had he fallen in love with someone? *Wanting what will never be. Love and its mysterious absence.*

I felt socked in the chest, and I didn't know why. He was the equivalent of a pen pal, after all; a confidant at most. Nothing had changed: if our paths crossed in the hall I still wouldn't recognize him. If he saw me, I would seem a stranger. He wouldn't wrap his arms around me, his beloved friend.

The bell rang, and every other student got up to leave, scraping chairs, laughing, stuffing books in backpacks, dropping papers. My time to help him was over, and I felt a rising panic that I would fail him.

I was no poet, I had no right to even try. But I hastily added these four lines, and I left the room without allowing myself to reconsider.

> *Powerless*
> *But for the stardust*
> *Unknowing*
> *I trail through her heart*

Wednesday
6:45 p.m.

Day Boy helped me into the back seat of the car, handed me Baby Boy Fitzroy, and put my seatbelt on for me. He went to the trunk and returned with a towel, to wrap the infant in an outer layer before handing him back to me. He was about to close the door, but on second thought he reached in and tugged off the baby's hospital cap, rearranging the towel to keep his head warm.

"Don't lie down," he ordered. "I don't want you falling asleep and dropping him. And if we get stopped by the police or Hour Guards, the story is that you just delivered at home and I'm bringing you to the hospital. But let me do the talking. Got it?"

"Kiss off," I said.

"Ah, it's like old times," he mumbled as he slammed the door.

A couple of blocks into our trip, in the pooled light of a street lamp, I saw two kids from my math class walking to school together, past a billboard that shouted SHARE SPACE FAIRLY BY SHARING TIME FAIRLY. I would never again have what they had, an ordinary life. I stared until they moved into the shadows and out of sight.

"Why weren't you in school today?" I heard myself ask Day Boy. My voice was hollow, like it was coming from inside a shell.

"I'm a senior," he said.

Implied in that answer was another bit of information he had left out.

"You have National Distinction," I guessed, with a huff. "That figures." I closed my eyes, promising myself I wouldn't sleep.

Seniors who had achieved National Distinction received stipends to do full-time advanced apprenticeships in their assigned fields, in effect being excused from their last year of high school and guaranteeing the most prestigious jobs after graduation.

"I told you I had a lot to lose," I barely heard him say.

The baby struggled a bit against his bindings. I opened my eyes, waited for them to focus, and then studied him. The lights of Lake Shore Drive strobed across his body. He was waking up, and his whole face was scrunched like a dried apple, as if he were in excruciating pain or dying, when it was probably just a hunger pang. There was no way I could have known that the little person in that hospital bassinet was a boy, I consoled myself. He looked so much like a boy to me now, I wondered why I hadn't seen it before. The pain passed as quickly as it had come, and his face reverted to angelic relaxation.

A black car zoomed past us on the right. It had a tall antenna waving to and fro on the back, and a license plate in the double digits.

"Unmarked cops," I said.

Day Boy only nodded in confirmation.

And then behind us, on the left, another car just like it. It sped up and pulled alongside us, too close.

Day Boy muttered something I couldn't hear and began to slow down, preparing to pull over to the right shoulder. I instinctively slid low in my seat. But the driver and the passenger of the black car didn't even look sideways. The car sped up and moved in front of ours, into our lane, and then pulled away. The baby's face contorted again in silent agony.

A feeling of dread washed over me that we were possibly the subject of the police urgency, but there was no point in mentioning it. In the last fourteen hours I'd done some exceptionally stupid things and now I would pay for them. The strange thing was, the only punishment I cared about was not saying goodbye to Poppu.

"Poppu," I whispered under my breath, as the baby let out a strangled cry.

"He's hungry," Day Boy said.

"I guess he'll eat soon," I said. "Lucky boy." I had the foul heartburn in my chest and throat of a person who'd had nothing in her belly for too long.

We took the next exit and waited at the light as three identical black cars, all with tinted windows, blew right through the stop.

"They're headed toward the hospital," I said, stating the obvious.

Day Boy dropped his forehead to the steering wheel. He looked up just in time to see the light turn green. He drove carefully, deliberately. He took the first left turn toward the hospital and slowed down, looking right toward the east entrance.

The street was dotted with the five suspicious cars. The exterior lights of the hospital and the sidewalk lampposts exposed a handful of men in suits with neat haircuts and shadowed faces, one texting furtively, a few plotting together in a business-dress huddle, all standing too straight, from years of discipline. I stared at them—at their brazen surreptitiousness, which was such a visual oxymoron. We weren't going to be able to sneak into that entrance, for sure.

"Get down, Plus One," Day Boy said all at once.

"You told me to sit up." It felt much less belligerent than it sounded. The baby started to mewl again.

"*Cache-toi*," he practically growled, using the familiar form, maybe out of exasperation.

I leaned over, lying with the baby, and I laughed—I didn't know where it came from, given the scrape I was in. "*Bon, enfin on se tutoie*," I said, joking about our lengthening acquaintance. *Finally we're addressing each other as friends.*

"Would you please shut up?"

The baby began to cry in earnest. I felt the car hover, in a moment suspended with uncertainty, and then pick up speed and veer away from the hospital. Day Boy was not turning me in. At least not at that moment.

As uncomfortable as I was—sliced in two by the seatbelt, sweating through my hoodie, my head beating like a drum, awash in the baby's wailing—the fact of reclining promised to knock me out for good. I wrapped my arms around angry little Fitzroy and fell asleep.

Night Minister

I learned the truth about our parents' deaths on the night I turned thirteen—the night Ciel gave me the necklace. In retrospect it was clear that he had been waiting until the moment I was a teenager to tell me. I was not as ready as he thought.

Before that night, I believed my parents had died in a car crash. In fact, they had. But the accident was not simply bad luck, or the fault of a drunk driver or a spinning semitrailer on slick pavement, or any of the other visions I supplied with my imagination whenever someone mentioned it. The crash happened because they were speeding away from Hour Guards.

Before Ciel got far in his explanation, Poppu stopped him. He took my hands over the table. He rubbed the tops of them with his cool, paper-skinned thumbs. His eyes became moist and pink-lidded, as they often did when he spoke of my parents.

"There isn't a person in the world who is perfect, Sol," he said. "There isn't a person who hasn't made a mistake he regrets, not a single human being."

"I know," I said gravely. But I didn't believe it, because Poppu had never once made a mistake, with me or with Ciel. Poppu was kind to everyone he met. He was brilliant and gentle. He was funny, and sometimes crude or obscene or profane— exactly when it was called for, exactly when the world felt so wrong for me I thought I might suffocate, which was more and more often, the older I got.

"Ciel is right that you should know more about them. You were so little when they died."

I was not yet two, and Ciel was five. Ciel had snippets of memories of them, including one I coveted, of my father tossing him in the air over and over and catching him, and I had nothing.

Poppu went on. "But after he tells you how they died, I want you to remember how they lived—all the things I've told you about your mother as a baby, and as a child, about how she and your father met, about the night they were married, and the way they blossomed after you and Ciel were born." Now he took a hanky out of his pocket and blew his nose. "Because the one thing you must always remember is that they loved you. They loved you both more than anything else in the world."

He sat back and looked at Ciel, who had waited through this message patiently and was a little too unfazed, as if he had heard it before. For my part, I needed to know that my parents loved me, and it wasn't until Poppu had said it in such absolute terms that I realized how much I craved it—how some deep part of me was an empty well that desperately needed a spring to refill it.

"Mom and Dad were part of the old resistance." Ciel started his story again.

All I knew about the old resistance was that both the Day and Night branches of the government called it a terrorist organization, and they had crushed it a decade ago by killing or imprisoning its leaders and strangling its money supply. The so-called new resistance was a bunch of young hippies led by a Ray teenager named Grady Hastings, who had only rhetoric and righteousness for weapons. They wanted curfews to be abolished, but no one took them seriously. They held rallies; they got themselves arrested on purpose. Still, it seemed like a wasted effort: most Rays and Smudges had jobs, if not always the ones they wanted, and roofs over their heads, and food on the table. We didn't live in revolutionary times.

"They rigged bombs," Ciel was saying, "and set them off in official government Day and Night offices and vehicles—"

Poppu interjected, "Your parents had never once hurt anyone."

Ciel said, "But they damaged a hell of a lot of government property. They were meticulous about detonating their devices after hours—nighttime if it was a Day office, daytime if it was a Night office—when their target was closed and empty. They tailored the size of the blast to the area they wanted to damage and placed the bombs so carefully that even security guards were never injured."

"I don't understand." I shook my head. The information was bouncing off me, not filling me. "Why did they pick on Night offices? They were Smudges."

Ciel shared a glance with Poppu. He had learned all this before me. I felt left out, and young.

"If they were terrorists, at least they were equal-opportunity terrorists." Ciel smiled with one side of his mouth. "Because they objected to the *system*, not to one population or the other."

Poppu took over for a moment. "See how old I am, Sol. I'm nearing the end of my years."

"You are not! Why are you saying that?"

"I was born twenty years after the Spanish flu pandemic. Twenty years *after* the Day/Night divide. I have known nothing else. In fact, there are perhaps only three or four hundred individuals in the world today who were old enough in 1918 to remember the change. Now every few days one of them dies, and soon the living memory of a world without the divide will be gone."

I wondered whether we should be talking this way.

"No one can help being born Smudge or Ray," Ciel said. "But Mom and Dad wanted to shake everyone—to make them think about why the law is still here all these years later, and whether it's right."

I had heard the history of the divide a thousand times at school and on television. I could recite it from memory; I'd regurgitated it for exams. It was familiar, it made sense, it was—permanent. It had never been presented as a point of discussion.

The pandemic was like a nuclear bomb in its human destruction, before nuclear bombs existed. Everyone lost family members, all over the globe. Entire villages disappeared. The virus hitched its way to the Arctic and to remote Pacific islands. People were buried in mass graves. No, not people: your mother, your brother, your aunt, your best friend on the block, your teacher. In Chicago, the streetcars were draped in black and used to collect the dead. Doctors and nurses collapsed from exhaustion; hospitals set up tents outside for overflow.

In the fall of 1918 Woodrow Wilson formed the Federal Medical Administration, and it had the clever idea of recruiting apprentices from colleges and high schools to boost the staffs of hospitals. Half of all doctors and nurses and new aides were assigned to day, and half were assigned to night, with mandated rest. It worked so well, the FMA expanded the dual curfew to include industries that supported hospitals: drug companies, medical supply companies, delivery services, morticians and morgues, police and fire departments.

There was an unexpected bonus when half the medical industry started working after dark: public transportation was less crowded, and that small change helped to slow the spread of the disease. Meanwhile, efficiency in medical supply companies soared with round-the-clock factories, setting new records in productivity, even though there were fewer workers because of the war and the pandemic. President Wilson was encouraged. He set up the Office of Assignment to make decisions about who would be Day and who would be Night. The Committee on Public Information helped people to accept and understand the change.

The United States began to recover—financially and medically—before other countries, which quickly patterned their own governments and industries after our successful Day/Night model. Two and a half years and more than fifty million deaths later, the pandemic was over, but the system stayed in place.

"So the day they died," Ciel said, "they were set up."

"Betrayed," Poppu corrected.

"By who?" I asked.

"By whom," Poppu corrected again. "And they never learned who it was." His voice broke, and he shook his head, wiping his eyes with the hanky. It took him a moment to be able to speak. "In fact, in Brussels I knew nothing about the inner workings of the resistance. I was alarmed when I found out that your mother was involved. She had been such a studious, gentle child."

"The Night Minister was tipped off," Ciel went on. "It was Minister Paulsen's first term. In her campaign she had promised to end corruption and terrorism, and she decided to be hands-on about it. She arranged to have a decoy leave the building before curfew, and then she hid, in her own office."

"Did she have a gun?" I whispered, having read too many thrillers with Poppu.

"No." Ciel smiled. "Her plan was less primitive than that. She had Day police cars stationed along each side of the building, on alert, so that the exits were covered. She wanted to catch them in the act, and she knew Mom and Dad would run."

I couldn't speak because of the suspense. Poppu's tears had forged paths from his eyes, and the ducts pumped so steadily that he just leaned the hanky on his cheeks to blot the tiny rivulets as they ran.

"Minister Paulsen wasn't being brave, although that's the PR she got when it was over. She knew they wouldn't be armed, other than the explosive. It was their MO *not* to harm people. But somehow . . . Dad was injured. We think he tried to disarm the bomb when the minister confronted them." Ciel's eyes became moist now, too, but with embers of rage behind them. "The bomb took off his hand and part of his arm."

Suddenly it was no longer a book or a movie, it was real people. It was my father, and he was flesh and blood, not just photographs, and he had been alive that night, and he'd had Ciel and me waiting at home for him. And now he was mutilated. My mouth was dry.

"Did he die?"

Ciel shook his head. "No, when they found him in the car he had tied a tourniquet around it, or Mom had. They got away from Minister Paulsen. What she didn't know was that they had gotten into the building through steam tunnels, not through a door or a window, and they escaped."

"They escaped." My heart pounded.

"Yes, they managed to get to their car, even though it was daytime and he was bleeding bad."

Poppu interjected, "Your mother's camisole was wrapped around the stump."

"They drove away," Ciel said. "But then they got stopped by Day Guards—random, fucking Hour Guards."

Poppu didn't flinch at the swear, which I knew meant the context was in a category he found acceptable.

"And even though the Day forgeries in their phones were perfect," Ciel said, "there was an APB out on them the moment Paulsen alerted the police." He told the rest of the story in short sentences, like bullets firing, making survival for my parents impossible, even though I already knew they wouldn't make it: "Mom drove away; the Day Guard must have pulled his gun;

there was a chase; the Guard shot a tire; Mom lost control at high speed, hit the median, and the car flipped."

His eyes glowed hot again, swallowing me, and dragging me to a dark place I wasn't ready for at only thirteen.

"I believe our father tried to save Minister Paulsen's life disarming that bomb, and she repaid him by murdering him."

Thursday
12:00 Noon

I woke up seventeen hours later in a real bed—a firm one with a feather mattress pad under me and a cotton quilt on top. My head had the thick feeling of too much sleep, and there was a horizontal line of pressure above my eyebrows. I lifted my right hand; my finger was re-dressed. It was sore, but not throbbing. I put my hand to my cheek: I was cool to the touch, no fever.

I sat up. I was in a bedroom—spare and masculine, with rich, rust-red walls and evidence of recent life: dirty laundry in a basket next to the dresser, and a stick deodorant on the desk with books, papers, and a computer. There was an Ansel Adams photo on the wall near the door: *Moonrise, Hernandez, New Mexico, 1941*. It made the night look positively enviable. What beauty would Adams have captured if he'd been allowed to photograph during the day? I lay back down and smelled lavender on the pillow.

In a moment I rolled over. My eyes drifted to the objects on the bedside table: an almost-empty bowl of chicken soup and Yukie Shiga's hospital lanyard. There was a bottle of prescription medicine—doxycycline, a non-penicillin antibiotic I remembered from when I'd sliced my palm open with a tin can on a camping trip—and a glass of water. A fuzzy image flashed in my head of a man, a stranger, spoon-feeding me, my head in a cloud of pillows, my alertness lapping in and out like wavelets on the shore, warmth and richness traveling down my esophagus. I would not have remembered any of it if I hadn't seen the empty bowl. I watched the digital clock move from 12:06 to 12:07. I meant to get up, but my eyes closed themselves. It was 12:29 when the door opened.

"Better, I think, yes?" the man said to me. He had the remnants of a French accent, and I knew immediately that he was the one who had spoon-fed me. He was tall, with an athletic build, and he looked like the middle-aged models from some fashion spreads. He had all his hair, which was mostly gray and spiky, and he was clean-shaven. His skin was the color of—I imagined—a person who went sailing on Lake Michigan on the weekends. I nodded, mute, and when he came closer I saw that his eyes were a soft hazel.

"Mr. Benoît," I said. Only Day Boy could have such a perfect father.

"Jean." He leaned over the bed, felt my forehead, and smiled. "In fact, you'll live."

I sat up, making him drop his hand. The world and my fate began reasserting themselves in a rush of dread. "Where is my phone?" I pulled the blanket and sheet from around my legs to get out of bed, only to see that I was wearing a man's shirt, with no underwear. I flung the sheet back over myself. "Crap. Where are my clothes? I have to get up!"

"I have washed them." He turned his face toward the door

and called quietly, *"D'Arcy, elle s'est réveillée."* He looked back at me and said, "You will want to take a bath."

"I don't have time for a bath. I need to find my grandfather."

"A shower, then," he said, deliberately misunderstanding me. "You cannot go out without freshening up. You will call attention to yourself. Take the moment you need to be healthy."

"I don't have time for a shower."

He put a clear plastic bag and a rubber band on the bedside table. "Keep your dressing dry," he said, turning to leave. He remembered something. "And take one of those pills. You're two hours late. You'll need to take it every twelve hours until it's gone. Drink it with a big glass of water."

Day Boy came to the door hugging a bath towel and my folded clothes.

His dad turned sideways to pass him in the doorway and said in a low voice, *"Je vois ce que tu veux dire. Elle est fougueuse, n'est-ce pas?"*

He was calling me feisty, but using the word normally reserved for a horse, and I resented that Day Boy had been talking about me while I slept.

"I can hear you!" I said.

Jean left. Day Boy hovered in the doorway. I tucked the blanket tightly around my legs and realized that I was at his mercy. "Bring me my clothes," I ordered.

"Ask nicely."

"Please," I begged, "at least give me the towel. I can't get up like this."

"This is an interesting situation . . ." He leaned against the doorjamb with his eyebrows raised.

"You're not funny. My grandfather is out there. Dying."

The corners of his lips turned down. "Promise you'll take a shower. We won't discuss going anywhere until you do."

He set the clothes on the bed and I pressed the covers to my chest with one hand as I reached for them.

"There's something you should know," he said.

"What."

"It took the two of us to put you in that shirt."

I scowled when I caught his meaning.

"I'm going to be a doctor, Plus One. You're a patient."

My brain raced through hazy images of my body, leaden and uncooperative, head aching, my finger on fire, and the two of them gently lifting my limbs, peeling my clothes off. I would not have remembered it if he hadn't told me.

Day Boy pinched his lips, maybe sorry that he had said anything.

"Meet us in the living room for lunch when you're clean."

The shower was hot and lovely. So lovely that I cried as it pounded on my head and rinsed the previous hours away, purifying me temporarily. The shampoo smelled like lavender.

I dried myself, rubbing hard with the rough side of the towel. I took the baggie off my right hand; it was damp, but from sweat. I changed into my clothes: fresh, a little gray, and stiff from being line-dried. There were a few stray cosmetics in the cabinet—not enough to indicate a woman lived there, just enough to suggest she visited. I used her deodorant. She had left a black elastic hair holder, and I took it. I braided my hair and tied the end off with it. In the mirror my face was shiny, the heat of the shower had made my lips crimson against the white of my skin, and the flames of my hair were muted by dampness, making my eyes stand out in their hollow, hungry sockets.

I was more than hungry. I was starving.

I walked barefooted down the hall, and the living room opened before me. Their home was laid out something like mine, a typical old Chicago railroad apartment, with bedrooms along a hall that led to the front foyer, then the living room, and a sun porch beyond. Their porch was winterized so that it was a real room, with expansive windows set high off the floor but reaching the ceiling. There was a desk with a computer, a chair, a file cabinet, and a reclining chaise: someone's home office. In the corner of the office was a treadmill. Day Boy and his dad were sitting on opposite sides of a sectional sofa in the living room, eating sandwiches over plates on the coffee table, resting their elbows on their knees. The television was in the corner, tuned to the local Day news. Like the bedroom, everything was tidy and comfortable and reasonably clean but not fussily so.

I saw that there was a third plate with a sandwich waiting on the coffee table. It was made on crusty French bread, with hints of white fresh mozzarella, red tomatoes, green basil, and a strip of prosciutto licking out like a salty, fatty tongue. I hadn't seen a sandwich like that since Poppu had gotten sick. A cluster of grapes sat beside the sandwich on the plate. A pitcher of iced tea was in the middle of the table. Obnoxious amounts of saliva poured into my mouth. I might have killed for that sandwich.

I stood in front of them and said, "I'm clean. May I have my phone?"

"Sit," Jean said, patting the sofa very far away from himself, as if I might bite.

"Food first, phone second," Day Boy said.

"First my grandfather, then jail," I corrected, not budging.

Day Boy and his father stared at me. The television was the only noise in the room, set to the Independent News Network, which prided itself on evenhanded coverage of Day and Night issues and was subversive enough to criticize the curfew laws in some of its reports. I was surprised to see Rays watching it. It had a reputation for outrageous, almost flamboyant radicalism outside the Smudge community. The weather segment had just ended: sunny with cumulus clouds and unseasonably warm with highs near twenty-seven degrees Celsius. It was almost like being in a foreign country, where my body still breathed, I still saw and heard, but everything was just a little different, everything made me slightly dizzy. *Sunny, with cumulus clouds.*

I was about to ask for my phone again, but the next item in the broadcast caught my ear with the words "Now some happy news for Night Minister Paulsen." I turned to see an anchor-woman I didn't know from the Day staff.

"In a press conference today at County Hospital, the minister's husband confirmed that his wife has had her baby: a healthy boy weighing twenty-eight hundred grams, and measuring forty-five centimeters. The delivery was by Cesarean section, but Mr. Paulsen and the doctor report that mother and baby are doing fine."

The video cut to Mr. Paulsen and the doctor, sitting in front of microphones at a table. Next to Mr. Paulsen stood a man in a suit, his eyes darting like a cockatrice, surveying everyone in the room to see who needed to be turned to stone.

"Jacqui is comfortable but tired," Mr. Paulsen droned robotically into the microphone, looking kind of ragged himself. A reporter asked a question, and Mr. Paulsen said, "His name? Oh, uh, no. We haven't chosen a name for the baby yet." He glanced up at the man in the suit, and something like worry crossed his face.

The anchorwoman came on for a new segment to interview the Hour Rights leader, Grady Hastings, who was organizing a march on Washington in which he would give a speech that deliberately overlapped the night curfew bell. I turned back to the men in my room.

"'Mother and baby are doing fine'? What the hell!" I said.

"Precisely," Mr. Benoît said, deadpan. "What the hell."

"Did you give the baby back?" My voice was verging on anger.

"No, my dear. We're not that wise." Jean stood up and took two sidesteps past the coffee table. "God help us, the child is asleep in my bedroom." He extended his arm toward the sofa. "Take my place, eat lunch, while I clean up and check on him. You need fuel to be of any use to yourself."

All at once I realized that the look of worry I'd seen flash across Mr. Paulsen's face was actually anguish. It was loss, and heartache, because his baby was missing. I clenched my teeth. No one cared about my heartache, why should I care about his?

"Sit down and eat, Plus One," Day Boy said. "And when your plate is clean I'll give you your phone. You look good, by the way." He pushed the plate in my direction, concentrating on that and not me. "Recovered, I mean."

I resented the way he was holding my phone hostage, and his patronizing tone of voice. But I had to have that sandwich, so I sat down and took an enormous bite, and then another. I inhaled the sweet aroma of the basil so deeply that my eyes closed while I chewed, and I was transported for a second to a day when, standing on a stool, I helped Poppu make packets of pesto to freeze for the winter. I willed the tears not to come, and for once they obeyed.

"Your dad is . . . nurturing," I finally said with my mouth full. A piece of mozzarella slipped out of the sandwich and onto my jeans. I picked it up with my fingers and popped it into my mouth.

"He raised me almost single-handedly," Day Boy said, passing me a napkin.

"But—"

"I know," he interrupted. "I have a mother. But she was the breadwinner, and he was the one who gave up his career to raise me."

"What was his career?" I asked, curious in spite of myself.

"In France he was a professor of psychology—neuroscience. He specialized in biological rhythms, and the evolution of biological timekeeping mechanisms. Growing up he always wanted to be an archaeologist, but only Rays can study archaeology."

It took me a moment to process the last sentence. I stopped in midbite. I stared at him.

He nodded, to confirm what I was thinking. "He's a Smudge."

I finished chewing and then swallowed.

"But you and your mom . . ."

"My mother is very good at what she does. She was invited to practice and teach in the United States. It was a chance to be reassigned to Day. She was pregnant with me at the time. It meant automatic Day assignment for me if she gave birth here. She was desperate to say yes. Plus, the Day government promised—at least, she thought they promised, but there was fine print—that Jean would be reassigned, too."

"Why wasn't he?"

"There were no posts in his field. The market for professors is drying up. He was supposed to wait until something opened at one of the local universities. After a year and a half of being apart from us, he gave up and came over as a Smudge. He chose retirement, to raise me full-time."

"How does a Night father care for a Day baby?" I asked.

"That sounds like a riddle." Day Boy smirked. "And the answer is: he lives like a prisoner in his own home."

"No, really."

"Really. The parents of other students walked me to school. Neighbors took me to the park and museums. Jean watched me play in the yard from the window. He cooked, he cleaned, he made my lunches, helped with homework, baked my birthday cakes. He makes the best chocolate mousse tart. He kept a

Day schedule and did the grocery shopping at night, when he was allowed to leave—when Hélène was home and I was asleep."

I finished the sandwich, which had barely taken the edge off my hunger, and started on the grapes. I watched Day Boy use a napkin to wipe the ring of condensation the pitcher had left on the coffee table. He did it carefully, just as he seemed to do everything. On the TV, Grady Hastings was being quizzed about the ethics of using teenagers in the nonviolent resistance movement. Day and Night high school students had been arrested for swapping their school hours in protest. Hastings was no longer a gangly teen. He was in his early twenties now and strikingly handsome, with skin so black it seemed to have a tinge of purple, and shocking tribal scarification on his forehead, cheeks, and chin in the form of patterned bumps. His hair was shaved to almost nothing, like he was too busy to bother growing it.

The reporter said, "How do you answer the critics who charge that you're deliberately exploiting children because their criminal records are wiped clean at eighteen?"

"I didn't organize this part of the protest movement." Grady was outraged, as he always was. "Pockets of students all over the country developed the strategy on their own. But if they don't embody courage in our pathetic, complacent society, I don't know who does. Unlike the adults who should be advocating for them, these kids are working to expose the daily inequalities and lies that both branches of government perpetrate on young people. So no, I did not recruit them, but *yes*, I commend them; *yes*, I will help them in any way I can."

I glanced at Day Boy watching the TV, focused and serious. I had judged him unfairly: he did not live in a high-rise, his family did not appear to be wealthy, he had been touched by the Day/Night divide in a way I had never suspected.

Jean came in cradling Fitzroy, feeding him a bottle, smiling as if he were his own son. "I had to wake him up to feed him. In these first few days they sometimes sleep too deeply, but their bodies need to eat every two hours."

I remembered how the baby had stayed so unbelievably still against me, a slumbering heat bomb, allowing me to escape the hospital with him. Was that only yesterday? I noticed Jean's hands—almost delicate, with long fingers made for pipetting, or typing, not for operating blister-pack sealing machines.

"You have a tan," I said, before I had the chance to edit myself.

He smiled. "So D'Arcy has revealed that we're compatriots, you and I." He glanced at the ceiling. "In fact, I sneak up to the roof for fifteen minutes a day to sun myself. I believe in making my own vitamin D."

"Where did you get the baby's bottle?" I asked, out of nowhere.

"Don't worry," Day Boy said. "We didn't go to the store wearing a sign advertising our new infant."

Jean said, "D'Arcy and I thought it would be safest for the purchase not to show up on either of our phones. I have a network of Day neighbors who have always bartered with me to pick up odds and ends that I have forgotten at night." He looked at his son and said, "It was Katherine—on the first floor—she has an infant granddaughter who visits on the weekends. It makes sense for Katherine to buy diapers and formula." He smiled at me. It created irresistibly charming creases above his cheeks. "In exchange, I will be making her pies for Unity Night."

"Speaking of fair trades," Day Boy said. He walked over to the TV stand and picked up my phone. He tossed it carefully onto my lap.

It had been right in front of me the whole time.

"You can't turn it on, though," Day Boy said, before I had a chance to do anything.

"Why?"

Jean said, "The police are looking for you; they would locate us by your phone's position."

"This apartment is the closest thing to a safe house we'll ever have," Day Boy added. "Jean is practically off the grid. He wants to keep it that way."

I wondered briefly where Day Boy's mother was, and what she thought of her husband and son harboring a fugitive. It didn't seem like her to let something like that slide.

"We can drive some distance away for you to use your phone." Day Boy interrupted my thoughts. "The trouble is we'll risk being stopped by an Hour Guard. And I hadn't thought of this till now, but it turns out that when you're rested and clean and not feverish you don't really look like my Plus One anymore."

"Thanks," I said, only half sarcastically. It occurred to me that no one was talking about turning me in. I wanted to know why, but for the moment I didn't dare break the spell.

Something clicked from my childhood. "I know how to get around the global positioning feature."

Day Boy raised an eyebrow, as if I'd surprised him with yet

another aspect of my criminality, while Jean said incredulously, "You do?"

I nodded. "My brother used to do it for money. He showed me once." Poppu had blown a gasket when he'd found out. It was the only time I'd ever heard them raise their voices in an argument. Smudges don't shout; they debate quietly. They master hurting each other with the choice of words, not the volume. I remembered hiding in my bed, under my comforter, hating being the cause of their fight.

"I'd need a computer, a mobile interface cable, and a pair of tweezers," I said.

"The first two are right in there," Jean said, using his chin to point to the sunroom study. "I'll get the tweezers."

"There are drawbacks," I warned, when he returned. "The instant I open the mobile case, the credit functionality is frozen. And if an Hour Guard stops me and happens to audit my position, he'll see that it's falsified, and I'm dead."

Day Boy said right away, "The credit functionality doesn't matter, because you can't buy anything or they'll track you by purchases. But the second part sounds risky—"

"Not necessarily," I said. "I don't think Hour Guards even glance at the accuracy of the phone's position when they stop you." My experience with their invasive scrutiny had always been creepier: checking whether I used birth control, looking at my family's income and my home address.

"No one has ever paged through to see my global position, as far as I know," Jean agreed.

Day Boy relented. "If she gets stopped while I'm with her I'll just hold my breath until I pass out."

I went into the sunroom. Jean opened a drawer and produced the cable that came with every state-issued mobile to download photos and records. I hooked my phone to his computer, pried apart the case, tweezed out the chip to reboot it, reinstalled it, and then reprogrammed it. It took no more than five minutes—and longer than necessary, because Day Boy was so curious his chin was over my shoulder the whole time, the breath from his nose wisping against my neck.

"Where should I put myself?" I asked, angling my cheek so I could see him, which put our faces too close. I turned back to the computer. "I can be anywhere on the planet. How about Japan?" Japan was one of the only countries—along with American Samoa and New Caledonia—that didn't follow the Day/Night divide, probably because they had survived the 1918 flu pandemic relatively unscathed by quarantining themselves.

"For now, let's choose something a little more believable," Day Boy said. "Somewhere you could have driven in this amount of time. How about Minneapolis?"

With the programming complete, I was free to move away from Day Boy. I unplugged my phone, got up from the seat, went to the living room, and tapped the screen.

"I should explain something—" Day Boy started, but I was already reading.

Someone had replied to the threatening texts on my behalf.

I'm here, with infant, ready to bargain, "I" had typed. The message was uncensored.

"You pretended to be me!" I said to Day Boy, irritated. But a bubble of admiration rose, too. It would never have occurred to me to use the word "bargain." I would have only thought to ask for instructions.

"That's what I wanted to tell you. We couldn't leave radio silence the whole time you were out cold, and you were of no use to anyone without sleep. I drove to the hospital to send and receive the messages so the cops couldn't trace you here."

I looked at the reply: **Bring the baby to Jackson Park outer harbor slip A12 at midnight.** It was time-stamped 10:12 p.m.

"This was last night!"

"Keep reading," Day Boy said.

I scrolled, and "my" reply said, **Need proof Poppu is safe. No meeting possible until tomorrow night.**

Delay is unacceptable, they had said, but there was a photo of Poppu attached, lying on an oval-shaped bed of what must have been a ship's cabin, with paneled walls and a porthole-style window. The photo was high-resolution—another violation of the censorship laws. I expanded it. He was awake and looked relatively comfortable, but he was two days closer to death than when I'd last seen him. He had a thin tube that wrapped around his ears and stuck into his nose, feeding him oxygen, which was alarming. Day Boy came and stood next to me, his shoulder just grazing mine. He reached out and dragged the close-up to highlight Poppu's forearm. Something was taped to Poppu's wrist, snaking out of the field of the photo. I swallowed.

"He has an IV and a nasal cannula," Day Boy said quietly. "So whoever they are, they have a medic with them."

The warmth and realness of Day Boy's arm and shoulder only made it more clear to me that Poppu was a bunch of

139

electronic pixels on a device. I edged just a hair to the side so that he wasn't touching me. I scrolled more.

Unavoidable, Day Boy had replied on my behalf. **Will be out of touch until tomorrow afternoon, at which time we will each provide proof of our possessions to negotiate.** It was so much his voice, his deliberateness, not mine. Anyone who knew me might have questioned whether I wrote it. And what a coup it was to receive a photo of Poppu without showing evidence that we had the baby.

I tried to scroll farther. That was the last message. I looked up at Day Boy, and at Jean across the room, swaying with Fitzroy.

"And now?" I asked. "What do I do now?"

Be Here

After Ciel told me the truth about our parents, the thought that they had died for a cause rather than raise me began to burn constantly, like a weak acid. When Poppu got sick I knew I would lose the person who had gracefully chosen to take their place.

In a fit of despondency one Monight I scrawled this on my desk:

$$death = abandonment.$$

I drew a picture of a crying baby—me—with soft curls that were destined to become wiry flames after puberty.

My drawing partner responded the next night by sketching a pacifier, floating above the open, wailing mouth of the infant, with a dashed arrow pointing as if to say "insert here."

> *Ah, Mistress of the Dark Non Sequitur,*
> *I missed you over the weekend.*
> *How can I help?*

141

It was such a simple, sweet offer. *How can I help?* No lecture, no arrogant presumption that he could interpret and comfort without further information.

I put the circled number ① next to the crying baby, the number ② next to his drawing of the pacifier, and for number ③ I re-drew the baby with the pacifier in her mouth, soothed, with only a vestige of a tear on her flushed cheek. Below her I wrote:

Just always be here.

Jean put the baby on his shoulder and said, "How strong do you feel, Sol?"

My name sounded good on his lips, like he'd said it many times before and burnished it to a soft luster.

"I'm well, thanks to you."

"D'Arcy did most of the nursing," he said dismissively. He turned to his son. "I think it's time for us to introduce her upstairs."

"Why?" Day Boy pleaded, almost whined. "They've already met."

"First, keeping secrets from your mother is unwise. Second, you said Fitzroy was transferred from the Night to Day nursery to avoid treatment, and I need your mother to explain what that means."

"But she'll turn her in!" he said, gesturing at me, his voice heavy with something I couldn't recognize. "And stop calling the baby Fitzroy. It's pissing me off."

It was curious to me the way Jean referred to his wife as "your mother."

Day Boy stood up and paced the room. Jean waited quietly, so I did, too. Finally Day Boy stopped in front of me.

"Let's go see Hélène," he grumbled at last. He started to walk to the rear of the apartment. I followed, with Jean behind me.

We passed the front hall and the bedrooms without stopping and finally ended up in the kitchen. It was a well-loved room, with copper pots hanging from a rack on the ceiling, and canisters of flour, rice, and pasta on the counters. An espresso machine. A butcher-block island that had been subjected to countless chef's knives. A marble pastry board just like Poppu's, with the same worn patina. The windows of the room were high, for privacy, and there was no back door. There was the inviting smell of something warm and rich bubbling in a pot on the stove, with the lid cocked and vapors curling toward the hood.

Day Boy climbed a steep, library-style ladder that led to a hatch in the ceiling.

I was thoroughly confused.

I put my foot on the bottom rung, my hands on the railings, and looked up at him. He knocked hard on the beaded wood paneling. Three series of three knocks. He waited for an answer, looked down at me, and said with a scowl, "What would you like written on your tombstone?"

I heard footsteps, and then a piece of furniture moved above us. The hatch lifted, and Hélène's face appeared, with her dark hair dangling and her cheeks plump from the pull of gravity. There was a look she gave Day Boy that I craved— the kind of unguarded joy that I saw on Poppu's face when I walked through the door after school—but it was there for only a second or two.

"*Mais enfin te voilà,*" she began with relief, as if he were simply late and she had finally found him. Her eyes caught on me, standing below him on the ladder. The look on her face morphed into something like intense confusion and escalated to horror when she caught sight of Jean and the baby.

"Now wait, before you—" Day Boy started.

"*Non. Non! Non! Je ne peux pas croire que tu as—*" and then she slammed the hatch in midsentence and Day Boy ducked. I heard her voice, hysterical, muffled by the floor, ranting in French about the police, her feet stomping like a teenager. Something swished across the hatch and plunked lightly—a rug maybe—and a chair pounded on top of that, perhaps, and I heard her throw her body into the chair. And then there was silence for a moment, followed by racked sobbing. That last sound reached into my gut, grabbed a handful of intestines, and squeezed. It was more awful to have caused such despondence than any amount of rage. I wondered when I'd gone so soft that I gave a damn about a woman who openly despised me.

Day Boy waited a minute, and when her crying quieted some, he knocked again. Three sets of three.

"Mum," he called. No answer. "*Maman.*" His voice was becoming puny. "*Je suis vraiment désolé.*" *I'm so sorry.*

Hearing him apologize about me with such profound emotion caused a surprising ache in my chest. It was as if I were a horrible mistake, a life-changing regret, a misfortune that he would wish away if he could.

But of course I was all of those things.

I turned to look at Jean, a couple of steps away from the ladder, but I couldn't read his face. He was cool, nearly stony.

I stepped down and waited, empty as a glass jar, hugging myself with a chill. It was warm in the kitchen, I knew, but my starved body had lost the ability to regulate its temperature at the most unpredictable times. Meanwhile Day Boy hadn't moved. He was so high on the ladder he was scrunched, leaning against the railing, his head bent and his shoulders curved.

Jean sighed. *"Tiens,"* he said, handing me Fitzroy, whom I took somewhat reluctantly and very clumsily. The baby growled at the transition. Jean went to the cabinet and pulled out a deep round mug. He used a hot pad to remove the lid of the pot on the stove. He ladled two scoops of steaming green slop into the mug, set it on the island near me, and reached into the dish drainer for a clean spoon. And then he gently took Fitzroy back, supporting his head and neck far better than I had. For the next several minutes I sat on a stool and sipped hot, rich split-pea soup with ham—so wonderful and warming—trying not to look at Day Boy, jammed against the ceiling and miserable.

Something thumped above us. The chair was dragged aside. The hatch crackled as it stuck slightly. Hélène stood above the opening, hands on her waist, her face red-nosed and shiny from scrubbing it. She stepped aside so we could mount.

"Merci." I heard Day Boy thank her, softly.

"Je ne promets rien," she replied, monotone. *I promise nothing.*

It was one of the hardest things I had ever done, to climb out of the hatch and feel her eyes on me as I moved into her

146

space. Dozens of people glared at me every night when I was in school, and the sum of them didn't add up to this.

But what was the space I was stepping into? It was another kitchen, and a quick glance down the hall showed an apartment that seemed to be laid out almost identically to the one below. Except this one, I noticed, had a back door in the kitchen. This one was perfectly appointed with modern furnishings, not the eclectic mix of old and new downstairs. This one was a little too clean, almost sterile.

"His and hers," Day Boy said, answering a question I hadn't asked.

As Jean climbed up the ladder behind us cradling the baby, Day Boy said dully, "*Maman*, you remember Sol." He hurried to add, "Sol speaks fluent French, so there's no hiding behind language. Unless you intend to speak Latin."

"Actually . . ." I said, looking at his sneakers instead of his face.

"Okay, forget Latin, I guess she knows that, too," he muttered.

Jean was in the room, and Hélène looked at the baby in his arms. "I hope that infant is in perfect health," she said, her voice cold. "Because if god forbid anything happens to him—"

"Perfect health," Jean said, just as stony as he was a floor below.

It occurred to me that they didn't like each other. That the his-and-hers apartments were separate homes. That Day Boy came from a so-called broken family. I glanced over and caught him reading my face, everything I was thinking.

Hélène turned on Day Boy then. "After all we've worked for

together, and the potential you have for a successful, fulfilling life, you risk throwing it away by aiding a *criminal*—an uncivilized, rude, unhappy . . ."—she couldn't come up with adjectives for me fast enough—"factory worker."

"Don't," Day Boy said.

"And you," she said to Jean, her voice rising. "You're an adult, you *know* better. You had *no right* carrying her through my apartment—involving me. That baby should have gone back immediately to its parents. You should have saved D'Arcy from himself and his naïve, misplaced . . ."

"Compassion?" Jean filled in.

"Folly!" she cried. And then she seemed to realize that the neighbors might hear and hissed, "Any compassion that is being handed out should go to this child's parents, who don't know whether he is even *alive*."

She was right again.

"And you answered my door when the police came searching for her," she said incredulously to Day Boy. "I'm outraged by how easily you lied to them. I'm ashamed that I helped you to do it, defending you against their accusations of incompetence . . . with her hiding downstairs the whole time!"

The police had come while I was asleep, and I hadn't heard a thing.

"I did not raise a liar," she said pointedly.

Day Boy's face became expressionless. And as much as he had looked like his mother when he treated my finger in the hospital, he looked entirely like his father at that moment.

"Our whole life is a lie, Mother. Jean lives in hiding

downstairs. You pretend to be happily married to him. We all act like the Day/Night divide hasn't destroyed our family."

She paused for a second, a heavy, wounded second. And although she was looking squarely at him, I felt her attention—her soul, if there is such a thing—directed fully at me. What he had said was too private, and it cut her that I had heard it. Her cheeks and neck flushed as she redirected the argument, the only thing she could do: "An abducted child will ruin you. You'll end up in jail. You'll lose your apprenticeship. Your life will be over. Why are you throwing everything away for the sake of a stranger who means nothing to you?" Her eyes welled up for the first time since her crying jag.

Day Boy didn't answer the question. "She was pyretic and dehydrated—"

"So you take her to a *hospital*, not your home."

Day Boy looked at the floor, pushed his bangs up, rubbed his forehead. "You should know I wrote a script for doxycycline in your name."

She shook her head, her lips compressed in a line.

He held her gaze with a courage I wouldn't have had. "I never wanted to disappoint you. You've given me everything."

This was the point in my apologies to Poppu where I would have thrown my arms around him in a frustrated, giant hug, and he would have been unable to resist me, no matter how angry he was, and the concessions would have tumbled out of us like an avalanche of rocks down a mountain. But I got the feeling that Day Boy and Hélène didn't touch each other much, that their love was reserved, and based on mutual respect—respect that my presence was eroding.

"I hid her from you so that you wouldn't have to lie to the police," he said. "So that you genuinely wouldn't know where she was. It was only a matter of time before Dacruz came to question me; he had given me responsibility for her at the hospital."

"You are a fool," she whispered, the air escaping her on the last word.

"I am a fool," he agreed, suddenly looking older than eighteen. "But I beg you to help me anyway."

We sat on white couches in her living room while Jean and Day Boy took turns relating what had happened since Hélène had treated me in the hospital. I noticed that Day Boy made my trip from lockup back to the ER seem medically essential, and that he didn't reveal that Ciel and I were on the outs. These tweaks to the truth left the impression that I was earnest and impulsive in my kidnapping, but not conniving, which was a kindness I didn't deserve.

Hélène was like her son: nothing escaped her. She asked, "Did the police summon you to the station to check her condition?"

Day Boy hesitated. He'd have to lie outright if he wanted to fudge this part of the story.

"No." He told the truth. "I went on my own. I wanted to make sure she was okay." Apparently he would only lie to make *me* look better. I couldn't figure him out.

He moved on, and when he came to the part about Poppu's blindness, Jean caught my eye.

"What was the cause of the blindness?"

151

I didn't see why it mattered, but I said, "Severe retinopathy."

"Retinopathy is usually the result of a systemic disease," Day Boy said. "Is he diabetic?"

I shook my head. "His hypertension was uncontrolled for too long."

"Hypertension, retinopathy, and cancer," Jean said thoughtfully. "The poor man."

"And gallstones," I said, "but those are the least of his worries now."

"Gallstones," Jean said, as if he were chewing the word. "Was your grandfather always a Smudge?"

I shook my head. "He was reassigned when he moved here from Belgium."

"Why would he accept reassignment?"

Was everyone in this family genetically programmed to probe? "My parents were killed in a car accident when I was little, and he moved to the States to raise my brother and me. We were Smudges, so he had to be, too."

"If your grandfather was a Ray in Belgium, why was your mother a Smudge?" Hélène asked, as if catching me up in a lie.

"Because she fell in love with a Smudge on a ship in the middle of the Atlantic." As the words left my lips I wondered for the first time whether those four days together without curfews had also ignited my parents' passion against the Day/Night divide. I added, almost to myself, "They were only eighteen."

Day Boy told Hélène that Poppu had been kidnapped by people who were threatening me by text, demanding that I hand over the baby, yet it was unclear how they knew I even had a baby.

I couldn't stop myself from asking a question: "Who were you texting when I collapsed at my apartment?"

Jean said, "That was me. I'm afraid I counseled him to take you to the hospital, Sol."

"But something was wrong when we pulled up," Day Boy said, looking squarely at his mother. "It was obvious they knew the baby was missing. I expected to see police, and news reporters, and satellite uplink vans. Instead there were undercover Suits, kicking dustballs." He gestured at me. "I couldn't put her in jail for something I didn't understand. I went with my gut, not my head.

"So we carried her through your apartment, and the rest you know," he said to his mother. He looked at me, sensing my confusion, and explained. "Jean's apartment has no entry or exit, except through Hélène's apartment. Like I said: off the grid." I nodded, understanding everything except perhaps why a person would want to live that way.

Jean had his knees together with Fitz lying faceup, asleep in the valley of his long thighs, which were swaying ever so slightly from side to side. "In the middle of the night I saw the first news report that Minister Paulsen had happily delivered her baby." He rubbed Fitz's tummy. "*This* baby, who was in my arms at the time. They were covering up his disappearance."

Hélène's gaze fell on me. It was almost unbearable. I knew that if she stared long enough she'd see every one of my flaws, all the sour anger packed inside me, curing like pickles in a jar, without my opening my mouth. I concentrated on not moving; I tried to loosen the muscle tone in my face—to be expressionless—as Day Boy and Jean had done.

"How is it you managed not to steal your brother's baby, if that was indeed your goal?"

I knew I was a liar, but hearing the accusation in her voice over something I had *not* lied about made my head heat up. I felt pricks along my scalp, like I was some sort of feral cat, hackles rising.

"I took him from the *Le Cœur* bassinet," I said. "You're the one who moved him to the Day nursery against hospital rules, maybe you can tell *me* how he landed in the wrong crib."

She froze for only a fraction of a second before I saw outrage bloom on her face.

"*Attendez, attendez,*" Day Boy said to us both, before whatever was building in her exploded, before I leaped on her like a real cat. "We don't have time to argue." He looked at me, pleading. "Please," he mouthed, with an expression that indicated, *Can you keep it together just this once?*

Before I knew what I was saying, I had apologized. "*Je vous prie de m'excuser,*" I mumbled in Hélène's general direction, using the strictly polite form Poppu had taught Ciel and me to use with adults.

Day Boy said to his mother, "I believe her when she says she took the baby from her brother's bassinet. So that means someone had already switched the babies before she got there. She stumbled into something."

"Hélène," Jean said. "Why was the Night Minister's child in the Day nursery?"

I glanced at her, and some of the color had left her face. She was silent.

Day Boy answered. "It was a political favor. We were allowing him to avoid the treatment that all Night babies get."

154

Jean leaned forward. "What treatment?"

Day Boy shrugged, shaking his head lightly. "I've never worked a Night maternity shift, but I've heard it's a first intravenous dose of melatonin and vitamin D, because the mother hasn't produced any during gestation." He looked at little Fitzroy, resting on his dad's legs, but his eyes focused through the baby, into the middle distance. "Come to think of it, why avoid that?" He turned to his mother. "Is there something unsafe about it?"

Hélène was silent. I watched Jean, whose face had lost the blank mask and was all astonishment.

"*Zut, non,*" he said to her, under his breath.

She dropped her head to look at her hands.

"*Hélène, dis-moi que ce n'est pas ce que je pense.*" *Tell me it's not what I'm thinking.*

"It's mandated by law," she said, her voice thin and strained. "It has been for almost two decades."

Jean said, "I was still sharing your bed a year and a half ago."

"I couldn't jeopardize D'Arcy's future. I couldn't risk that you'd call attention to it because of your . . . your . . ."

"My what? My research?"

"Your fundamentalism!"

"*Every* Night infant?" he asked.

She nodded.

He stood up with the baby. His eyes found me, and they had a profound sort of sympathy. "And all adult Night transfers, too, I am sure."

Day Boy said exactly the words that were unspoken in my head: "What the hell is going on?"

Balanced Rock

My desk partner disappeared after the first week of the fall term of my junior year. If I had understood his last message in time I might have been able to say goodbye.

I sat down one night to a drawing with the word *Quiz* above it. There was a distinctive natural formation sketched out: a blockish, oblong rock—made of limestone I thought, because of the faint cracked layers he had drawn—balanced on another giant boulder or wall. There was a wooden boardwalk and stairway leading up to it, making the location seem distinctly like a state park. For scale he had drawn a crow on the railing, which, if it was accurately depicted, as his drawings usually were, implied that the rock was positively enormous and the balancing act impressive. The rock had ferns poking out from cracks and a full head of leafy, twiggy hair on its flat top.

I had never seen it before.

"I'm stumped, but this is incredible!" I wrote, and I spent the rest of the period giving the rock texture, and drawing the deep shadows that would be there if it were in moonlight, happily unaware that it was my last collaboration with him.

The next day he had practically written a treatise: the longest message he'd ever composed in the two years we'd corresponded, with no further drawing. I copied it down into my phone before the teacher made me wash the desk, and I read it enough times at home to have it memorized:

"This is Balanced Rock, in the Maquoketa Caves State Park, in eastern Iowa, near the northwestern Illinois border. The rock weighs about seventeen tons. The whole park is stunning: it escaped glaciation in the last Ice Age so that nothing was buried under drift and everything has been eroding naturally since the Paleozoic era. There are bluffs, caves (along with thousands of bats), hidden springs, sinkholes . . . In the fall the rocks are covered with green moss after the rains, the woods are misty, the overgrowth from summer is beginning to turn red and gold. There are cool streams and brooks carving archways through sandstone, and pools that are almost tidal in their beauty. You would love camping there. I wish I were there right now, listening to the creeks burble and the trees whisper. I wish I could show it to you. I wish my life weren't as precarious as Balanced Rock, and that my twin masters, Duty and Stealth, would give me just a little breathing room before they pass me off to Endless Responsibility. Try to go see the caves. And think of me when you do."

Thursday
4:00 p.m.

Jean and Hélène's fight escalated, in French. It became clear that Jean had resumed his research ever since his son had become school-age. His partners overseas did the lab work, he crunched the numbers. I learned that the projects they were working on were permissible in France, but questionably legal in the United States.

Day Boy finally raised his voice over theirs, saying, "Do you care at all that the neighbors can hear this sensitive discussion?" He turned to Jean, chafed. "What have you guessed, that you can share with me?"

"Since your mother refuses to say the word, I will: *pinealectomy*."

Day Boy hesitated only a second. "Are you saying the Night babies are all getting pinealectomies?"

Hélène said, "It's an actionable offense for a doctor to divulge that information to anyone other than another doctor." She grabbed Day Boy's hand. "Do you understand that? You don't *say the word* or your medical license is immediately revoked."

I knew that an "ectomy" was when something was surgically removed from your body. I knew that the word "pineal" was usually followed by the word "gland." And although I had probably learned where the pineal gland was and what it did at some point in a science class, I could not dredge the information up on the spot. But I had seen a few newborn babies in my lifetime, and I would have thought a surgery would have been obvious—that we Smudges would have noticed something like that happening to our babies and talked about it to each other.

Day Boy was thinking the same thing.

"Why is there no incision or portal on the scalp?"

That's right. The pineal gland is in the brain.

Hélène clamped her lips together.

Jean said, exasperated, "If it is done the same way that they do it in France, it's not a true surgery; instead they destroy the tissue with radiation. The pineal gland is smaller than a grain of rice in an infant, but it takes up fluoride faster than other organs in the body. They attach a tiny seed of quickly decaying radiation to a molecule of fluoride and inject it into the subject. Then they run a positron emission tomography scan to be sure the seed hit its mark."

"Are you getting this?" Day Boy had the courtesy to ask me.

I nodded dumbly. "But I forget what the pineal gland does."

"It secretes melatonin," he replied.

I should have remembered that, being a Smudge. Melatonin was a daily concept for us.

"Melatonin helps to regulate the body clock," he went on. "The pineal gland produces melatonin after the sun goes down and makes you feel drowsy. The trouble is, Smudges are supposed to sleep during the day. So theoretically I guess if you destroy natural melatonin production at night and then add CircaDiem supplements in the morning, the body clock could be reset."

Jean said, "Except the scientific evidence that supplemental melatonin recalibrates circadian rhythm is totally nonexistent."

I could have told them that, based on personal experience.

Jean said, "The only evidence that performing a PinX destroys the body clock comes from experiments on Siberian hamsters—an animal that is hyperphotosensitive because of its evolution. When you remove the pineal gland, hamsters 'free-run'—their cycles drift regardless of the light hours. For them, introducing melatonin infusions at prescribed times does re-create the cycle, but I must emphasize that *no one* has ever replicated the results in humans." He glared at Hélène. "Certainly not enough to merit blanket tissue destruction in half the population, using a procedure that is questionably safe."

"Complications are rare," Hélène said.

"But greater than zero!" Jean said instantly. "No amount of risk is justifiable for a procedure that has not been proved to be efficacious."

I asked Hélène, in a voice weaker than I expected, "Did they do this to me?"

She looked at me only long enough to say in a monotone, "If you were born within the last nineteen years in a hospital in the United States . . . yes."

The reality of it made me feel fragile, or damaged. I resisted the urge to touch my head, to see if it was whole. I was the same person I'd been five minutes ago. I would not show her that I cared.

I looked at Jean. "My grandfather?"

"I suspect he had the procedure when he arrived. There's far less data in the area of adult PinX procedures, because there are so few adults who transfer from Day to Night. But we do know that the pineal gland becomes calcified with age. The uptake of fluoride is not the same, and the amount needed to hit the mark may be higher, requiring repeat injections. The effect of systemic radiation may be increased. There are data, though statistically weak until we get larger sample sizes, that show health detriments for this procedure that correlate with his illnesses." He came over to me, the baby on his shoulder, and said gently, "The changes are seen in older patients only, not in infants, whose new, flexible bodies adapt in ways we don't understand. But in adults, melatonin suppresses tumor production. It has vascular effects, which might explain your grandfather's hypertension and retinopathy. It inhibits cholesterol secretion from the gallbladder—"

Hélène interrupted. "This is all theoretical, with little empirical evidence." But she would only look at Day Boy, not at me or Jean.

Day Boy scrabbled his hair with one hand, thinking. It messed him up perfectly.

"You say complications are rare. What are they, and what is the incidence?"

She said, "The vast majority of infants have no adverse reaction. Some infants have soreness at the injection site. Infrequently, exhaustion and lethargy from the radiation."

161

"Is that all?" Day Boy encouraged her.

She looked at her hands. What came out next was practically wilted. "Rarely—*rarely*—the radiation misses its mark, or doesn't decay fast enough for that individual's physiology and seems to . . . it causes a leukemia or lymphoma."

"Blood cancer," Day Boy said, stunned.

"One in fifty thousand. But it is most often treatable."

"How many births are there in the United States every year?" He shot the question at Jean, who shook his head.

"Four million," Hélène said.

Day Boy clawed his hair again, back and forth. This time he created a giant cowlick that I had the urge to reach out and coax back into place. I shook my head to snap myself out of it.

"Four million babies." He was doing quick math. "Divided by fifty thousand—"

"Forty babies a year," I said.

"Eighty," he corrected.

"Only two million of those births are Smudges."

The edge of a smile lifted on one side of his face. "Right you are, Plus One." He quickly became serious again. "Forty children with cancer."

Hélène said, "There is a similar incidence of complications with vaccines that are given in the first few days of life."

"Not *cancer*. And those vaccines prevent serious childhood illnesses—they prevent epidemics," Day Boy said. "If Jean is right that this procedure confers no health benefit to the patient *or* the general population, administering it and causing random cancers is a public health disaster."

When there was a pause in the discussion, I found myself blurting, "I'm sorry, I have to go now."

Day Boy swung around. "What?"

"None of this medical talk can help me, or Poppu." I held up my phone. "They said he's at Jackson Harbor. I'm going to see him before he dies."

"Just like that," he said. "What makes you think they're still there? How do you know they won't hurt you? We don't even know who *they* are!"

"I'll take my chances and leave now. If they're still docked maybe I can talk my way in." I put my phone in my pocket. "I'll wing it."

"That's the stupidest plan I've ever heard," Day Boy said.

"By definition 'winging it' is not a plan," I said, too crisply.

He stepped between me and the sight line to the front door. "You have no way of traveling safely in the daytime." He pointed toward the couch. "And hell if we're going to let you trade that baby for your grandfather."

I looked at Jean, who was changing Fitz's diaper across his lap, which I had never seen done before.

"I kind of guessed," I said. "I'll wrap a football in some blankets as a decoy and hope that it gets me as far as seeing Poppu before they discover there's no baby."

"Look at me, Plus One, do I look like the kind of guy who has a football in his house?"

I knew him for what he was now: a slightly disheveled, unconventionally handsome National Distinction scholar, with a fearsome stage mother and a renegade scientist for a dad. Plus he was French. There would be no football.

"A loaf of *bread*, then, it doesn't matter." A jumpiness had started to thrill its way from my brain to my arms and legs, making me want to run, or shake someone. "I couldn't take Poppu home even if I tried—we don't *have* a home anymore. My last hope is just to say goodbye to him, and *time is running out*."

Hélène stood up. "You should in fact leave, Miss Le Coeur," she said coldly. "But the correct plan is for you to turn yourself in. You must depart at night, in your proper sphere, without D'Arcy's or Jean's help, carrying this baby, and hail the first police officer you see."

"That's not happening," D'Arcy said.

She ignored him and continued to pin me with words. "If you had a single compassionate cell in your body, you would understand that D'Arcy worked his whole life to be where he is now, that he has already shown exceptional kindness to you at great personal risk, and that this is the only way to safely convey the baby to its parents, where it belongs, and to absolve

D'Arcy entirely of responsibility, after which for his sake you shall forget any interaction you had with him other than receiving stitches and a dressing in his care."

"I won't turn myself in without seeing my grandfather one last time." I felt my shoulders and neck tense—no, almost flare, like a cobra's hood. "So if that's what you want you'll have to tie me up right here." And then I heard my voice rise slightly in pitch but not volume as I said, "Do you understand that other people live, and hope, and love each other? Or is the only room you have left in your heart filled with your son?"

Jean hastily finished the diaper change, nested the baby faceup where the seat of the sofa met the back, and stood to move between us. I had gotten closer to Hélène, and something fierce was spewing out of me like water from a broken levee. Jean spoke, but I couldn't focus; I felt light-headed, with sounds of the ocean rushing around my ears; and from the corner of my eye I saw Day Boy storm off into the kitchen.

I heard a buzzing noise through the surf in my head. I blinked. It was the doorbell. Hélène had already bolted toward the sunporch and leaped on the office chair to look down at the sidewalk.

"Three men," she whispered breathlessly to Jean, leaning away from the window so they wouldn't see her, just as I had done when it was her son at my apartment door. "Men in suits."

"Crew cuts?" I heard Day Boy ask behind me. I felt an irrational flush of relief that he was back, that he hadn't given up on us all. Hélène nodded.

He said, "It's the men from the hospital."

He scooped Fitzroy off the sofa, grabbed the rolled-up dirty diaper, handed it to me, and tugged me out of the room by my sleeve.

"Please don't turn her in," he pleaded to his mother over his shoulder, and led me briskly into the kitchen with Jean following after. I hurried down the ladder first and Day Boy followed, taking obvious care with only one hand for the baby.

Before Jean closed the hatch door, Day Boy looked up and said quietly, "Switch on the intercom."

Jean nodded. "Keep the baby happy." I knew "happy" meant "quiet," and that Day Boy had probably never had to cry much when he was young. After the hatch was closed, I heard the heavy rug slide across the floor and the chair clomp on top of it.

At the foot of the ladder there was a blue vinyl bag that hadn't been there before, shaped like a soft rectangular suitcase. Day Boy must have dropped it down the hatch during my argument with Hélène. It was about the size of the old sewing machine and case that Ciel had rescued from the dumpster when our Day neighbors had moved to the "safer" suburbs.

Day Boy picked up the bag, and I hurried to take it from him so that he'd have both hands free for Fitzroy. On our way through the kitchen to the hallway, I tossed the diaper in the kitchen garbage can. We went to his room, where I set the bag on his desk. He pointed with his chin and said, "There's a receiver in that bottom drawer." I retrieved it, something like a baby monitor. He tipped his head toward the wall. "And an outlet next to my bed." I plugged it in and switched it on.

". . . my husband, Jean François Benoît," I heard his mother say.

"How do you do, sir," a man's voice said. "Now, Mrs. Benoît . . ."

"Dr. Benoît," Jean corrected.

"Yes, of course."

Day Boy eased himself onto the bed, propping his back against the wall, and laid the sleeping baby on the quilt, resting his hand on him. I sat in the stuffed chair beside the bed. In my mind's eye I suddenly recalled a hazy image of Day Boy sleeping in that same chair while I was feverish: his elbow on the armrest, his temple resting on his knuckles, his eyelashes like black fringe on his cheeks.

"Dr. Benoît, may we speak with you in private, please?" the voice on the monitor was saying.

"With all due respect to you, Mr. Benoît," another voice said.

"Dr. Benoît," Jean corrected again. I smiled. He was being deliberately maddening.

"Are you an MD at the hospital, too?" the first man said.

"No, I'm a medical researcher. I have a doctorate."

"Then I'm sorry, I'm afraid you'll have to leave the room. Mr. Smith here will take you outside for a walk."

"Not now he won't," Jean said. "I am . . . how do you Americans say it? A Smudge."

There was a slight hesitation.

"Really?"

"Really. Would you like to see my phone?"

"Why yes, I would."

Another pause, during which I murmured, "He's surprised Jean doesn't have two heads." Day Boy tightened his lips.

"Huh," the Suit said. "You don't see much of that. I mean, for a Smudge and a Ray to . . . to . . ."

"To love each other?" Hélène suggested crisply.

"To be married, I meant," he said. "In any case. Well. To each his own. That's fine, sir, Dr. Benoît. We have a Day pass at our discretion. Go ahead, enjoy yourself. Stroll around the block, soak up some sun." The last part of the sentence was muffled, as if they were walking away from the transmitter. The door opened with a click and closed with a gentle slam.

Hélène did not offer the remaining men a seat.

"Dr. Benoît, I'm here to ask you about the Paulsen baby. My colleague, Mr. Jones—he's just going to have a look around your apartment while we talk."

The men in suits searched Hélène's apartment but failed to find Minister Paulsen's baby, who woke up hungry, just one floor below, but whom Day Boy successfully stalled with gentle attention until they'd left. I stole glances as he paced the room with Fitzroy, rocking him, nuzzling him, and making quiet clicking noises, like an affectionate uncle. The baby had a sweet look of unfocused bewilderment.

The Suit who interrogated Hélène, whose name was supposedly Mr. Thomas, knew that she had handled the baby in the Day nursery before he'd gone missing. He knew that the ankle bracelet said "Baby Boy Fitzroy." He knew that Fitzroy was Hélène's mother's maiden name. He was full of all sorts of information, but he was as dumb as a post, the kind of guy whose good grooming and punctuality had gotten him promoted past his natural ability. Hélène was specific and accurate about when she was in contact with the infant and who was in charge of the nursery when she left. The rest of the day she was in the constant presence of the hospital staff in the ER, in a meeting with the director of emergency services, and had gone to the restroom only twice. In short, she had an alibi for nearly every minute, and he and Mr. Jones were welcome to leave now. Her sharp tongue was sort of kickass when I wasn't on the receiving end.

Mr. Thomas reminded her of the sensitivity of the information she possessed: it was vital that the public not know about pineal destruction. "Sharing time fairly" meant keeping the Smudge population happily and healthily adjusted in their time zone. It was considered by the executive branch to be a matter of domestic security. Mr. Thomas's mandate from his superiors was to return the Paulsen baby with no fanfare, without the public's knowledge that he had ever been missing.

I had a sudden picture of Mr. Thomas in my head: I'd have bet anything he was the Suit who was sitting next to Mr. Paulsen at the press conference.

Mr. Thomas let Hélène know, with puffed-up importance, that he reserved the right to return, and that he was sending her a text message with his business card attached. She was to contact him at any time of the day or night if she remembered something that might help them recover the infant.

Jean returned to her apartment a moment after the men left. He announced in French that he was going downstairs and would speak with Hélène after he checked on us. On his way to the hatch, he flipped the switch of the transmitter, and the receiver hissed static, so I shut it off.

I stepped halfway into the hall and heard Hélène's voice on the ladder. She was following Jean. Of course she was.

"Your mom, too," I told D'Arcy.

He ushered me out with Fitzroy in his arms and closed the door. The blue vinyl bag was not something he wanted Hélène to know about, I guessed. Fitz had begun a full-on cry of hunger, and by the time we got into the kitchen, Jean was already warming up a bottle of formula, the old-fashioned way, in a pan of heated water.

"Thank you for not turning her in," Day Boy said to Hélène, ladling Fitzroy into Jean's waiting arms.

"How could I?" Hélène said sharply. "She was down here with you, and you would have both been arrested!"

I spoke up. "I have an idea that would allow me to take the blame for the kidnapping, return the baby to his parents, and still give me a chance to see my grandfather." Day Boy swung around to glare at me, and for the life of me I couldn't figure out why—why I couldn't have a say in my own demise. Fitzroy's cry became guttural.

"Would you mind checking the temperature of the milk?" Jean asked Hélène. When her back was turned, he gave me a pointed, nervous look.

She took the bottle out of the water, dried it with a dish towel, capped it with a nipple, shook it, and then dribbled some of the formula on her wrist. She nodded at Jean perfunctorily and handed him the bottle.

"So what is this plan?" Hélène asked me. Day Boy's lips were pursed, Jean's brow was furrowed. I could see that they didn't like not knowing the script.

"Your son and the baby stay safely out of it," I began, by way of reassurance. "But it may pose a risk to Jean. My idea is that I text the people who have my grandfather to confirm a meeting tonight after dusk. I bring a fake baby. I don't let them touch the decoy until I'm in Poppu's presence, until I've seen him with my own eyes. Meanwhile Jean leaves the real baby somewhere safe, like a church—we can agree ahead of time on which one—and I hit 'send' on a text that I've prepared in my phone, telling the police where to find the baby. Since the message will come from my phone, I'll be the one they blame for kidnapping the Paulsens' child."

"Fine," Hélène said, after only a second or two to process the explanation.

"Too many holes," Day Boy said.

"What holes?" I asked.

"Jean might be seen dropping off the baby."

"It sounds easier than many things I've done," Jean said.

Day Boy shook his head at me. "It's still flawed. Why would they take you to your grandfather without demanding to see the baby first?"

"I'll agree with them ahead of time that the trade-off only happens when he and I are in the same room together."

"You're right, we'll just make them pinky swear, what was I thinking?"

I frowned at his sarcasm.

He went on: "These people could just as easily grab the 'baby,' not let you see your Poppu, and kill you when they discover you brought a fake. They may already be planning on killing you the moment you show up. They'll definitely kill you when they see the Paulsens on TV with their son. Who knows whether they'll even have your grandfather with them? And if they do have him with them, what incentive do they have to show him to you, if you seem to be carrying your only leverage in your arms?"

He was right, and I could only blurt, "Well, what bright idea do you have?"

"*Du calme, D'Arcy.*" Jean tried to soothe his son.

Day Boy sighed. He rubbed his forehead hard. In a moment he said, "Your plan isn't far off, I'm sorry. It's good that you're bargaining to see your grandfather without having the real baby with you—I mean, it's good strategically, and not just for the baby's sake. Your safety depends on their believing that *only you* know where the baby is, and even then it's not guaranteed."

I watched little Fitzroy sucking on the bottle—the way his lips reached with such frank need around the nipple. Everything about him was fresh and new, with no artifice. A blank slate, ready to be ruined by the world.

Day Boy said, "How about this: you bring a decoy, but just to get within talking range; you preemptively announce that the real baby is in a secure place that only you know. You agree to divulge the location in a text after you've seen your grandfather and are a safe distance away. We can pray they understand the argument: that you'd lose your ticket to safety if you brought the real baby."

I asked, "What if the kidnappers won't let me leave until they confirm where Fitz is—until they go to retrieve him?" But I knew the answer: they would see that I had lied, and eventually they'd see that the Paulsens' boy had been returned to his parents.

Day Boy shook his head, bewildered. "If there's absolutely zero trust on both sides, how does anyone ever exchange prisoners?"

Hélène said clinically, "In the event that you are detained I hope you understand we will still return the baby."

"It doesn't matter," I said, meeting her eyes. "As long as the baby is safe, and I have a chance at seeing Poppu, we've all got what we need." But I couldn't hold her gaze for long, and so I said to the floor, "I'm as good as in jail right now—how would being held captive be any different?"

"They could hurt you, that's how," Jean said.

Day Boy turned to Hélène and held her shoulders gently. His touch was tentative, civil. I wondered disjointedly whether the number of giant hugs Poppu wrapped me in had been weird by other families' standards.

"You can't return the baby until she's safe. Her life may depend on it."

She pulled away with a small, stiff tug. "The child cannot stay in this apartment—*my* apartment. It makes me an accomplice to have him here and I want to end that as soon as possible."

"*Je t'en prie*," he begged in an earnest whisper. "Just until we know she's away from them."

Hélène said, "I can only promise to delay until I decide action is absolutely necessary."

It was a too-carefully worded promise, but it was the best he would get.

* * *

The details were a matter of bargaining between mother and son over the next ten minutes. Day Boy insisted on driving me; Hélène would only accept that condition if it was daytime, so that he was legal to drive, and demanded that he drop me off no less than half a kilometer from the meeting site, whereupon I would walk the rest of the way; Day Boy would return immediately home after leaving me; I was to text Hélène the go-ahead to release the baby as soon as I was clear of the kidnappers, and turn myself in to the police, either by flagging down a squad car or by texting emergency services.

When they had reached a familial détente, Hélène went upstairs and Jean put the baby down for a nap on his bed. Day Boy and I went to his room, where I wrote a text opening negotiations with the people who had my grandfather.

As we waited for a response, Day Boy unzipped the blue bag. A layer of thick foam covered whatever was inside.

"Shh," he said, with a sideways smile. "We're borrowing this from Hélène."

There was an invoice lying on top of the foam. I picked it up and read it. Whatever it was, it had cost twelve thousand dollars.

He tipped his head to read the paper alongside me. "When she discovers this missing, you'll have to compose something for *my* tombstone."

He lifted the top layer to reveal a giant block of foam beneath, specially designed for its contents. In the center, nested in a cutout the shape of a baby, was . . . a baby. Or something that looked very like a baby. It had on a diaper and a knit cap, and its mouth was eerily open. It was wrapped in a clear bag, which had the macabre effect, given how much it looked like a real infant, of making it seem dead.

"This is Premie Gort," Day Boy said, lifting it out. "It's a medical training patient simulator the size of a premature baby."

"No, this is more than half the income Poppu and I earn in a year," I corrected him, feeling certain that I couldn't take something so valuable.

In my peripheral vision I sensed a glance from him that lasted a fraction of a second too long, and then he concentrated on the doll. I had reminded him that I was just a guttersnipe. How much money did Medical Apprentices with National Distinction make, I wondered?

"Well," he said, "that's because it's pretty sophisticated. It has little veins you can catheterize, a heartbeat, fake lungs that respire; it even moves its arms and legs a bit and cries. If you program it to do those things."

"Why does Hélène have this?"

"They're made in Canada by her uncle's company. She negotiated a discount for the hospital. The only reason she hasn't delivered it is that she's expecting a toddler, too, and she'll be training the staff on how to use both. Normally they're sixteen thousand dollars."

"Oh, great," I said. "I can't borrow an electronic baby that costs as much as a new car."

He removed the plastic bag, found the AC adapter, and plugged the doll in to charge it.

"Really," I insisted, "a loaf of bread would be fine."

"It takes an hour to charge." It was maddening the way he ignored me when he disagreed with me. He pulled a computer tablet and stylus out of their foam cutouts. "In the meantime, I'm going to figure out how to program it, and you're going to rest up until we hear back about your grandfather."

Thursday
6:20 p.m.

The final text from Poppu's captors had said simply, **Monroe Harbor, pump-out dock, 6:30 p.m.** On the global map, the pump-out dock was clearly the straightest shot into and out of the harbor—they were preparing for a quick exit if they needed it. But I didn't understand the meeting time: sunset was at 6:40, which meant I'd be outside, fully exposed and very illegal. Why couldn't it have been 7:00 p.m., to cloak me in comforting darkness? But the hour was not negotiable, and I consoled myself with the fact that those ten minutes of daylight were almost enough for Day Boy to get home before his curfew, which would keep him safe and go a long way toward satisfying Hélène.

When we were nearly there, on Columbus Drive passing Roosevelt Road, Day Boy glanced at me in the back seat and announced a change in plans.

"I'm dropping you off when we reach Monroe Street, just like we said. But do you know the little parking lot that's hidden under Lake Shore Drive north of Randolph?"

I forced myself to process what he was saying. "I . . . think so."

"It's the lot for the DuSable Harbor. I'm going to park there and wait for you."

"What?" I said, genuinely confused. I couldn't imagine that Hélène would tolerate deviations. I looked at the robot baby in my arms. It was stiff and almost monstrous in its preanimated state, its mouth gaping. I recalled holding Fitzroy in this same position and how expressive his little face was, already full of character. I might have had a soft spot for infants if I'd lived a different life.

Day Boy's voice became strained. We were almost at Monroe, and I could tell he felt his time was running out. "You're not turning yourself in after you see your grandfather. You're going to hit 'send' on that text to the police about where Fitzroy is, but you're going to run back down the dock and—are you listening?"

I looked into his eyes in the rearview mirror. I nodded, but I had already planned on disregarding his instructions.

"Good. You're going to meet me at the car. The lakefront trail north is the easiest route for you to take, and then duck west under Lake Shore Drive at Randolph. But I don't care how you get there, just find me in the lot, okay?"

"Sure." I said it maybe a little too quickly.

"Plus One." There was a reprimand in his tone.

"Why bother?" I said, launching straight from feigned cooperation to rebelliousness. "It's just delaying the inevitable. I'm going to jail, and no one can stop that."

"If the baby is returned, Hélène will have half of what she wants. We'll hide at Jean's place and think for one more day."

We had reached Monroe, and the light was red. I draped a corner of the blanket over the doll's face to cover its silent scream.

I slid out of the seat, and just before I shut the door I said, less casually than I meant to, "I'm really sorry I messed things up for you." I'd thought a lot about it at Jean's apartment and decided that I did in fact hope Day Boy would have a nice life. I took the first steps away from the car and then made the mistake of looking back. He was rolling down the window.

"No!" he shouted, flustered. "Meet me at the lot!"

I turned and ran—uncomfortably, with my upper body stiff because of the rubber corpse in my arms—toward the Chicago Yacht Club.

All at once I understood the choice of time: the streets were slightly chaotic, with Rays running home and Day tourists hustling to their hotels. My mild panic blended right in.

I waited at a red light to cross Lake Shore Drive, sweat drops forming on my nose, which I couldn't wipe away while holding the baby. I saw from that distance that there was a white yacht at the pump-out dock. A big one—one you'd expect a mob leader or a drug lord to own, with its deck high above the water and a spinning satellite dish of some sort on top. My legs suddenly felt trembly, and I looked back toward Columbus Drive to find that the car was gone. I was on my own from now on.

I had achieved one thing, at least. I had ditched Day Boy.

"*Bonne chance*," I sighed to him.

A taxi with an orange stripe similar in color to the Hour

Guard vehicles sped by, reminding me that the whole thing would be over instantly if I stumbled into a routine Day check. The light changed and I hurried across Lake Shore Drive and down the path past the yacht club. When I stepped onto the dock I slowed, and then stopped altogether. My throat was dry, and I was breathing too hard. I needed time to get a grip. I adjusted the baby in my arms, but carefully, as if it were a living thing, because I assumed that I was being watched. I startled when it began to move slightly. Day Boy's programming was kicking in. It made low grunting noises that must have been digitally sampled from a real baby.

As I approached, I saw a figure waiting at the stern, where there was a platform on the same level as the dock. It was a man—tall and spindly, with his arms crossed nervously over his chest. I stood straighter; I walked deliberately. I tried to make my body lie to him that I wasn't scared out of my mind. From a few yards away our eyes met and I recognized him. It was the male nurse from the maternity ward. I froze.

"Come on, Le Coeur," he called irritably, as if I were dawdling and not just paralyzed with confusion. "I won't bite."

I took a few steps toward him. There was a railing around the platform, and he reached over it to offer me a hand. I shook my head. If I lost my footing, the space between the boat and the dock was just wide enough to accidentally drop a baby through. I needed to be in control—of myself and of the doll.

"Pass me the baby and you can board on your own, then," he said. Premie Gort's grunts got louder, and his legs and arms moved. It felt so odd: a reanimation of the dead.

I shook my head again, mute. Pass him a fake baby? Not on his life.

"I need to talk to whoever is in charge." I started my prepared speech.

Something made me look up then. I had a sensation I couldn't have described before that moment: an awareness of a person's presence, from years of knowing what he *feels* like when he's silently in a room with you, off in the corner, reading or thinking. There, gazing down from the top deck at me, dissecting every part of me with his eyes, was my brother, Ciel. He was a man now, broader in every way, with defined muscles, a thicker neck, a sparse, clipped beard, and spiky, mussed hair.

I let out a cry, and I stumbled backward, nearly dropping the baby. I couldn't process what was happening fast enough, and I was bombarded instead with useless snippets of thoughts:

the male nurse, I knew him

the courtroom

hyena laughter

Ciel

a yacht

Ciel, grown up

Poppu, on a ship with Ciel.

And then one last thought began to gel, made of all the incoherent pieces: my own brother had blackmailed me using my grandfather.

My reaction was pure and unedited. Something like a hand grenade went off in my core, exploding up and through my head, and I found myself shaking, saying, "You bastard," and then shouting, "You bastard! You horrible bastard!" I clutched the baby to me and collapsed my frame around it, as if it were a living thing that needed protection from him. But I wasn't acting a part; it was an automatic, visceral response to Ciel's betrayal, to my feeling that he was more of a monster than I had ever imagined, that nothing was safe or sacred near him.

"Stay there, Sol," he yelled angrily, pointing at me, as if to pin me in place with his finger. The male nurse had climbed over the railing and had one foot on the dock. But I was stumbling away now, my gaze riveted on Ciel, though I never wanted to see him again. My vision was blurry, and I quickly wiped my eyes with my wrist but they wouldn't clear. I heard a thumping deep in my ears—my heartbeat?—and I saw flashing, strobing lights, like I was having a seizure. I started to run, but the beating was not my heart, it was the resonant *wub wub* of a helicopter. The strobes were police cars on Lake Shore Drive.

Premie Gort let out a feeble cry.

The sky behind the city's massive buildings was brilliant orange and purple.

Ciel was shouting orders at the male nurse, who responded by untying the lines of the boat and leaping back onto the platform for the getaway. The engines had already started. The ship belched dark smoke as it revved to pull away from the dock.

I ran all out now, the baby mannequin more like a football than an infant, and from the corner of my eye I saw Officer Dacruz spilling out of his squad car in the turnaround of the yacht club. The helicopter was above him, with a rifleman leaning out of the side, training his gun on me, just like in the movies. It was surreal. He wouldn't really shoot, would he? A spotlight beamed down, blue and too bright, throwing shadows off me and the posts of the dock. I had a cramp in my stomach that threatened to hobble me.

"Stop!" Dacruz yelled, but I was already off the dock and on my way up the grassy hill toward Lake Shore Drive. I looked frantically ahead and saw Day Boy, zigzagging through lanes of speeding cars on the road to meet me. I couldn't believe what I was seeing. Any one of the cars could have killed him.

I tripped and fell, twisting my body midway to avoid landing on the "baby"—a stupid instinct that I would pay for with deep bruises if not a real injury. I rolled off my shoulder and struggled to sit, the wind slightly knocked out of me. Dacruz was just leaving the path, just starting up the hill, and Day Boy was coming down from the Drive. They would converge on me—and each other—if I didn't get up.

Dacruz lifted something in his two hands that looked like a gun, but it was bright yellow and black.

"Stay where you are!" He stopped and planted his boots to take aim.

Day Boy shouted, "GET UP."

I scrambled to my feet. I heard a puffing explosion of air from Dacruz's gun. It was a taser.

The son of a bitch shot me while I was holding a baby.

I felt the probe end of a wire filament pierce my sleeve, and I saw the other filament drop uselessly to the ground. *He missed.*

In the reprieve of that second, I yanked the probe off my arm, stinging my palm with the sharp wire, and ran up the hill, straight into Day Boy.

"Stay away from me!" I yelled at him, wrenching away as he juggled to grab me, my tears streaming again. I launched myself into the traffic of Lake Shore Drive without even looking, Day Boy right on my heels.

It was a miracle that we didn't get hit. It was like the videos I had seen of traffic in India—we somehow weaved between cars, drivers screeched to near stops, a lane was blessedly empty, another car swerved—with multiple horns blaring for so long that their pitches dropped as they receded, and the constant beating and whine of the helicopter blades and engine above us. The police cars driving north couldn't cross the concrete median to follow us; officers started piling out of their cars to chase us on foot instead. And then I looked back and saw Dacruz leap onto Lake Shore Drive and get immediately clipped by an SUV.

Don't you dare die, you bastard.

His comrades refocused their energies on stopping traffic and helping him. One pursued us, but was trapped between lanes by moving cars, buying us precious time.

Day Boy and I scrambled onto the grass north of the southbound lanes and ran down the hill under Lake Shore Drive, where the helicopter couldn't see us.

"Follow me!" he shouted.

I was out of breath, my chest ripped raw from heaving too much air, but I wanted to cry, "No." *No, I won't follow you.*

I should have separated from him, should have taken my lumps alone, with dignity. But I could hardly see through my tears, I was gutted by Ciel's betrayal, I was terrified of the rifle in the helicopter, I was totally out of ideas, and he was leading with conviction. And so I followed.

Telemachus

The *Odyssey* meant nothing to me when Poppu and I first began reading it. It was about a time period so long ago the people dressed, ate, and lived entirely differently from us. They had conventions I didn't understand. While Odysseus was lost, his wife, Penelope, seemed to host nonstop parties for her suitors. Why did she do it if she despised them—these "guests" who refused to leave, ate her food, and argued over her as if she were a piece of meat? She even dangled out hope that one of them would win her. It was odd to follow characters who lived during the day, as if they were Rays, but were free to go out at night, like Smudges. The settings were countries I could never go to, and even if I could, they wouldn't look anything the way they did thousands of years ago.

But Poppu brought books to life and made you forget what you didn't know. To hear him tell it, Odysseus's son, Telemachus, was a boy like Ciel, a good person, stronger than average, but green. Telemachus had lived in the shadow of a father he had never seen—a man who left for the Trojan War when Telemachus was a baby but who was extraordinary enough to have earned Penelope as his loyal wife, Athena as his protector, and the god of the oceans, Poseidon, as his enemy.

"That's a lot to live up to for poor Telemachus," Poppu said. "Just at the age when he wants to be like his father, having never *had* his father in his life. He presumes that Odysseus would smite all of those bastard suitors while eating a sandwich. So why is he, Telemachus, powerless to protect his mother?"

As for Penelope, she was living with the kind of uncertainty that digests your insides, waiting for word of her husband that might never come. She could have lost everything to violence. Instead, she played the suitors against each other to keep them in check. She made promises she didn't intend to keep. She stalled for years, which only a wily woman could do.

Poppu pointed out that Odysseus loved Penelope above everything, enough to fight for two decades to get home to her. But as clever as he was, he was also a man who gave in to temptation again and again, and screwed himself over because of it. What sort of person makes his companions put wax in their ears and tie him to the mast so that he alone can hear the song of the Sirens without losing his ship against the rocks? The answer is: a badass who's teetering on the knife's edge of genius and recklessness, that's who. A man who is so cunning that he is sometimes stupid. Odysseus was indeed extraordinary—so gifted that the gods bothered to take notice and openly intercede in his life—but he was also a man with ordinary weaknesses. Because everyone—*everyone*—makes mistakes.

In twenty-eight hundred years, Poppu told me, not a thing has changed about people.

Day Boy had left the car unlocked. We tumbled into the back seat and sat on the floor, scrunching low, our backs against the doors, with our feet practically in each other's faces. I was sobbing out loud now, barely able to catch heaving gasps between sputtering, deep-throated moans. Day Boy was breathing hard but quietly. He shut off Premie Gort and shoved him under the front seat. He let me cry for no more than a minute, and then he said, "You have to stop now."

"Ciel," I blubbered.

"Quiet!"

"He was on the boat . . ." Convulsive breath. "Poppu! It was Ciel . . ."

He leaned forward so that his face was closer. "Do you hear me? *Shut up.*"

It was so unexpected, like he'd slapped my face. I sprayed a cough and gulped breaths in and out, but there were suddenly no tears. He had no idea what I'd just been through. He had no right to bully me. He was such a controlling, condescending ass.

I leaned forward, too, so that my nose was practically touching his, my chest still heaving. "That was my *brother* on that ship, screwing me over! My own *brother*! Don't you tell me what to do *ever again*." I threw my back against the door and clamped my mouth shut, air blasting in and out of my nose like a charging bull's.

"That's better!" he said, energized, almost triumphant. And then he actually smiled. "The wrath of Plus One I can handle. Bring it on." He leaned back against his door, sliding down as low as possible, put his finger to his lips, and whispered, "But quietly."

Flashing lights lit up the windows as a squad car drove slowly past—painfully slowly, with its spotlight swinging back and forth, surveying the lot. I wiggled myself to a nearly lying position, tucking my knees under his bent legs. If I could have become part of the floor I would have. I closed my eyes and concentrated on slowing my breathing, realizing that he had shut me up just in time.

And so we stayed motionless, undiscovered, for two dark, cramped hours. Day Boy whispered questions about what exactly had happened on the dock, and I whispered answers.

"Do you think Ciel set you up?" he finally asked.

"What do you mean?" It was obvious to me that Ciel's gang—whatever it was—had planned to kidnap the Paulsen baby at the hospital. I had thrown a wrench in the works by accidentally taking Fitzroy in place of Ciel's daughter. Ciel was just trying to get Fitzroy before the Paulsens did. *Yes, of course Ciel set me up*, I thought. He had set me up the moment he embraced being a Ray and left our family. He had set me up to nurse Poppu to his death—to be utterly alone in this world.

Day Boy said, "What I mean is, would Ciel have called the cops?"

I was quiet as I thought about this. It was true that the police had arrived almost exactly on cue for the meeting; they had dispatched a helicopter; this wasn't a crime they had just stumbled upon.

I whispered, "Ciel's a jerk, but he really wanted that baby. He wouldn't bring in the police."

A full minute later Day Boy said with heavy certainty, "It was Hélène."

I felt a squeeze in my chest. "She didn't trust me to turn myself in."

"Right."

"She thought you'd be safely on your way home when the cops arrived."

Silence.

I said, "After my arrest, the police would have read the unsent text in my phone, with the information about where to find Fitz, linking me with his abduction." It was a fail-safe plan to distance her son from my crimes, except he had blown it by following me.

"So," he said, barely audibly. "You don't have a monopoly on family betrayal."

Eventually the helicopter went away and the cops stopped searching, or moved their search elsewhere. Day Boy left me on the floor in the back, climbed into the driver's seat, and took us into the shadowy bowels of Lower Wacker Drive, where he eased the car into a dark loading dock. He got out, and I followed him. He lifted the trunk, his mouth a determined straight line. He looked weary, for the first time since I'd met him. He opened a toolbox and took out a socket wrench, and then he tugged on the edge of the carpeting at the bottom of the trunk, pulling it up until he revealed something flat and rectangular, folded in newsprint.

"Unwrap these," he commanded, as he squatted and started to remove the little bolts on the license plate, setting them in a neat pile on the ground.

I knew immediately what was in my hands. If Dacruz had seen Day Boy with me, the police would be searching for the Benoîts' car, with the Benoîts' license plates. I unwrapped the paper.

"But why would you have—" I started.

"Because this is Jean's car." It was slightly irritating that he so often knew what I was going to say before I said it. He could at least have the decency to pretend I wasn't completely transparent to him. He went on, "And Jean is nothing if not prepared." He finished removing the bolts and reached for the plate, his eyes catching mine. I must have been scowling. His face softened, as if my sour look cheered him. He left his hand out, patiently. I gave him one of the plates, and then I squatted to help hold it in place as he began tightening the first bolt. I picked up the other three bolts and handed them to him as he needed them.

"When you said Jean was practically off the grid, did you mean that he's an undocumented immigrant?"

"No, he has a green card. As long as he and Hélène are married. And technically at least, they're still married."

"Then why—"

"He's cautious, that's all, because of his research. And he does a lot of bartering with Rays, which I'm sure you know is—" He dropped a bolt, which rolled away from him in an arc. I picked it up and handed it to him.

"Against the law." I finished his sentence this time.

He nodded. "We've never needed these plates, but there's a first time for everything. They belonged to the car of a very old friend—a car that was the same make, model, year, and color as ours. He gave the plates to Jean before he died. The car itself is currently a habitat for fish in Lake Michigan."

Jean was a surprising guy.

I picked up the old plate and put it in the newsprint. We went to the front of the car and started the process for the second plate.

I said quietly, "If Dacruz saw that it was you on Lake Shore Drive, your parents—"

He nodded, twisting the socket wrench.

I let the rest go unsaid. He had obviously worked this out: Jean and Hélène would be—very soon, if not right now—the focus of a lot of police attention. And if Dacruz had noticed the baby under my arm, god help us.

In the yellow sodium-vapor lights of the dock I watched Day Boy work, watched how taking a license plate off a car, like every task he undertook, merited his full concentration and was done with care and organization. I looked at the skin of his cheeks and forehead, smooth and unmarked—betraying a life spent reading and studying, and probably not much of that playing in the yard that he had described at his dad's apartment.

"Why are you doing this?" I asked. What I meant was "Why are you breaking the law for me?" But he understood, and he didn't answer. He furrowed his brow as he worked on a rusted, recalcitrant bolt. I thought I saw him try to put something into words and then give up, but he could have been struggling with the hardware.

I didn't know how to ask again. And so I waited, which was unlike me. I waited until he was ready to talk about it.

When the job was finished, he took Premie Gort out from under the front seat, wrapped it tightly in its blanket, and put it in the well of the spare, under the carpeting in the trunk. I tucked the old plates in before he smoothed the fabric down, and then he put the socket wrench back in the tool kit. He walked to the rear door and opened it.

"I think you should lie on the back seat and pretend to be my feverish Plus One, don't you? I need a reason to be out after dark." As an afterthought he said, "Speaking of fever, I remembered your pills." He pulled the bottle from his jacket pocket and handed it to me.

I put it in my hoodie pocket and climbed in. When he got in the driver's seat I said, "Where are we going?"

"On a vacation." He sounded tired, or maybe defeated. "I deserve it."

I didn't understand, but his voice wasn't inviting discussion, and with cops all over the lakefront I had no plan of my own.

"If it was your mom who reported me to Dacruz," I asked, "do you think she told him outright that I was Fitzroy's kidnapper? Or do you think she trusted that the text would implicate me?" I lay down with my head on the right so I could see the edge of his face as he drove—his cheekbone, nose, bangs, and that level concentration. It settled me, somehow.

He shook his head. "I don't know. But I'm guessing those Suits would have been there if she had mentioned the minister's baby, not just the cops, and we'd be dead right now."

I closed my eyes. I didn't want to fall asleep, but my crying jag and the rush of adrenaline from the chase had worn me out.

Friday
1:00 a.m.

When I awoke it was with a start. I was still in the car, and it was slowing as it turned. It was dark. We ground onto a dirt road. Stones and pebbles kicked up, pinging the wheel rims and undercarriage of the car. I worked hard to sit up. Without Modafinil and caffeine being pumped into me on a regular basis, my body wanted to sleep when it was dark, as if I were no longer a Smudge—as if the human body were predisposed to sleep at night and would happily revert back, if only it were allowed the chance.

"How long was I out?" I asked groggily.

"Forever," he said.

"Why didn't you—"

"You need sleep to get better. I knew it would be a long ride."

"Where are we?"

"You'll see."

"We're in the country," I said stupidly.

"Mm."

"The moon starts its last quarter tonight." I realized that my comment might seem out of the blue to him. The lunar phases were ingrained in me the way musicians know their scales.

"Cool," he said distractedly, turning on his high beams. "I forget what that means."

"It's waning, about fifty percent illumination, but only visible toward dawn. Which means: no light to help guide us," I said. "Wait. How far out of town *are* we?"

"Three and a half hours." He looked at the odometer. "Three hundred and nine kilometers."

"*What?*" I said, climbing into the front seat.

"Hey!" he said when I crashed into him and made him lose the steering wheel for a second. He pulled into a small parking lot off the road.

"We can't be here," I said, my voice rising. "We're wanted by the cops. I need to see Poppu."

"We're safe here, as safe as anywhere. We need time to think." He leaned past me to open the glove compartment and remove a flashlight. I reached for my holster, but of course it wasn't there. Dacruz had taken my torch a long time ago. Day Boy popped the trunk. His voice became hard as he opened his door. "But more than that, I've decided I won't go to jail and lose everything I've worked for without coming here one last time."

I had no idea where "here" was. I got out of the car with him. He opened the trunk and removed a small, bulging day pack that I hadn't noticed before. Inside were bottles of water, bags of beef jerky, and granola bars. He pulled everything out except two bottles of water, a bag of jerky, and four granola bars. A late dinner, I supposed, or after-school snack for me, the Smudge.

"Take your pill," he said, handing me water. It didn't sound like an order as much as a reminder from my doctor. I obeyed.

"Let's go for a hike." He turned on the flashlight and walked down the path ahead of me, careful to keep the spot of light at his feet, rather than in front of him, so that I could share it.

We were in a forest preserve or state park of some sort, with railroad-tie stairs that descended from the lot through the woods to a stone hut on the left and a boardwalk on the right. The hut had restrooms, a Day snack bar that was closed for the night, and an external hearth with a pretty fire that lit up the picnic benches next to it. Smudges were eating quietly, and they nodded to us in greeting as we passed.

We followed the boardwalk for a short way, and Day Boy turned left at the first opportunity, down a stairway. I had to concentrate on the beam of light so that I wouldn't trip, but with brief glances I could make out the shadows of stone walls that rose around us. The air was all earth-smell: damp rock, dust, decaying leaves. We went down, and down—it must have been a few dozen stairs and several landings—into what felt like a cool grotto. The wood stairs transitioned to stone steps covered with claylike dust. Piles of small boulders lined the path to keep us from straying. A quick flick of the light over the walls and ceiling showed that we were in a cave. The rock looked like an exuberant version of gray limestone—jagged, pockmarked, riddled with holes.

"Pretty stone," I said.

"Dolomite." He wasn't in a verbose mood, and the whole experience was so surreal for me I was at a loss for words. Because of my nap, I had gone from being chased by a helicopter and a bastard with a taser gun to being plopped in the remote woods of a state park.

I followed the bob of his flashlight along a cobblestone walkway, beside a trickling stream. Thousands of years of this running water must have carved the cave, with a serene patience that only nature and cancer victims had. Watching my feet, I had the distinct sensation that I might bump my head—he hadn't aimed the flashlight up in this part of the cave, so I had no idea how high the ceiling was over the path—and I found myself wincing and ducking. I reached up, but there was just air above me. Day Boy marched on.

"Slower," I said, with a nervous laugh. "I have no idea where I am!" He had only gained a few meters on me, but I was already unsure how the path curved between us.

"Sorry," he said, lighting the way, his voice genuinely apologetic. "If I remember correctly, we're coming up on a stretch without much headroom." When I reached him, he stood still and shone the light in every direction, carefully, allowing me to survey the cave. It was stark, eerie, and utterly lovely.

We had to duck for a little while, walking very slowly so that he could shine the light both up and down for me. And then the ceiling opened into a cavern again. There were no other Smudges in the cave. The sound of the water tripping over stones next to us was so magical, I smiled in spite of everything: in spite of being a fugitive, separated from Poppu; in spite of not knowing where I was; in spite of Day Boy's stern mood. For just this moment, the world was turning, there was no city, Nature was in charge of everyone's fate. I had only to relinquish myself to her. I heard Day Boy sigh—not a sad sigh, not a weary sigh, but exactly the sigh of beauty that I felt—and I knew he was beginning to loosen up, too.

"This is Lower Dancehall Cave," he said. "The entrance to Upper Dancehall is on the other side of the road. It's all connected, if you're prepared to crawl through some terrifying, tight spaces, which I will never be."

"Spelunking freaks me out," I agreed.

We exited the cave up stone steps that segued into wooden stairs and then another boardwalk. It was a clear night, but the moon hadn't risen and the tree cover was thick, so that only the pinpricks of stars shone through.

We stopped at a fork in the boardwalk. He aimed the light at the sign in front of us. The beam crawled up the post, slipped and slid, until it found the letters printed at the top. I read quickly, but not as fast as he did. An arrow pointed left to a few sites, including one that may have been "Rainy Day Cave," and another pointed right to "Parking Lot" and "Balanced Rock."

His light returned to the boardwalk.

He had chosen Rainy Day Cave.

I froze. Had I read that correctly? Balanced Rock?

Balanced Rock.

My desk partner's goodbye.

"No really, Day Boy, where are we?" My voice surprised me with its quaver. I crossed my arms in front of my body, hunching a little and hugging my sides to hold myself in, to regain control of my suddenly trembling body. I hurried up a few wooden steps and onto a dirt path to catch up. His flashlight was getting too far away.

"Iowa," he said.

I stopped, but he kept walking, saying, "It's called Maquo-keta Caves State Park. It's not the Grand Canyon, but for some reason—maybe because I was conceived in a cave—it's my fa-vorite local park."

With no warning, my knees buckled and I dropped to the ground. D'Arcy heard me fall and he spun around. I put my hands on the dirt in front of me to steady myself. Too much air escaped my lungs before I remembered to replenish it. I closed my eyes for a moment.

It was him.

My mind raced to put the pieces together. He was a year ahead of me in school. He had left just as the seniors were awarded National Distinction. He was organized, neat, and in-telligent. He was exactly the person to know what a virion looked like, for crying out loud.

It all made sense.

"Are you okay?" he asked. He bent on one knee beside me. "Oh, hell, you're not well enough for this."

"I'm fine." I looked up at him in the dark. He had aimed the spot of the flashlight on the dirt and stones to the side of me, trying not to blind me by pointing it in my face. But that made the light in my peripheral vision too bright; it put his face completely in shadows. I wished the flashlight were angled toward him. I wished for moonlight. I wanted to see him—I needed to see him again—now that in a matter of seconds every-thing had changed, and nothing between us would ever be the same, at least for me. I needed to see his eyes, to see what he saw when he looked at me, and who he was now that I *knew* who he was. I needed to see him so badly, as if I'd never seen him before.

As if I couldn't draw that nose, those eyes, that barely combed hair by heart now.

"Really, I'm *fine*. I . . ." I wiped tears away quickly with my sleeve. "I tripped."

He offered his left hand across his body, so that I would reach with my left, my good side. He pulled me up.

"I should take you back," he said, letting go sooner than I wanted. "This was stupid and selfish."

"No, let's go on." The tremor in my voice began to annoy the crap out of me. "Please."

I saw the beams of two flashlights bobbing behind us. I cleared my throat and said, "Is it possible we were followed?"

"We're fine," he said in a low voice. "It's just other Night visitors." He let out a little laugh. "You've forgotten how to be a Smudge, Plus One."

We hiked for ten or fifteen minutes more, stopping to peek into Rainy Day Cave and Ice Cave before entering the woods proper. The night was blue-black all around us, and there were no other hikers on the path we chose, even though it was perfect late September weather—unseasonably warm, clear and dry.

He turned to me. "How are you doing?"

"Maybe a little shaky." I told the truth.

"Mm," he said, not knowing what to make of that. "Let's rest for a minute. Your body is still fighting a bacterial infection, after all."

"It's not that. The antibiotics are working great." And then, because everything had changed—because *I* had changed—I said, "Thank you for those. And for remembering I can't have penicillin."

He led the way to a fallen tree. It had landed on an old metal fence with barbed wire on top, crushing it. He shone his flashlight on a sign that indicated this was the edge of the park.

Beyond the fence was private property—a field or meadow of some sort, with what might have been hay clipped short for the fall. I sat down on the trunk of the tree. He put one sneaker up on it, crossing both arms on his knee. He leaned his chin on his arms and turned off the flashlight. We were quiet for a minute. I was so aware of his presence, it was heady and disconcerting. Two years of imagining him had never included the possibility of his being a real person—someone I could reach out and touch. And yet here he was.

"I can't wait for the sun to rise," he said to the open air.

"Why?"

"Because I want to show you how beautiful this place is."

I was quiet, remembering how much he had wanted to be here when he last wrote on the desk. There had been a sadness to his message that I didn't understand, that I wanted desperately to ask him about now, but couldn't. He misinterpreted my silence, maybe thinking he had insulted me.

"I mean, no offense, but it turns out nature is not as fun at night."

"I think you're mistaken," I finally replied, remembering how to be acerbic.

"How so?"

"In your Day prejudice, and your lack of Night skill, you're neglecting a massive amount of beauty."

I was relieved that he detected the sarcasm in my tone.

He put on a snotty voice. "Well, then, perhaps you could educate me."

"Give me the flashlight."

I climbed onto the log and scooched my feet along it like a tightrope walker, up and over the mangled fence, hopping off at the end. I turned around and illuminated the route for him.

"Brambles when you land," I warned.

I walked to the middle of the clearing and located the North Star. The lack of a moon was now a great bit of luck. It was the perfect night for stargazing.

"Come on," I called, to hurry him up, using my deep, stealthy Smudge voice.

I lay down, facing west, in the clipped hay. It was dry and a little pinching, even through my clothes. He took off the day pack to lie down beside me.

"It hurts," he complained, at full volume.

"Get comfortable." I folded my arms behind my head. He did the same.

"Look at the midsky, about halfway up from the horizon, and wait for your eyes to adjust," I said softly. "It will take five to ten minutes."

He was quiet. The sky was full of stars, and the spaces between them were not fully black, because the longer we stared, the more the pricks of other stars peeked behind and next to them. I stole that time to listen to him breathe. I soaked up his presence, storing it for the future, burning it into my memory. I said his name in my head, the name I had avoided for so long.

D'Arcy. My dear friend.

D'Arcy, my mind sighed.

Soon the sky had become a blanket of stars; and then it became heavy, bulging down on us, so thick it was like soup that

I might reach up and stir with my hand if I tried. And finally, to my relief, Cygnus the Swan and the Great Summer Triangle began to emerge from the cosmos with the faint, cloudy dragon spine of the edge of our galaxy.

"Oh my god, is that the Milky Way?" he whispered.

My throat got hot. It was the most beautiful thing I could ever have hoped to show him. I could be grateful for one thing that night.

"You're a brave guy," I said, my voice cracking just to make sure I felt like an idiot.

"Why do you say that?"

"It took me ten years not to wad my body into a tight ball every time I saw the Milky Way."

He burst out laughing. It was too loud. Night people don't belly laugh outside of their homes. He really was a Ray. I shushed him.

He laughed again, but softer, and then turned his head toward me and said in a low, smiling voice, "A ball?"

"Four hundred billion suns spiraling through space together. Our solar system just one grain on that galactic carousel. The carousel itself a speck in the cosmos. And here I am in this small clearing, on the surface of the earth, as transient and unnoticed to the universe as the dry blades of grass that are poking into my shirt. It's too much to comprehend up there, too enormous, and I'm so small when it's on top of me. It frightens me, like I'm being crushed."

I could feel him staring at me, although it was almost pitch-black around us, as I poured out my childish thoughts.

After a moment he said, "Holy cow, Plus One."

"What?" I said defensively.

He settled his head in the cradle of his arms again and refused to answer. Then he said, "Here on earth, where it counts . . . you're not unnoticed."

We gazed up together in silence at the stars. Eventually D'Arcy sat up and opened his day pack. I flipped on the torch to rest it between us. The light from below caught his cheekbones and set his eyes in shadow. He took out two granola bars and handed me a water bottle. I opened it and took a swig. I offered it to him. He drank from it and handed it back. I rested my lips on the rim of the bottle before I drank, trying to differentiate between the warm wetness of the water and the warm wetness of his mouth, disappointed that I couldn't. He tore the end of his granola wrapper with his teeth. I tore mine with my fingers.

"*Bon appétit*," he said.

"*À toi aussi*," I replied quietly.

We took another sip of water. I was careful to offer it to him first, for that indirect lip contact. It was juvenile, but it was all I had. He opened a bag of jerky, took a piece out, and ripped a section off with his teeth.

He passed me the bag, chewing, ruminating. Finally, after he had swallowed, he said, "Why does your brother want the baby?"

"I don't—I don't know Ciel anymore."

He accepted that answer. We sat quietly eating, perhaps both imagining a reason—D'Arcy maybe assuming that Ciel's motives were political, me knowing they were more likely to be self-serving.

We ate our second granola bars and more beef jerky. D'Arcy opened his bottle for a last drink of water, since mine was empty. The food, as usual, barely took the edge off my hunger. I would need a Unity Night–size meal to feel sated, and maybe even that wouldn't work. Maybe the hunger was a permanent part of my being.

I asked, "Do you think Hélène has returned the baby by now?"

"I can't believe she hasn't, but without your text, I wonder what method she used." He added with grim sarcasm, "Ring the doorbell and run?"

The songs of the crickets had swelled around us: trills from all directions—a sea of sound, an audio imitation of the stars. I thought, *Without the Paulsen baby, I'll never see Poppu again. I have no bargaining power against Ciel. And I've dragged my only friend, my desk partner, down with me.*

D'Arcy leaned back on his elbows and breathed in, letting himself become part of the sky. I recognized the feeling, and I realized there was something I was neglecting about the Milky Way—a corollary to its gravid weight. It was the infinite possibility of time and space. There *was* a way to salvage good from bad, if only I could slip myself into the orbits of all those billions of stars, make myself a part of those distant light-years, return D'Arcy to his pre-Sol life.

A tiny plan was sparking in my brain, trying to become a flame.

"You know," D'Arcy said, sitting upright and smacking dirt off his sleeves, "the Milky Way might just be worth a little jail time." He began to pack up his bag. "But now it's my turn. I get to show you the park in sunlight this morning." He stood up. "And then we'll text your brother."

I didn't argue. "Will we sleep in the car?"

"It's not allowed here. And we can't risk getting questioned. But don't worry, we'll be safe."

We walked back the way we'd come: through the woods, the long saber of our flashlight slicing through the trees; down the dirt path; passing single file between two giant boulders with stairs cut into them. When we reached Ice Cave, he grabbed my hand and guided me inside, silently. He swept the beam of light along the walls, evaluating the space. "We can stay here tonight. No one will come in."

"Why?"

"Because the caves have been closed for the last couple of years to protect the bats from white-nose syndrome."

"Awesome," I said. "Bats."

There was a jagged, jutting wall to the side of the entrance—it would block a casual flashlight beam if someone were to peer in. I showed him how to quash the light of the torch against the stone, so that it created ambient light around us.

We sat down near the wall. He slid the pack off his shoulders and took his phone and keys out of his jeans pockets to put them in his jacket pocket. The soil was sandy and, to my relief, dry. But the air was cool and damp in the cave; I didn't know how we would last the night without feeling the chill. He reached deep in his bag and pulled out a plastic packet, not much bigger than a deck of cards. He opened a snap on the packet and pulled out something that sparkled silver in the dim light and crinkled like cellophane. It was a Mylar first-aid blanket.

"Jean," I said.

"Jean," he confirmed. He shook it out and put it on my shoulders. He lay down, setting the pack next to him. "You can use this as a pillow if you'd like."

"We should share the blanket."

"My jacket is heavier than your hoodie." He ended the discussion: "Time to sleep."

I hesitated until I saw the car keys in the sand. They had fallen out of his jacket pocket. I crawled next to him, scooping up and hiding the keys in my fist.

I pushed the day pack toward him. "I'll use my hood, you take the pillow."

He switched off the light. The only sound outside was the occasional owl and the slow creak of a branch swaying in the breeze. We heard the swish of an animal in the brush. D'Arcy and I lifted our heads to look out the mouth of the cave, and at that moment, in the first light of the moon, a deer tiptoed past, froze midstride to stare into the cave, and walked on.

Petite Daine, I thought incredulously.

"*Petite Daine*," D'Arcy said under his breath a beat later, erasing any possible doubt about who he was.

I pulled up my hood, rested my head on my arm, and pretended to sleep.

It took him a long time to fall asleep after that, shifting from side to side, sighing. Eventually he turned his back to me, with his arms crossed on his chest, and sometime later his body jerked with a hypnagogic twitch, and then utter stillness told me he was asleep. I sat up, holding my breath, the Mylar making the sound of a hundred candy wrappers as I lifted the blanket away.

It's almost impossible to be quieter than a still country night, but I was a Smudge, I'd gone camping my whole life, and I had confidence I could do it. I felt the ground next to him for the flashlight. I rose to my feet and waited a few seconds more, letting my body acclimate to being vertical, giving my legs time to gain their balance. I barely displaced the sand inside the cave as I left, I was such a lightweight. Once I was sure the glow of my phone wouldn't wake D'Arcy, I checked the time. It was 3:57. I would not make it back to Chicago before sunrise, but it didn't really matter: the goal was to turn myself in to the police anyway.

I was selfish enough that I couldn't part with D'Arcy forever without leaving him a message. I had no paper or pen to write with, so I crept into the brush with the flashlight and selected a large handful of twigs, which I quietly snapped into shorter lengths. I carried them just inside the opening of the cave, where I hoped he'd see the message as he left, and I laid them in bunches that formed thick letters. I debated long and hard about what to say in the fewest words. "Sorry" sprang to mind first—I was stranding him in another state without a car, after all—but eventually I settled on something that expressed a tiny bit of what he meant to me.

THANK YOU

I gathered rocks and pebbles and left them in a ring around the letters. And then I walked quietly back to the car, to accept with whatever grace I could muster the disaster that was my real life.

Friday
4:30 a.m.

Just to remind me that it was in charge, and that my planning anything good for someone I cared about was always laughable, the universe made sure that I couldn't start the car. The battery was fine, the tank simply had no gas. Not even enough to turn the engine over. I couldn't believe it: D'Arcy had driven it dry. I had no way of getting back to Chicago.

I stood by the car, my thoughts muddy and slow, until I saw a flashlight coming up the railroad-tie stairs through the woods. I dropped low and snuck off the gravel of the parking lot, crouching in the brush nearby. It was a park ranger, on a routine check of the cars in the lot, making sure they were empty. I welled up with tears and sank all the way to the ground, lying down on my belly. I pulled my hood over the top of my head and buried my face on folded arms, waiting for him to either discover me or leave, and eventually I fell asleep.

It was after dawn when I heard footsteps by the car. I was on my back now, so stiff and cold I couldn't raise myself quietly enough to see who it was, so I listened instead. My heart

thudded as I realized in the low light that I was hardly camou-
flaged by the narrow trees, and that the bushes between me
and the lot had already lost most of their foliage. I had felt
so sheltered in the dark, but it was an illusion. Whoever was
creeping around the car had only to take a few steps in my
direction and I'd be revealed. I closed my eyes, lying flat
and still.

"What do you think you're doing?" D'Arcy said above me.

My eyes cracked open. How had I not heard his steps?

"I thought you were lying dead there." His voice was a mix
of relief and exasperation. "Why would you take such a stupid
risk, leaving the cave?"

I opened my mouth but nothing came out. I was a codfish at
the bottom of a boat, gulping air. My mind ran through lies
but landed on the truth. "I was going to drive to Chicago to turn
myself in."

He looked up at the trees and then rubbed his eyes with the
heels of his hands before staring at me, his head tipped to the
side. I had no idea what he was thinking. I sat up and my mouth
motored on, stupidly filling space, never knowing when enough
was enough. "If you were abandoned in the park, it would
be believable that I carjacked you, that you were innocent. I
thought that once I was arrested and you were found a whole
state away, Hélène—and even Jean—would have the sense to
back up that story." And then this tumbled from my mouth,
loaded with emotion, before I thought to edit it: "Leaving you
here was the only thing I had left to give you."

His body stiffened almost imperceptibly.

"What did you say?"

I got up off the ground and dusted my hands on my jeans, not meeting his eyes.

"It's believable that I abducted you—"

"After that. The nice thing."

I had regretted saying it the moment it left my lips. I had hoped he hadn't registered it. Looking out at the misty woods surrounding the parking lot—the reds and golds, the green leaves and moss slowly becoming vibrant with the dawn—I repeated myself, careful to cover with practicality the raw, exposed feelings that had escaped me the first time. "You and your dad helped me so much. It was the only way I could think to repay you."

I heard a puff of air escape his nose. "Giving me a heart attack? That's how you want to repay me?" There was a smile in his voice, a warmth that my heart reached for. My head knew better though, refusing to let me look at him.

He waited briefly for me to say something. Eventually he said, more guardedly, "Well, you're stuck with me, despite your heroic efforts. The car is out of gas."

"I know," I said to the ground.

"I saw a gas station last night. Ten kilometers back, while you were sleeping. I was already driving on fumes. I pulled in to fill up, but I drove right out again."

I looked at him then, trying to figure out what he was saying.

He went on, "I realized I had a choice: gas the car up or spend the day here with you."

I shook my head, mute. How important was the "with you" part of that sentence? He took my silence for confusion.

"If I had turned my phone on to pay for the gas, the cops would have known our position, and we'd be caught by now," he explained.

I finally spoke, but my voice was punier than I wanted. "The park is special enough that you ran the tank dry rather than miss it?"

"Apparently."

I wondered when Day Boy, the uptight Medical Apprentice with National Distinction who'd turned me in at the hospital, had become D'Arcy, who flouted responsibility with an equal but opposite conscience. Was it when he sprung me from the cell? And then I remembered my desk partner, who routinely defaced school property and never cleaned it up. I felt the corners of my mouth turn down under the weight of things that were lost.

"You're not giving up on seeing your grandfather, are you?" D'Arcy asked quietly, reading my expression.

I shook my head. "Ciel could be anywhere on Lake Michigan by now. And I'm only hours away from being arrested and taking you and your parents down with—"

"Stop," he interrupted. And then he said too calmly, as if he were speaking to a child, "State park first. End of the world later."

I pointed out that after a night of sleeping in the brush, with my hair flyaway, no shower, and no breakfast, there was no way I would be able to walk in public like a Ray, which is to say, like I belonged.

But D'Arcy had anticipated my need for food.

"The Smudge campers are under curfew in their tents. Let me show you something." He guided me through a stand of trees to a nearby Night campsite, and from a distance away we squatted in a two-man huddle.

He pointed to a tent. "They have a cooler," he whispered so low I could barely hear him. "Which means perishable food— maybe fruit if we're lucky—and they've hung a bag of dry goods in that tree."

"We're going to steal food," I said. "Is that what you're telling me?"

He grinned. "I know, right? I *am* a miscreant now. And it's your fault."

My stomach grumbled, like the muffled creak of an old hinge. "They probably only just got settled in," I whispered. "They may not be asleep yet."

"Then we'll have to be as sneaky as . . ." He stopped.

"As sneaky as Smudges." I finished the pejorative saying for him.

"Sorry."

"Not at all. I'm actually worried you can't pull this off, with your galumphing about and booming voice. Maybe I should do it alone."

His eyebrows knit together, and I allowed myself a tiny smile, no bigger than the Mona Lisa's.

"Touché." He laughed under his breath.

He pulled a small Swiss Army knife from his pocket. "I'll handle the bag, you get the cooler. We'll meet here on the path and go straight to the car." I nodded. The division of labor was good: the bag was a fair distance away from the campsite in the woods, which meant D'Arcy could approach it from behind;

and the cooler was probably heavy, which would have made it difficult for him to walk quietly.

The trick to being stealthy in the woods is landing on your feet balls first, like a dancer, keeping your ankles and knees limber, and avoiding branches that might snap and stones that might skitter or crunch. You can't move too slowly, or your caution sometimes paradoxically causes loud mistakes. You have to move with a level of confidence that allows you to keep your weight fluid, so that you practically glide.

The cooler was just outside the tent, but the screens had shades, the way all Smudge tents did for light control, so I was pretty sure I wouldn't be seen unless the occupants opened the flap. When I was just a couple of feet away I crouched for a long minute, listening. I heard nothing, but just as I reached for the cooler one of the people inside shifted in his sleeping bag and whispered, "Sorry," to his partner. The other man just sighed "mmm" in reply, nearly asleep. My heart was pounding, and the muscles in my thighs ached from squatting too long. I glanced up at D'Arcy, who had cut down the bag and was tying something to the end of the dangling rope. I peered closely and saw that it was his watch. His eyes caught mine when he had finished, and I mimed that the occupants were not entirely asleep: I wagged my finger "no" and then made the sleepy *fais dodo* sign that Poppu used when I was very young, laying a cheek on praying hands. D'Arcy shrugged sympathetically and put his finger to his pursed lips, impishly shushing me.

I took a silent breath in, stood slowly, and bounced my weight back and forth on my forefeet without leaving the ground, to stretch out my cramping leg muscles. Then I lifted the cooler by the handle, emptied my mind of worry, and padded back to our meeting spot. I discovered en route that the cooler contained ice—of course—and bottles, and that I had to hold it away from my body so that it wouldn't bump my leg, which tended to shift the contents against one another.

"Smooth, Plus One," D'Arcy whispered, his eyes fairly sparkling with adventure. "Very impressive."

"Not bad yourself," I said, thinking what an incorrigible softy he was for leaving his watch as compensation. "For a Ray."

"Well, you know I have Smudge genes . . ."

I snorted quietly. "There's no such thing."

He smiled, lips closed, suddenly somber.

Back at the car we opened the cooler and bag and examined our spoils. It was a hungry thief's dream: a breakfast of oranges, bread, and soft Brie; a lunch of Italian cold cuts, hard-boiled eggs, provolone, and pears; and a dinner of cold roasted chicken parts with a salad of French beans in a plastic tub, plastic forks thoughtfully included. There were even two mini-bottles of champagne—the origin of the clinking sound in the cooler. I couldn't believe how lucky we were to have blindly robbed a pair of gastronomes.

I lifted the bread and started to tear off a hunk. My mouth was watering, and my stomach felt like it would eat itself if I didn't put something else in there to distract it.

"Hold on, hold *on*," D'Arcy said. "We can't just tear into this like barbarians. The least we can do after stealing a spread like this is to treat it with some respect."

He opened the trunk and put all the dinner items away, tucking breakfast and lunch into his day pack, including a mini-bottle of champagne and two water bottles.

"Let's go to the Milky Way clearing," he said. "I have a sentimental attachment to it."

"Already?" I said.

"Uh-huh, and it will be nice to see how the landscape changes in the light."

Twenty minutes later, I was weak with hunger but we were there. There were no Day guests in sight yet, and the air around us had a post-dawn stillness. It was a beautiful little spot, surrounded by a mix of quaking aspens, hornbeams, and a few ancient oaks. The sun was up enough that the mist was beginning to burn away in fading patches, but there were chrome beads of dew on the stubble of the meadow.

"The ground will be pinchy and wet," I warned unsentimentally.

"There's some rusted old farm equipment over there we can perch on," he said, marching across the field toward what looked like a giant axle with two huge metal wheels.

I followed after, secretly growing delighted at the idea of a picnic. Maybe D'Arcy was onto something. Maybe our chances at happy lives were so far down the toilet we should cram as much joy as possible into our last day of freedom. Maybe I shouldn't throw away the few hours I had left with him by trying to ditch him or hide behind my gruffness. This day might be the last good memory I would ever have, one I could revisit in the privacy of my mind in jail, to sustain me and keep insanity at bay. He turned to look at me, sensing my pensiveness, and I allowed myself to smile at him. My real smile—the one I reserved for Poppu, and formerly, Ciel. D'Arcy startled almost imperceptibly, and then not only returned my smile, but went on to open his mouth wide and laugh that belly laugh of the night before. I was embarrassed at his unbridled pleasure, so I closed my lips into something more prim and shook my head, a little bewildered by how even a wordless interaction between us could carry so much meaning.

After breakfast we hiked and talked for four hours, with half my energy going toward not giving away how much I knew of his camping exploits and reading interests, until finally I said, with a weaker voice than I expected, "Would it be ridiculous to eat lunch at ten-thirty?"

He looked concerned, I realized for the first time since we'd started hiking. "Did you take your doxycycline this morning?"

I felt for the bulge in my hoodie pocket. "I forgot."

He handed me the water we'd been sharing and there was only one swig left. I was so parched I downed the whole thing with the pill. He took the bottle from me, and before he capped it up, he put the rim to his lips, glancing at me with a smile I couldn't name, and tilted the last nonexistent drops into his mouth.

"I know just where we should have lunch, and Balanced Rock is on the way."

We started walking again, passing several Rays on the path. They all called out cheerful hellos and good mornings. I was becoming used to saying hello back, even though the custom among Smudges in public spaces was a perfunctory nod of the head—always there, but only visible if flashlights were bright or if the park had spotlights for Smudges.

At Balanced Rock, I climbed the stairs of the boardwalk while he stayed below in a sort of mossy gully, staring up at it, quiet. I wondered whether he was thinking of our desk drawing, of saying goodbye. The structure was more impressive in real life, because of the scale of it, and because I could walk around it to examine three out of four sides and see just how precarious it seemed. I wondered how it had stood there through storms, falling trees, and the freezing and thawing precipitation of thousands of years. Perhaps, I decided—analyzing the point of contact—when something is already so solid and symmetrical, all it needs is a small, level surface to keep it anchored and steady.

For lunch we found a pretty spot to sit down, in a bed of dry leaves beneath the trees near the creek. D'Arcy made rustic cold-cut sandwiches—just meat, cheese, thick slices of bread, and totally wonderful—while I gobbled down an egg and one of the sandwiches before he had even finished cutting the pears for us to share. Toward the end of lunch he reached into the bag and pulled out the mini-bottle of champagne.

"This is cold now and it won't be later. If we leave the park this afternoon we'll have to have our wits about us—be good and sober, I mean. What do you say we open it?"

Because it was a single serving, it had a screw top rather than a cork. He passed it to me after he had opened it and, still immaturely wanting his lips on it before mine, I said nonchalantly, "That's okay, you first."

A smile crawled open on his face. "No, I insist," he drawled.

I smiled back, unsure whether he was being playful about what I thought he was being playful about. I felt my face flush—which on a redhead can be alarming. I took a bite of pear and said, "Oopsh," cheerfully pointing to my full mouth, and then busily chewed with my lips closed.

"That's okay," he said, setting the bottle next to me and easing to the ground with his hands under his head. "I can wait for you to finish your pear."

I swallowed my bite, broke down with a dramatic huff, and took a sip. The champagne was cool and acrid, a hint of stinging fruit with tiny bubbles that effloresced on my tongue. I took another sip, bigger this time. It turned into warmth as it made its way down my insides.

"Mm," I said. "Quite brut."

He sat up and I passed him the bottle. He grinned as he took a drink where my lips had been, and then another. I took it from his hand, looked in his eyes with all seriousness, pressed my mouth to the bottle, and drank again.

After his last turn, the champagne was gone, and I felt not exactly tipsy, but super relaxed and oddly hopeful. We both lay down, looking up at the trees. I closed my eyes. My belly was, if not bursting, the most satisfied it had been in a long time. The sun filtered through the branches, warming my cheeks and nose and forehead. In fact, searing a bit.

In a moment he said quietly, "What was the thank-you for?"

"What thank-you?" I asked, my eyes still closed, thinking back no further than lunch.

"At the edge of the cave last night."

"Oh," I said, sighing. He meant my stick message to him. There was no way to say it all: thank you for nursing me to health; thank you for trying to rescue me from Dacruz at the harbor; thank you for making me look less horrid in Hélène's eyes. And the biggest one of all, which I'd never be able to say out loud: thank you for comforting me with friendship in high school when nothing else gave me joy.

"Just—everything," I finally murmured. "Someday I'll make you a list."

He was quiet for a moment. I started to drift off.

"I hope there will be a someday."

His voice was too melancholy. I wouldn't allow it. "If there isn't," I joked, "I'll send it to you from jail." I fell asleep for a blissful nap.

That afternoon we hiked along a path that promised a "natural bridge." It was a formation that had been shaped by erosion over the course of thousands of years, even though the river that had originally carved it was long dry.

The sun was as high as a midwestern sun can get in late September, which D'Arcy informed me was not very high, so that as we approached the natural bridge the light was hitting it somewhat from the side, highlighting the red ferns and lichens and moss that grew on it and throwing extravagant shadows on the rough surface of the stone.

The bridge was geologically ancient, an impassive observer, surrounded by life that was fleeting in comparison: trees that would only survive hundreds of years, tourists who would live decades, insects that would thrive only for weeks. From a distance down the path, it was shaped almost like a man-made bridge over a creek, with sturdy rock abutments on either side, anchoring it, and a deck crossing the span.

But from up close the bridge turned out to be massive. As the people ahead of us walked under it they shrank in size, until the bridge was a gutted cliff over them. Some of the delicate, filigreed plants I had seen from afar were actually trees and bushes, anchored in and around the stone.

"Oh," I whispered. D'Arcy said nothing, trailing behind me a little ways.

There was a cluster of boulders at the base of the arch, off to the side, and I clambered up one and then the other until I was on top of the mound. I turned around, saw that D'Arcy had dawdled enough to be several meters away, and I smiled, widemouthed, at him.

"It's gorgeous!" I called, as loud as a Ray. I tilted my head back and put my arms out, as if the scenery could soak into me and warm my insides, the way sunshine did. And then I flopped them down with an exhale of satisfaction.

"Beautiful," I thought I heard D'Arcy agree.

In a moment he stood at the base of the rocks, shielding the sun from his eyes with his hand. "Your hair is on fire in this light. I wish you could see how it looks against the black rock and green moss."

"You know," I said with a sudden revelation, grabbing the ends of my hair and holding them in front of my face, "I have no idea what I look like in sunlight." I realized too late that I was broadcasting that I was a Smudge. I scanned the faces of the visitors nearest us, but none of them had reacted.

He shook his head gravely. "If I could turn on my phone, I'd snap a picture to show you."

"If the camera on my crappy phone had *ever* worked, you could have used mine," I said, laughing. "But I guess you'll just have to memorize the scene, and draw it for me later."

"I'd never do it justice."

There was the same sort of quiet seriousness to his voice that I'd heard before our nap, and I wouldn't tolerate misery—not now, not in our last hours together, so I said, "Poo. False modesty does not become you. I'm certainly no harder to draw than a hungry chipmunk."

The moment the words left my lips I wished I could crawl after them and eat them up. I clamped my mouth shut, hoping that he hadn't heard me, or that he wouldn't make the connection. But this was D'Arcy I was with; D'Arcy who missed nothing. His eyes met mine, and they were instantly questioning, already analyzing. I had to look away—at the boulder, at the bridge wall, at a fern growing so unlikely from stone—at anything but him, examining me.

"Sol," he said, using my real name, so achingly soft on his lips. I didn't answer. "Sol," he said again, but this time it was directed inward, to himself.

"I'm such an idiot," I mumbled. How much fonder would the memory of his drawing partner have been without knowing what a mess she really was? When I finally looked at him, his eyes had a reflective glint of tears.

"Was it you?" he asked simply.

I nodded. "The desks," I said incoherently, "the drawings."

"It was you."

"I'm sorry," I said, shaking my head. Sorry that I was a Smudge; sorry that I hadn't thought to say as much all those months and years our desk friendship grew; sorry that the person he believed was his friend back then was about as worthwhile to him and to society as a blister-pack sealing machine;

sorry that I was on the cusp of ruining his life, and selfishly stealing hours with him beforehand. But deep inside, I was also sorry for me. Sorry that I had to add D'Arcy—kind, quick-thinking, organized, generous, rule-following, rule-exploding, sentimental D'Arcy—to the list of people I couldn't bear to lose and yet somehow had to say goodbye to.

From the corner of my eye I saw that D'Arcy was climbing up the boulder. In the time it took me to draw in a gasping breath, he had swept me into his arms in a bear hug. I remembered the moment I had figured out who he was, and how desperately I needed to see his face. If I had been braver, I would have wanted *this*.

He wrapped himself around me so tightly the air came out of my lungs. All I could do was cling to him, teetering on the uneven surface, relishing the squeeze of his arms. Our chins were crammed across each other's shoulders. He started swaying from side to side.

"Sol," he said. "Oh, Sol."

Tourists passed under the arch, watching us like we were on television, not on top of a rock in the middle of a state park.

For a moment I closed my eyes and felt he would never let me go.

"D'Arcy," I whispered his name out loud for the first time, giving myself over to an eternity of wanting what could never be.

"I knew you were the most remarkable person I'd ever met." His voice was muffled by the bunched hood of my sweatshirt.

A minute later he loosened his hold only enough to tuck his chin to his chest and look at me. Our faces were so close, and he seemed to be studying every freckle. I felt a prickly heat in my cheeks.

"I missed you after you got National Distinction," I said, to distract him. "You ditched me—and for what? For some silly award that a whole . . . *handful* of people get."

"I worried it might be goodbye forever."

"If you had known I was a factory Smudge, you would have been sure it was forever." I laughed.

"I knew you were a Night student."

"What? How?"

"Several times you seemed to wish me happy weekend on a Monday. I figured out that you had written it on Frinight. Plus"—he laughed—"everything was weirdly shaded, like it was lit by the moon."

I frowned. He had seen through me back then, before even meeting me. Yet I had been too dense to notice any signs that my drawing partner was a Ray.

"My face hurts," I said.

He broke into a broad smile and squeezed me again. "Oh god, I love your non sequiturs."

And then he took one hand out from behind me and brushed a strand of hair from my cheek. I winced.

"You have a little sunburn. I'm sorry. I should have known you would need sunblock, even in late September. Your poor, sheltered, ginger skin." He kissed the hair on my temple, as close as he could get to my tender face without touching it.

"I would roast on a spit in exchange for today," I murmured, wondering exactly what sort of kiss that was.

He hugged me again and said, "There's only one spot in the

park we haven't been to yet—the tallgrass prairie restoration, along the western edge. Are you game to see one more site before the end of the world?"

I nodded, game for anything that meant being by his side for just a little longer.

As we approached the edge of the woods I noticed the increasing chatter, all excitement and bother, of birds above me. I looked up at the trees—some of them were impossibly tall in this park—and the highest branches were dotted with hundreds of iridescent black birds, calling to each other with a metallic sort of *twick*, repeated again and again, in a dither. I stopped, tilted my head up, and stared. I knew birds who hunted after dusk, like owls and nighthawks, but in general birds were not part of my world, and when they were, they were quick, elusive shadows overhead, sometimes indistinguishable from bats. Poppu and I had studied Day birds in books when I was very little, but I remembered almost nothing because I never experienced them enough to make them belong to me.

"Starlings," D'Arcy said.

"So many."

"And multiplying."

It was true: more and more of them were flitting from the sky, roosting with the others, joining the chatter, convening from other locations to form a growing starling conference.

We stepped out onto the prairie, which had a clipped path down the middle of it but was otherwise a sea of tall, wild grasses, like something you'd see in a movie, with greens and blues and browns, and feathery seed heads at the tips of long stalks, swaying in the breeze. There was a family with three small children who were running back and forth on the path, screeching with delight. There was a couple in the distance, holding hands. I longed for what they had—I just stupidly, openly let myself want what I could never have, which I knew was like stabbing myself in the heart.

The birds chipped and babbled, preened and communed above us everywhere. Something occurred to me, a question I had long wondered about, that I was now free to ask.

"Why would someone as smart as you sit in the back of all your classes?"

He looked sideways at me and smiled. "Should I tell you the story?"

"Please."

"I missed the first day of school my sophomore year, because I was sick. On the second day, I went to what I thought was my immunology class. I was late and the teacher had already started talking. The room was jammed, and there was only one desk free in the back, so I squeezed past the other kids and stepped over backpacks and inched my way down the aisles until I finally sat down. I thought it was kind of weird that immunology would have so many students, but it wasn't until I was already settled that I knew I was in the wrong room. This class was basic biology, also known as Bio for Trees, because you can be as dumb as a tree and still pass it. I was trapped: I would have had to disturb the entire class again to get up and leave, and what do you know, there was this excellent drawing of the Council Overhang on the desk to distract me for that period."

I smiled. The clatter of the starlings became like the sound of metal scraping against metal. He raised his voice over the din.

"The next day, on a lark, I skipped my immunology class on purpose—just that once, I told myself—so I could go back and see what the artist thought of the virion I had added to the drawing. In fact, I ended up dropping immunology and registering for basic bio, and I taught myself immunology on the weekends."

"You took Bio for Trees just to draw on my desk?"

He nodded, with a little closed-lip smile.

"That's the nicest thing anyone has ever said to me."

"After that, on the second day of every new term—the second day because by then I'd figured out that you were a Night student—I scouted the desks in the back of each class to see if we shared a room, and if I found another kid sitting at your place I made him move, to stake my claim to it for the rest of the semester."

"You bullied other students to sit in my seat?"

He had to practically shout over the birds, raising a finger for each item he ticked off. "First: *charmed*; second: *bribed*; then, only when options one and two failed: *bullied*."

At that moment the trees exploded. The starlings, on a mysterious mass whim, burst from their perches like thousands of synchronized windup toys. They formed a zeppelin-size cloud that seemed to levitate into the sky, swirling as each bird adjusted instantaneously to the smallest movement of the bird next to it. The cloud shimmered, flashing black and silver in the light, twisting on itself, blowing above us like a plume of smoke on the wind. D'Arcy and I, and every other person on the prairie with us, turned our heads and swiveled our bodies, following the path of the birds.

"A murmuration!" someone shouted.

Back and forth the cloud of starlings swirled: now as concentrated as a tornado, then unfurling like a massive flag in the wind, finally rolling in on itself into a tube, and a ball, becoming blacker and smaller in its density, then breaking apart into two midair groupings and shape-shifting seamlessly together again. The cloud ebbed and flowed through the vast sky— wheeling like a wave cut loose from the ocean, pouring over the farmland across the road—and suddenly disappeared high above the trees, only to reappear just as quickly, swooping back over the prairie, so low over our heads that D'Arcy and I ducked instinctively, my hair whipping in the downdraft the birds generated, their wings beating like the rush of the surf, deafening as they passed. I screamed involuntarily, my chest bursting with the marvel, the joy, the miracle of nature. It gave me the sort of exhilarating edge of fear that I had whenever I experienced something astonishingly beautiful. The mass of birds flew up, straight up, headed for orbit, and then curled and plummeted in a limp waterfall of tiny bodies behind the trees, falling straight toward the ground into utter silence.

The people around us laughed in overt wonder. I was gasping for air, and my heart was beating frantically in my chest. D'Arcy's face fairly glowed.

I shoved him in the shoulders, making him lose his balance,

blurting, "No fair!" and then caught him before he fell. We steadied each other—I grabbed his elbows, he held my waist—as I said, forgetting to conceal a smile that was probably transparent with adoration, "You just *had* to top my Milky Way, didn't you?"

And then, because he was in my arms and he hadn't let go, and holding him gave me a feeling of being planted firmly on the earth, and because thousands of starlings knew exactly how to live without questioning themselves, I kissed his cheek without thinking. It wasn't a quick peck, it was one of unabashed appreciation. It happened, for me at least, as if it were in slow motion. His skin was warm and firm and so real, with that soft stubble I had felt in the hospital, and the smell of D'Arcy.

The kiss was very near his mouth, and because he didn't flinch, didn't waver even a millimeter, didn't take his eyes off mine, he just exhaled a moist vapor of intimacy, I kissed his lips, but only lightly, because now I knew for sure what I was doing, and half of me understood it was a mistake. The other half was defiant, despite the fact that giving him up, as I had to do in every conceivable future scenario, might kill me.

He wouldn't let me pull away. He moved his hands from my waist to the small of my back and drew me closer instead.

He said with a playful smile,

"*Powerless*
But for the star destroyer
Unknowing
She crash-lands in his heart."

"I knew I was a bad poet," I said breathily, because being that close to him was knocking the wind out of me.

"You kept me going." He touched his forehead to mine, closed his eyes, and brushed his beautiful great nose against my stinging cheek, caressing and breathing me in at the same time. I shivered with pleasure. And that was when I realized that the poem and the cleaved heart were references to the lost love between his parents, not the lost love of another girl. Again without thinking, I lifted my arms to encircle his neck and pressed myself against him, because I was sorry that Jean and Hélène had caused him anguish. I kissed his mouth, but harder this time.

His lips parted, as if he had only been waiting for me, and my body was taken aback by the welcome. It felt like someone had scooped out my insides and dumped them on the ground. I opened my mouth wider, our tongues touched shyly, and a rope from my heart to deep in my pelvis pulled itself taut. It didn't seem possible that my body had remembered desire after months of dying alongside Poppu, but a surge of inner heat burst into flames inside of me. I was greedy for his lips and his warm saliva and the exquisite pressure of his chin against my sunburn. I needed to wrap my legs around him, if only they weren't supporting my weight. I moved my hands up, through his hair, and braced the back of his head so I could push harder.

I had the alarming sensation of wanting to devour him, and I remembered his once saying, "You're like a wild animal, do you know that?"

He nibbled my upper lip to slow me down, to get me to listen. I stopped, reluctantly, my mouth poised for more near his, my heart thudding in my chest, my breath coming furiously, as if I were sprinting. He whispered, with both a definiteness and a quaver of vulnerability, "I want to be alone with you."

There were other Day visitors around us, walking quietly past on the path, affording us the only privacy they could by averting their gazes.

"Me, too." I heard my voice, husky and hungry.

"Where?" His eyes were penetrating, and I could see in them that his quick mind had already ruled out the obvious candidates and he hoped I'd have an idea. None of the locations I could think of was secluded in the afternoon light—not the meadow, not the woods, not the caves—not with all these visitors.

"If only it were night," I said.

"I know, right?" His voice had a mix of irony and exasperation. "But we can't wait for night, we need to find gas somehow and get you an audience with your grandfather before it's too late."

I shook my head, bewildered. How powerful a drug was desire that it could make me temporarily forget about Poppu? And what sort of heroic friend was D'Arcy that he would remind me at a moment like this?

He squeezed me against him, his hips pressing mine, tourists be damned. He kissed me, harder even than I had kissed him, our teeth knocking together once. And then he forced himself to stop and he bear-hugged me, as he had on the rock near the natural bridge, and exhaled the words "Don't forget" near my ear.

"Don't forget what?" I gasped.

"Don't forget you want me."

He loosened his hold, and I nearly collapsed from the trembling weakness of wanting him.

"I couldn't possibly forget." I almost laughed.

He dropped his head back, face to the sky, and called out a strangled, "*Zut.*" And then he straightened up, sighed, tipped his head in the direction of the parking lot, and said, "We gotta go."

Remembering Poppu, remembering that the real world was about to slap me in the face, didn't mean that I couldn't hold D'Arcy's hand—his right and my left because he hadn't forgotten my injury. We laced our fingers as we walked, and he rubbed his thumb along the side of my hand up to my wrist.

When we got to the car he opened the trunk and we searched inside. Thievery was the plan, again, but to siphon gas from another car we'd need a hose, which turned out to be one thing Jean's off-the-grid car didn't have.

"If I jogged to the gas station it would take me about an hour," he said in a low voice. "Walking back with a full gas can would take another hour and a half, maybe two. The Suits would lock on my position as soon as I made the purchase, and they'd have too much time to find me. I'd lead them straight to you."

"We could push the car to the station, so that we take off as soon as we're gassed up," I whispered.

"Push the car ten kilometers?" he asked rhetorically, shaking his head "no."

"Maybe one of the RVs in the campsite has a hose we could steal."

A hand reached out the open window of the car next to us and tapped the heavy ashes of a cigarette onto the gravel. I had assumed the car was empty, and I startled. I saw red nail polish on short, bitten nails, multiple bracelets and bangles, and intricate tattoos snaking up the skin of a tanned-looking arm.

A girl sat up slowly—she had been in a completely reclined position in the shadows—and rested both forearms on the window ledge of her car. She had black spiky hair, short on top and long in back, perfectly round circles of rouge on her cheeks, red Cupid's bow lips, black painted eyelashes above and below her eyes, and when she smiled one of her front teeth had a silver cap. My stomach clenched at the memory of Dice's beating, as it did whenever I saw the Noma.

"You two seem to be a bit fucked, no?" She got a good look at D'Arcy and drawled appreciatively, "Well, aren't you interesting?" She was chewing gum, but she still took a drag on the cigarette.

"Why aren't you under curfew?" I asked, pulling rudeness out of fear.

"Shut the fuck up," she said, dropping her cigarette out the window. She forced the creaky door of her jalopy open. She was smaller than I was, but insanely wiry. Her shirt was cut off to show powerful weight-lifting abdominal muscles. There was a giant bulge in the front pocket of her black shorts. She used a red shoe—it had a stylish heel and strap, but a rounded oversize toe—to grind out the butt. "Do you really think you can out-bitch me?"

It was the strangest thing. She was so cocky that I felt instantly inferior to her—physically smaller, and like a total square, like a geek. Me, the rangy girl who could barely keep a job and stay in school, the outsider who caused other students and teachers to pretend to check their phones as they passed her in the hall.

She took a step closer to me and said without emotion, "I'll cut you to pieces and feed you to my dogs if you look at me wrong. That makes you an amateur."

D'Arcy put his left arm around my shoulder and stuck his right hand out. "D'Arcy Benoît."

She chewed her gum with noisy pops and dragged her eyes to meet his, like it was almost not worth the bother. He didn't drop his hand, but from the corner of my eye I saw him eventually tilt his head and raise his eyebrows with a little half smile, wordlessly asking, "Are you going to shake it or not?"

The answer was not. She leaned back against her car, picked a piece of tobacco off her tongue, and flicked it away, saying, "I could prolly help you, if you make it worth my while."

D'Arcy hugged me to him with one squeeze and let me go, successfully conveying two messages: *She's apparently not going to cut you to pieces at this very moment* and *Let me do the talking.*

"Help us how?" he asked.

"You need gas, I have a car."

"You'd get us gas?"

"Depends on what you give me in return."

"We don't have money." He tipped his head toward me. "She can't . . . access hers, and I can't turn my phone on."

"So I heard. You're running from the cops."

We didn't have the advantage of asymmetric information, that was sure.

D'Arcy looked at me. "Is there anything of value in the trunk?"

Only a sixteen-thousand-dollar mannequin, I thought. Out loud I said, "Your day pack, a toolbox."

"There are a lot of expensive tools in it," D'Arcy confirmed.

"That's not enough," the girl said, shaking her head. "I'll get you a full tank of gas, so you won't have to stop before you get to Chicago."

"What makes you think we're going to Chicago?" D'Arcy asked.

She rolled her eyes like he was an idiot. "Illinois plates, city sticker, helpless Rays." She was right about almost everything.

"What's your name?" I asked.

"What's it to you?"

I shrugged. "I just like to know who's screwing me over."

D'Arcy sighed, as if he'd forgotten what a loose cannon I could be and had just been reminded.

"Well, isn't that a coincidence," the girl said. "When I'm screwing someone I like to whisper my name in their ear." She stepped over and put her cheek next to mine, on the side away from D'Arcy. It was eerily like the tactic I had used in the emergency room. Her hot breath smelled like mint and rancid smoke. Her lips reached for my lobe, which she took in her mouth for a second and sucked, making me shiver. She stuck her tongue in my ear, wet and alive, so that I heard her disconcertingly inside me, and whispered, "It's Gigi, and after I screw you I think I'll do your boyfriend."

I was an amateur; she was right.

"Please stop," D'Arcy said, ridiculously calmly. "I'm sure we have something else." I knew that he was about to trade away Premie Gort.

"You can have my necklace," I said to Gigi, before he could continue. She already had about a dozen of them on, and I wondered whether they were like shrunken heads, or notches on a spear: a physical tally of her victims.

D'Arcy narrowed his eyes. Gigi said, "Let's see it."

I reached into my shirt and pulled out Ciel's gift. I had always thought I was a sap for wearing it; I'd nearly chucked it in the trash a hundred times. But maybe years of being spineless were about to pay off.

Gigi reached out to hold the charms, deftly flipping each piece over to examine it. I almost expected her to pull out a jeweler's loupe. She paused midinspection to study my face, her eyes darting over my features and my hair like minnows in a moonlit pond.

I said, "They're white gold and eighteen karat gold, and the stars are—"

"I'll take it," she said, like a businesswoman and not a thug. She knew her stuff. And then she grinned at the charms, chewing her gum madly. Something about the sun and moon seemed to please her.

"Sol," D'Arcy said, obviously thinking it was important to me.

I shook my head at him. *It doesn't matter.* I reached behind my neck and unclasped it. Gigi put her hand out.

I glared at her, holding the necklace tightly in my fist, not relinquishing it yet. "This is worth a lot of money." In fact, Poppu suspected that it had cost over a thousand dollars, and we both knew that Ciel had come by the money illegally. I felt a little naked without it around my neck, and that surprised me.

"Sol—" D'Arcy started, again.

I stood up straight, so that I was looking down on her. "I want more than a tank of gas."

"Or how about this? I stab you in the gut and take it from you," she said, rubbing her hand on the bulge near her groin, which I now assumed was a switchblade.

"No, you won't," D'Arcy said, taking a protective step toward me.

"You think I can't take you both?"

I was pretty sure she could.

"I don't think you will," he said diplomatically.

I said, slowly, so she couldn't misunderstand me, "On top of the gas, I want you to make me over."

"What the fuck," she said, like I was out of my mind, which I probably was.

"Make me look like you."

Gigi brought the fuel back in three bright red, twenty-liter gas cans, loaded in the back seat of her car. She made D'Arcy take each one out and pour it into our tank, while she smoked a cigarette.

When he was done she stood in front of me with her hand out.

"What about my disguise," I said.

"I wouldn't skip out on that part of the deal for anything, Red."

I fished the necklace out of my pocket and dropped it in her hand. She grinned, smacking her gum, and found the two ends of the chain. She turned her back to D'Arcy and said over her shoulder with a fake pouty voice, "Will you help me with this, honey?"

I saw that D'Arcy wasn't pleased, but he took the ends of the chain from her, moved the black mullet away from the nape of her neck with his wrist, and put his clinical concentration toward the task of securing the necklace. I had a sudden vision of the inevitable: D'Arcy as a settled adult; D'Arcy without me;

D'Arcy clasping a necklace around the warm, pretty neck of the woman he would eventually love in my place. I had to lean against the car. It was like I had been shot in the chest.

"You okay, Sol?" he said with forced casualness, still fastening the clasp. Observant as ever, he could only have been watching me in his peripheral vision.

"Kinda hungry," I mumbled.

"You're bottomless," he said, finished with his job.

Gigi said, "You look like a concentration camp victim."

We followed Gigi's car, eating the dinner that we had stolen from the Smudge campers, as if we were on an ordinary road trip and not wanted criminals trailing after a possibly homicidal Noma who liked to stick her tongue in people's ears. Gigi had said we'd be driving for almost an hour, which would bring us uncomfortably close to curfew while we were on the road. But there was no point in my sitting in the back, pretending to be ill; the police were looking for me, and if we were pulled over, breaking curfew would be the least of our worries.

We were driving roughly southeast, judging from the setting sun. Gigi was taking back roads, and the current one was dirt and only one lane wide. Who knew what would happen when we arrived at our destination. Who knew where she was taking us, and whether she would slash our throats somewhere in rural Iowa. Even if she didn't kill us, I suddenly realized, we could easily get stopped on the way to Chicago, and I might never learn all the things I wanted to know about D'Arcy.

"Were you," I said, all at once shy, "were you really conceived in a cave?"

D'Arcy guffawed, that beautiful belly laugh. A bubble of a smile started in my chest and burst open on my face.

"At least in a town with caves," he answered. "I've only suspected that it happened inside an actual cave, but I don't think I want to know the answer badly enough to ask."

"Which cave?"

He glanced at me. "I'm lucky not to be named Lascaux or Chauvet, I guess. My parents had their honeymoon in Arcy-sur-Cure, in Burgundy, in north-central France. The cave paintings there are the second oldest in the world."

"D'Arcy," I said, understanding. *From Arcy.*

"Did you think French scientists would name their son after the love interest of a nineteenth-century British novel?"

"I didn't think that was it, not with the apostrophe."

We were quiet for a moment and then he said, "It's pretty great that they explored caves on their honeymoon."

I thought about how compatible they must have been. How in love. How in *lust*, to grab a moment in a cave, if his suspicion was true.

Gigi slowed down ahead of us, tapping her brake lights hesitantly so that they blinked through the cloud of dust her car had kicked up. We passed a stand of trees and my stomach tightened: out of the corner of my eye I saw the orange flash of an Hour Guard vehicle nested inside.

"Oh, shit," D'Arcy said.

The pulse of a siren sounded. I glanced back, and the SUV had pulled out of its hiding place.

"I'm sorry," I said. Every bad thing was my fault. I took credit for it all.

D'Arcy slowed to a stop. The Guard pulled up behind us. There was no escaping. We had an old sedan and the Guard had four-wheel drive. Not to mention a firearm.

Gigi backed up, gunning so hard that her wheels spun impatiently on the gravel. D'Arcy rolled down his window. He looked at me with his lips tight. "The odds were against us, huh?"

The Guard took his time approaching. He wasn't as put-together as the city Guards were: his helmet was unstrapped; he was unshaven, with the puffy skin of someone who drank too much; his black jacket was unzipped; he had a cigarette dangling from his lips.

Gigi marched toward him. His body language told me he was hyper-aware of her, like he could draw his gun and shoot, but he chose to pretend he didn't notice her. He removed his mirrored sunglasses, took a drag from his cigarette, leaned toward D'Arcy's window, and drawled, loud enough for Gigi to hear, "Destination?"

D'Arcy was required by law to respond, but when he opened his mouth, Gigi spoke first, venom in her voice.

"You're lying in wait for me now, asshole?"

"Gigi, you little skank, what's up?"

"You know they're with me, Brad. It's a cheap trick, stopping them."

He smiled, but it was creepy. He said to her, pointedly, "Destination?"

"Fuck you."

His doughy face went dark. "Your ID, please, Noma slut? Oh, wait. It's daytime, isn't it? Lemme guess . . . your phone says you're a *Ray*."

She closed her eyes for a beat, trying to resist stabbing him maybe. I could see sinewy muscles roll in her clenched jaw.

"So let me see," he went on. "Why might you care if I check your friends out? And more important, *how much* do you care?"

"I said they were with me. I didn't say they were my friends."

"Twenty-six minutes till curfew. Yes or no."

There was a subtext of some sort that I didn't understand. D'Arcy was more focused than I'd ever seen him. I wanted to be restrained and analytical like him, but I had an urge to say something, to get out, to run . . . anything but sit there, helpless.

Gigi finally took a step toward Brad and snatched the cigarette from his mouth. He let it go, grinning like the bastard he was. She took a deep drag and blew smoke out with the words "Six months, no stops."

"Two."

"*Six months.*"

"You can have three if you act like you want it, and now it's time to ante up."

She dropped the cigarette and stepped on it. "Your car or mine, dickwad."

"Something new. The bushes."

"Wait a minute—" D'Arcy said. He understood the deal before I did.

"Shut the fuck up, you *fucking* City Ray," Gigi exploded, shoving her finger in his face. "Sit in the car and keep an eye on your *fucking bitch.* Don't let her *move* from that spot, or I swear I'll *kill you both.*" She reached through the window past him and flipped on the radio, loud. It was set to Independent News Radio.

. . . and sisters, warriors of the hours. Fourscore and fifteen
years ago the government worked to heal the nation of a
physical illness, a cataclysmic pandemic.

My mind registered Grady Hastings's voice, speaking like a
preacher in a pulpit, his words passionate and drawn, echoing
slightly with the reverb of outdoor speakers.

Gigi stormed off toward the tree blind where the Guard vehicle had been hiding.

The Curfew March on Washington, I thought disjointedly. *It's
today. Or it was today, and this is a repeat broadcast, because D.C. is an
hour ahead.*

Brad followed Gigi, lifting off his helmet and dropping it
through the SUV window on the way.

*But in doing so our leaders inadvertently introduced a moral
pestilence—a virus that infects the declaration that "all men
are created equal"—a cancer on the Bill of Rights and the
fourteenth amendment, which promised freedom and equal
protection of the law. You, gathered here, are the doctors who
will excise the tumors of lies.*

*It is fitting that we stand before the memorial of this great
American who once said, "Let the people know the truth, and
the country is safe." Let the people know the truth! We are
here to reject the proposition that time can be shared fairly.
We are here to declare that our fundamental rights to travel,
to sojourn, and to assemble are violated by the division of
hours. We declare that arbitrary distinctions between citizens*

are odious to all people, to this great nation, whose institutions
are founded on the doctrine of liberty, and justice for all.

I craned my head back and saw Brad unbuckling his belt before he disappeared into the trees, and I whispered, "Oh god." D'Arcy reached for my hand without looking at me.

The dark nights of the Smudge's righteous grievance will not pass until he feels the warmth of the sun on his face. The prison of the Ray's day will not be unlocked until she knows the magnificence of stars on a country night.

"The truth is on the march, and nothing will stop it." And you, my brothers and sisters in resistance, are on the peaceful front line of the formation. Your presence—oh, you beautiful sea of faces!—is a thundering cry of urgency—it is a testimony to the human thirst for what is right.

Why had Gigi agreed to such a horrific bargain? Why hadn't she just ditched us? And why was she doing it if her phone said she was Day, if she thought *we* were Day?

Seneca said, "What is true belongs to me." It belongs to you . . . and to you . . . and to you. The truth is inside you. "Re-examine all that you have been told . . . dismiss whatever insults your soul."

"What is true belongs to me." Look around you. Smudges and Rays, side by side, veterans of suffering. You are men and

women who accept these verities: "You can only be free if I am free"; and your children will reap the blessings of justice only if you are strong enough to fight for it. Look at the Smudges being arrested as I speak! The gratitude of generations goes with you, brothers and sisters! Our spirits will soar together someday, unshackled from clocks and alarms!

My heart pounded, urging me to get out of the car, to help Gigi, to stop Brad. I reached for the door latch, but D'Arcy's hand squeezed mine powerfully and held me back.

"What is true belongs to me." Every moment of light and dark is a miracle. Every child is entitled to both.

"What is true belongs to me." You can close your eyes and have repose or speak the truth. Choose now, you can never have both.

Over the microphone I heard the curfew alarm of Grady's phone and the phones of multitudes ring simultaneously. The din of electronic bells was louder than I had imagined possible, an aural testament to Grady's claim of hundreds of thousands, and the prick of gooseflesh rose everywhere on my body.

"What is true belongs to me." I will speak the truth until I can no longer speak! I will never be freer than I am now, as the Hour Guards take me! Yes, come, gentlemen. It is night and my phone says I am a Ray, but my heart says I AM A MAN.

I tried to yank my hand away from D'Arcy, and when I looked up at him with a flash of anger, his eyes were glassy and shadowed. He shook his head. He was not going to let me go. I turned in my seat to face him, pushing my bad hand against his chest to get away.

D'Arcy launched himself at me and roughly wrapped his arms around my back. I twisted my body, I wrenched my arm away, I shoved him hard. I fought scrappily, but I was weaker than he was, frustratingly weak, and as I slowly lost the battle I realized that Gigi had told him not to let me move from this spot, and that she somehow knew I would try to intervene, and the radio was meant to cover whatever noise her abuser made, and that D'Arcy was following her instructions, even though the look in his eyes revealed that he could hardly bear it, and I stopped resisting—collapsing instead while Grady Hastings's shaking, buffeted, physically muffled voice shouted "WHAT IS TRUE BELONGS TO ME!" as the Hour Guards subdued him—and I sobbed with helpless rage into D'Arcy's shirt.

Brad left the tree blind first, tucking in the last stray tail of his shirt and fixing his hair. I glared at him as he made a special trip to our car to gloat. D'Arcy flipped off the radio.

"Woo." Brad practically whistled the sound as he zipped his fly in D'Arcy's face. Much of Gigi's makeup—pancake white and red rouge—had transferred to his face. "I doubt you geeks were worth that, but Gigi must be keen on you. That was her personal best."

Gigi came out of the trees, fully arranged, but with her makeup smeared and an ugly red bruise on her neck in the shape of an oval, which had the sick effect of a tag advertising Brad's conquest.

She strode past him on the way to her car and said, "Who the fuck said you could talk to them?"

"Fuck you, whore," he called after her. And then to us he said, "I'll catch you later. Get it? *Catch you* later." He laughed at his own joke as he walked to his car.

"Where is a taser when you need one," D'Arcy muttered,

putting the gearshift in drive. I slid down in the seat and wiped my eyes with the sleeve of my hoodie.

The Noma compound was an enormous piece of farmland outside of Clinton, Iowa. It stretched as far as the eye could see, until gentle hills muted the edges. Part of it was planted with summer and fall vegetables, and part of it was planted with mostly battered, weathered trailers and RVs. I had heard that the Noma were wanderers, but this camp, with homemade gravel walkways, makeshift electrical poles, and dirty garden ornaments, had the feel of something that had been around for a few years, like it would be a lot of work to uproot those trailers and get on the road.

We parked in a dirt lot. Gigi got out of her car and I could see that she had reapplied most of her makeup while she was driving. Around us were Noma kids and wild dogs, running and yelling and barking in the twilight, all of the girls with spiked black mullets and all of the boys with white-blond shaved heads, some of them barefoot, playing what appeared to be a game of cops and robbers with alarmingly real-looking guns, but without an adult in sight. The Night bell sounded on dozens of phones—the children's, Gigi's, and mine included, but the kids just kept right on pretend-shooting each other.

Gigi led the way in stony silence past trailers and suddenly gawking children. The walkway was narrow, and D'Arcy was behind her. As we made our way, he put his left hand behind him. I reached for it with my left, and he gave me a comforting squeeze. It was so reminiscent of the squeeze below the flirty hospital receptionist's desk, I wondered for a moment exactly when it was that D'Arcy had started to find me tolerable as a human being, in the evolution of his somewhat miraculous affection for me. It could not have been as early as the hospital. Strung out on lack of sleep, food, and mostly hope, I was not remotely tolerable then.

We arrived at by far the biggest trailer, roughly in the center of the makeshift city. Before she got to the door, Gigi pointed at me with her chin and said, "Her first."

I followed her up three short stairs and when she opened the door I saw that the room was packed full of Noma, filling dozens of chairs, with standing room only along the walls. I instinctively stumbled back down a step, bumping into D'Arcy, who caught me before it could turn into a real fall.

"More Noma than you've ever seen in your life, I know," Gigi said, stepping in. "We won't hurt you. At least not right now."

The room was buzzing with conversation, and a booming voice rose above the rest saying, "Well, well. Who could have predicted it? Soleil Le Coeur."

I glanced at D'Arcy. How did they know my name?

D'Arcy's eyebrows were at quizzical angles, as if I had surprised him again. "Sol is short for Soleil?"

"We haven't got all night, dummy," Gigi said, so I reached for D'Arcy's hand and stepped inside, bringing him with me.

The atmosphere was close in the room, from too many bodies crammed into one space, and the people who were standing shifted uncomfortably, irritably, like they could hardly bear another second of being cooped up. There was a strange uniformity of color—black clothes, red makeup, glinting piercings. The man with the big voice was younger than I'd first thought—maybe in his twenties—but when he stood up he was gigantic in every dimension, with a bushy black beard in contrast to the bleached stubble on his head.

Gigi said, "Gimme your phones."

D'Arcy and I looked at each other, affirming that we didn't have a choice. I reluctantly let go of his hand to pull the phone from my pocket. We passed them to Gigi, who gave them to the giant bearded guy, who put them on the table in front of the skinny kid next to him, who might have been all of fifteen.

D'Arcy said, "Don't turn mine on, unless you want the police here."

"We suspected," the giant said.

Gigi said to me, "Red, this is our tribal leader, Fuzz."

His eyes scoured me. He put out his beefy hand, the size of a small ham, which I thought was an oddly formal gesture for someone named Fuzz. I shook my head, held up my bandage, and said, "I'm kind of protective of this." I turned to Gigi and said, "I never told you my name."

She said, "You think I'm an idiot, don't you?"

I didn't think she was an idiot. In the few hours I'd known her she'd taken advantage of the fact that D'Arcy and I were stranded, she'd bartered for the only thing of value I owned, she'd somehow anticipated my suicidal outrage at Brad's assault, and had used D'Arcy to subdue me.

Gigi lifted the chain of my necklace from her neck and slid her fingers back to find the clasp. "I put two and two together as soon as you showed me this." She easily removed it, without

D'Arcy's help, and lowered it onto Fuzz's outstretched hand. She asked him tersely, "Can I show her?" He nodded.

She turned to me and pulled the collar of her black T-shirt down in the front, almost to the nipple of her right breast, where there was a tattoo. I took a step closer. It was the full moon, about to eclipse the sun, whose rays were blazing in all directions, ending in little stars near the moon. Fuzz lifted his shirt, and over his right nipple, buried in a phenomenal amount of curly hair, was the same image. The skinny kid sitting next to him unbuttoned his black shirt and showed me the same tattoo on pale skin.

"Your pendant," D'Arcy said in a low voice.

"No, the symbol of the Noma," Gigi corrected him, still staring at me. "Very few non-Noma have seen it. We generally marry them or kill them if they do. Your brother must have figured it would protect you."

"And it has. This once," Fuzz added.

Gigi said, "Just how many redheads three years younger than Ciel Le Coeur do you think there are in the Midwest, wearing a solid gold symbol of the Noma around their necks? You're the only one, babe." She reached out to lift D'Arcy's chin, admiring him. "Besides, the minute you pulled that necklace out, your little boy toy here clinched it by calling you 'Sol.'"

I found myself blurting, "This *boy toy* happens to be the most brilliant, decent person in the room."

Fuzz burst out laughing, a spit-spraying, cynical guffaw. "So Gigi's texts were right: you have Ciel's legendary temper. Not to mention his exaggerated loyalty."

I felt a fire blaze in my chest, maybe proving half his point.

"You guys throw Ciel's name around a lot, but if you really knew him you'd realize he's the least loyal person on the planet."

Gigi whispered to D'Arcy, knowing I would overhear, "I'm thinking if you serviced her more regularly, that would go a long way toward taming the shrew."

They took D'Arcy and me away separately, with no sappy reas-
surances that they'd bring us together again. After three days
of trying to ditch him it was like pulling my heart out and
leaving it behind. I had let my guard down so thoroughly in
the last eighteen hours that I'd as good as guaranteed a continuous drip of acid, burning a hole just like this in my chest
until I was senile or dead.

D'Arcy caught my eye and said over his shoulder, "See you
soon," and the acid burned paradoxically deeper because he
sensed what I needed.

There were several trailers dedicated to the bleaching, dying,
piercing, and tattooing that were involved in being Noma. Gigi
reminded me that I could be killed for knowing their secrets,
and the number of vicious fenced-in mutts around their ram-
shackle homes made her previous threat to feed me to the dogs
feel real.

It turned out that in order to dye orange hair black, you had
to add an intermediate step of a warm brown first, so the hair
wouldn't look muddy in the end. If I had been even slightly

more feminine, I probably would have known that. The brown step alone took an hour. Rinsing, conditioning, adding the black, rinsing again, and finally cutting the spiky mullet took another couple of hours. The camp's resident hairstylist, a middle-aged woman named Zinnie with a surprisingly sweet smile, had no trouble giving me the cut: it was the only style female Noma wore; she must have done it thousands of times. Like Gigi, she chewed gum nonstop the whole time I was there. She asked if I wanted a stick, and when I said no she offered a chocolate candy bar, which I accepted gratefully and tried hard to eat slowly. It wasn't long before she had given me an apple and a can of tomato juice, too—snacks she had clearly brought for herself.

My eyebrows were deemed too conspicuously ginger, and so Zinnie made me put on swim goggles in order to brush a bit of developer mixed with brown dye on those, too. When she was all done, I was shocked at the result: my murky blue eyes were enormous, in deep sockets; my skin was ghostly; my face was all angles, topped with black spikes of hair. The mullet, hanging on sharp shoulders, was ugly and punk.

"Shit," Gigi said. "As an emaciated redhead you kind of pulled off 'ethereal.' Now you're all savage hunger."

I was scary; it was true. And I still didn't have the piercings or tattoos, which Gigi informed me would be temporary: makeup and a magnetic nose ring.

"But we'll do that tomorrow," she said, yawning. "It's midnight, and I'm on a Ray schedule right now. Fuzz wants to see you at eight, so I'll get you up at seven for the finishing touches."

I'm on a Ray schedule right now, I repeated dully in my head. I was too exhausted to understand it.

She took me outside and I followed her flashlight as we made our way around the dark hulks of trailers. When we got to our destination, she held up the light to use her key and I saw the graffiti-like tag "Gigi" scrawled on the door. Inside, she flipped on the light, and it was like a filthy bachelor pad, with a weight-lifting bench in the middle of the room, free weights strewn on the dinette table, multiple ashtrays full of squashed cigarette butts, empty bottles of beer and whiskey on the kitchen counter, and dirty dishes in the sink. She locked me inside with her—it was a dead bolt—and showed me to the bathroom. From a cabinet she dug out a used toothbrush, used toothpaste, and a questionable towel, and I was grateful for them all.

When I came out, she was already curled up on the built-in sofa, with a pillow and a blanket, and the bedroom door was open with the light of a single lamp streaming out. She was giving me her bed. I stood still for a moment, stealing a look at her. She was wearing a very un-Noma white night-shirt. Her eyes were closed and her face was relaxed. She had removed her makeup and it was easier to see the contours of her face. She had fleshy cheeks with high bones. Her lips were full, her eyes slanted upward. She was quite exotic-looking.

"Shut the light, dummy," she said. She wasn't asleep.

"Where's . . ." I hesitated, still becoming accustomed to my own vulnerability on this point. "Do you know where D'Arcy is?"

"He's in Fuzz's trailer. He's fine. Go to bed or you'll be a useless fuck tomorrow and you'll put him in danger."

I started for her room. When I got to the doorway I turned around. "Thanks, Gigi."

She sighed, a long sleepy sigh. "Fuck you, Red."

Saturday
7:00 a.m.

I slept more deeply than I expected, and about half as long as my body wanted me to, until a pile of clothes hitting my face woke me up. I opened my eyes, disoriented, not remembering where I was. I picked an article of clothing off my neck: a black jeans miniskirt. I sat up. Black fishnet stockings and a black long-sleeve T-shirt fell from my chest to my lap.

Gigi was already smoking and chewing gum.

"You have gigantic feet, so I had to get these from my ex-boyfriend. No heels for you." She tossed a pair of red high-tops at me, one of which I had to bat away with my left hand before it creamed my face.

"I'll give you three minutes to shower. That's two minutes more than you'll want anyway, because I don't have hot water."

While I was undressing in the bathroom she yelled through the door, "And don't wash your hair, just rinse it."

The shower was bracing, but that was a good thing. It focused me, it woke me up. I had no baggie to protect my bandage, so I hooked it over the top edge of the shower stall and did all the washing with my left hand. I toweled off, covered in gooseflesh, and pulled on the Noma clothes she had given me. When I stepped out of the bathroom, she had a bowl and a spoon waiting on the dinette table with a quart of expired milk, a box of bran flakes, and a four-pound bag of sugar for sprinkling.

She pointed to the chair in front of the bowl. "I sniffed the milk. It won't kill you."

I ate three bowls of cereal while she put product in my hair, spiked it, dried it with a hair dryer, and then applied so much hair spray my scalp felt like it was made of plastic. She let me brush my teeth before she put on my makeup: an off-white foundation that covered my sunburn, freckles, and lips; black eyeliner in the pattern of giant, comical eyelashes; two circles of bright rouge on my cheeks; and lipstick just in the middle of my lips, like a living Betty Boop. As she was applying the lipstick she said, "No macking on lover boy today—you'll mess up my work."

I felt my muscles relax just a bit, the way they did when the Night alarm sounded on my phone. There was the promise of D'Arcy.

She gave me a magnetic nose stud and a pair of earrings shaped like tiny knives, and then she led me to the mirror. She had more than carried out her end of the bargain: I was not Sol Le Coeur anymore; I was Noma.

"Time to go to the meeting hall," she said. I turned, and she handed me a baggie full of doxycycline pills, which I recalled were last in my hoodie pocket. "You can't have your old clothes back, in case the pigs stop you. And you sure as hell don't get to keep a prescription made out to Sol Le Coeur."

I took a pill and sipped from the faucet to wash it down. And then I stuffed the baggie in my skirt pocket.

"Am I ready?" I said.

"You never looked better." She grinned, showing the silver tooth.

In the daylight I could see that her trailer was near a large vegetable garden, which at this time of year was still carrying some green and pink tomatoes on drying, brown vines. There were rows of healthy kale and patches of squash and pumpkin. I had never seen entire broccoli plants before—sturdy and thick—or broad-leafed stalks studded with Brussels sprouts. Those were things I had assumed only Ray farmers and Agriculture Apprentices saw. My hairstylist was picking from the plot with the help of four boys, and she looked up in time to smile at me. She said something to the tallest, whom I recognized as the boy Fuzz had given our phones to. He nodded, grabbed a small paper bag from the ground next to her, and started walking after Gigi and me. He had long, lanky legs, and he caught up quickly.

"Hey, Gigi," he said.

"Zen." She greeted him perfunctorily.

"Um," he said. She kept walking. He stayed with us, in uncomfortable silence. His bleached, shaved head looked good on him, I decided, which was not the case for many of the Noma men. Perhaps it was because he was a real blond. I looked closer. His lashes were as pale as his eyebrows.

We arrived at the meeting house. The door was open. Gigi hopped up the three stairs, and Zen said to me in a hurry, "I'm

Zen, Zinnie's son—the woman who did your hair?" He put out his hand for me to shake. I looked at it, stunned for a second to be offered a left hand. He nodded at my bandage. "I saw . . . at the meeting house yesterday. Um, Fuzz tried to—"

"Just hump her already, Zen," Gigi said.

He dropped his hand and glared at her. "Why do you have to drag everything into the gutter?"

I reached out with my left hand. "I'm glad to meet you, Zen. Your mom was really nice to me." He grinned and pumped my hand, and for a moment it was oddly like I was a celebrity. I added covertly, "And by 'nice to me' you should know I mean she fed me chocolate."

He laughed, and Gigi rolled her eyes.

"May I take a picture of you, Sol?" Zen asked, holding up his phone.

"Uh, I guess," I said, and he snapped it before I had a chance to smile.

The room was less crowded than the evening before, and the first thing I saw was D'Arcy, speaking privately with Fuzz, who was at the head of the conference table. D'Arcy was on Fuzz's right and had been made over as Noma, just as I had. But even with the buzzed blond stubble, red earring, and black clothes, he was all D'Arcy: distinctive nose, seemingly longer without his hair to distract, hazel eyes, beautiful bone structure, and the bonus of a surprisingly pretty head shape. He glanced at us as we entered. I saw his eyes fall on us in succession—Gigi, me, and then Zen—registering each in that observant way he had, while still carrying on a conversation with Fuzz. He found Gigi again, to nod hello, and then he focused on Fuzz, jotting something on the paper in front of them, and I suddenly realized that he didn't know me. It was the strangest feeling to have D'Arcy look at me but not see me. As if what was Sol in me had disappeared.

Gigi tilted her head to murmur, "Tough break, dummy. Turns out it was just a perverted fetish for redheads."

But then D'Arcy's head jerked up again, as if on second thought. His eyes locked on me, scanned my features, slid down my body and back up to my eyes. I saw his smile peel open and I read the word "Sol" on his lips, but I couldn't hear over the buzz of conversations in the room. He interrupted whatever Fuzz was saying by putting a hand on the paper and excusing himself. He got up from the table and walked around it to greet me. I couldn't stop myself from running to him.

"Your makeup!" Gigi called to my back, irritably.

I slammed into him and he grabbed me in a bear hug. The room groaned and hissed at the spectacle of our greeting.

"Sit down now," Fuzz commanded. We obeyed.

Zen had taken the seat at Fuzz's right hand, and I recalled he had been there the day before, too. Fuzz began by saying, "I understand you want to see your grandfather."

I nodded.

"And Ciel has him, on a yacht."

"Yes."

"And . . ." He hesitated. "You and Ciel don't get along."

I wondered how much D'Arcy had been responsible for this information. What else had he divulged to Fuzz, a stranger and a potentially dangerous Noma?

"Gigi and I had a deal," I said. "My necklace for gas and a makeover."

"Uh-huh."

"So can we have our phones back, and the keys to the car?"

D'Arcy covered my hand with his. "We might be able to use their help getting to town."

"We don't know them," I said, not caring that everyone was listening. "How can we trust them?"

Gigi barked, "You trusted me to save your ass when I went in that blind with Brad."

"Gigi." Fuzz's voice had a warning.

"I didn't ask you to do that!" I said.

"You ungrateful little bitch," Gigi said through her teeth.

"Shut up, both of you," Fuzz said.

Gigi backed into a corner, but it seemed more to keep herself from throttling me than to concede.

Fuzz turned to me. "Listen, Sol. Listen and shut up for one single minute. Shit, you are so like your brother."

I'm nothing like him, I thought.

"Let me start by giving you back your phone, and maybe you'll consider trusting us."

He nodded at Zen, who opened the paper bag in front of him and pulled out our phones. I had assumed the bag had a couple of green tomatoes from the garden, or his lunch. It was becoming clear that I had underestimated Zen.

Fuzz said, "Zen has added the ability to initiate uncensored texts. That should be worth something in the friendship bank."

Zen said, "I also repaired your global positioning feature, Sol. Did Ciel disable it?"

"I did," I said.

"Cool." He grinned. "But you won't need that sort of camouflage anymore."

He walked around the table and placed D'Arcy's phone in front of him. The girl on my right gave up her chair to Zen without his even asking. He sat down and said, "May I?" I nodded, and he tapped the screen of my phone to turn it on. He leaned toward me so I could see what he was doing. D'Arcy got up and stood behind us to watch over our shoulders. Zen opened my text messages and pulled up a photo attachment of me in full Noma regalia—the picture he'd taken outside just a couple of minutes before, which he had sent to my phone in high resolution. With my black hair and no smile I looked like dark clouds before a storm. He tapped away, his fingers magically making it my profile photo—something I thought only the Office of Assignment could do.

Zen is their Ciel, I thought.

"I'll do the same for you after the meeting, D'Arcy," he said, glancing back. He turned his attention to my phone again and pulled up my vital stats.

My name was Sunny Puso.

"*Puso* means 'heart' in Filipino," Zen murmured. "It was Gigi's idea."

"You made—" I stuttered. "You made me a *Ray*. How did you do that?"

"I didn't do it," Zen said. "Ciel did."

Fuzz said in his booming, rumbling voice, "This is the part where we kill you if you divulge our secrets."

Zen said, "Several years ago Ciel figured out how to pro-gram our phones so that we switch instantaneously from Day to Night at the precise moment of each curfew." He waited, so that we could process what he said. D'Arcy and I were mute. "This means," he went on, "Noma papers always categorize us as legal, no matter what hour of the day or night it is. During the day we appear to be Rays, at night we're Smudges, and the designation changes automatically on our phones."

I remembered Gigi saying, "I'm on a Ray schedule," and Brad saying to her sarcastically, "Let me guess, your phone says you're a Ray."

"The Hour Guard knew it was a trick," I said.

"The government knows it's fudged," Zen confirmed.

Fuzz interjected, "The authorities think it's Noma technology—so for the moment they feel the problem is contained. They know we protect the code like fighting dogs, and that we don't hang with Rays *or* Smudges if we can help it."

"Except when we're beating them or robbing them," someone shouted. The room exploded with laughter.

Fuzz put his hand up to quiet them. "The point is, the government is patient while it works on busting open Ciel's programming. But when it succeeds, we're dead."

Something nagged at me. My mind flitted to the trial, to Ciel being denied bail because people he knew had "disappeared" from the Day/Night rosters—they'd vanished from the government's radar. I remembered Ciel's voice and his face perfectly when he told me no one knew how they did it.

Ciel knew. Ciel was the one who had developed the technology.

My eyes got hot with tears. "That bastard lied to me about everything," I said to myself, my voice breaking. But Zen heard me.

"If I had to guess, I'm pretty sure any lies he told you were to protect you. I would do the same if you were my sister."

D'Arcy asked, "At the moment of curfew—at that very second—what if an Hour Guard was holding your device? What would he see in your papers?"

Zen said, "He'd see the switch. He'd see a Day assignment flip to Night, or the other way around. And if the device wasn't protected, the government hacks would be able to back out the programming. The game would be up, for all Noma everywhere."

"How can thousands of Noma never get caught?"

Zen said, "First, we try not to be on the road right before either curfew."

Gigi had cut it too close yesterday because of us.

"Second, each Noma phone has a personal code. You and Sol have one now, too. We have a self-destruct command on all our phones. If anyone tries to access the programming on the device without entering the personal code first, the phone's drive fries itself."

"Destroying your papers is a federal offense," D'Arcy said. "You get life, with no parole."

Fuzz nodded gravely. "We lost people in the beginning, before the government figured out it was pointless to actively hunt us down—that they were just filling their prisons without gaining any information. Someday I'd like to . . . bargain for the release of those prisoners."

"Is this how Ciel got rich?" I asked, frowning, thinking of the yacht. "Selling you this technology?"

"He didn't sell it to us," Fuzz said. I saw him glance at Gigi in the corner. She raised her eyes to the ceiling, the way you do when you hope tears will drain into their ducts instead of spill onto your face. I began to understand that something had happened between Ciel and Gigi—something he'd hidden from me and Poppu. Fuzz was saying, "Ciel *gave* the technology to us. Which is the only reason we're helping you now—why Gigi went to so much trouble to get you here." He got up and put his beefy hand out, with the palm open. My necklace was nested in it. He was giving it back to me. "It's pretty damned lucky that Gigi found you—for you and for us. We've been waiting a long time to pay Ciel back."

D'Arcy and I agreed to let the Noma drive us back to Chicago.
They insisted on splitting us up, which I had to acknowledge
made sense. If one of us got caught, the other might get away.

Gigi drove me in her car with one of Zen's little brothers,
Cake, sitting next to her in the front, while I was stuffed in the
back. Fuzz drove Jean's sedan with a burly guy named Dope in
the back seat and D'Arcy up front. A Winnebago and a pickup
truck with a camper top anchored the two ends of our little
train. Fuzz had explained that the Noma always traveled by
caravan, and a trip of this distance could be no exception without seeming suspicious.

In the minutes before we left, Gigi brought me to her mobile home for a rest stop and to fix my makeup, and Zen silently trailed after us.

"May I come in, Gigi?" he asked, with the same unassuming
voice he had used when he'd taken my picture. I was starting to
appreciate his quiet depth, and I wanted Gigi to let him in if
only to see what was on his mind.

"Don't get in my way," she said, holding the door for him.

Inside, while Gigi touched up my face, Zen asked me to take out my phone.

"I installed a gift for you—with Fuzz's permission," he said. "I didn't put it in D'Arcy's device, because only three other people in the world have this technology."

I took the phone out of my pocket, ready to hand it to him. He motioned for me to keep it.

"Enter your personal code—the one that disarms your self-destruct command—and then hit a one."

I tapped my code and the number one.

"Now hit the text message icon."

An ordinary text message box popped up. "Okay . . ." I said, with a little laugh. "At least it didn't blow up."

"It looks like a simple message box, but do you see how the rim is black, instead of blue?"

"So it is!"

"This is a thing of beauty, Sol." His eyes were wide, his voice was breathy. I loved how passionate this kid was about his work.

"She's Sunny until we get her to Chicago," Gigi corrected.

"It's one of Ciel's finest creations—not the application itself, which is relatively simple, but the way he cloaks it from the censors."

My mood sank like a stone in a pond. *Enough with the adoration of Ciel.*

"When your phone is in this mode, you're able to send a future text." He paused, in that Zen way he had, so that I could think about what he had said.

"You got me," I admitted. "What's a future text?"

"It's a preprogrammed text. It gets delivered at a set time, unless you call it off with your personal code, plus one. You enter the number of days, hours, and minutes until delivery, and type in the message. Want to try it?"

"Sure," I said, feeling my own enthusiasm kindled by his energy. "But what . . . what will I use it for?"

He grinned. "You'll think of something. Never say no to geek software."

"Are you in my contacts?" I asked. He nodded.

I pulled up his name, entered the number in the correct field for one minute, and then held the device close to my chest, like a hand of cards, so neither he nor Gigi could see what I was typing. I hit "send" and we waited while Gigi added more spray to my spikes.

Find another hero to worship was the message I had sent.

A minute later, his phone made a *ping*, he tapped the screen, and let out a bursting laugh.

"What?" Gigi said.

"It worked," he said simply, and got up to leave. He reached for my left hand with his right and I clasped it willingly. "Stay safe, Sol Le Coeur. I would really hate it if anything happened to you."

My phone pinged. "That's from me," he said, smiling. "Naturally I'm one of the other three who has the technology." He squeezed my hand and dropped it.

After he left, I tapped the message open and it said, **Give Ciel a chance.**

As I got in her jalopy, Gigi handed me a piece of gum. "Chew this. The whole way. And don't say anything if we get stopped by cops or Hour Guards, do you understand?" I nodded, knowing I was not Noma enough for a confrontation with police.

"You, too, Cake. Let me do the talking, and just sit there acting pissed as hell." She shot me a look filled with distaste. "That should be easy for you, Sunny, since that's your default setting."

An hour into Illinois we did get stopped, by a posse of Day Guards, which I had never seen before. They seemed to deliberately target the caravan. It took forever for a Guard to swagger to the window.

"Destination, Noma bitch?" the Guard said to Gigi. He bent to look past her at Cake, who gave him the finger—such a thin little child's finger—and then examined me, sitting in the back. Following Cake's lead, I gave him a wild look that said *Screw you*, but inside I felt like the skinny redhead who was wanted by police.

"We're taking Cake here to the Licking Puke Zoo, pig," Gigi said, as if she were ready to spit on the officer, "and then we're going to the observatory at the John Handcuff-Your-Mother-to-the-Bedpost."

"Your ID, freak?" He shoved his open palm in the window. She slapped her phone onto his glove. He tapped it on and said, "I need to see the devices of the freak in training and skeleton freak, too."

Cake and I handed them up. I had an instinctive moment of panic: it was daytime and I was being assessed by an Hour Guard. I needed to trust that this would work—that Ciel's programming was as flawless as Zen believed it was—but every Smudge instinct in me cried out that the game was up. My guts had turned to slush in my belly.

He studied each phone one at a time, slowly scrolling through our data, checking our faces against the photos. It felt like he lingered longer on my phone. He opened several pages. I realized that I had taken only a cursory glance at what my made-up vital statistics said before we left. I could not reproduce any of it other than my name if he asked me questions. I glanced at Gigi. She looked like this was the biggest pain in the ass she'd ever encountered. She was so cool, and I was such a wreck. I tried to take strength from her. I focused on the Guard, I chewed the gum with my mouth open, and in my head I chanted at him, *I hate you, I hate you,* to distract myself and to make my face believably Noma.

"Wha'd you know, you're all *Rays*," he finally sneered.

When he shoved the phones at Gigi and Cake, they each snatched them back and said, "Fuck you," instead of thank you, so I did the same. Before he left, the Guard leaned in and hissed in Gigi's face, "I can't wait until we bust the lot of you and rid the streets of Noma filth."

"I can't wait until I track down your wife when you're not home."

He punched the side of her face so hard that my whole body startled, and I almost let out a cry.

As the Guard walked back to his motorcycle, I said, "Oh god, Gigi, are you okay?"

"Shut your trap," she said in a low voice, bracing her cheek with her wrist. "Never let down your guard until the last bastard takes off."

Saturday
12:30 p.m.

The caravan got off the expressway at Lake Shore Drive and moved south. Lake Michigan was the turquoise color that I had seen from Dacruz's car on the way back to the emergency room from lockup, with little wavelets giving the water the texture of fish scales, and glints of early-afternoon light winking at me. I thought back to that moment, to being in the back seat of the squad car, hot, nauseated, and utterly alone. If I had known D'Arcy was my desk partner then, having been freshly betrayed by him, would I have given him a chance?

As we passed the Fifty-seventh Street beach, I caught sight of Ciel's white yacht cruising the shore, and I felt a ball of lead lodge in my chest. Somewhere on that boat was Poppu, whom I hadn't seen for three nights, who could already be dead or moments away from death. And I would have to navigate Ciel in order to see him.

I tried to prepare myself for changes that might have occurred. I tried to remember what Poppu looked like in the photo, which had been deleted with my old identity, tubes snaking from his arm and his nose. I planned for the worst: that he was in pain, or doped into unconsciousness. If he was awake, he might not recognize me. If I couldn't speak with him, I hoped against hope that he might know I was there, if only subconsciously. I needed him to believe that I hadn't abandoned him, that I never would. In a flash of selfishness that I knew I would have to subdue, I wanted to tell him it was Ciel who had taken him from me.

We got off Lake Shore Drive at Science Drive, and the caravan snaked through park district lots to the Fifty-ninth Street Harbor. Ciel's yacht was still visible offshore. We parked next to the harbor house, and Gigi and Cake got out of the car.

"Stay with the other guys in the Winnebago, Cake," Gigi ordered. "There are snacks in there. And use the little boys' room." He nodded and ran off to the trailer, which had stayed in the larger lot with school buses full of Ray students on a field trip to the Museum of Science and Industry.

D'Arcy's car pulled in next to ours, with his door already opening. He headed straight for me and said in a low voice, "You okay?" I nodded. He said, "I've been given strict orders to 'shut the fuck up.'"

"Walk home now, D'Arcy," I urged under my breath. "You're so close."

He smiled. "I knew you'd say that. Tell me, how far would I get in my old life as 'Skin Russell'?"

I'd forgotten about his new ID. It had allowed us both to travel freely from Iowa, but now it was imprisoning D'Arcy. "We'll make Ciel change you back," I said.

Dope and Fuzz got out of the car and stretched, unfurling their impressive bulk.

"Ciel is waiting, Sunny," Gigi called. "And lord knows Ciel can't be kept waiting." She came over to claim me, linking her arm with mine the way Poppu said Belgian sisters did and steering me toward the viaduct that led under Lake Shore Drive to the lakefront. I glanced back at D'Arcy; Fuzz and Dope were escorting him, too. Something about their body language was off—but maybe they were always ready for a fight.

On the other side of the viaduct we walked up a path to the breakwater. The yacht was hovering near the end of it, not moored, but poised for a quick stop, engines running. Ciel was on the top deck, with binoculars. I had the uncomfortable feeling that he was looking at me, and only me, even though Gigi was gripping me so tightly my hip was nested in her waist. When we were halfway down the breakwater, he signaled to the captain to dock up alongside it. The captain did it effortlessly: pivoting, swinging slowly, gently into place, with the male nurse lowering fenders to protect the side of the boat. The nurse leaped onto the breakwater and hooked some lines to a metal post, and then he turned to watch us arrive. The engines never stopped idling. Ciel had disappeared from the upper deck.

When we were a few meters from the male nurse, Gigi stopped.

"Hi, Gigi," he said. "It's been a long time."

"William," she said, emotionless.

He turned to me and laughed. "You look a little different, Le Coeur."

D'Arcy, Fuzz, and Dope hung a few meters back, waiting.

Ciel emerged on the lower deck, hopped over the railing, and stretched to step onto the breakwater. He went straight for me with his arms spread, like he was greeting me after a trip, swooping in for a hug, and I felt myself cringe. The last time I saw him I had called him a horrible bastard. Had he forgotten?

Gigi said, "That's far enough." I was grateful for her intervention, even as I didn't understand the tone of her voice.

Ciel froze, stunned. "Gigi," he said, his voice oddly pleading.

Fuzz stepped up past me, moving fast. I looked back, and Dope had hooked his arm around D'Arcy's neck in a choke hold. I turned instinctively to help him, but Gigi grabbed me from behind, pinning my arms and smashing her stomach and chest against my back. Faster than I thought possible, she had grabbed my left wrist in her right hand and my right wrist in her left hand and pulled, so that my arms were crossed and locked under my breasts. Holding me too tight, she turned her body to the side and shoved her hip against my butt, tipping me just a bit off balance. It was like a professional wrestling hold; I was completely incapacitated.

Ciel burst toward me and I saw him slam into Fuzz like a brick wall. He stumbled back, recovering his balance.

"You can't have her yet," Fuzz said in his rumbling voice, his feet planted and his fists up offensively.

Have me?

William was on his way to help, but Ciel put his hand up and commanded, "No."

The two of them stepped back from Fuzz, who looked more like a mountain than any other time I'd seen him. Now Ciel had both palms up in front of his chest, like he was calming Fuzz down or proving he had no weapons, or both.

"I haven't seen her in two years, Fuzz. I can't stay docked here for more than a minute. Just let her go, please."

Let me go?

"I don't want a hostage, Ciel. And frankly, she'd be a handful."

Ciel smiled at him and dropped his hands. The dynamic between these people was confusing the heck out of me. I looked back at D'Arcy, but the hold he was in forced his head down, and I couldn't see his face. I struggled to pull away from Gigi, but I only succeeded in losing what little balance I had, which churned an instant, angry outrage in my core.

"Dope is choking him!" I blurted at Fuzz. "He's a nerdy Medical Apprentice, not a freaking karate sensei."

Dope loosened his hold and D'Arcy was able to lift his head some. He gave me a look through his eyebrows that was not appreciative.

Ciel said, "I gotta take off, Fuzz. I don't have a permit to land; I can't afford to be inspected. I'm grateful that you found her—more grateful than you'll ever know. And now her grandfather needs her."

I felt myself nearly collapse with relief; Poppu was alive. He was still alive.

"I don't want your gratitude, I want remote programming."

"I can't give you that, Fuzz, you know it."

"Then you can't have Sol." He was oddly firm, like he'd be happy to just turn around and drive three hours back to Iowa with me.

"Ciel," William said, his jumpy eyes scanning everywhere—the lake, Lake Shore Drive, the bike path. "We can't stand on this breakwater negotiating."

"Let us aboard," Fuzz said. "She can visit with your grandfather while we talk this over in open waters. That's more than fair."

Ciel shook his head. "I don't have room."

"Then no Sol," Fuzz repeated.

Ciel's temper flared. "You're wasting precious time!" He jabbed his finger toward the yacht. "My grandfather is *dying*. I need to be with him, not standing here arguing with a pack of ungrateful bullies!"

It pissed me off to no end to hear Ciel talk about how important it was for him to be with Poppu, after disowning us. I wanted to strangle him.

"*Ungrateful bullies,*" Fuzz said. "Is that how you're gonna write this history? Well, *fuck you* and *fuck* our old alliance, you sniveling Ray minion." He pointed at me without looking at me. "I'm making one last offer before I pick her up and carry her back to the Winnebago: bring us aboard for talks, and we'll agree to stay completely out of your way until your grandfather dies."

Until your grandfather dies. It was so practical, and so coldhearted. Poppu's death was an inconvenience to him. I could suddenly no longer bear to be this close to my grandfather without seeing him.

"Let me go aboard!" I shouted at Fuzz. "I don't give a damn about this asshole who used to be my brother, or your precious 'removed programming,' or whatever the hell it is. I don't care about any of you *filthy liars*. None of you is worth one-tenth of Poppu."

Ciel looked at me like I was a stranger. And then I saw his

mind quickly begin recoding, adjusting to unexpected field conditions.

"Okay, I get it," he said to Fuzz, tearing his eyes away from me. "You'll come aboard and we'll talk later. I can take two of you, in addition to Sol."

"Me and Dope," Fuzz said.

Ciel shook his head. "You and Gigi."

"Fuck you," Gigi said to Ciel, with real venom.

I spoke up. "D'Arcy is one of the two, or I throw myself off the boat at the first opportunity. And I'll do it." There was silence.

Ciel was starting to look irritated by me. He switched his attention to D'Arcy and quickly studied him. He asked Fuzz, "This is the Benoît kid from your texts?" Fuzz nodded.

Ciel sighed, wiping his forehead with the sleeve of his shirt. "Benoît and Gigi then," he said.

"Benoît and Fuzz," Gigi corrected.

Ciel shook his head, but he kept his eyes on Fuzz, not Gigi. "Benoît and Gigi."

"Done," Fuzz said.

"*Fuck you*, Fuzz," Gigi said, spitting on the ground next to him.

Saturday
1:00 p.m.

As soon as the deal was struck, Dope released D'Arcy from his stranglehold, and Gigi let me go with a shove toward the yacht for good measure. With no parting words, Ciel and William jogged to the boat, Gigi only a step behind, while Dope and Fuzz strode briskly back to the parking lot. They all seemed to be conditioned from years in the underground to minimize unnecessary exposure to the Day/Night authorities. D'Arcy and I glanced at each other and hurried after Ciel.

On the boat, Ciel bounded up the stairs to see the captain. William unlashed the lines and leaped aboard. The engines rumbled, belching diesel fumes. William reached his hand out to help me aboard and then thought better of it. D'Arcy climbed in after me.

A young woman appeared in the doorway to the cabins. Something about her looked so familiar, I startled.

William said, "Miho will show you to your bunks. They have small bathrooms, where you can freshen up if you'd like. Everything is cramped, but nice."

"You're . . ." I started. She was the person in the photo on the hospital lanyard. "You're Yukie Shiga," I accused her.

She smiled. "I was Yukie for the job at the hospital. And Ciel needs to talk to you about that ID you took. But later." She held her arm out, welcoming me inside. "I left a quick snack for you in your room. You look hungry."

A snapshot of a memory blinded me. "You were the reporter at Ciel's trial! And you"—I pointed at William—"you were that crazy homeless guy."

I turned to D'Arcy. "I'm such an idiot. I should have recognized him in the nursery."

D'Arcy shook his head. "In a surgical mask?"

I said to William, "Who was the other spectator in the court, the older one?"

"Ah, well, that . . . that's actually our captain, Richard. If you'd like, I'll bring you to the bridge to meet him. Dang, you don't miss a trick, Le Coeur. Just like Ciel."

"I'm nothing like Ciel," I said, following Miho through the doorway.

She took us down a low-ceilinged corridor, lit with small amber bulbs at the top of the walls. The rooms were marked with numbers, odd on one side of the hall, even on the other. We stopped in front of number three, which Miho said was my room. D'Arcy would be in five.

"Gigi will stay in two, Ciel and Kizzie are in four," Miho said.

Ciel and Kizzie. Ciel was part of a unit now.

"Your grandfather is in the first room," Miho said somberly. "Ciel and I will be waiting for you there."

I started toward the room marked "1," but D'Arcy caught my arm, shaking his head. "Bathroom break. Food," he said, like there would be no discussion. "And you might want to wash your face."

He was right. Of course he was right. I was chilled with hunger, and my bladder felt like it might burst. I had waited this long to see Poppu, I could force myself to endure a brief pit stop. I remembered Jean saying, "Take the moment you need to be healthy," and Gigi's crasser warning that I'd be a "useless fuck" if I didn't rest. Everyone I had ever met was less impulsive than I was.

"Meet back out here in five minutes?" I asked him.

"I'll be here."

I had to duck through the doorframe. The room fit only a double bed, a night table, and a chair. There was a long, narrow window looking out over the lake, tinted for privacy. It was like a classy RV in its decor, including the bathroom. A bottle of sparkling lemonade and a plate with wedges of cheese and apples and crackers was laid out for me. I gobbled a piece of cheese on a cracker, and as I did I tugged open the night table drawer to see scattered earplugs, a book on hospice care, dental floss, and a tube of lip balm. This was someone's room—probably Miho's—that had been given up for me. I shoved the drawer closed. The bathroom was filled with little travel sizes of everything I might need: a toothbrush, a comb, toothpaste, soap, and shampoo. I peed, and as I was washing my hands I saw my reflection in the mirror, and I understood why D'Arcy had told me to wash my face. There was no need to be Noma now, and I was already smeared. I soaped up a washcloth and scrubbed off the makeup until my skin was pink and angry, and then rinsed and patted my face dry. Back in the bedroom, I ate as much of the cheese plate as I could and gulped some of the lemonade before my impatience took over.

D'Arcy was waiting for me in the hall. He was unchanged, except that he smelled of soap and his earring was gone.

"They really pierced you," I said, reaching up to his lobe. He flinched.

"A needle and a cork. It wasn't the most antiseptic procedure you've ever seen."

I wrapped my arms around his neck; his arms looped tightly around my waist. I pressed my cheek on his. He said very quietly in my ear, "My window was open, and I heard William mention that Fitz is still missing."

I pulled my face back to look at him, surprised. I couldn't understand why his parents would still have the baby.

He shrugged, equally mystified. "All I can figure is that Jean doesn't know where I am and he's not letting Fitz go until he does."

"But Hélène."

"I know. Why is she going along with it?"

"I'll send Jean an uncensored text," I said. "We'll arrange the church drop-off, just as we planned: I take the fall."

D'Arcy shook his head. "Ciel wants him and we don't know why. Maybe we can do better."

I hugged him again. I breathed a big lungful of him in. *We can't do better.* I exhaled the words "Why are you here?" But I meant it rhetorically.

He kissed my cheek. "I'll make you a list later."

We let go of each other and walked to Poppu's room.

"This is where I stop," D'Arcy said when we got to the door. I opened my mouth to protest, but he added, "Check on him, spend time with him. I'll be waiting."

I knocked on the door and Ciel opened it. Miho stood behind him, taking the tips of a stethoscope out of her ears. This time Ciel was wary. This time he didn't hold his arms out. He stepped to the side so that I could enter. As I looked back, I saw D'Arcy nod at him, but Ciel didn't return the greeting. He closed the door.

It smelled like Poppu's bedroom at home, stagnant and musky, because death was with him no matter where he went. This was obviously the master bedroom of the boat. In addition to the large oval bed built into the wall, there was a small walk-in closet, a TV hooked to the ceiling, and a desk with a chair. I recognized the wood paneling from the "kidnapper's" photo—the kidnapper who was my own brother.

Poppu was lying on his back, a living skeleton in a flimsy hospital gown. His silver hair was in sparse strands across his scalp. His eyes were closed, but not fully, so that a crescent of white showed behind crusted lashes. His mouth was open and his breathing was audible, like he was partially underwater. An oxygen tank hissed, pumping the air he couldn't catch on his own into his nostrils; an IV bag hung on a pole nearby, but the tube dangled, crimped at the end, not attached to him anymore; a catheter bag was hooked to the edge of the bed, holding a scant amount of dark amber urine. Someone had punched my gut, or may as well have, and I found myself wanting to double over from the blow.

"He asked to be taken off the morphine as soon as I located you," Ciel said in a low voice. "It makes him light-headed and drowsy, and he wanted to be here for you. We also made another decision with him . . . he's not . . . we're not hydrating him anymore."

He moved toward Poppu and touched his arm gently. "Poppu. Sol is here." He bent down to kiss his cheek. My heart turned over at the sight—at Ciel's open love for my grandfather—and I hated it for betraying me. "Sol is here," he repeated.

Poppu's eyelids fluttered, but didn't open. A low sound came from his throat.

Miho reached for a sponge swab on the night table, dipped it into a small bowl of liquid, and lightly ran it on his tongue and inside his cheeks.

I went to Poppu's bedside—the side away from Ciel—and immediately crawled beside him, trying not to jolt the mattress, wanting not to hurt him.

"We'll leave you alone with him," Miho said, putting her arm around Ciel, forcibly turning him, making him come away with her.

After Ciel left, I draped my arm over Poppu and I cried. I sobbed as if my life were draining out of me. Eventually I realized from the noises he was making that he was awake, and distressed, and that I was the thing that was distressing him.

I was a thoughtless idiot.

I sniffed hard and wiped my eyes with my sleeve. "I'm sorry," I whispered. "I'm so sorry. I'm fine now."

His hand twitched feebly, and I knew he wanted to reach for me. I slid my arm under his fingers.

He tried to say something, but only a rasp came out.

"You don't have to talk," I said. I lifted my face to his cheek and kissed it.

His head moved almost imperceptibly. No, he was saying.

"Missed you," he said, with no volume, no diaphragm, dry as a desert wind.

"I missed you, too. I'm sorry I never came home." I wondered what Ciel had told him.

"Have you . . ." He stopped, panting too fast, blowing out harder than he breathed in. How weak is a person when saying four words is an effort? I waited, letting him pretend to hold my arm, cradling what was left of his body because hugging might crush him. "Have you seen," he tried again, and failed.

Tears squeezed out of my eyes, but absolutely silently. There was no way I'd let him hear me cry again.

"Fleurs?" he finally said, it felt like minutes later.

Have you seen . . . fleurs?

I stayed still for a long time, suddenly sick with dismay that I was too late, that he was no longer lucid. *Fleurs* was the French word for "flowers." Poppu had a particular passion for flowers. He said they were the bit of day that Smudges could bring into their homes. Before he got sick, he used to buy small bunches and keep them on the kitchen table: daffodils and tulips in the spring; nosegays of lily of the valley; irises in the summer; roses in the fall. After he went blind and couldn't see them, he still enjoyed smelling them, especially the lilacs and the roses. He took meticulous care of them whenever they were in the house: trimming the stems, refreshing the water, arranging them by touch.

Have I seen which flowers? I thought. I heard his chest rattle painfully.

"Yes," I finally said. "Yes, I have."

He smiled. His mouth still hung open, so the smile was a gruesome, pitiful thing. "Isn't . . . she . . . beautiful?" he asked. I almost couldn't hear him.

I didn't answer.

Several minutes later he whispered, "She feels . . . beautiful."

"Yes," I said.

"*Même elle sente . . . jolie—*" he struggled to say. *She even smells pretty.*

He seemed to sleep then, and I listened to the frightening pattern of his breathing. There were long—too long—moments when he didn't seem to breathe at all, and then he'd draw in a rattling wheeze and my own body wanted to cough—wanted to cough up whatever it was that was suffocating him.

I stayed where I was, and I closed my eyes, remembering what it was like when he was alive, even though he wasn't yet dead.

Almost an hour later, he woke up again. I felt his finger move on my arm, which had fallen painfully asleep, but I refused to move it.

"Sol," he said.

"I'm here, Poppu."

"Sol."

"I won't leave you again."

"Please . . . forgive," he said.

I couldn't forgive Ciel, but there was no way I was going to tell Poppu that. Not now.

". . . me," he finished. He was back in a panting cycle, and I wondered whether I should fetch Miho.

"Shhh," I said, lifting my numb arm to touch his face with my fingers.

A tear dripped out of his eye. It wasn't plump enough to roll off his face. He was so parched it just wicked into the creases of skin by his eyes and disappeared.

"I didn't . . . didn't . . ."

"It's okay," I said softly. "Really, Poppu, don't."

Don't cry.

"Didn't know. Oh, Soleil, *je me déteste* . . ."

"No," I said, not understanding why he would hate himself in his last days. "I love you."

"*Ta mère . . . ton père . . .*"

I was quiet. He was thinking of my parents in his last hours. It was natural.

Another tear slipped out and evaporated.

"It was me." He panted furiously, all exhaled puffs, with seemingly no inhales.

"Stop," I said. "Oh, please stop."

And then he got a burst of energy, which a hospice nurse once told me sometimes happens with dying patients, and croaked out this long thought: "I called . . . the office of the minister. I reported my own daughter." A crackling sob heaved out of the shell of his body so violently that I thought he might break.

I froze, both understanding and not accepting what he had said. It bathed every crevice of my body but would not soak in.

Agonizing moments later, he breathed again and took up his cause with a pitiful desperation. "They were making explosions. Bombs . . . I didn't want them to hurt anyone . . ."

My Poppu, the man who had raised me, had betrayed my parents.

"Soleil," his lips mouthed, but almost no sound came out.

"I'm here."

I forced myself to listen. Not to take a single step beyond hearing him. Not to judge, because I was incapable of rational thought while he was dying. I lifted myself on my elbow and put my forehead on his temple.

"My baby," he said.

My mother.

"I . . . didn't imagine she would die. Forgive me, Soleil."

"Of course I forgive you."

There was no question in my mind. Nothing could bring my parents back; nothing would stop Poppu from dying. He needed to hear that I forgave him. It was the last gift I could bestow.

"I have never told Ciel." I barely heard the words. "I would have lost him."

He drifted out of consciousness again. I raised myself to a sitting position and rubbed my arm, exploding with pinpricks. I wiped my eyes with my sleeve. My nose felt swollen, my eyelids puffy. I took in a shaky breath and blew it out in a thin stream.

There were quiet voices in the hall. A moment later, a knock at the door. The handle turned and a woman I recognized as Ciel's wife poked her head in. I stared at her. I was too drained to be angry.

"Can we come in?"

We. She had a baby in her arms.

She closed the door behind her. She looked hard at Poppu's too-still shape, perhaps worried that—

"He's drifting now," I reassured her. "I don't know if he sleeps or loses consciousness. But it's merciful." I had never planned on meeting this woman, had never practiced any words, and now I had nothing more to say.

She came over to the bed and sat on the end. "I'm Kizzie."

Of course I knew that. I recognized her from the pixelated wedding photo. I stole a look at the baby, who wasn't swaddled but was wearing a simple white unisex one-piece outfit. She had wispy black hair with loose curls that were sparse enough to show scalp, black eyes, and a lovely round forehead, which would probably be like her mother's. She grimaced and squirmed, and I saw a flash of Ciel's dimple.

Kizzie caught me staring. "This is your niece, Fleur."

Oh god, Fleur the name, not fleurs, the noun for flowers. I opened my mouth, but no words came. Finally something antagonistic popped out. "Are you sure?"

She laughed. It was like a bell ringing, and she had the most beautiful teeth I had ever seen. Everything about her was gentle and composed. I could imagine her being very soothing to a fiery redheaded geek.

She said in a low voice, smiling, "We got the DNA test back today, just to be sure. She's ours." She looked nervously at Poppu, and that's when I understood that he knew nothing about the disaster in the hospital. I gave a tight-lipped nod to indicate that I wouldn't mess up in front of him.

"Do you want to hold her?" Kizzie asked. I shook my head no.

"Did Poppu get to . . ." I began.

"Yes, he's held her. Or more like, cuddled on the bed next to her. Many times."

Tears welled irritatingly in my eyes. It was what I had wanted all along, wasn't it, for him to hold her? Even though I wasn't the one who had made it happen.

Kizzie's eyebrows went up at worried angles. "Will you talk to Ciel?"

I glanced at Poppu, not wanting him to hear the answer. I shook my head. *I'd rather not, thanks.* But I didn't really believe I could have my way, not on Ciel's boat. Not when we had to share our grandfather's last hours.

"I just want to tell you one thing, and then I think you should take care of your friend out in the hall."

D'Arcy had waited for me, as he'd promised. The tears spilled out now. I pushed them quickly away with my fingers. I had done nothing to deserve him; it was incomprehensible to me that he was here.

"Ciel loves you like a lioness loves her cub," Kizzie went on. I wanted to cover my ears and shout like a child, to keep from having to hear. It was obvious Ciel had sent her. "He couldn't see you, couldn't contact you these past two years. He's being monitored all the time, Sol. The truth is, Ciel made a choice: he chose Day so he could help you. So that he'd be able to send you money; so you and Poppu would survive."

I shook my head, violently this time.

"Do you think Poppu's pension and your factory work supported you all these years? He's been secretly adding money to Poppu's account every month, and in order not to arouse suspicion, he only allowed himself legal texts to you, like a dutiful Ray transfer, knowing each one was being scrutinized." She stood up to leave. "Whether you choose to believe it or not, I saw it. And it killed him to be apart from you."

Before she opened the door she paused for a moment, looking at Fleur in her arms, thinking. And she said to me, "I've wanted to meet you so much this last year, because of everything I've heard. I never knew anyone as ferociously loving as you and Ciel and Poppu. I didn't have that growing up. It's—it's not typical, you know. As soon as I met Ciel I wanted in. And now I want to be your family, too. If you'll have me."

I stepped into the hall after Kizzie left. D'Arcy was sitting against the wall, with his knees up and his heels tucked near his bottom. He moved to stand, and I held out my hand to pull him all the way up. I tugged him into Poppu's room—too briskly for his stiff legs—and closed the door after us.

I couldn't tell if Poppu was awake, so I went over to the side of the bed the way Ciel had, to kiss him. The skin on his cheek was cool crepe paper, and he smelled of antiseptic wipes. "Are you awake? I want you to meet someone."

Poppu's breathing changed, and his eyelids fluttered.

"*Laisse-le dormir,*" D'Arcy said. *Let him sleep.*

"*Je ne dors pas,*" Poppu said, clear as night. *I'm not sleeping.*

I reached my hand out for D'Arcy, and he came to my side.

I introduced him formally. "*Poppu, je te présente mon cher ami, D'Arcy Benoît.*" To D'Arcy I said, "*Voici mon grand-père, François Harcourt.*"

D'Arcy reached for Poppu's hand lying motionless on the bed and gently clasped it. "*Je suis enchanté de faire votre connaissance, Monsieur Harcourt.*"

Poppu breathed through his mouth and said nothing. But his hand was not limp in D'Arcy's, which I realized with a pain in my chest was the best he could do.

To me D'Arcy said, "Has he been on his back since you got here?"

I nodded.

"That's more than two hours. He should be turned. Is there a chart anywhere?"

There was a paper on the night table. I handed it to him.

"His right side is next. Will you help me?"

I nodded again.

D'Arcy squatted and said, "Mr. Harcourt, Sol and I are going to turn you onto your right side now. We'll be careful, but tell us if we're hurting you."

He rolled the blanket down neatly until it was past Poppu's feet. Poppu was lying on a folded sheet. There were pillows under his ankles, his knees, between his legs, and under his elbows—everywhere that his bones protruded the most. At D'Arcy's instruction we gently pulled the sheet to slide Poppu more to one side of the bed, and slowly shifted him onto his right side. He groaned, and his breathing increased. D'Arcy inspected his skin at all the pressure points with the mattress and gently lifted his leg to put a pillow between his knees. He straightened and checked the catheter tube. A smaller pillow went between Poppu's ankles and another under them. D'Arcy moved him carefully and slowly, making subtle adjustments to his hip alignment and the position of his arms. And then he lifted the blanket to cover him.

"Can you mark on the chart that we moved him?"

I couldn't find a pen on the nightstand, so I crossed the room to look in the desk. As I did, D'Arcy bent so that his face was near Poppu's. He put his hand on his arm. Poppu's eyes were open but unseeing. His mouth was still hanging. As I rummaged in the drawer I heard D'Arcy say quietly, "It's been a privilege to meet you, knowing how important you are to Sol."

I marked the time and left the paper and pen on the desk. When I turned back I saw that D'Arcy had whispered something more in Poppu's ear, and that Poppu had heard him, letting out a gurgled gasp of acknowledgment.

"Secrets, already?" I asked.

"Uh-huh," D'Arcy said. He reached out for me as I approached. I sank into his arms, leaned my head on his shoulder, and watched Poppu's labored breathing.

The door opened. It was Ciel. He saw D'Arcy holding me and something flashed in his eyes, something irritable.

"Who turned Poppu?" Ciel said.

"We did," D'Arcy said. "I hope that's okay."

"I was coming to do it."

"Well, it's done," I said.

"I'd like to be alone with Sol and Poppu," Ciel said to D'Arcy. He was a man of few words now.

D'Arcy looked into my eyes. "Stay, or go?"

"Go is fine."

Stay forever.

"I'll be in my cabin if you need me." He gave me a quick, warm kiss.

Ciel said nothing until the door closed, and then he mumbled, "A Ray Medical Apprentice."

It wasn't a question, so I didn't reply. But "Ray Medical Apprentice" hardly summed up D'Arcy. It left out his family, broken by the Day/Night divide; it left out the poet and artist and scientist, coexisting in one mind; it left out all of his sacrifices for me, from the moment he had picked up that stupid black phone in lockup. Or maybe from the moment he decided to take Bio for Trees in order to write on my desk.

Ciel said, "Can he be trusted?"

Outrage bloomed on my lips—*You're the one I don't trust!*—until I remembered that Poppu might be listening. "With my life."

Ciel went over to Poppu and bent to put his cheek on his forehead. I closed my eyes, because it still hurt like hell to see it.

"*Poppu, tu ne dors pas?*" he asked. "*Sol et moi, nous sommes ici.*" He looked up at me. "I don't know how much he can hear."

Poppu's breathing was hard work. His face was contorted with the effort, and whether he was conscious or not, it looked like pain. Pain that it was senseless for his body to endure.

At home I had watched the world contract around Poppu until it was only what was in his room, and soon it was what was at the edge of his skin. Now it had tightened further until all that seemed left was what was inside of him: pain and the desire for peace.

"Can he have some morphine now?" I asked.

Ciel pulled his phone out of his pocket and sent a text.

He got the chair from beside the desk and brought it next to the bed. "I bet you didn't even remember it's your birthnight," he said somberly.

I was stunned for a moment. "I lost track of the date."

"You're seventeen." He shook his head, as if it were his fault. "Not even a cake."

"I don't need cake," I said.

"What about tarte au maton?"

That thought almost knocked me over, and my eyes rimmed with tears. "Yes, I could do with one of those."

He leaned on the chair and studied me. "I wish you weren't in that Noma getup."

I didn't know what to say. I couldn't be whatever it was he expected me to be, or wanted me to be. The girl he had left was long gone.

"It's somewhat empowering," I finally said.

Miho knocked lightly, and when Ciel opened the door she had a tray with food—hamburgers and asparagus. There was also a syringe.

"You two eat dinner while I check on him."

I didn't move.

"Eat," she repeated to me. "Everyone else is eating." I knew she meant D'Arcy. I knew she already understood something about me. Of course Ciel would surround himself with perceptive people.

It was as if I had no taste buds, but I ate the burger just for the calories. I ate the asparagus. I drank the bottle of water Ciel handed me. I dutifully pushed fuel into my body. I watched as Miho took Poppu's blood pressure with a portable cuff by the side of the bed. She listened to his heartbeat and breathing with her stethoscope. And then she lifted the blanket to inject the morphine into his buttock. She carefully replaced the blanket and came over to Ciel and me.

"He's very close to the end. But he won't suffer."

These are the criteria for a good death: not to suffer, to be with people you love, to be home. I was grateful Poppu had two out of the three.

Miho said to me, "I'm really sorry, Sol." And then she left the room.

I went over to the bed and sat beside Poppu.

"You're still wearing the necklace," Ciel said. "From your thirteenth birthday."

I didn't reply.

He sat in the chair, so we were both near our grandfather, so we could both see his face. "I was . . . with Gigi when I gave you that," he said quietly. "I hurt her a lot." But I had already guessed. He said, "Even taking that into account, she's the only Noma we can trust right now."

We.

I dragged my eyes from Poppu to look at Ciel: my grown brother, the father of a child, the boy being bloodied by Dice on the gravel path at Wooded Island, the tech genius the Noma sought, the boyfriend Gigi wanted, the teen who looked over his shoulder and shouted that he loved me. They were all Ciel, and I had to make sense of them somehow.

He said, "I asked William to grab a book . . . from your apartment . . . when he picked up Poppu."

Our apartment, once—Poppu's and yours and mine.

"Would you like to read it to him?"

I nodded. I very much wanted to. I wanted to read one last time to my grandfather—to do something, anything, to comfort him when he was beyond help.

Ciel went to the shelves above the desk and pulled out a thick book. When he put it in my hands, dog-eared and dingy, it was like a last vestige of my old life, the life I had lost. I wondered what would happen to the apartment—what had happened already. The police had taken it over, I was sure, and when I went to jail, everything would be confiscated by the state. I would never go back. This book was all that was left of my home.

I lay down next to Poppu, facing him, with my back to Ciel, and I opened to the first page. Ciel sat in the chair and listened.

I began, the words like dear friends:

> *"Sing in me, Muse,*
> *and through me tell the story*
> *of that man skilled in all ways of contending,*
> *the wanderer, harried for years on end,*
> *after he plundered the stronghold*
> *on the proud height of Troy."*

I stumbled to my cabin the way a dry, curled winter leaf blows down a street—carried without a will, tumbling, cracking, and splitting as I grazed objects in my path. I landed on the bed, facedown, and I wanted to cry but I was empty. I was suspended for this one moment between a world with Poppu and one without; stuck between seventeen years of his love and presence in the past, heavy and real, and his never-ending absence in the future, oddly light and ephemeral in its unfamiliarity. Tomorrow the scales would tip, and I would fall into the world that was empty of him. Right now, for an hour, a night, I was on the precipice. My life both included Poppu and it didn't.

I thought sleep might come, but soon I opened my eyes and stared at the blanket without seeing it, because what I saw in my mind was D'Arcy, next door, probably asleep at this hour, his face relaxed, his eyelashes black on his cheeks, the way they were when he held vigil during my fever. I pushed myself up, opened the door, checked both directions to make sure the hall was empty, and padded in my fishnet-stocking feet to his room.

The door was unlocked. The hinge cracked quietly as I

opened it. D'Arcy startled, his body swishing against the sheets, and took a surprised breath—a light sleeper. He lifted his head and stared. There was a night-light in his room, plugged in near the floor. But with the amber lights along the ceiling of the hall behind me, I could only have been a shadow. A lanky, broken shadow. I held my breath for the beat it took him to process what he saw. He pushed himself up on an elbow.

"He's gone," he said softly, his voice thick from sleep.

I let out my breath, shakier than I expected.

"Je peux entrer?" I whispered, all at once feeling exposed and frail and hanging. *Can I come in?*

"Viens." His arm threw back the sheet and blanket and reached out to me. *Come here.*

I took three steps and climbed into the bed with him, his warm arm reaching around me, scooping me into his space. He had nothing on but boxers. He pulled the covers over us, and a waft of heavy, close, sleepy skin scent filled my lungs. I breathed it deep. He nested himself around me, his stomach to my back, his arm around my waist with the hand tucking all the way under me, our knees bent. I entwined our feet, locking us together.

"I'm so sorry," he whispered.

His breath on my neck, humid and surprisingly sweet, the softness and firmness of his skin, the hair on his arms, the firing synapses in his brain—everything was the opposite of Poppu's corpse, every cell of D'Arcy was dynamic and alive. The tears finally came.

He wrapped around me tighter as I cried. Now and then he kissed my shoulder, my ear, to let me know he was there. I felt him aware of me, and of every rise and fall and turn in my emotions; so present, so solid. Eventually I stopped crying. Eventually my body became heavy and I dozed. In my sleep I felt him kiss my hair and begin to pull away. I held his arm. I growled in protest. I scrunched back an inch so we were touching again. He pulled me close, a puff of a laugh leaving his nose and tickling my neck.

"Do you know how much I love you?" he whispered.

My heart tumbled, caught off guard for a sluggish, sleepy beat.

He curled his knees up tighter. "It's as big as the Milky Way."

He rubbed his nose against my ear. "It's as wild as the murmuration."

There was a pause. "It's as stuck as the *Morazan*."

"*That's* why I'm here," he said, answering my question from the hallway. I couldn't speak, couldn't attach a single coherent word to the lake of feelings his declaration had filled me with. He said, "Do you remember when you were feverish on the sofa in your apartment?"

I looked back at him, craning to see his face in the shadows, catching only the outline of his high cheekbone and his beautiful nose in my peripheral vision. I nodded.

He went on. "You admitted you were throwing your life away so that Poppu could hold Fleur just once, and it was like the floor of your apartment opened under me. You had the balls to condense the whole screwed-up world into this one pure thing, this crazy act of love. Everything I was working for collapsed through that hole with me, and I went into a free fall. And then you kissed me on the prairie and I wanted it all—I selfishly wanted what Poppu had."

I realized suddenly that for the first time—and probably the last—I was alone with the person I desired beyond reason, and that we were safe for a single moment, in a quiet room. Sunrise would likely take him out of my life forever. I whispered, hoarse, into the air above us, "I want to have sex with you."

He laughed out loud, a belly laugh. And then he buried his face in the pillow to cover the sound. When he lifted his head, he whispered near my ear, "Please never stop saying exactly what you think."

"Does that mean you want to, too?"

He took a deep breath of my neck and exhaled in something like frustration. "Will you think I'm a jerk if I admit I've been comforting you *and* lusting after you for the past half hour?"

I turned to face him and he tipped back a bit to accommodate me. I hooked my arm around his neck and pulled his mouth on mine. I curled my leg over his hip so that we could press our bodies all the way together. We kissed until my lips felt swollen and raw and his stubble angered the skin of my chin and I'd do anything for more. I pushed him over to be on top.

I sat up and grabbed the sides of my shirt with my arms crossed, pulled it over my head, and dropped it on the floor. I unhooked my bra, slid it off my shoulders, and tossed it on top of the shirt. He breathed in with a sort of surprise, sat up with me on his lap, put his arms around me, and buried his face in my neck, timid and tender, all at once.

"Hold on," I whispered. I climbed off him to stand on the floor.

"Nooo," he groaned jokingly, stretching for me as if I were leaving.

I wriggled out of my skirt and stockings, pulling my panties off with them into one big wad that I ditched on the rug. I saw him lift his hips and squirm out of his boxers. I felt the chill of standing nude and vulnerable, and my whole body turned to gooseflesh. He pulled the covers open, inviting me. I clambered in, our cool skin everywhere.

"Do you know how to do this?" I whispered.

He laughed a hot cloud of air. "I have a good handle on the scientific theory," he said. "But I don't have much . . . lab experience."

"Impossible. I would have eaten you alive if I had been a Ray in any of your classes."

"I would have fed myself to you." He added more seriously, "But you weren't there."

"There must have been someone."

"I went on a few dates, but mostly I hung out with groups of people. I was busy, and I didn't mind being alone." He lifted his head from the pillow to bite my lower lip, and something in my pelvis pulsed, warm and demanding. "No one was as smart, and insightful, and in tune with me, and just—raw—as the girl who drew on the desks. It was a high standard you set. I didn't have any second dates."

In a moment he said, "How about you? Where did you learn to kiss like that?"

My eyes were accustomed to the dim light, in a grainy, monotone way. He was looking at me like he was glad to see me, even while I was in his arms. I said, "Mostly I try not to hurt you."

He laughed, not knowing it wasn't a joke.

But I wanted to answer his question. He wasn't my first kiss.

"Once, the summer before I turned twelve, I was playing curfew violation with my brother and his friends—"

"Curfew violation?" he interrupted.

"It's a running game. A chasing game. Outside."

"In the dark?"

"With flashlights." I nodded. "And nearly silent, of course. But even Smudges need to play."

"Go on."

"I was a pretty rabid competitor."

"You? Rabid?" He traced his finger around my jaw.

"I was 'it'—I was Hour Guard—and I thought I was holding my own with the older boys. I cornered one of them in the gangway of our apartment. His nickname was Ace. He was in the grade above Ciel. He shoved me up against the brick wall and started kissing me."

He got up on his elbow to watch me and listen.

"It was confusing, but also sort of exhilarating. It lasted a long time—minutes. I copied whatever he did. I thought kissing me must have meant he liked me.

"I remember feeling embarrassed because he had jammed me against the wall holding my armpits, and he started massaging my breasts with his thumbs. I was just developing—they weren't breasts, really, they were nubs, and too sore. I didn't know how to ask him to stop.

"For a long time, whenever he came over to visit Ciel, I tried to find ways to be alone with him, hoping he'd kiss me again. It wasn't until I was fifteen myself—the same age he was when he did it—that I understood what happened."

I had never uttered that story aloud.

D'Arcy was quiet, thinking. Finally, he put his hand on my cheek and angled his face to kiss me sweetly, gently. It was the opposite of what Ace had done.

I pushed him onto his back and straddled him, saying, "So I guess we're both rookies."

He nodded, but there was a hint of worry in his voice. "Reassure me this is what you want."

I leaned down to whisper against his lips, "This is what I've wanted since the prairie."

"The same night that . . ." He couldn't finish the sentence.

"The same night that Poppu died."

"There are—I saw condoms in the bedside table," he said almost shyly.

I reached for the drawer, leaning my chest on his, feeling his lips on my shoulder in a stolen kiss. I sat up again, tore the foil wrapper open, and we worked together, our hands bumping— mine trembling with the frankness of the task. When we'd finally got it, there was a loud thump that made the room quiver, followed by a low voice.

D'Arcy pulled the blanket around my legs and said quietly, "Was that against the hull or in the hallway?"

"Couldn't tell," I whispered.

We waited, staring at each other silently, for another sound. There was nothing. With the passage of time and D'Arcy under me nude, his chest rising and falling with anticipation, whatever it was became unimportant.

A tiny smile spread on his lips, and I felt my own face open with warmth. I leaned down to kiss him, softly at first, affectionately, deliberately trying to make the pressing of my mouth convey "I love you" without using any words. The air around us became our breath. He playfully flipped me onto my back, with his body three-quarters on top.

I encouraged him all the way on me. I tried to guide him.

"Wait. I—" he said, suddenly flustered, "I don't want to hurt you."

"You won't."

"I *will*," he objected.

"I need it to be you."

"Tell me if we should stop," he begged.

I knew I wouldn't, because I was experiencing what Grady Hastings had called a thundering cry of urgency—and mine had to do with being as close to this person as humanly possible before the morning tore us apart.

He was so careful, so concentrated, so D'Arcy that tears came to my eyes and dribbled down my temples into my hair.

He faltered, alarmed.

"I'm fine!" I said.

He watched me, to see for himself whether it was true. And I needed him to understand that unlike every other source of pain in my life, this was temporary, necessary, and very much wanted. I pulled his neck down and reached my face up to kiss him—to hide the tears, spilling uncontrollably now, and to stop him from fretting.

Sunday
5:00 a.m.

While I was in the bathroom I heard the sound of a fist banging on D'Arcy's cabin door and the noise of someone barging into the room.

"What the *hell*," D'Arcy said at the intrusion.

"Where is Sol?" Ciel's voice boomed, accusing.

There was a robe on the hook of the bathroom door, and I threw it on as quickly as I could, tying the belt in a knot.

"She's not in her room," Ciel barked. "Is she here? *Shit, she is.*" I heard smothered rage in his voice. He had seen something. My clothes on the floor? I burst out of the bathroom, my hackles raised, ready for a fight. The lamp was on.

"Sol," he said, with a kind of hysterical relief that seemed genuine, mixed with irritation, or disapproval, or . . . what was it?

"What do you want?"

Ciel pointed at D'Arcy but held my eyes. "How long have you been here with him?" It wasn't as much of an accusation as I expected; it was, oddly, a question.

"It's a little late to play the protective older brother, isn't it?" I asked.

"*How long* have you been here with him?" he repeated.

"What business is it of yours?"

"Has it been since you left me?"

"Yes!"

He glanced at D'Arcy. I saw a quick assessment. A reluctant acceptance. A hint of understanding that this person was someone I would defend to the death. He looked back at me. "Fleur is gone," he said.

I'd heard what he said, but I couldn't grasp the meaning. I couldn't adjust to what the conversation was really about.

"Gigi stole her," he said. His voice was thick, his eyes watery. "When I didn't find you in your room I panicked. I thought . . ."

He thought what? That I had something to do with it?

D'Arcy threw off the blanket, modesty be damned, found his boxers, and started dressing. "Why would Gigi take Fleur? As a bargaining chip?"

I hoped that it wasn't because she wanted to hurt my brother. The outcomes between the scenarios could be terribly different.

"Fuzz set me up. I can't believe I fell for it." Ciel picked my clothes up off the floor and tossed them at me. "Get dressed. In these. I need you to be Sunny Puso. Kizzie has makeup and hair spray you can use."

I caught the clothes but I was paralyzed for a moment, clutching them to me.

"I'll help," D'Arcy said without hesitation.

"*Sol, I need you,*" Ciel said, snapping me out of it.

"You need me?" I found my voice rising. "For two years I was alone—where were you? Where were you when I slogged

319

through every school day without hearing a single kind word? When there was shopping and cooking and cleaning and hot blister packs and force-fed Modafinil coming out of my ears, and hospitals and appointments and radiation and chemo and vomiting and Poppu dying before my eyes and I couldn't do a thing to stop it?" It was pouring out of me now. "I was fourteen when they took you away, Ciel. I was a *kid*. It was too much. You abandoned me in the dark, while you had freedom and daylight and William and Miho and *Kizzie*. And now I'm supposed to gird myself for battle and help you?"

It was too late to fend him off. He was storming toward me and before I could put up a fight he had grabbed me hard—but he was holding me, not hurting me. He was wrapping himself around me in a Harcourt–Le Coeur trap, squeezing me until I couldn't breathe, ignoring my pathetic writhing to get loose, subduing me the way a parent holds a toddler whose tantrum is a danger to herself, saying, "Sol, Sol, Sol," through his teeth, over and over again until I stopped resisting against his vise arms and I stopped saying "Let me go, let me go," and my muscles caved and I let him hold me and I found myself putting my own arms around my brother—the brother I had hated for so long and had given up forever but somehow got this one chance to hug again despite everything.

"Oh god, I've missed you so much," he growled into my hair.

I've missed you, too, my brain volunteered instantly without permission. But I knew it was true. I knew that my hate was really battered, bloodied, devoted love, and that I would do anything if I could be his sister again, just as I'd do anything to have Poppu back and be D'Arcy's lover for more than one night. And

I knew that none of those wishes could ever be granted, and that whatever had happened with D'Arcy, whatever was happening right now with Ciel, was temporary, was a bittersweet goodbye, that the galaxy would keep spinning without a thought for me, a blade of grass on a meadow in Iowa, and I would be ripped away from them all, as permanently as I had been torn from Poppu. So I held Ciel, I wrapped my arms around him as tight as I could for this one frozen second. I hugged him to me, and he squeezed in return until we both knew how we felt without having to say it.

D'Arcy spoke up. "Sol and I heard a noise against the hull maybe an hour ago. It must have been a smaller boat or dinghy. Gigi has a head start."

Ciel and I released each other. My Noma clothes, which had been trapped by our hug, dropped to the floor between us.

"Meet me on the captain's bridge?"

I nodded. "I'll be right there."

After he left, I scooped up my clothes, and then I paused, thinking. It was going to be a long day. Jean—sweet, maternal Jean—would tell me to bathe.

"I'm going to take the world's fastest shower," I said to D'Arcy.

He nodded. "Did you take your doxycycline last night?"

"No."

"Take it now, and again at the usual time this morning. And don't worry about protecting your bandage from the water. I'm sure Miho has a medical kit, and I want to re-dress the wound."

As I washed, I saw the muted shape of D'Arcy through the frosted glass of the shower stall, brushing his teeth. I pretended for one juvenile moment that we lived together, that we did this every morning, that it would go on like this forever. And that little fantasy turned out to be a mistake, because a pool of sorrow welled in my core and filled me to my eyes, where it began to spill out, and I had to tip my face up to the spray of water and let it wash away the thought.

I toweled off quickly, took my pill, brushed my teeth, and pulled my clothes on. When I emerged from the bathroom, D'Arcy was waiting. He had even made the bed.

"I'm ready now," I said.

He stopped me before I got to the door. "Wait," he said, with a husky vulnerability that reached straight into my chest and squeezed the air out of my lungs. "One second more?"

I nodded, understanding him perfectly, and wrapped my arms around him. As long as we lived, we'd never forget what had happened between us in this room. We held the feeling for one last moment, a breath before the unknown.

It was well before dawn as we climbed up to the bridge. The sky was watery black, with a waning wedge of moon smeared with Vaseline. As a girl I'd often tried to imagine what it would feel like to walk on its surface from shadow straight into light, to plant one foot in each. Nothing else filled me with the wonder of the moon. Dinosaurs had seen it. Ciel's grandchildren would look up at it. The moon would watch the death of us all; it would itself be incinerated by our sun. D'Arcy and I might someday gaze at it simultaneously, miles and a lifetime apart.

Ciel was with Kizzie, Miho, William, and the captain, Richard, who told me how glad he was to finally meet me, how much he had heard about me from Ciel.

Kizzie's eyelids were puffed from crying, but she sat me down and began working on my hair, adding product, teasing it, spiking it. D'Arcy sat next to me with gauze, tape, and ointment that Miho had fetched from a cabinet on the bridge, and he got straight to work on my finger.

It turned out that Kizzie had left Fleur sleeping on the bed to check on Ciel, who hadn't gone back to their room after

Poppu died. In the half hour that Kizzie spent comforting Ciel and cleaning and covering Poppu, Gigi had snuck into their room, taken the baby, and escaped by water.

"You said Gigi was the Noma we could trust," I reminded Ciel unhelpfully.

"I hoped she was," Ciel answered. "I wasn't sure. A lot of good happened between us. But I knew that even if I was wrong about her—" He stopped.

"What?"

"I'm not proud of this," he went on, "but right before we broke up I put . . . I planted a tracer program in her phone. I never ended up using it. I put it there because . . . I don't know, I imagined I could protect her. I wanted to know I could locate her within a three-meter radius if I had to."

I thought of Gigi going into that blind with Brad. A blip on a map would not protect her, could not transmit the horror she'd endured.

"Where is she?" Kizzie cut to the chase.

"She's on the campus of the University of Chicago." Ciel pulled out his phone. He tapped the screen, his fingers flying like Zen's, totally facile, as if the device were a part of him. He found the right screen, expanded the map, held it up for Kizzie. "She moves around fluidly, but she keeps coming back to this building, Harper Library."

He got up and brought the phone to me. D'Arcy looked over my shoulder. It was a satellite view of a six-square-block radius, with trees and grass in a central quad, and pretty red-tiled roofs. There was a blinking red pin on the image. Gigi was on the south end of campus, in a building across from the Midway

Plaisance, which was home to a skating rink that Poppu had brought Ciel and me to every winter before Ciel's trial. I remembered the bright spotlights flooding the ice, racing with Ciel in endless circles, fingertips burning with cold, blisters rubbed open by my hand-me-down hockey skates, and the scalding, watery, inexplicably satisfying cocoa Poppu bought from a vending machine in the warming hut afterward. Ciel took his phone back and moved around the table, showing the location to William, Miho, and Richard.

"None of the crew can leave the boat, Sol," Ciel said, motioning to himself and the others. "We're being watched."

"You mean, literally?"

He nodded. "There's a boat tailing us—it's been there for the last hour."

"Who's on it?"

"My boss."

"Why?"

"In the grand scheme of things? She's worried that I'll disappear with my new family—that she'll lose her favorite pet. But I know you and D'Arcy can slip away, as Noma. She'll assume that you're old friends of mine."

"How will I persuade Gigi to give up Fleur?" I asked, skipping straight over whether I would accept this mission or not. It was a given.

Ciel looked at me with grateful relief. "I'll be with you constantly by text, to help and advise. I have nothing else to offer. But, Sol, I don't know anyone who wings tough situations as well as you."

"I do," I said. "D'Arcy."

"D'Arcy." Ciel sighed, as if D'Arcy weren't sitting right next to him. As if D'Arcy were some sort of problem that needed to be solved. "Yes, this brings me to D'Arcy."

William piped up. "We need D'Arcy to bring us Minister Paulsen's boy."

"I'm not sure what you mean," D'Arcy said.

"Give it up, Benoît," William said, irritably. "We know you know where her baby is."

"Please, D'Arcy, hear us out," Ciel almost begged. He said to me, exquisitely gently, "We figured out within minutes that you took the Paulsen baby, Sol. William tried to go after you, but he was delayed by D'Arcy's attention in the nursery."

"It was *Fleur's* bassinet!" I said, ruining D'Arcy's bluff with my big mouth. "Why the hell wasn't Fleur in it?"

Miho said, "We had a carefully orchestrated plan—"

William finished her sentence. "—that didn't involve you trying to steal your niece."

Ciel said, "When we learned Kizzie was due within days of Minister Paulsen, we couldn't pass up the chance. It was too serendipitous. Minister Paulsen's husband is biracial, like Kizzie. Plus, we knew the minister had scheduled a C-section a week before her due date, and that her baby would be moved to the Day nursery—"

"How did you know that?" D'Arcy asked.

"I have sources that are very close to the family," Ciel said, but he didn't elaborate. "So we decided we'd have Kizzie induced on the same day. William switched our baby with the Paulsen baby in their respective bassinets and was going to wheel the Paulsen baby to our room, where we'd be discharged with him as if he were ours. Miho had falsified the computer records so that we'd had a boy, and William was getting ready to put a fake Baby Boy Le Coeur band on the Paulsen baby, but you and D'Arcy showed up just then, so he had to busy himself with something else."

Kizzie had started putting pancake makeup on my face, and I had to hold her arm still to ask, "How did William know which baby was the Paulsen baby? The bassinet card and ankle bracelet said Fitzroy." I saw D'Arcy nodding his head, keeping right in step, as usual.

"Miho again, on the computer. There was no mother in the ward linked with the last name Fitzroy, so that was the odd baby out."

"Why were Miho's lanyard and stethoscope on the Fitzroy bassinet?" I pressed, as Kizzie started on the rouge.

Ciel became agitated. "We don't really have time for questions."

"Yes, we do," I said. "Real Noma would never leave your boat this close to curfew."

He opened his mouth and then clamped it shut. I was right and he knew it. He let out an exasperated huff of air. "Miho had been working in an administrative post in the hospital, as an operative—she was our eyes and ears there. She was supposed to pick up the lanyard and stethoscope for the same reason you grabbed them: to look more like maternity staff. As Yukie Shiga she was going to take Fleur for a 'test' but then slip her out of the hospital as if she were a mother with her child visiting the pediatrician, and we'd all meet up back here. We had to let her take Fleur rather than the Paulsen baby because there was a strict 'no tests/no removal' order on the Fitzroy file."

D'Arcy spoke up again, asking the most important question. "Why were you stealing Minister Paulsen's baby?"

"I was doing it for Sol," Ciel said instantly, with pinched lips. "I was going to barter the baby to bring her to Day with me."

"What about blackmailing me using Poppu? Were you doing that for me, too?" I demanded, messing up the lipstick that Kizzie was applying to my lips. She got a tissue to blot the mistake.

"I'm *sorry*, Sol," Ciel practically whined. "I knew he didn't have long to live. I needed to see him. And yes, I admit it, I didn't want you giving that baby up to anyone but me, and I thought it would have the added benefit of getting you on the boat, of reuniting us. But it was stupid of me to strong-arm you. When I saw you on that dock, a foot taller than when I'd left you, so thin, and hurt . . ."

I felt steam coming to a head inside of me. I would have exploded if D'Arcy hadn't put a hand on my arm.

"Not now, Sol," he said. He wasn't commanding, he was counseling.

"Yes, now!" I insisted.

"It won't help," D'Arcy said, shaking his head. "And Fleur is out there." He took my hand, grounding me.

I forced air out of my lungs, and my shoulders down. Kizzie began painting clown eyelashes above and below my eyes. I focused on her face and saw wet tracks of tears on her cheeks. She was making me up like a Noma, like the woman who had stolen her child. She was placing her hope in me, and I was balking.

I closed my eyes, quashing the confusion in my chest. Fleur was my niece. She belonged with Ciel and Kizzie. I was the right person for this job; I was the one with guts and nothing to lose.

"When I bring Fleur back, I want two years of answers," I said, my throat hot and full.

Hearing that I was back on track, Ciel switched gears, the way I was learning terrorists do, in the interest of efficiency. "I'll put you on a dinghy and you can row to the Fifty-ninth Street Harbor. The lake is calm this morning. D'Arcy's car is there. He can drop you at Fifty-ninth and University and then get the minister's baby. Richard will keep us hovering just off-shore until you're back. William will look for your return with binoculars all day."

Kizzie finished her work and stood back to look at it.

"Do you have a tracer on my cell or on D'Arcy's?" I asked.

"No," Ciel said. "Of course not."

"Put one on mine." I handed him my phone and stood up. D'Arcy stood with me.

When everything was agreed, Ciel took me out onto the upper deck alone. The air was cool but calm, and the lake smelled heavy with fish. It was still dark, but there were lights running along the exterior wall, casting our shadows so that they criss-crossed each other.

"Listen," Ciel said in a low voice, "when you talk to Gigi it's as simple as this: I haven't successfully developed remote programming yet. Tell her that when I do, I promise I'll talk to Fuzz and Zen. But so far it doesn't work. I have major hurdles to get over before it's functional."

I held his eyes for a long time. They were bluer than mine, so clear they were almost see-through. And fourteen years of a childhood spent looking into them had served me well.

"I'll tell her that. But in exchange for getting Fleur I want a favor from you."

"If I can. Anything."

I looked at the door to the bridge, hollow and flimsy. I took a few steps toward the stern of the boat; he joined me.

"I want you to remotely program D'Arcy's phone back to his real profile later today. Zen said he stored the old information somewhere in a blinded buffer—you'll find it. Make it kick in the second William sees that I've returned with Fleur."

"Sol, I just told you—"

I shook my head. *Don't even bother.*

He pursed his lips and bit his cheek. And then he smiled, but there was a melancholy corner to it. "Will do." He pulled me into a hug. "I love you, Sol."

William and Ciel planned to lower the dinghy at sunrise.
D'Arcy and I stood at the railing, facing east. I had never seen
the sun rise over the lake, but neither had he: the precise moment of legal curfew happened when the upper edge of the disk
of the sun broke the horizon, and unless you lived in an apartment near the lake there wasn't enough transit time for most
people to witness it. Ditto sunset.

Ciel appeared next to me, on my left. "Do you know what a
green flash is?"

I shook my head.

"It's a flash of emerald light that appears at sunset and sunrise, the instant the upper rim of the sun breaks the horizon.
It's not that easy to see one; the conditions have to be just right—
the sky has to be clear, of course, and it helps when the air is a
little colder than the water, the way it is this morning, because
the temperature inversion creates a mirage that magnifies the
refraction between red and green light."

We were already in twilight, with the reflected light from
the sun in the atmosphere beginning to bring the world to life.

Seagulls called overhead, embarking on their scavenging missions to the city's beaches.

"The trouble is, the flash occurs directly above the sun and it only lasts for a second or two, which—on a sunrise—is how long it takes your eye to fix on the location, so you're almost always too late. It's a lot easier to see it on a sunset for that reason, from the Michigan side of the lake." He pulled out his phone and tapped the screen. "I wrote a program to predict where the sun rises on the horizon using the state's global positioning software." He held it out for me, and I passed it to D'Arcy. "Line up the horizon with the dashes, and then watch the point of the vertical arrow as the curfew clock counts down—that's where the sun will break."

The clock was at SR-00:02:11 and tenths of seconds that were counting down faster than I could see them. Two minutes before sunrise. Two minutes until Smudges had to be in their homes, off the streets.

D'Arcy handed it back to him. "Nice. But maybe I'll try it on my hundredth sunrise with Sol, not my first."

Ciel nodded, his glance revealing something—either that he was still struggling to accept the idea of D'Arcy and me, or that he knew there wouldn't be a hundred sunrises for us. He moved to help William get the dinghy ready.

"I *would* like to see a green flash with you someday," D'Arcy said in a moment. "Sunrise or sunset."

I looked out at the lake, the water finally acquiring the glistening blue hue that made it seem like liquid and not just a massive shadow that rimmed Chicago. It was unbearable that this was the only sunrise I would ever see with D'Arcy. I hated that every first was also our last. I couldn't allow myself to enjoy the moment, for the crushing sorrow it produced, a weight heavy enough to force me to my knees if I let it. I gripped the railing, willing myself to stay standing. His left hand slid on top of my right, and then lightly trailed along my knuckles, coaxing me to relax them.

"You're being kind of quiet for Sol," he murmured. "What happened to the girl who says exactly what she's thinking?"

I turned to face him. There was finally enough light to see the green splotch in his left iris. I fixed on it. "You want to know what I'm thinking?"

He nodded, staring back, unwavering.

"What I'm thinking, exactly," I said rather than asked. He nodded again. I swallowed to try to smother the dull heat that burned where my heart was. "This is what I'm thinking . . ." My voice trailed flimsily, and I had to stop to take a breath.

Oh, why the hell not? It was superstitious idiocy to hold it back, as if not saying it would fool the universe into letting me have him.

"I love you," I said, and it came out defiantly. "I love you more than I've ever loved anyone. There are times when the amount I love you hurts so much, I have to sit down. And at this particular moment, it's debilitating."

D'Arcy let out a sort of surprised exhale. The right side of his face began to glow, and he must have seen the same thing on the left side of my face, because we both turned to look at the lake. The watery orange disk of the sun had shown its edge above the horizon, and it was reflected in the rippled water, with streams the colors of flame lying like ribbons low in the sky and pink-tinged clouds fading into a pale robin's-egg blue of the upper atmosphere. I felt his arm slip around my waist and pull me against his side. Tears welled in my eyes, and everything became an impressionist painting, swimming in color. We tipped our heads until they were touching.

"Thank god I asked." His voice was rumbly, exposed. "It would have been a shame if that had gone unsaid."

William lowered the dinghy—an inflated raft big enough for two—and D'Arcy got in first. As I prepared to board it, a vessel the size of a lifeboat moved swiftly toward us. It had no identifying features at all, no Coast Guard stripes.

"What is that, Ciel?" I asked nervously.

"My boss's boat. Just ignore it, climb down." As I ducked under the railing and put my leg over the side, he said to D'Arcy and me, "Make sure to act Noma."

"Identify your departing passengers, Ciel." A man's voice exploded in my ears through a loudspeaker. I glanced to see a rifle pointed in my direction. My foot slid off the rope ladder, and I flailed, burning my hands on the plastic twine to save myself from falling. D'Arcy scrambled below me to catch me, slipping himself, toppling with the squeak of skin against rubber. I gripped the ladder with the crook of my right arm and raised my left middle finger high in the direction of the boat.

"We can speak for ourselves, asshole," I shouted.

"Sol . . ." Ciel hissed. Obviously he didn't have Noma instincts.

"Identify yourselves," the bullhorn said again.

"Sunny Puso and Skin Russell, and you and your metal cock are . . . ?" I shouted again, climbing onto the raft, where D'Arcy's hands caught my thighs and then my waist. I tumbled in and we both instinctively crouched low, looking over the edge.

"Please state your destination."

"WE'RE GETTING THE FUCK OFF CIEL'S YACHT."

Pause. "Please state your destination."

The boat was close now, close enough that I could see three figures on board: two men and a woman—the two men were wearing neat suits. I lost the air in my lungs for a second, at the precise moment that D'Arcy said, "What the hell." And then I saw what he saw: the third figure was Jacqueline Paulsen.

I froze for a second, stunned, and she disappeared from the deck into the cabin. I yelled, but my voice had a quaver to it, "What, are you fucking Hour Guards in training?" I sat up, and D'Arcy followed my lead. I forced air into my lungs to yell with more conviction, "We're going ashore to hook me up with some C-4, so that I can come back when Ciel least expects it and blow his lying ginger ass out of the water."

I glanced up at Ciel, my chest burning with real anger. His eyes were riveted on me, with the whites showing in a stark rim around the blue.

"Hold while we check your papers in our database," the voice announced.

"Go ahead and put the oars in their locks," I muttered to D'Arcy.

"C-4?" he asked, as he clicked the second oar in place.

"Putty explosives."

"I figured, but . . ."

My heart was still pounding from the confusion of seeing Minister Paulsen. I refused to look up at Ciel again. "My family had an eclectic library, what can I say."

After D'Arcy started rowing, the bullhorn said, "Your papers check out. You may proceed."

"Thank you, Zen," I whispered, my shoulders rolling and my back curving in a premature collapse that Gigi would have scorned.

D'Arcy rowed toward the Fifty-seventh Street Beach. Soon we pulled in at the southern tip, where the beach ended and the riprap was piled high—giant boulders of limestone with an overgrowth of volunteer trees and bushes that created a mini urban wilderness. We climbed out of the dinghy and lashed it to the scrub. We picked our way over the riprap to the bicycle path and ran south for a half a block to the via-duct at Fifty-ninth Street—a beige-tiled, graffiti-tagged tunnel under Lake Shore Drive—and back to his car in the harbor lot.

Minutes later, D'Arcy stopped the car in front of Harper Library, put the gearshift in park, and turned to me without cutting the ignition.

I said too sharply, "You're coming with me."

"I can't. I'm sorry."

"Please." How could he leave me to hunt down a gangster Noma and wrest a baby from her arms? The anticipation of loss settled on me—as familiar as an old sweater, with the worn-soft feel of Ciel's betrayal.

"You saw what I saw on that other boat." He pushed the scraggly ends of my mullet behind my neck. "I can't follow Ciel's order. I've got to take Fitz back to his family before your brother gets his hands on him. It's not right for Ciel to barter using someone else's life—not even when he's negotiating for something that would benefit me quite as much as your reassignment. You of all people agree with that, don't you?"

You of all people. I knew what that meant. I, who grew up without parents. I, who had a gaping hole in my life where they should have been. I, who miserably wrote "death = abandonment" on my desk.

"How will you get the baby back to Paulsen? She's out there on the lake!"

"I'm going to try that whole 'leave him on her doorstep, ring the bell and run' method." His smile was thin. "And if she has Suits guarding her house, I'll leave him somewhere safe nearby and send an anonymous text. That boy is so wanted, someone will come within seconds."

"And then where . . . where will you go?"

"We'll text each other to meet up." He studied me, reading my expression. It took about one second for him to figure me out. "Are you worried that I'll leave you?"

I didn't answer. Instead I said, "I'm going to screw this up without you." I hadn't relied on just myself in days. I had become soft and D'Arcy-dependent.

"You're going to kick ass, the way you always do."

"I can't not see you again." I hated how needy I sounded.

"Me neither."

He leaned in to kiss me. "This is a down payment. I'll put you at risk if I mess up your makeup." It was a peck, slim and friendly.

I knew there had to be a last kiss between us. But as I opened the car door, I wished for that one not to be it.

Harper Memorial Library was a Gothic-inspired building with leaded-glass windows, a limestone façade, and crenellations at the top like a small castle. As theme-park as that description sounded, it had a stolid scholarliness and aged patina that gave it genuine gravitas. I thought disjointedly that I might have enjoyed going to college in another life—to read Homer in the original Greek, or something equally useless to society; whatever the opposite of pill packing was.

I received an uncensored text from Ciel as I was pulling open the heavy door.

Target is NW of you 20 m

Twenty meters was damn close. After a second set of doors I was in the main entryway with a cluster of four students, three men and a woman. They whispered something hastily and split up, the two young men flying in separate directions and the couple scurrying down the west hallway. I had forgotten that I wasn't ethereal anymore, I was ravenous. Another message:

Target is N 5 m!

At five meters she should have been right in front of me, but the large foyer was empty. I suddenly understood. I hit reply.

Need altitude

A sign indicated stairs, so I followed a long hallway to my right, past intimate classrooms, and pushed through a door to the east tower of the building. I ran up the stairs. The second floor was all office spaces, marked "Dean of Students" and "Academic Advisers." I ran to the third floor, and at the top of the stairs I burst through double doors. There was a café in front of me, and a sign that said "Reading Room" to the right. Every student in the café turned to look at me. I had no college ID in my phone to wave in front of the reader, but I didn't need it; I was Noma. I hoisted myself with my arms and swung my legs over the turnstile; it was surprisingly effortless for someone who weighed fifty-two kilograms. I ran west into the Reading Room and I stopped short when I got there.

It was the most beautiful room I had ever seen, like something out of an old British movie. There were two massive chandeliers at each end of the cavernous space. The walls were lined with hand-carved shelves loaded with books. The arched windows above the bookcases stretched to the ceiling and were not just leaded glass, as they seemed from the outside, but also had stained-glass pieces embedded in them: the crests of many universities, and Jesus flanked by a couple of robed men with halos, one of them holding a book and a quill. The window casings were carved limestone; the ceiling was vaulted with ribs that formed enormous stars, like a cathedral, with brick inlays in a herringbone pattern between the stars. Students were camped at long study tables dotted with lamps glowing a honey gold, surrounded by their books and sweaters. I walked to one of the bookcases on the north side of the room. I dragged my hands along the spines, just to touch books again, while also looking at every face in the room, searching for Gigi. Wherever I stepped, students packed their bags, preparing to give me the space a Noma might need. My phone vibrated.

Directly N 2 m. Are you with her??

I was still on the wrong floor. I replied:

Not unless she's dangling out the window. Will try basement.

Ciel replied:

She's heading W

I grabbed a terrified blonde before she skirted past me. I pointed to the west exit and said, "Are there stairs through those doors?" She nodded with her mouth open. "Do they go all the way to the basement?"

"I—I've never been to the basement!" she cried, horrified, as if she knew she was giving the wrong answer on an oral exam. I ran to the exit and down a staircase, taking the steps two and three at a time. The basement door was locked. I banged on it in frustration. Ciel texted:

She's too far W and S now to be in Harper. On the Midway?

How could she have been two meters away from me at some elevation less than a minute ago but not be in the building? And the answer bloomed in my mind from my long-dead childhood: steam tunnels.

The university had a warren of underground tunnels connecting every building, bringing heat in the form of steam, and electricity in conduits from the power station across the Midway. Smudge delinquents avoiding curfew sometimes hid out there for the day, lifting metal grates all over campus to climb in. Lovers who could stand sweltering, forty-degree-Celsius heat entwined themselves down there; potheads made their deals and smoked weed. But the tunnels had been locked down by the university when I was still in middle school. A text from Ciel:

She's on the move

I replied:

Steam tunnels. All grates locked?

Immediately, another text:

Brilliant. Entrance in loading dock of UC hospital, under dumpsters, no padlock.

Leave it to Ciel, high school hoodlum extraordinaire, to have this insider information. I hoped it was still current. I started running west on Fifty-ninth Street toward the hospital. An uncensored text arrived from D'Arcy:

Hey, I need to hear from you.

I couldn't stop to answer. When I got to the hospital I texted Ciel:

Which loading dock?

Ciel: **Sorry East of ER on 58th**

I had to run all the way around the building, which covered an entire city block, only to discover that the loading dock was behind two giant wrought-iron gates that were locked with a chain. I was losing my energy fast. I didn't have the reserves for this kind of effort. I bent and put my hands on my knees, trying to catch my breath. From that angle I could see the grate under the dumpster. *I was so close.*

D'Arcy texted again:

SOL. CHECK IN.

The chain was loose on the gate. If I pulled hard, I might be able to create enough space to force my head through. For someone as undernourished as me, the skull is the widest part of the body—the only completely inflexible part. I had learned that from a Harry Houdini biography in Poppu's fourth grade "curriculum." I took two seconds to reply to D'Arcy, mimicking his urgency with all caps:

SOON.

I wedged my head under the chain, scraping my cheeks against the painted iron of the gate as I did, leaving white pancake makeup and red rouge behind, but my head was through. I wiggled my body sideways. The chain levered the gates back together, crushing my chest, preventing me from breathing. My instinct was to suck in precious air, but I knew it would only expand my rib cage. Instead I exhaled as hard as I could and pushed and wriggled until I was jack-knifed by the gates at the hips. I saw stars, but I could breathe again. I yanked the rest of me through with only a couple of scraped knees to show for it and tumbled onto the ground. I was in.

Pushing a dumpster is not a job for a featherweight. My most forceful shoves resulted in precisely a centimeter of move-ment, and I felt an explosion of frustration that I would fail Fleur because I was a pathetic bag of skin and bones. Eventu-ally I got the grate one-third exposed, which was enough. As Ciel had predicted, it was unlocked—why lock it when there was a chain around the gate to the dock and a half tonne of steel and garbage resting on top? I was able to lift the grate half a meter and slither in.

The heat and humidity wrapped around me and invaded my lungs as I climbed the ladder down to what felt like a tropical nightmare. Every pore of my skin released sweat instantly. The tunnel was louder than I expected, with the hum of machinery, hissing, and the occasional metallic bang like an old radiator. There were lights along the ceiling, which was convenient since I was supposedly a Ray and had no flashlight holster. I stopped to text Ciel.

I'm in, which way

His reply was immediate:

Like a boss. Directly E two blocks. Phone sounds off?

The low light was familiar, soothing, concealing after the bright daylight. I started running, but I had to slow it to a brisk walk. Deep breaths were like swallowing a hot lake. Two minutes later, a text:

She's 10 m SE

But I already knew I was close. There was an intersection up ahead, and a baby's strong cry echoing above the noise of the chamber. It was Fleur's voice. Her tiny human voice, husky, like Ciel's. Tears came to my eyes, and I wiped them away. I padded on silent Smudge feet and peeked around the corner. Gigi was slumped against the wall. Her makeup was running, and she was crying along with the baby. Fleur was dressed in a T-shirt and a diaper only, with her hair plastered wet to her scalp. Gigi looked up at me and her whole body startled. She almost dropped the baby. She tried but couldn't scramble to her feet with the bundle in her arms.

My instinct was to show that I was alone by stepping around the corner. I didn't want to threaten her by approaching. She caught my body language and stopped flailing to get up. I could have run to her, fought for the baby, tried to take advantage of her position. But something calm rooted me to the spot. It was the fact that Gigi was crying. Gigi, the powerhouse. Gigi, who credibly might feed you to her dogs. Gigi, the toughest girl I had ever known, hands down, was crying. And I understood.

I sat on the ground. It had a layer of powdery dust and dirt that must have been a century old. Fleur wailed. Gigi stared at me.

After a couple of minutes of intolerable screaming, I got up and moved next to them. I sat down again, leaning against the wall, as Gigi was. The heat was making me dizzy.

"She's too hot," I said.

"Duh."

Seriously, Fleur's tiny body would dehydrate in a matter of hours in this hellhole.

"Let's get her out of here."

A minute more, and Gigi reluctantly started to get up. I stood first, clapped the dust onto my skirt, leaving handprints, and helped hoist her by the elbow. I didn't try to take Fleur. Gigi led the way through the labyrinth, back toward Harper Library, carefully avoiding hot, asbestos-lined pipes. Our feet crunched in the mineral deposits that seeped from the walls; I ducked almost in half through some passages.

Five minutes later, we were in a subbasement, in a room that itself looked like a library, or maybe a storage area for spillover books, with metal stacks and carts full of forgotten hardcover tomes. It was cool, with the musty, mildewed odor of ancient books. My damp body shivered.

"Now she'll need her clothes," I said. But Fleur was also starving, or something, because she was screaming so hard her whole body had tremors.

Gigi raised her voice over the baby's cries. "There's a bottle in that mini-fridge, and a microwave in the corner."

I got the bottle ready while she changed Fleur's diaper and gently maneuvered her tiny, quaking body into a black long-sleeve shirt and pants. She put a red knitted cap on the baby's head, and Fleur was Noma, too. I shook the bottle and tested the temperature on my wrist as I had seen Hélène do with Fitzroy's milk. It was tepid, not really body temperature like mother's milk, but at least the cold edge was off. I handed it to Gigi. She sat in a battered office chair.

At first, Fleur was so hysterical she couldn't focus on the nipple, ripping her mouth from side to side, her face an alarming shade of red. But eventually she figured out that this was what she had demanded, and she began sucking, began breathing through her nose, wet snot spraying in and out with a gurgling sound. And finally, I heard with each swallow the outraged grunt of a need barely met. Gigi's shoulders dropped. I stood where I was.

"I didn't want this job," Gigi said.

I recalled her on the breakwater, spitting at Fuzz's feet. The whole thing had been planned from the compound, and D'Arcy and I had unwittingly played into it. Someone had even prestocked this room for her with rudimentary baby supplies. I said nothing.

"I never wanted to see Ciel again."

Me neither. But I had been lying to myself.

"I knew it would kill me to meet Kizzie. *Shit*, I can't even say that name without wanting to puke." Silver pools welled on her lower lids until the tears spilled over. "I can't stand to hold her baby."

Was that my cue? I wasn't sure; it had a rhetorical edge. I stayed where I was. Again, I said nothing. The baby's suckling became noisy and smacking. Her grunts segued from urgent to ecstatic. It was comically adorable. It was wrong of me, while Gigi was in such agony, but I laughed through my nose. Gigi looked up at me.

And then she smiled, too, a flimsy smile. "She's pretty fucking cute."

"Uh-huh."

"When she's not pitching murderous fits. Damn, I could never be a mother right now."

"Uh-huh."

We watched Fleur suckle, drift off, remember that she was hungry and suckle desperately again, and then drift off, only to repeat the whole cycle.

"You prolly shouldn't hang around here, Red. Fuzz is on his way."

"From?"

"The compound. But he left almost three hours ago."

"So, any minute."

She nodded. There was a long silence. My phone vibrated. She looked at it in my hand.

"Ciel?" she asked.

I put it in my pocket without reading the message. "Mm." I didn't have much to say, not because I was at a loss for words, but because I felt an unusual calm. Fleur was safe. For the moment that was enough.

"I would have liked you, you know, in another life," Gigi said to me out of the blue. After a long pause she said, "If Ciel had made a different choice."

I put my arms behind me and leaned against a desk, bracing my butt on the back of my hands.

"Hell," she went on, "I might've even loved you. While simultaneously wanting to strangle you every minute I was with you."

"I would have loved you back," I said finally, and it was the truth. I already sort of did, in an always-off-balance, somewhat terrified way.

She stared at me. "I can't give her to you, Sol."

"I know."

"No. No, you don't. Fuzz would kill me. I mean that literally: he'd kill me." She watched the baby, who had temporarily won her battle against sleep and was drinking steadily. "Unless I was willing to disappear, and give up everything."

There was nothing I could do but listen. I would never win in a physical fight with Gigi. She would slash my throat, I would bleed out onto the floor, and that would be the end of me, in a forgotten subbasement of a library at a small midwestern university. Thousands of strangers would walk above my rotting, undiscovered corpse, living their lives of the mind.

"You wanna know what was unexpectedly shitty about this whole mission? Something that blindsided me?"

I waited.

"Knowing that your grandfather was dying in the room across the hall and I had never met him. Realizing I had no right to see him, and Kizzie did. That he was going to die without knowing I existed. And that it didn't really matter anyway, because I didn't matter to Ciel anymore. Who the fuck could have known that would slay me?"

I looked at the floor. It was true that Poppu and I knew nothing about Gigi while she was in Ciel's life. I still didn't know how he'd met her, how long they were together, whether he spent time in Iowa or she in Chicago. I was pretty sure she was his first lover, though.

"I don't think this will help," I said eventually, hoping I was doing the right thing. "I'm imagining myself in your position, and I'd need to hear it. But ultimately it wouldn't help." That old image of D'Arcy clasping a necklace around the neck of another woman flashed in my mind for a second, as fresh as the first time, and I had to close my eyes.

"What."

I took a breath and opened my eyes. "Ciel does care about you, he never stopped. Knowing Ciel, he physically can't stop."

She shook her head, rejecting my theory.

"It's true. Listen." The decision to spill was suddenly easy. "You need to talk to Zen when you get back to Iowa, because Ciel put a tracer on your phone."

"What the fuck."

I nodded. "It was his assbackwards way of keeping in touch with you after you broke up. He couldn't let you go—not all the way."

"Son of a bitch."

"I wouldn't know," I said. "I have no memory of her."

She smiled, crooked, at my macabre humor. "Yeah, sorry about that."

The baby finished the bottle. She had a mighty little appetite. Gigi wiped her milky chin with a sleeve and carefully put her over her shoulder, confidently thumping her fragile back. She must have taken care of siblings. Or maybe the Noma raised their children like a wolf pack, with everyone helping.

"And here I thought he chose me over Fuzz and Dope because he trusted me," she said cynically. "I wasted a lot of energy feeling like shit about betraying him."

"He did trust you. *And* he had a Plan B. That's Ciel."

Fleur belched, a little newborn *blurp* that resulted in a mucousy mess on Gigi's shoulder. Gigi didn't flinch. She rubbed Fleur's bottom gently. She lowered the baby so that she was lying on both of Gigi's strong forearms and studied her. Fleur was out cold, sated.

"Okay, tit for tat, Le Coeur," she said to me. "One sucky piece of Ciel information for another. I think your loving brother wants the Paulsen boy so he can blackmail the minister for his freedom."

"What?"

"Jacqueline Paulsen is his boss. Hadn't you figured that out? She plucked him out of jail to be her own personal computer geek. She probably had him arrested, too."

"I learned that she was his boss today. But how does that work? She's a Smudge, and he was transferred to Day."

"He's an employee of the federal government under the

supervision of the Office of Night Ministry. That's why she has him on a boat. When they're both in open water, Night and Day don't matter and she can ride herd on him. She assigned him the remote programming project a year ago, and he hasn't produced. She's starting to question why it's taking so long." She smirked, and it was bitter. "Everyone wants Ciel's magic."

Ciel had told D'Arcy he wanted to barter Fitz for my reassignment to Day. He hadn't hesitated with that explanation. His face was earnest; I had seen it myself. I moved toward the only other chair in the room—an outdoor wooden bench so weatherworn it was a mass of splinters. I sat down anyway; I needed to.

"Fuck this," Gigi said abruptly. "Fuck *all* of this and everyone." She stood up and strode toward me. I got up defensively; I even lifted my arms to block a blow. But what she did was totally unexpected.

She handed Fleur to me.

Gigi led me up and out of the building, and then she ditched me, running north through the quadrangles, not stopping, not looking back once, until she was a speck of a black figure turning onto Fifty-seventh Street, out of sight. I wanted it not to be the last time I would see her.

I needed a moment, so I sat on a bench on the quad holding Fleur. The air was cool but the sun was out, bathing the baby and me in a dry, early-fall warmth. I sat cross-legged so I could cradle her in a nest on my lap. She was a dusty, greasy mess, and I knew I was no better—with smeared makeup, filthy clothes, and limp spikes from the humidity of the tunnels. I took my time composing and sending three texts, the first much longer than the rest, and possibly the most important thing I had ever written in my life. The second one I sent to D'Arcy:

Miracle: I am holding Fleur. Where are you?

The third one I sent to Ciel:

This bundle needs a bath. Remember your promise about Skin's phone this morning.

Ciel responded first:

Speechless. Thanks are not enough. Kizzie weeping. I didn't forget.

I replied:

Can't row with baby. Pull up to 59th Street breakwater again?

Ciel: **Watching for you. Careful.**

And then D'Arcy replied to me:

Oh god you're safe. 2nd Sol-induced coronary averted. My job done too. I dread Ciel's wrath. Meet?

Me: **Ciel idling at 59th breakwater. Setting off on foot. Eta 20 min.**

D'Arcy: **Will run to make 20 min. Relieved Gigi didn't gut you.**

I was starting to feel the exhaustion of stress, too much running, and not enough food, and even though it was a straight shot down Fifty-ninth Street to the lake, it was still almost two kilometers for my rubbery legs. I didn't bother to worry about police or Hour Guards. I didn't have the energy to spare. And there was something about my natural demeanor as a Noma—more secure than Sol but less antagonistic than Gigi—that felt almost like a force field to me. I would be a little sorry to drop my costume and all the superficial strength it afforded.

As I walked, I wondered whether Ciel would already know that the baby was safe at the Paulsen home before D'Arcy got to the ship—whether Jacqueline Paulsen had received word already and was gone, with her Suits and their rifle in tow. I wondered whether she even knew that Ciel was aware that Fitz was missing. The kidnapping was such a guarded secret, and I had no idea what her relationship with Ciel was. And then I worried about Ciel getting angry at D'Arcy. It had been a long time since I'd seen my brother's cheeks flush and the tendons in his neck flare, and our childhood fights had only ever been over silly things like leftovers and borrowed books, not stolen babies.

My left bicep was seizing, hot and tight. Babies are not meant to be carried in the arms for any great distance. It turned out there was a reason women strapped them to their backs and chests all over the globe, or pushed them in strollers.

As I approached the Fifty-ninth Street viaduct, I looked through it and saw that D'Arcy was at the end of the tunnel, waiting for me. He had seen me. He was walking toward me. An odd flood of joy and confusion washed through my body.

The joy: D'Arcy was like a planet to my meteor. The gravitational pull was similar to a hurtling sensation. My body *needed* to collide with his. And, the universe be praised, this planet welcomed the impact.

The confusion: he had a baby in a sling that draped over his left shoulder and looped under his right armpit.

A baby. And a crying baby at that. I opened my mouth to say something startled, but before anything came out, two burly men in suits rushed him from the bike path, grabbed him, and hauled him in the direction of the breakwater.

I hurried after them as quickly as I could while still toting a living human being in my arms, and when I emerged on the other end of the viaduct into the bright sunlight, I saw D'Arcy being hustled by the Suits to the end of the breakwater. They forced him onto Ciel's yacht, one holding each elbow as he climbed aboard over the railings, trying to brace the baby with his hand as he did. Ciel was there; Minister Paulsen was there; the rifle was there.

"Leave him alone!" I shouted. William leaped onto the break-water and ran straight for me. I turned away from him and squatted instinctively into a defensive position with Fleur folded inside the envelope of my body.

"Get up, Sol," William said when he reached me. He had the sense not to touch me. "Get the hell up and carry your niece onto that boat. *Do you understand that Paulsen can never know Fleur was missing?*"

I was frozen in place. It was one of those moments when I needed to think faster than I could—to assess my options and find a cleverer way out than the only one that presented itself to me, the one I had committed myself to as the least bad evil. Why couldn't I ever get exactly what I wanted—*everything* I wanted?

And through it all, there were only three coherent truths bubbling to the surface in the bog that was my brain. First: none of this was Fleur's or Fitzroy's fault. Second: Fleur needed to be with Kizzie and Ciel, and Fitz needed to be with the Paulsens. Third: there were things in this world that mattered more than what Sol Le Coeur wanted. I stood up.

"Good girl," William said.

"Fuck this," I replied, hugging the baby to me. "Fuck *all* of this and everyone."

I strode to the boat.

Sunday
10:30 a.m.

D'Arcy was huddled against the cabin wall, holding Fitz away from the Suits, who turned out to be none other than Mr. Thomas and Mr. Jones. Minister Paulsen was bullying D'Arcy verbally, threatening him with a life sentence in jail.

"I won't let your son go until I know Sol is safe!" D'Arcy yelled. Fitzroy was wailing.

Minister Paulsen ordered the Suits to take a step back.

Kizzie was waiting for me with her arms outstretched, but I still wouldn't pass a baby across the gap. Ciel and William helped me aboard, with Ciel whispering, "Thank you." Once I was safely on deck I slid the baby out of my arms into Kizzie's. She scurried with Fleur into the cabin, with Miho right behind her. The first part of my job was done.

"I'm here," I called to D'Arcy. To Minister Paulsen I said, "I'm Sol—Sol Le Coeur, Ciel's sister."

"Ciel's sister." She shook her head, like she'd been a fool for overlooking the possibility.

D'Arcy uncurled his body, and Thomas and Jones kept their distance. Minister Paulsen wiped her eyes with her sleeve and took a seat on the lockers, wincing in pain. I realized she was five days out from major abdominal surgery, and reluctantly acknowledged that it was somewhat badass she was here at all. Fitzroy's cries had turned to exhausted whimpers. It was palpable to me how much she wanted to hold him.

"Give him room," she ordered. "He's not going anywhere." To D'Arcy she said almost heartrendingly, "Have pity on a new mother."

"I've given you what you asked for," Ciel said to Minister Paulsen. "I caused your son to be recovered, and you promised me a reward."

I exhaled, closed my eyes, and allowed myself a wish.

Ciel went on, "In exchange I want my freedom, plus this boat."

Wishes are stupid and pointless. They're self-inflicted injuries—open wounds that you have to tend for the rest of your life just to contain them, to keep them from festering and consuming you.

"Is anything you say ever the truth?" I asked my brother.

"I've always told you the truth!" he said defensively.

"You *said* you were going to ask for my reassignment to Day."

"He would never do that," Jacqueline Paulsen said.

"Right," I said. "Not when he can get something for himself instead."

"Bringing you to Day *would* be something for myself, you little idiot," Ciel hissed. "But it's also something Jacqui has no power over."

My brother was on a nickname basis with the woman he once told me had killed our parents.

Minister Paulsen was herself again, in control. "Ciel wouldn't waste leverage on something out of my jurisdiction. Reassignment is a federal Day directive."

I hated that she acted like she knew my brother better than I did, after stealing him from me.

Ciel said to her pointedly, "When I stop working for you, I'm leaving Chicago forever and taking Sol with me on this boat, and on the open seas her assignment status will be irrelevant." And there, *there* was the ambiguity that defined my brother: freeing himself also freed me from the Night. Everything had a Plan B, a redundancy, a fail-safe. Maybe Fuzz was right: Ciel was fiercely loyal. But it was his own brand of loyalty, not mine.

"How can she live on a boat when she's incarcerated?" the minister asked coolly.

And all at once I saw that poor Ciel was still her lapdog, and the full weight of his two years away began to hit me. It was turning out that I understood nothing of the world except perhaps how to love people with every cell in my body.

D'Arcy stood up, as if on cue. "I'm afraid I have to insist on a different trade." I suddenly realized that Fitz had grown silent. In fact, he was too silent, and he had stopped squirming. In those moments I seemed to be the only one who noticed it, and D'Arcy caught my eye with an intensity that I had never seen before, which was saying a lot.

"It's not Fitzroy," he said to me, as if we were alone on the boat.

"What the hell is going on?" Paulsen demanded, her voice clipped.

"Minister Paulsen," D'Arcy said, "I respectfully request that you drop the curfew violation against Sol, and arrange to absolve her of responsibility for Officer Dacruz's accident. I believe these favors *are* within your jurisdiction. I'm not asking a lot. It's pathetic really: I just want her to be able to go back to square one—back to eleventh grade and her factory job. She has lost so much in the last couple of years. Don't you think it's enough?"

"Give me my son and I'll consider dropping the charges against you," Minister Paulsen said in a counteroffer.

"Your boy is safe. I have his location entered in my phone."

It took only a fraction of a second for her eyes to show understanding. "You son of a bitch," she whispered. *"Where is he?"*

D'Arcy spread the folds of the sling and pushed aside the hospital blanket. He pulled out the lifeless gape-mouthed body of Premie Gort.

I now had a quantitative measure of Mr. Thomas's denseness, based on the amount of time it took him to process that the baby wasn't real. He finally exploded from a standing position into a lunge faster than I've seen any human being move—speed and strength and grooming being his comparative advantages—and tackled D'Arcy against the wall of the cabin, throwing him to the deck facedown, pinning him with the full weight of his body. Gort was crushed beneath them. Jones was by Thomas's side instantly, shoving his hand against D'Arcy's head, forcing his cheek hard against the deck. With his other hand he rifled through D'Arcy's pockets.

"I have a self-destruct code on my phone," D'Arcy struggled to say, his voice distorted and strained from the weight of Mr. Thomas on his lungs. I tried to go to him, but Ciel anticipated me, locking his arms around me. When I fought him, William joined in and I was subdued.

I understood D'Arcy's plan. He was going to send the text with Fitz's location after Paulsen fulfilled her end of the bargain, after she promised to drop the charges against me, after she let me off the boat. It was a hopelessly unenforceable deal and riddled with all the same hostage-negotiation dilemmas we had already discussed in his apartment, but it socked me in the chest that he had even dared to try it. He had used the only card he had to try to rescue me, to erase my mistakes of the last week.

Jones held the phone out for Minister Paulsen.

She took it and said, "Destruction of your papers sends you to jail for life, Noma. Did you really want to throw everything away for a factory Smudge?"

"He's not Noma," Ciel said. "You can access his data."

Minister Paulsen tapped the screen. D'Arcy closed his eyes, expecting the end.

All I wanted was to be at his side.

And then I saw Minister Paulsen scroll with her finger. Her eyes darted around the screen, taking in information. When she came to what she was looking for, she let out a choked sound, something like a sob—a release of anguish that startled me.

D'Arcy's phone had not in fact fried itself. And I knew why. It was because of me. It was because I had asked Ciel to set his profile back to D'Arcy Benoît, Medical Apprentice with National Distinction.

"Let him up," Minister Paulsen commanded Mr. Thomas.

"Send a unit to the County Day nursery." And then her voice caught with emotion. "Tell them *Baby Boy Harcourt*."

I was stunned at D'Arcy's resourcefulness. He had somehow returned Fitz to the nursery. Or Hélène had done it, but it could only have been at his request with that touching surname. I briefly wondered how you smuggled a baby *into* a nursery, given how difficult it was to secrete one out, but this mother and son were both brilliant hospital insiders.

Thomas climbed off D'Arcy and yanked him to his feet, where Jones held his elbows behind his back. I let out a guttural grunt of frustration as I ripped out of Ciel's and William's grasp to tumble forward into D'Arcy's chest. The descent of the meteor was complete. I wrapped my arms around him. He leaned against me and rubbed his cheek against my hair.

"D'Arcy Benoît," I heard Minister Paulsen say, still examining his phone. "I recognize you, now that I see a photo as you were. Such a distinctive face. You're the one in the news footage with Sol. The video camera from one of the police cars caught you dashing across Lake Shore Drive the night Dacruz was hit." I heard a smirk in her voice. "They're looking for you."

"They can have me, if it frees Sol," he said into my neck, refusing to untuck his face.

"No they can't," I said back to him.

"I'll switch to Night," D'Arcy whispered.

But Minister Paulsen had heard him and answered before I could. "There's no chance on god's earth with your résumé that the Day government would permit a reassignment." Her voice became trailing, hesitant, like she was simultaneously composing a text on her phone. "And you'd better have told the truth about the location of my son."

It was time for me to try to accomplish my second goal.

But before I did, I concentrated on the feeling of D'Arcy's body against mine, and I squeezed him tighter, wishing his arms were wrapped around me in one of his nourishing bear hugs. I closed my eyes and pulled a deep breath of him into my lungs, letting my nose and throat taste him on the way down. I nudged his face with mine until he understood I wanted his lips. I felt every part of his mouth in a kiss that was firm and urgent. I imprinted it in my memory. I prayed to a universe that sometimes granted me unexpected gifts: *Please don't let me forget.*

"What are you about to do?" D'Arcy murmured, his voice on edge. He might have read my kiss for what it was: a goodbye.

"I'm so glad I crushed my finger during your shift," I whispered back.

"Sol, no . . ."

I made myself pull away from him, and with Jones holding his arms he couldn't stop me. I turned to Minister Paulsen and said, "Let's make a deal."

Jacqueline Paulsen looked at me as if I were an alien, and then she put on her jacket, which had been draped over the locker.

"I don't think you people understand the definition of a *deal*. You have to have something of value to trade." She turned to Mr. Thomas. "Get an expedited Day pass for the arrest of these two"—she meant D'Arcy and me—"and one for my transport home. I have a baby to nurse. And tell Richard to take us to Monroe Harbor while we wait."

Her phone pinged, and she took it out of her jacket pocket to read a text message. Her face softened and her whole body settled like pills in a counting machine. It wasn't until that moment that I realized how tense she had been. She put a hard look on her face and held up the screen for me, to show me definitive proof of my lack of leverage. It was an uncensored, full-resolution photo of Fitz in the arms of a female Suit who was beaming. And even with his eyes closed, the baby was wearing a defiant frown.

"He's beautiful," I said. "Ornery and opinionated . . . I hope you never try to take it out of him. As a Smudge, he'll need that strength. Also, you might seriously consider naming him Fitzroy. It suits him."

"What the hell are you babbling about?"

"Tell Mr. Jones to let D'Arcy go."

"Excuse me?"

"I can't make it any clearer." And then I said to Mr. Thomas, "You might want to hold off on sending that text for a minute."

Minister Paulsen said, "Just what do you think—"

"Do you know what a future text is?" I interrupted. I knew it would make her listen. She stared at me. Her eyes were small and brown and wired to a very smart brain, the cogs of which I could practically see turning. For a moment I was taken over by the sensation that my parents had held her gaze like this, too, and suddenly those fifteen years were compressed, that moment joined with this one, and I felt them alive in me.

She said to Mr. Jones irritably, "Oh, for heaven's sake let him go. He's not Noma, he's just a Medical Apprentice." To D'Arcy she said, "Jones can kill you with his bare hands, so don't try anything."

Mr. Jones unhanded D'Arcy, who rubbed his upper arms and shoulders.

I took a breath and said, "Really, I don't give a damn if Mr. Thomas sends that text he's still working on, but *you* might want him to stop once you've heard what I have to say."

"You're quite the little bitch, aren't you?"

"I'm not little." In fact, I was looking down on her. "And you made me what I am when you killed my parents."

"I didn't kill them."

"When you didn't stop them from dying."

"Your parents made a choice."

She was sort of right on that score. There was an entire web of failures making up my life, fabricated of the finest strands, tangled and knotted over the last century. From the moment on March 11, 1918, that Mess Sergeant Albert Gitchell reported to Camp Riley Hospital Building Ninety-one with a high fever, throbbing head, and sore throat, every stupid decision after that had led to me, standing on this boat, without parents, without a grandfather, with a Telemachus of a brother, without a home. Without D'Arcy.

"They made a choice, and then you made a choice," I finally allowed. "And now I've made one. I've programmed my phone with a future text."

I glanced at Ciel. His eyes were narrowed, reading my face. He knew instantly where I had gotten that text capability. And I knew that I could be putting him in danger by divulging a new technology—one that his boss hadn't been gifted with—so I said to him belligerently, "You're not the only one with talent in our family, asshole. You've been gone a long time."

Minister Paulsen looked at Ciel for a moment, gauging his reaction, but Ciel was convincingly agape. She turned to me. "I don't, as a matter of fact, know what a future text is."

"It's self-explanatory, really. A future text is a text sent now, to be delivered at a later date. The only way to call off a future text once it's been sent is to enter a personal code."

"You have my attention." She didn't take her eyes off me as she said, "Mr. Thomas, pause what you're doing."

I went on. "One month from now exactly, a text message

will be received simultaneously by three recipients: Grady Hastings, and the Day and Night desks of the Independent News Network. Unless I stop it before then, the text will reveal the existence of secret, mandatory pinealectomies for Night babies."

The muscles in her face became loose, making her skin look doughy and detached.

"From what I understand," I said, "this information will help the rhetoric of Grady Hastings and his followers *a lot*. It's one thing to deceive people that time can be 'shared fairly,' and another thing to mutilate their children without telling them."

She stared at me for a long time. Silences were hard for me not to fill, but I stood still and pressed my lips together to keep my mouth shut. I put my shoulders back. I was getting better at waiting. I would never be a patient person, but I might be able to survive jail time now without spontaneously combusting. It was something of a comfort to realize it.

"So you're demanding to be reassigned to Day with Ciel and have the charges against you dropped," she said. As if she could know what I wanted. As if the power to do it had been hers all along.

I shook my head. "Not even close."

"Take the deal, Sol," Ciel begged.

"Look again at that remarkable baby of yours in the photo, Ms. Paulsen," I said, ignoring Ciel. "And then think of the world he was born into. You had to break the law to make sure he didn't have a part of his body nuked on his second night of life. Is that really how you want things?" I wasn't being eloquent, but I didn't care. No one was writing this down for the history books. "I can't have my freedom, and you know it. I screwed up: I broke curfew, I escaped the custody of an Hour Guard, and then I caused his injury. On camera."

"Are you forgetting about the kidnapping charges?"

Ciel interjected here. "No one but you knows that Fitzroy was missing, Jacqui. There don't have to *be* charges."

She glared at Ciel. "I'm going to name the baby after his father."

"Someone has to go to jail after that spectacle at Monroe Harbor," I said, "and I'm the logical person to do it, not D'Arcy. You saw his records just now—he's an asset to the Day community. I corrupted him; I used him. Without me, he's as straight as they come."

"Stop it, Sol," D'Arcy said, his face full of an anguish I couldn't stand to watch, so I turned away.

"I'm a factory Smudge," I went on. "Some other grunt is manning my blister-pack station as we speak, and there wasn't even a hiccup in the transition. No one will miss me. I'll have a trial and I'll go to jail. I don't demand special treatment."

"So Mr. Benoît gets off with a slap on the wrist, I can arrange that," Minister Paulsen said crisply. "Although I'm a bit surprised that someone who's resourceful enough to program a future text into a mobile phone would waste blackmail leverage on a boy."

I laughed. It was a tired snort, but genuine, and it came out of me without my even knowing it was bubbling up. She shook her head like I was a lunatic.

I said, "D'Arcy's exoneration isn't all I'm asking for."

Ciel said, "Sol, *fais attention.*" *Be careful.*

I looked into my brother's eyes. God, I would miss them. Again. "I really *don't* want to set the world on fire," I admitted to him, feeling a sting of tears at the thought of Poppu's song.

"I just want to start a flame in your heart," he replied quietly, right in step with me.

I turned back to Minister Paulsen, to finish the job. "The text includes the information that privileged members of the Night government routinely have their children spared the procedure. It names you and describes how Fitzroy took a little vacation in the Ray nursery while his Smudge peers had their pineal glands destroyed with radiation."

Her eyes were wide. There was a stunned silence around us.

"I've had longer to think about this than you have," I said. "But with time, when you stop trying to find ways to cancel that text, I believe you'll understand that *you* should be the one to expose the existence of the PinX procedure and take a public, political stand against the policy, rather than have your complicity with the Day government revealed in the news.

"So this is the deal I'm offering: when you begin your campaign against pinealectomies, I'll cancel the text. Just get my phone to me in jail somehow. I assume the police will confiscate it in the next few minutes."

"Why are you doing this to me?" There was a hairline fracture in her stony façade. I prayed that, with time, the truth would eventually cleave her open along that crack, revealing whatever decency she had inside.

"It has to be you," I told her. "Just like it has to be me."

"Do you understand that my career is over no matter which path I choose?"

I thought about that. There was a small chance that she'd be a hero and public opinion would insulate her from political backlash. And then I recalled the power of the Day government over Night and I knew it was more likely she would be crushed.

Finally I said, "You'll have your husband, and Fitz, and your health. And you'll know you did the right thing. Given what my grandfather went through—where he is right now—that doesn't seem too shabby."

Within twenty minutes the cops arrived on a police boat with their lights flashing and took me away. D'Arcy and Minister Paulsen were dropped off at Monroe Harbor, where he was free to go and she made her way home with a Day pass to see her little boy.

I spent those last twenty minutes flanked by Mr. Jones and Mr. Thomas, in the company of the person I valued more than life itself, while Ciel retreated to the bridge with Minister Paulsen. I knew she was going to put heavy pressure on him in the next month to find a technical solution to her "problem"—a technical solution he in fact already possessed and would have to hide from her. Everything depended on Ciel's strength.

I wasn't worried.

D'Arcy wasted too much time talking about how we would find a way to have the charges dropped, how his parents had friends who were powerful Smudge lawyers, how I couldn't be tried as an adult, how if it came to a trial we'd win, and if we didn't win, I would get off with time served. I had to stop him. It was like hearing Poppu's oncologist talk about treatments we hadn't yet tried that had near-zero probabilities of success, when all he wanted was to enjoy the last weeks as pain-free as possible, curled in his bed listening to me read, or reminiscing about all the beautiful places we had been together.

What D'Arcy didn't understand was that I had gotten more than I dreamed possible when I'd stubbornly watched that heat-sealing plate descend on my finger. Poppu had not only held Fleur before he died, he'd seen Ciel again and he'd met Kizzie. Both Fleur and Fitz were with parents who loved them. The medical procedure that had killed Poppu would be exposed for what it was and—if there was any sense left on this planet—might be discontinued.

But most unexpectedly, I had met my desk partner. I'd grown to know and love the real person behind the drawings, and we had somehow snuck a moment of passion past a world designed to keep us apart.

"Will you tell Hélène thank you for me?" I asked D'Arcy, not revealing to Thomas and Jones that the thank-you was for returning Fitzroy to the hospital.

D'Arcy nodded, understanding perfectly. "She's not half-bad when she's being subversive."

"And tell Jean that I only really started to fall in love with you when I saw what you might look like when you're fifty."

He laughed, and then got too serious and said the words I didn't want him to say, but I knew he would. "I'm going to wait for you, Sol."

I shook my head, having practiced what I would reply. "Always remember that I won't hold you to that."

"It's my choice—"

"And if you change your mind, that's fine."

"You're starting to infuriate me."

I wasn't fooling myself that there was only one person in the world for me or for D'Arcy. He was young and he was a Ray. I was a Smudge, and I had no future, even in the Night. If I got something as long as a five-year sentence, he'd be a different person at the end of it, with thousands of days spent living and working in the sunlight, while I might become stunted and isolated. He'd make friends, he'd grow into adulthood, he'd begin practicing medicine as a real doctor. I wasn't naïve enough to think that no one else could ever attract him, that no one else deserved him. There was a smart, sunny girl out there right now somewhere, a Ray on a trajectory that would cross his path, a girl who made sense with him. I was just as glad not to know her this very minute, but she existed, and he would run into her, and with time I would accept it.

No, that was wrong. I wouldn't accept it so much as continue to breathe, the way I somehow did after Ciel was taken away and Poppu began dying: fifteen inhalations a minute, twenty thousand times a day, eight million times a year, each breath a bit more work than it should be.

"You don't have to think about it now," I said. "Just remember someday, if you need it, that I didn't ask you to wait."

"May I kiss her?" D'Arcy asked Mr. Thomas, his voice irritated.

"As if this conversation isn't torture enough," Mr. Thomas replied.

D'Arcy took that as a yes. With the low September sun creating a sort of halo behind him that seemed pretty damned fitting, he held my jaw in his hands and pressed his lips on mine. He did it with such gentle authority that the only message I could possibly receive was "I'm going to wait for you."

Acknowledgments

I wouldn't have set a word of this book down if Eric Fama Cochrane had not challenged me to a novel-writing duel in the summer of 2011. The manuscript he produced was more fantastical than mine in every way.

The poem D'Arcy wrote on his desk was inspired by a 2011 online *Forbes* article by journalist Susannah Breslin about her cancer diagnosis.

Grady Hastings's "What Is True Belongs to Me" speech is a composite of the thoughts and words of many authors more eloquent than I: Seneca, Abraham Lincoln, Martin Luther King, Jr., Émile Zola, Walt Whitman, Thomas Paine, Clarence Darrow, and Ralph Waldo Emerson.

Special thanks to Simon Boughton, Angie Chen, Sara Crowe, Susan Fine, Kate Hannigan, Linda Hoffman Kimball, and Carol Fisher Saller for insightful comments; to Sally Fama Cochrane for suggesting pinealectomies and for teaching me about the biological rhythms of Siberian hamsters; to Lydia G. Cochrane for French consultations; to Dan Carey and Dave Vargas for showing me around the University of Chicago steam tunnels; to Gary A. Becker for stargazing help; and to Dana Pietura, who makes me seem outwardly put together.

Discussion Questions

1. In *Plus One*, the government took a series of steps that gradually split the population in two: a Day group and a Night group, with mandated curfews. Though dramatized, the origin of the division is based on historical events during the Spanish Flu pandemic. For instance, the mayor of St. Louis controversially closed schools, churches, and non-medical businesses for months, and severely restricted the movement of all people. As a result, St. Louis had the lowest death rate of any big city in the U.S. In your opinion, should a government be able to make restrictive laws if the end result is good for citizens? Who gets to decide when the loss of freedom outweighs the added security?

2. Can you think of ways in which we've denied groups of people their constitutional rights and civil liberties in this country? Does the Day/Night divide seem better or worse? Does the reasoning for it seem more or less sensible?

3. Do you think it would be technically possible to live divided by day and night? Can you think of ways the Day/Night system would be complicated by reality? For instance, in the northernmost-inhabited area of Norway, the sun is visible for twenty-four hours from roughly mid-April to mid-August. In those months, how would Night people shop for groceries or go to school? More generally, how would transcontinental travel be possible?

4. If you had to choose, which would you be, a Ray or a Smudge? Why?

5. The story describes the possible health consequences of living without sunlight. Can you also think of emotional or psychological ways living at night might affect you?

6. Do you think there are some industries that lend themselves to the domain of Rays or Smudges? Which ones, and why?

7. Gigi is subjected to sexual coercion by the Hour Guard, Brad. How could this sort of abuse of power be controlled in the society of *Plus One*?

(Note: the answers contain spoilers!)

JEN OF THE STARRY-EYED REVUE (starryeyedrevue.blogspot.com)

Where did the idea for Plus One *come from? When I hear "plus one," I automatically think of an RSVP, but what importance does the phrase have with regard to your story?*

Some readers have suggested that *Plus One* is based on a fairy tale called *The Day Boy and the Night Girl*, which I have never read. I think of the world of *Plus One* as a metaphor—an allegory about separate never being equal.

As with many of my ideas, the inspiration for the story started with a daydream and a lot of questions. My daughter's friend had back surgery late one day, and she was told she could visit him when he got out of recovery at 10pm. We flew up Lake Shore Drive—all the lights were timed, the roads were empty—and got there in about thirteen minutes, when it would have taken thirty-five during the day. As my daughter popped up to see her friend, I waited in the car outside—it was dark and peaceful and the street was empty—and wondered, "Why do we all try to live on the same schedule? Why don't we stagger the time of day that we live and work, to spread the resources around the clock?" Then I thought, "What if we *had* to live at alternate times? What would life be like if you lived in the dark? How would it be enforced? Who would choose your assignment? Would one group fare better? Could there be health consequences?" And of course, my mind moved to the political and social analogies in our real world, which became the most important focus of the book.

The phrase "plus one" refers to the permission some health care workers have to transport patients beyond curfew. And you're right, the phrase is borrowed terminology from an RSVP. But "plus one" took on a more personal meaning as I wrote. When Sol realizes in the hospital that she can't bring herself to say D'Arcy's name (which really means she refuses to humanize him in her own mind), she blurts out "Day Boy" instead, and D'Arcy understands immediately in that astute way he has. Out of principle, he holds back her name as well, calling her "Plus One." A few early readers have called these phrases nicknames, which isn't how I think of them. For me, they represent an inability to acknowledge the other person fully. Later, when Sol whispers his name in her head, and he uses her name aloud for the first time, I hoped you'd see that they've each grown to respect the other as a person.

There are some small elements typical of a dystopian novel in your story, but this book is anything but typical. And the cover of the book makes it look like a romance novel. How would you categorize Plus One? *What (sub)genre do you think it falls under? What would you tell people to entice them to read it?*

I'm such a nerd, I would tell people, "It's an alternate-history thriller exploring issues of civil liberties and social justice," and they'd fall asleep before I finished. I'm sure I would have chosen a much less romantic cover, and it might have been a mistake because the jacket design is so moving and dynamic. A blogger who read the book in digital format claimed that the romance doesn't start until 70% in, which is probably technically true. (Although I can't think of a more swoony scenario than two smart people who don't like each other running away from the law together . . . or am I weird?) Some readers have tagged it as dystopia on Goodreads, which surprised me. I often think of dystopias as being set in the future, which *Plus One* isn't. But it makes me wonder, would I say our own United States was a dystopia before the Civil Rights Act of 1964? Is the growing level of government invasiveness today (for example, monitoring phone calls in the name of protecting us, or detaining people in Guantanamo Bay indefinitely, without trial) dystopic? If the answer is yes to those questions, then you could argue that *Plus One* is a dystopia.

You're not weird. I, too, thought Sol's and D'Arcy's animosity and flight was one of the most romantic scenarios I'd ever read.

How did you settle on Chicago as the setting for your story? It's a pretty popular setting for dystopian novels these days, but you utilize the city in unprecedented ways in your book. What is the importance of the city to you and the story?

I was born in Chicago and have lived there my whole life, with the exception of one and a half years in Brussels, Belgium (that's the source of Poppu and the French language), and a year in L.A. So, the feeling of Chicago at night is a part of my core. I see this book as a love song to the South Side, which is my favorite part of the city—gritty and slightly unmanicured, but real, and hardworking. The steam tunnels and the University of Chicago came up organically, because they're a part of my young-adult life. My brother spent some . . . er . . . leisure time in the steam tunnels when he was in high school.

In your story, there are three different groups of people: the Rays, the Smudges, and the Noma. Would you mind elaborating on the differences between these groups and how you came up with their characteristics and lifestyles?

While the privilege of the Rays is obvious (the federal government is run by Rays), if you look closely, everyone suffers from the restrictions on their freedom. Fleshing out the two lifestyles presented subtle problems I had to try to solve, and I had to do a lot of imagining. There are so many ways in which you and I move fluidly between day and night without thinking about it. Even if particular issues didn't show up in the book, I had to answer questions in my head like, "How is intercontinental travel possible in this world?"

The Noma are a semi-nomadic group who form loosely into tribes and are less rebels than criminals, out for themselves, and who have figured out how to straddle the Day/Night divide. Their way of dressing and talking is inspired somewhat by Alex's delinquent gang in *A Clockwork Orange*. As I explored their individual characters, though, I discovered what's true of all people: There are good and bad among the Noma.

One of my favorite aspects of this novel was all of the contradictions: night and day, light and dark, beauty and roughness, etc. And I loved how Sol and D'Arcy were complete opposites themselves, yet they complement each other well. What do you think each character would say the other brings out in them?

I love how different Sol and D'Arcy are, but how fundamentally similar: They are both loyal to the bone and family-oriented. I love how they slowly discover it. When I began writing, Sol presented herself fully formed to me. She was angry and wounded and *fierce* . . . and already crushing her finger in that machine (although I didn't know the name of it at the time). So I think Sol would say that D'Arcy reins in her impulsiveness, which keeps her safer, and his love is an unexpected refuge in the absence of her family.

As for D'Arcy, at first you can't figure out why a studious, ambitious, and rule-oriented person like him would be drawn to helping such a loose cannon (in his own words) when he has so much to lose. But for me, even before he met Sol, D'Arcy was already questioning his path— conforming dutifully, but not comfortably, to a system that had hurt his own family. His loyalty to his mother and his lack of alternatives had kept him marching along the safe path. (Recall the Spanish Flu virion, looming over Sol's first drawing, and how symbolic that is.) It took meeting this enigmatic, totally raw, openly hurt young woman who put one thing (love of family) above anyone's laws to make D'Arcy confront his life decisions.

JEN FROM THE BEVY BIBLIOTHEQUE (thebevybibliotheque.net)

I'm not usually a poetry person, but I love the little pieces of poetry written by your main character Sol and a "mystery" writer. Were the pieces inspired by anything in particular?

I *wish* I were a poetry person! I've always suspected that authors who write the most beautiful prose actively read poetry, that it changes their brains and gives them a nuanced facility with words. Poetry immerses you in a kind of "language of inner thought" that makes you see and feel primal parallels between disparate objects and emotions. I think it would train me to be less literal.

The "Stardust" poem was inspired by an online *Forbes* article by journalist Susannah Breslin about her breast cancer diagnosis. She said that when she heard the news, she felt like she was "something that had come loose from a spaceship" and that she stepped outside to see that the world was "thrown into sharp relief." Those feelings stuck with me as being so characteristic of loss.

I found the novel structure where we move with Sol through her present day to flashback chapters growing up with her brother and grandfather particularly effective. What made you decide to use that structure?

That structure seems to be part of my DNA! It surfaced in *Monstrous Beauty*, too. But it's actually a risky writing strategy. Most readers want to feel like they're a fly on the wall, watching the action unfold. It's distracting to be taken out of the moment into the past, herky-jerky. I tried to keep those flashback chapters short for that reason, but they felt necessary to me because we need to know the depth of Sol's family connections. In the flashbacks with her desk-writing companion, I enjoyed showing two people who are apparently unaware of the other's Day/Night status developing a real friendship without prejudice.

One of my favorite names in the book is Soleil, the French word for "sun," particularly ironic because Sol is a Smudge. Can you talk a bit about how you chose the names of other characters?

I knew that the Le Coeur parents would be rebels when I began brainstorming, so I wanted the names they chose for their children to be defiantly Day. Pretty early on, I knew that Sol and her brother, Ciel, would be of Belgian heritage, so I started thinking of French words that felt "sunny" to me. (Ciel means "sky," or as Gigi points out in the short story *Noma Girl*, it can also mean "heaven.") The Noma names were fun because they often choose ordinary nouns as nicknames, like Fuzz and Cake, and you can imagine how they might have arisen and "stuck."

Having read both Monstrous Beauty *and* Plus One, *I have to admire how well you carry out two different writing styles. What was your favorite thing about each style?*

I hope that every book of mine will be different! I'm a life-long learner, and I always want to be growing and exploring. I'll probably never develop a "brand" as a result, but I'll be challenged every day. With *Monstrous Beauty*, I loved the way third-person past allowed me to see everything and to "tell a story" in the more classical sense. The plotting had to be meticulous, and I worked from a detailed outline. I think you can sense the tight control of that book as a result. The historical fiction sections required precise language—no anachronisms—and transporting myself back in time to get it right. Those were total nerdy pleasures. With *Plus One* on the other hand, I loved how speaking in first person made me inhabit Sol and her life, and how her passion flowed through me as a result. I wrote mostly by the seat of my pants, and I woke up uncontrollably early, working well before dawn. It was a surreal, Smudge experience. Also, I continue to miss Sol and D'Arcy, and I worry about them, whereas I feel very good about where I left Hester.

SHAE FROM SHAE HAS LEFT THE ROOM (shaelit.com)

As my regular followers know, I love Ms. Fama and her work, so I'm tickled to have her here today to talk about how writing Plus One *almost turned her into a Smudge.*

An odd thing happened to me while I was writing *Plus One*. Somehow, my body clock reset itself. I wouldn't say I became a Smudge, exactly, but it was close.

Plus One is set in contemporary Chicago, but imagines that history took a different path during the Spanish flu of 1917–18. The world has been divided into Day- and Night-dwellers, with mandated curfews. The policy helped to curb the pandemic and increase post-WWI productivity, but now, ninety-six years later, it has become nothing more than an entrenched loss of freedom. People who live at night are colloquially called "Smudges," those who live during the day are "Rays."

While writing the first draft, I found myself waking up uncontrollably at 3:30 in the morning, eyes wide open, thinking about Sol. I'd try to go back to sleep, but the quiet house called to me. The silence outside felt more compelling than the bustle of the day. My laptop was waiting. Sol was in trouble. I couldn't empty my mind and rest.

I'd get dressed as quietly as I could, trying not to wake my husband, and tiptoe downstairs carrying our wobbly, ancient, fifty-pound dog, Angie. I'd empty the dishwasher, make a cup of tea, and start working. There was something about that hour that made me feel *simpatica* with Sol—I understood her completely before sunrise. I shared her world. Angie knew the drill and would flump down next to me, waiting.

I wrote at the kitchen table by my patio doors with the dark yard outside, the sky feeling cavernous, even though I live in the city. I'd watch the cycle of the moon and the brightest stars through the glass panes of the doors. They become important companions when you can't see much else around you. It was usually just before the birds began to sing, well before the paperboy went on his rounds, hours ahead of garbage pickup. It gave me a sense of isolation that I knew Sol lived every day, watching Poppu slowly leave her. After a while, I'd take the dog out—Angie and I would pad around the block as Smudges. She had always been a quiet dog. With her black curly hair, she disappeared into the night. I began to understand how you could move easily in the city at that hour, how you might come to feel at home in the dark.

After I had finished a full draft of the manuscript, my sleep habits returned to normal, as quickly as they'd changed the first time. Angie adjusted with me, agreeable as ever. We still got up early, but it was a reasonable "early." I had set down Sol's urgent story. I no longer had to keep her company in her Smudge world.

KAREN JENSEN FROM *SCHOOL LIBRARY JOURNAL*'s TEEN LIBRARIAN TOOLBOX (teenlibrariantoolbox.com)

I first contacted Elizabeth when I read Monstrous Beauty *and wrote a post about the common, everyday sexual abuse many girls face that we don't normally talk about, like street harassment. In* **Plus One,** *I again find sexual violence to be a compelling part of the story. Elizabeth, would you tell us more about why you included sexual coercion in* **Plus One?** *Of course, there is also the scene with Sol and D'Arcy that is really a beautiful scene about consensual sex and caring.*

Readers: For trigger purposes, you should know Elizabeth's answer discusses sexual violence, but without graphic descriptions.

Two major sexual encounters, and one minor one, tie in with the politics of the world in *Plus One*, and with the theme of lost liberties.

Gigi's circumstance is obvious: Brad the Hour Guard is able to abuse his authority by putting her in a position where she has to barter for ordinary freedoms using sex. This is a case of sexual coercion via asymmetric power. Although Gigi technically consents to the encounter, she would say no if she could; she is forced to make this "choice." This scene with Gigi and Brad is upsetting, but I believe it's crucially important to the themes of the novel. In particular, the scene acts in tandem with the healthy scene you mention, in which Sol is able to express sexual agency, and to act on her desires responsibly and without guilt.

But wait! Even the consensual scene is more complicated than that, as it continues to tie in with the theme of lost liberties. Yes, Sol and D'Arcy are equal partners when they have sex, but a different kind of pressure is present for them. There is a sense of "rushing" to love. Sol believes she'll never see D'Arcy again, and she's taking the one and only opportunity she has to be with this person she cares so deeply about. Who knows how their relationship would have progressed if they'd had the luxury of time? We already know, for instance, that D'Arcy has never had a second date, and has been thoughtful about what he is and is not ready for. His fear of hurting Sol is strong enough that it may have led them to delay physical intimacy. But because of the politics of this world, they choose not to take it slowly. (I've written more about this on Keertana's blog, Ivy Book Bindings.)

There's a third sexual encounter in the book that's also related to the political theme, but much more subtly: Sol's encounter in the gangway with Ace when she's only eleven. It's an experience I think a lot of girls have, and it's on the spectrum of sexual aggression (even though it may seem relatively harmless, and Ace himself is underage). Sol believes his kissing and fondling are affectionate—that Ace must "like" her. She has a crush on him after that, and thinks she wants it to happen again, until she's the same age he was when he did it and she sees his behavior for what it was (an older boy taking advantage of a child). To me, this has a symmetry with the Day/Night policy, which people have accepted at face value as a restriction that was put in place to protect them, and are only slowly coming to realize is wrong. Sometimes breaches of rights present themselves as benign at first, and confuse us into not resisting.

While there are many other freedoms the characters have lost (such as the ability to choose their own education and career), sex and love are powerfully relevant issues in the adolescent experience. I wanted teens to understand the violation of the Day/Night divide for what it was, and to imagine themselves coping with it.

CARINA OLSEN FROM CARINA'S BOOKS (carinabooks.blogspot.com)

What was the hardest part about writing Plus One?
I find it hard to start writing a new manuscript at all, even when I already have the basic story idea and I'm excited about it. I procrastinate horribly! It's a kind of fear of failure, I'm sure. Once I'm solidly on my way, though, I become obsessed with what I'm writing and the work comes easier. My son, knowing that I was about to stall again in the summer of 2011 (after the editing process for *Monstrous Beauty* was complete), challenged me to a "novel-writing duel." We agreed to write 500 words a day, and we verified each other's progress on Sundays. I wrote *Plus One*, and he wrote a sci-fi fantasy called *The Mile Corpse*. (By the way, our three judges voted him the winner.)

If you could be one character from your book, who would you be and why?
Well, I want to be someone daring and subversive, like Grady Hastings

or Gigi, but if I were to magically transform one night, I'd probably wake up as D'Arcy's mother, Hélène Benoît. I was premed in college, I always got straight As, I was a rule-follower, and like her, I collaborate a lot with my creative young-adult children. (I am much fonder of D'Arcy's mom than many readers will be. But honestly, do you think Jean would have fallen in love with her if she wasn't secretly awesome?)

A lot of **Plus One** *focuses on Sol's grandpa, Poppu. Do/did you have a good relationship with your grandpa?*

My grandfathers died when I was fairly young (eleven and fourteen). I love what I remember of them, but I never got the chance to experience them as a true young adult and adult, which I regret. My own kids have grown up just steps away from their grandparents, and it makes a big difference in how deep the relationship is. As you know, I'm super family-oriented, and we have a big, close-knit family (one that shouts boisterously around the dinner table), so it was easy for me to imagine how attached Sol would be to Poppu, who has raised her since she was a toddler.

Did you always plan that Sol and D'Arcy would be together? They have such an amazing romance.

I always knew the story would include "romance after initial animosity," but I thought it would be a little more of a lighthearted road trip between Sol and D'Arcy, and a sweeter, funnier coming together. Originally, I imagined their relationship to be a little bit like Jack Walsh and Jonathan "the Duke" Mardukas in the movie *Midnight Run*. But the stakes became so high in the novel that the intensity and urgency of their romance necessarily changed. Time is running out for them, and they know it.

I'm curious: If you had to live in the day or the night, which would you choose and why?

Unfortunately, no one gets to choose. The Office of Assignment chooses for us all. I suspect, because my ancestors were poor Italian immigrants, I would have been born a Smudge. But living at night would kill me because I'm a day person through and through. I get up early and go to bed early. I don't like to go out at night. I like to feel cozy and snug in my house when it's dark.

ERIN AND JAIME OF FIC FARE (fictionfare.blogspot.com)

Can you talk about what great writing means to you?

All my favorite authors seem to think not only about "Is this a great adventure?" while they're writing, but also, "Is this story meaningful? Does it change how readers think?"

Here are three additional hallmarks of smart writing for me:

1. **Every word counts.** Beautiful writing is like poetry: The author has considered every single word before putting it down, and then pared out the unnecessary. Franny Billingsley once gifted me with a comment that her late editor, Jean Karl of Atheneum, had tossed out while Franny was revising *The Folk Keeper*. Jean told her that each word had to exist in service of the plot. She told her to remove any passage or word that was not "wholly necessary." That phrase has stuck with me for fifteen years as a litmus test: "wholly necessary." As when you sculpt marble, you probably can't crank out beautiful writing at 2,000 words a day. You can certainly carve the crude form quickly, but you have to go back to chisel and polish it meticulously to make it come alive, to make it deceptively simple and beautiful. That means revisions . . . lots of them.

2. **Characterization.** Each character should not only be fully fleshed out, but also beautifully, believably flawed. For example, in Jane Austen's *Pride and Prejudice*, Elizabeth Bennet has a mischievous sense of humor, and she delights in the ridiculous, but it gets her into trouble and brings up that very contemporary (and I think mistaken) literary criticism, "Is she likable?" Lizzy's wit is sometimes caustic, and even the people who love her misunderstand her humor. For instance, she jokes to Jane that she fell in love with Darcy when she saw his

estate. We panic a little: Is her love for him actually mercenary? Austen makes both Elizabeth and Darcy imperfect so that we can see their growth, until there's no question by the end that their marriage will be a meaningful partnership.

3. **Nuance without heavy-handed explanation.** This happens when the author trusts the readers to understand a character's actions without letting him- or herself intrude to explain it. It's essential to a good book.

These hallmarks of great writing are the ones I aspire to every day.

LENORE APPELHANS FROM PRESENTING LENORE
(presentinglenore.blogspot.com)

I asked Elizabeth to share with us what kind of dates a Smudge might go on. And here's what she had to say:
Top Ten List of Date Ideas for Smudges:

10. **Watch the sun rise over Lake Michigan from a boat.**
In the world of *Plus One*, the open seas (and Great Lakes) are the only places that are not subject to curfew. (The curfew bell sounds exactly when the upper edge of the sun breaks the horizon, at sunrise and sunset.) Thus, many Smudges and Rays in Chicago may never have seen a sunrise over the water, unless they live in a high-rise along the lakefront or own a boat.

9. **Hide from Hour Guards in the steam tunnels under the University of Chicago.**
Granted, the tunnels are *really* hot and humid, but in a pinch, you can spend daylight hours there, all alone together.

8. **Meet the 'rents!**
You're taking your relationship to a new level. Time to figure out

the complexity of his family dynamics, and endeavor not to say something stupid, all while feeling feverish!

7. **Hunker down under Lake Shore Drive and whisper into the night.**
   Your feet near his face, his feet near your face. Hey, it's a lot more romantic than it sounds.

6. **Run out of gas in another state.**
   Oh, darn! *snaps fingers in dramatic resignation* You're stuck with each other now!

5. **Look at the stars while lying in a field.**
   Contemplate something bigger than yourself, savor the moment of being quietly together. Seeing the Milky Way was on your bucket list anyway.

4. **Sleep side by side in a cave.**
   Ugh, it's damp and chilly and sandy and there are *bats*! But the guy you're with is awesome. You're feeling warm after all!

3. **Get a (Noma) makeover.**
   Mullets were in fashion once. Maybe it could happen again? Besides, nothing signals togetherness more than getting pierced, dyed, and tattooed together!

2. **Negotiate a hostage situation.**
   Anyone can grab a pizza on their date, but only power couples can navigate the game theory of kidnappings and come out on top.

1. **Steal a baby.**
   The basis for many great relationships in history! (Hmm, come to think of it, maybe there's only one other: Hi and Ed McDunnough in *Raising Arizona*.)

FOR GENERATIONS, love has resulted in death for the women in Hester's family. The reasons are waiting in the graveyard, the crypt, and at the bottom of the ocean—but powerful forces will do anything to keep Hester from uncovering the truth.

ELIZABETH FAMA

Monstrous Beauty

"FRANNY BILLINGSLEY, National Book Award Finalist for *Chime*. "Dark and sensuous as the sea itself."

Keep reading to uncover monstrous mermaids, ghosts, and a century-old curse!

Prologue

1522

Sᴛʀᴇɴᴋᴀ ᴡᴀɴᴛᴇᴅ ᴘᴜᴋᴀɴᴏᴋɪᴄᴋ.

She watched him but never spoke to him. She never dared to approach or reveal herself. A year of stealth had taught her his language, his habits, his dreams, his ways. The more she knew, the more she loved. The more she loved, the more she ached.

The sachem's eldest son did not go unnoticed by the women of his tribe. A quiet keegsqua watched him, too. Syrenka noticed the way she smiled at him, the way she brought her work to the shore while Pukanokick burned and scraped his first dugout canoe. And why shouldn't the keegsqua want him? His glossy black hair glinted blue in the morning sun, his skin beaded with sweat, his eyes shone as he worked with single-minded passion on the boat. Syrenka read the keegsqua's shy silence for the desperate proclamation that it really was: the girl wanted Pukanokick, too; she wanted a smile that was meant only for her; she wanted to know his deepest thoughts; she wanted to see him lift beautiful sons onto his shoulders and hug their warm, bare feet to his chest; she wanted to grow old with him. She wanted him to save her from emptiness.

Syrenka's smoldering ache ignited into a fire. She spent all of her time near the shore now, and ignored her sister's beseeching to join her below, where it was safe, where she was supposed to be. Where she could not tolerate being.

On the day Pukanokick finished the boat, his younger brother and his mother's brother helped him drag the charred dugout to the edge of the water. They watched as he paddled it out, and they leaped and shouted with pride to see how true it glided and how stable it was, even in the heavy chop of that day, even when he stood and deliberately tried to tip it. One corner of the keegsqua's plump lips lifted silently with joy, while she pretended to bore holes into stone sinkers. Syrenka studied them all from behind an algae-green rock.

But early the next day, the keegsqua was gone. Pukanokick's brother and his mother's brother were gone. Pukanokick was alone when Syrenka became entangled in his fishing net. Swimming a short distance from the dugout, she was distracted by the rhythm of his body as he plunged the paddle in the dark water, lifting his weight off his knees, stroking a heartbeat into the quiet morning. She forgot that he had set a net the evening before—it was cleverly anchored with rocks and suspended with cattail bundles—until the fiber mesh collapsed around her and her own surprised thrashing caught her fin fast.

Working quickly, she was almost free by the time he had turned his boat and eased it over the net. She was curled upon herself, tugging at her dark tail with her thick white hair in a bloom around her, when she felt the cool shadow of the dugout move across her skin. She looked up and her eyes caught his—they were brown-black, the color of a chestnut tumbling in the surf. Her own eyes would alarm him, she knew. She saw him take in a breath. He did not reach for his club, although he could have. He did not reach for his bow. He watched.

She attended to the net and her tail. She lifted her arm and slashed at the remaining strands with the fin on her wrist, cutting herself loose. She looked back up and slowly rose from the deep, shoulder hunched and face to the side.

Her cheek broke the surface first. He didn't recoil. She smiled, careful not to show her teeth.

"Kwe," she said, in his own Wampanoag.

"Kwe," he whispered.

She tried to keep her voice smooth and quiet, unthreatening. "I am sorry. I broke your net."

He shook his head almost imperceptibly from side to side. He wasn't angry. She saw him swallow.

"This is the finest mishoon I have ever seen," she said, sliding her fingertips along the hull of the boat as she swam its length.

"Thank you," he said. And then he seemed to remember something. Perhaps that he had a club, and a bow, and that he was the sachem's eldest son.

"Who are you?" he demanded.

"I am Syrenka. You are Pukanokick."

"How do you know my name?"

She had never been this close to him. The muscles in his forearm extended as he unclenched his fist. She followed his arm to his shoulder, to his angular jaw, to his broad nose and then his unwavering eyes.

"I have seen you. Fishing. I hear others call you. I follow you. I listen."

"Why do you follow me?"

She stroked the edge of the boat. "You are not ready for the answer."

He stood up, balancing easily in his dugout. "I am."

She whipped her tail below her, rising out of the water like a dolphin—but carefully and steadily so as not to splash him—until she was eye to eye with him. She reached out with her hand and stroked his cheek. He did not flinch. He allowed her touch.

"Noo'kas says I must give you time. You must grow accustomed to me. You are yet too young," she recited.

"I am a man." But his breath caught as she traced the line of his jaw. He lifted his chin. "Who is this Noo'kas to question that?"

"Noo'kas is the mother of the sea. I must obey."

Pukanokick's eyes widened. "Squauanit. You mean Squauanit thinks I'm not yet a man?—the sea hag who brought the storm that killed my mother's father?"

"Shhhh," she said, putting her fingers on his lips. Her nails were long and sharp, but she was gentle.

She sank down into the water again and swam away.

"Come back!" She barely heard the muffled shout. She stopped, astonished. She felt her skin tingle with hope.

She turned and swam underneath the dugout. Back and forth, with his shadow above her as he knelt in the boat. She needed time to consider. To be calm. To choose wisely.

He waited. She gathered strength from his patience.

She rose to the surface.

"You are right. Noo'kas is a hag. She has become ugly as the seasons circle endlessly. She will live forever, but she will never be beautiful again. She missed her time. What does she know? I will decide myself."

Pukanokick rested his forearms on the edge of the dugout and leaned his head over the side so that his black hair nearly grazed the water. He asked her his question again, but softly this time.

"Why do you follow me?"

She brought her face close. "I follow you because I love you."

She brushed her lips against his. Warm breath escaped his mouth. He put his arms around her and kissed her. His lips were nearly hot on her skin, but firm and gentle. She felt a hunger for his touch that she could no longer hold back.

The dugout did not tip, but Pukanokick lost his balance. He fell into the bay, clutched in Syrenka's embrace. She released him instantly. But of course he knew how to swim—she had seen it many times—and he came up laughing. She joined him. He kissed her again, and they sank under the water together. She saw him detach his buckskin leggings from the belt at his hips. He swam up for a breath.

Syrenka surfaced and saw the sunrise, spilling pinks and purples and blues into the sky, as if for the first time.

Pukanokick touched her cheek. "I want to be bare-skinned in the water, as you are."

She sank under again and tried to undo the belt of his breechclout, but it was foreign to her. His hands pushed hers away and fumbled with it while she pulled down on his leggings to remove them. She brought him deeper and deeper as she tugged.

Lost in concentration, she misunderstood his struggles. She

thought he was wriggling to pull out of the leggings. She did not see the bubbles that escaped his mouth in clouds. She did not remember the passage of human time. She forgot her strength.

Finally, triumphantly, she peeled the first pant from his right leg. When she looked up, she realized with an agonizing start that his head swayed against his chest slowly in the swells, and his body floated lifeless.

She screamed underwater, a high-pitched wail with a rapid burst of clicks that caused the sea life around her to scatter. It was as Noo'kas had foreseen. She had dared to love, and she had lost everything.